A CHANGE of PACE

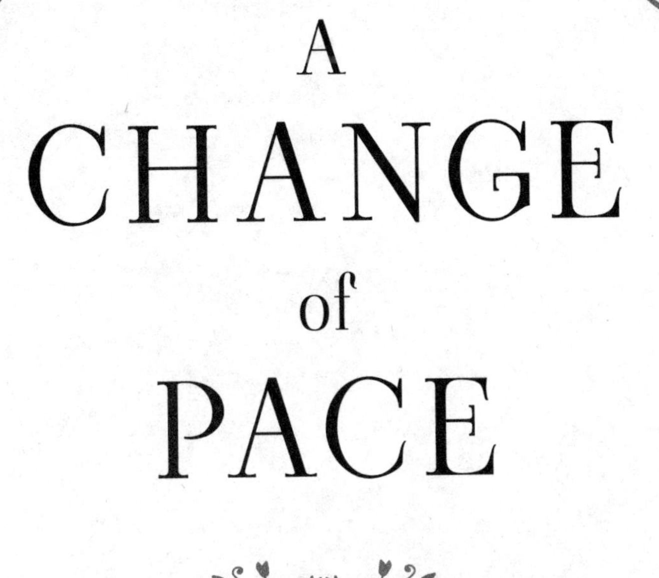

A CHANGE of PACE

A *Reimagined* Regency Romance

J.A. STEVENS

Generous Press
BELLINGHAM, WA

Library of Congress cataloging-in-publication data available upon request

ISBN 9798998759611 (TP)
ISBN 9798998759642 (eBook)

Printed in the United States

Distributed by Microcosm Publishing and Distribution

Interior book design by Alison Cnockaert.
Cover illustration by Anna Rabko. Cover design by Kenzie Sitterud.

Author photo by Britt Spring.

First edition
10 9 8 7 6 5 4 3 2 1

For Lily and Rebecca

Dear Reader,

My inclusive and colorful historical romance novels are a new twist on an old theme. All are welcome here.

A Change of Pace is set in a reimagined Regency London. In this world, trans and queer identities are not shunned nor hidden away, racism does not reign, and people with disabilities and neurodivergence are valued members of society. As you read this book, you might ask yourself, "If we could rewrite history to be fully embracing of human diversity, how would the world be a better place today?"

I never mean to minimize or deny the true histories experienced by marginalized people. *Because* we live inside these very real and entrenched systems of oppression, I wish to provide a whimsical and *not-so-realistic* reading experience for all to enjoy. My goal is to offer a softer, kinder—though not perfect—trajectory for protagonists who might otherwise have lacked an invitation to the ball. Deliberately, this is a world and history where certain painful conflicts simply did not exist.

As a cisgender white woman, I am privileged to be able to see myself reflected in the many thousands of regency romance heroines depicted throughout literary history. However, I am also a member of the LGBTQI+ community; a person with Autism (ASD); a partner to an amazing transgender woman; and the mother of a beautiful daughter with Down Syndrome. Not all readers can easily imagine themselves as a main character, swooning over a dashing hero and getting a happily-ever-after to sigh over. Realizing that my daughter and my partner belonged to demographics that history either excluded or punished for being themselves, I decided to create an alternate history for my family—and for you, Reader—to enjoy. And I hope you do!

Still believing in happy endings—for all of us,

J.A. Stevens

Content Note

The following pages include vivid descriptions and plenty of action. Little will be left to the imagination. *A Change of Pace* includes:

Coarse language

Disability themes

Gambling

Grief and Loss

LGBTQI+ themes

Manipulation

Sexually explicit content, including depictions of age-gap pairings, casual sex, infidelity, sex work, and sexual activities engaged with and without explicit verbal consent

Violence, including references to murder (off-page)

The author has undertaken a consultation process with members of various communities represented in *A Change of Pace*, with the aim of creating a world that is respectful, sensitive, and *pleasurable* above all.

Thank you for reading. Please take good care.

Author-Created Terms

The following terms were created by J.A. Stevens. In the reimagined history the author has invented for *A Change of Pace,* Regency London is a society inclusive and accepting of true diversity. In this world, these terms are used not as slurs or limits but in a descriptive and respectful manner, unburdened by cultural bias. You can find a full glossary at the back of the book.

Electora: Author-created term to describe non-binary individuals. Derived from the Latin words "Electio" meaning "choice" and "Ora" meaning "edge/border".

Honorian: Author-created term to describe individuals with disabilities (broadly). Derived from the Latin word "Honor" meaning "honor/dignity".

Lorian: Author-created term to describe males who were assigned female at birth. In modern terminology, this refers to transgender males. Derived from the word "valor" and the common masculine suffix "ian".

Mem: Author-created non-binary personal pronoun, similar to Mr./Miss/Mrs.

Miris: Author-created term to describe individuals born with Trisomy 21 (Down Syndrome, or similar chromosomal abnormalities). Derived from the Latin word "Miri" meaning "wonderful/to admire".

Velina: Author-created term to describe females who were assigned male at birth. In modern terminology, this refers to transgender females. Derived from Latin word "Vellus" meaning "gentle" and common feminine suffix "ina".

Veris: Author-created term to describe intersex individuals. Derived from the Latin word "Verus," meaning "true".

1

WITH TEARS OF laughter cascading down her cheeks, Miss Georgina Pace ran down the cobbled street, grateful that she had pulled her breeches on before climbing out of the first-floor window of her lover's town house. She clutched her other garments to her naked breasts, concealing them from the curious eyes of the late-night London revelers.

What a disappointing end to an otherwise delightful evening. She lamented having to leave the soft warmth of the lady's embrace, yet the inopportune arrival of a husband had made her presence rather awkward.

Panting for breath, Georgina slowed down as a rather prim lady—a large black plume curling from her elaborate coiffure—came around the corner. From her raiment, the lady may have just stepped out of Almack's, one of London's finest theaters. She gasped in astonishment, and on impulse, Georgina exposed one rounded nipple at her and winked.

The lady shrieked and hurried away, leaving Georgina chuckling. Her sides hurt from laughing at the absurdity of her own behavior. She had only been back in London for a few short hours, and already she courted a scandal. Her friends would think it most typical of her to be making mischief already; Sarah would lament her want of conduct, while Coulthurst would likely encourage her efforts, spurring her on to greater nonsense.

Georgina slipped into the shadows of a dark alley and shrugged into her shirt. She had scrunched her coat and shoved her cravat into one of her boots; now she unwrapped her makeshift bundle and dressed herself.

She tied her cravat loosely, wishing she had a mirror to make it more respectable. Never mind. Her next destination would not be fastidious about her attire. For now, she needed to track down her groom, Buckby, and have a word with him about his failure to keep watch for returning husbands and wives. This kind of mad dash from peril would not do at all. A proper dressing-down, and then she would ask him to escort her to Mem Lavigne's.

ONE OF GEORGINA'S hands, adorned by a heavy signet ring, cradled a glass of port. The other hand massaged the fleshy hip of the lass seated on her lap, a beauty with long, strawberry-blonde locks named Lottie. Some hours had elapsed since Georgina decamped without warning from the arms of her lover. Her plans for an evening of light entertainment had gone to pieces. Since arriving at Mem Lavigne's establishment, Georgina's performance at the card table had deteriorated. Her bloodshot eyes, heavy with alcohol and fatigue, scanned her opponents for signs of weakness. She sipped her drink, waiting for the next round of cards to be dealt. This would be her final game, she promised herself, knowing she had already extended well beyond the resources she'd intended to gamble with.

Of all the houses of iniquity, Georgina favored Mem Lavigne's enterprise the most. Not only was it located conveniently in the heart of Pall Mall, but it also offered the perfect blend of opulence and discretion. Anytime she came, they warmly welcomed her. Shutters and heavy damask curtains darkened the room and protected Mem Lavigne's guests from the scrutiny of the public milling by. Whilst many patrons opted to while away the hours shrouded in plumes of smoke at the gaming tables, equal numbers came to enjoy the *alternative* entertainment. Georgina often enjoyed both. Beautiful bodies, in varying states of undress, wandered amongst the patrons to be touched and enjoyed, and small alcoves allowed couples or groups to retreat for more intimate exchanges as desired.

The dealer presented the cards, and Georgina winked up at Lottie and squeezed her bottom, signaling for her to get up. The comely maiden had promised to bring Georgina luck. Not only had she failed to do so, but the constant wiggling of her hips against Georgina's lap dragged her thoughts repeatedly away from the game.

"Wait for me over there, Lottie." She gestured behind her. "I shall not be long."

With a giggle, Lottie retreated, letting her flimsy, diaphanous negligee slip open just enough so that patrons could see the shape of one ample breast before she took herself out of view.

Georgina appreciated this tactic periodically employed by the house to distract its sponsors from card play. The house always won in the end, but at least it made the losing pleasant.

Her eyes tried refocusing on the cards, as reds, blacks, spades, and diamonds blurred amongst clubs and hearts; her head pounded like an insistent drum, thrumming along to her heartbeat.

Georgina had enjoyed some good fortune earlier in the evening, but now that Lady Luck favored the house, she knew it was a fool's game to continue.

The house dispatched Georgina one final time, and she let out a resigned sigh, folding her cards in defeat. She thanked the dealer for their game and drained the rest of her port before going to find Lottie.

Seeing her companion waiting patiently nearby, Georgina snaked an arm around her waist and led her in search of a free alcove set off along the side of the suite.

Guests already occupied several of these chambers, some with shades securely closed to maintain their privacy. The primal grunts, groans, and squeals coming from behind the feeble barriers whetted the imagination of anyone wandering past. Other guests, meanwhile, did not even bother to shield their activities with a curtain.

Georgina suspected this formed part of the amusement for many people. That spectators were watching their lustful pursuits was exactly what drove such patrons wild with hunger. She did not indulge in this whim herself, though she basked in the openness and freedom that Mem Lavigne's establishment offered to those of such tastes. Few places could rival the liberal and diverse service offered here, and Georgina enjoyed being able to do what she wanted without judgment.

Lottie unfastened the silk tasseled cord that held back a thin curtain. The drape tumbled free, protecting them from prying and voyeuristic eyes.

"You are looking well," Georgina said, allowing Lottie to remove her midnight-blue coat from her shoulders.

Lottie tossed the jacket aside and drew Georgina farther into the room. "It's been a while since you left town. Why did you not come back after Christmas like you promised?" She pushed Georgina down into the thick-satin chaise longue and straddled her legs.

"A necessary change of plan, my dear." Georgina blinked blearily at the large bosom confronting her face.

Lottie placed a trail of kisses along her temple and brow, and

Georgina closed her eyes. Lottie's lips were full and moist against her skin, yet her best efforts were failing to haul Georgina from her inner reverie.

"What's amiss?"

Georgina should have known Lottie would be too astute to allow her mood to pass without remark. She also knew her fair friend would doggedly inquire until she received a satisfactory answer. A sour taste seeped into Georgina's mouth. "My visit to Cornwall over Christmas did not go as anticipated, and I needed to rusticate in Yorkshire for a while . . . removing myself from society while the dust settled."

Lottie froze, leaving her luscious breasts pressed against Georgina's face. "Was it another woman?"

Georgina dragged herself away from the succulent bosoms and smirked up at her. "The sweetest auburn-haired debutante you have ever seen."

Lottie's eyes flashed.

Georgina chuckled. Her relationship with Lottie was, and always had been, a mutually pleasurable one, free of the emotional drama that plagued so many connections. She remunerated Lottie handsomely for her companionship, and this served them both well. Whenever Georgina referenced other women, Lottie would admonish her for disloyalty, then promptly recover with the offer of a sovereign or sparkling trinket. Georgina appreciated the token gesture of jealousy, but Lottie knew not to extend it too far.

"I thought you only ever reserved your romantic interest for married women, widows, or . . . girls like me." Lottie had stopped kissing Georgina and placed her hands on her hips, as though awaiting an explanation. "*You* said that young ladies were impressionable and often mistook a flirtation for warmer feelings."

"True. Typically, I recoil from such entanglements. *However*, this

Christmas, they brought me to *point non plus.* It was a monstrously dull affair, and there was no one else to dally with."

"You could not resist, then?"

Georgina yawned. If only she *had* fallen in love. Then the penance she served in her freezing cold Yorkshire estate would have seemed justified. Sadly, she only had herself to blame. As usual. She was incredulous at how a small misdeed had escalated into such a spectacle.

"More that boredom overtook me. It was reckless. And regrettable."

"Why? You cannot have left the lass with child?" Lottie's argument held merit.

That would have been a simpler fate to reconcile herself to, Georgina thought wryly. "No, but she expected everlasting love and marriage."

Lottie released a peal of laughter, which, while warranted, grated on Georgina's nerves tonight.

"So, the notorious Miss Pace fled to the country to escape a scandal, like a scared little mouse running from a cat?" She scurried her fingers up Georgina's belly and over the landscape of her breasts, mimicking the movements of a rodent.

Georgina shrugged away from her hand. "Yes, I dragged my father away from his friends and rushed at breakneck speed to Yorkshire as though the devil himself pursued me. There, I waited, freezing to the bone, for four God-awful months, hoping she might forget the interlude."

"And did she?"

On the contrary. The time apart had done little to quell Prudence's interest. Georgina remembered the letter that rested like a lead weight in her pocket.

She shook her head. "Far from it, I am afraid. She sought me out the moment I returned to town." Georgina retrieved the missive from her breeches. The sender had liberally doused it with floral perfume.

Lottie's eyes widened in disbelief, and she snatched the letter from Georgina. "You've only been back a day. Did she hunt you down already, seeking wedlock?" She scanned the page, unable to conceal her mirth.

Georgina gave a cynical grunt. "Indeed, no. The lady writes that she is now married, as per my requirements, and she looks forward to engaging me in a discreet liaison at my earliest convenience." She took the letter back and shoved it into her pocket. "In my departure from Cornwall, I had foolishly cited my preference for married counterparts." While this was truthful, Georgina also loathed being pursued. She derived enjoyment from seducing ladies, and Prudence's overbearing conduct did not appeal to her.

Lottie grimaced. "She sounds a trifle *unhinged.*"

"Hence my distraction."

"You should have stayed in London with me! Avoided this loose screw completely," she added cheekily.

"Can we not talk about it anymore?"

Lottie grinned and planted an apologetic kiss on Georgina's lips. "What would you rather do?" she purred.

With her left hand, Georgina reached beneath Lottie's robe, over the curved mound of her belly, and down to the patch of bright ginger hair at the intersection of her legs. Lottie lifted herself upwards to allow Georgina easier access, as a little cry erupted from her.

Georgina's eyes held Lottie's as she sank her middle finger inside her easily. "You *have* missed me."

"I've missed your *touch*," Lottie said with an impish smile. She began rotating her hips.

The sound of a throat being cleared made Lottie whip her head around.

Mem Lavigne stood in the doorway to the alcove, the curtain parted around them. "I am loath to interrupt you, Miss Pace." They offered an apologetic smile.

Georgina craned her neck to look around Lottie and arched an inquisitive brow. "Indeed, Lavigne. An inauspicious moment, as I'm sure Lottie will agree."

"You have a most . . . *earnest* visitor."

"Could you not deny me?" Georgina suggested.

"Sadly, he has it on good authority that you are here," Mem Lavigne advised.

Georgina gave a little groan of despair and dropped her head back on the sofa. Whoever her caller was, she wanted to consign them to hell. And Lavigne too. She reluctantly slid her finger from the heat of Lottie's body and patted her behind with her free palm. This had better be worth it.

Lottie huffed and climbed off Georgina's lap.

Georgina caught Lottie's wrist as she retreated and drew her back for one deep, passionate kiss, in lieu of an apology.

Flashing a disdainful glare at her employer, Lottie flounced out of the cubicle.

Mem Lavigne came farther into the chamber and retrieved a clean handkerchief from the folds of their robe. They extended it to Georgina, who accepted it with a murmur of thanks and used it to wipe the residue of Lottie from her fingers.

While Mem Lavigne procured her a fresh glass of port, Georgina admired their energy. Estimating their age proved difficult, although the gray curls pinned atop their head hinted that their youth belonged to a distant past. The fine lines on their countenance denoted that they had enjoyed many experiences, and their ability to talk openly about anything made them an exemplary confidante. Their stature was moderate, and these days, they relied upon a cane to move around, but they did not let this diminish their presence. They wore a flowing black-and-gold wrapper over their well-formed figure, and many bangles clinked together up their wrist. Mem Lavigne was a striking individual.

"Who is my earnest visitor?" Georgina accepted the glass.

Mem Lavigne ambled over to the curtain and swept it back to reveal a harassed-looking young man on the other side.

"George!" the man said, stepping into the alcove and eyeing his surroundings. He was Georgina's childhood friend, the Viscount, Lord Edmund Telford, and he now glared at her in an accusatory fashion, causing her to shrink back in her chair. She sensed he meant to disturb her peace. The throbbing in her head resumed with renewed vigor; Georgina pressed her fingertips into her temples before running her hand back through her tousled curls.

"Edmund. What are you doing here, my boy?"

Lord Edmund Telford, a young dandy, could not have been more out of place in an establishment such as this. He directed an indignant scowl at her. "Have you forgotten our engagement, George? You undertook to meet me for tea? You may recall I had something of great importance to discuss with you?"

Georgina sipped her port. "I have not forgotten, Edmund. But we are meeting tomorrow morning, I believe?"

He blinked, a furrow of confusion between his brows. "Yes. You are late."

He *was* in a state. How curious.

With a befuddled smile, Georgina put her port down and groped for her fob watch. "It's past midnight now. The tea shop will hardly be open."

"It's noon, George. You've lost twelve hours, dash it." Edmund sighed and exchanged a look with Mem Lavigne. "Kindly fetch Miss Pace's coat, cane, and any other of her belongings in your custody."

Mem Lavigne nodded.

"It's time to go, George."

The opportunity to enjoy Lottie's pleasurable company had officially slipped out of Georgina's grasp. She wished they had not wasted so many minutes discussing that blasted trip to Cornwall. This had better be worthwhile.

2

MOMENTS LATER, THE front door to the street opened, and the midday sun cast its unforgiving light over Georgina. She recoiled from its welcome, head down and eyes in full squint, and leaned on the railing at the top of the stairs for a moment. Mem Lavigne's impressive drapes had effectively blocked out the light and preserved the darkness within. Georgina had successfully lost all sense of time.

Edmund tucked his hand under her arm and guided her down the few steps onto the sidewalk below.

The daylight splintered into her skull, and the fresh air made her head reel, though she would be damned if she would admit that to Edmund.

She had been back in London for less than twenty-four hours when her dear friend had dispatched an urgent communication, inviting her to meet him. Aware that if she did not agree, he would pursue her at home on Half Moon Street anyway, she had accepted without hesitation. She had then stumbled across Lady Victoria Dawson, an old friend of hers, which had resulted in her running partially naked down Albemarle Street in the middle of the night. Once she had located her groom, she had asked him to set her down at

Mem Lavigne's for some light entertainment. Though how the entire night had escaped her, Georgina could not fathom.

On the sidewalk, Edmund flagged down a passing hackney carriage, and they both climbed in. He directed the driver to an unfamiliar address on Mount Street.

"What is going on?" Georgina finally asked, unable to tolerate the ambiguity.

Edmund was a youthful man of only one and twenty, who aspired to dandyism and regularly attempted to execute styles made modish by Brummell himself. He wore his stiff collar unnecessarily high, making it challenging for him to turn his head far in any direction. His noticeable cravat, tied with perfect accuracy, showcased a multitude of intricate lace ruffles. The well-tailored coat and fitted pantaloons complemented his slim form, and his boots glinted from every angle, thanks to the efforts of a much-praised valet. Sensitive and naïve, Lord Edmund fell in love often.

Over a decade his senior, Georgina had long ago developed into a sister-figure for Edmund. Their families owned neighboring estates in Yorkshire, and she had enjoyed spending time with the little fellow from when he was still in swaddling-cloths. As a youngster, she'd witnessed many of his milestones, including his first ride on a pony and his first tumble. She had wiped his dirty face with her handkerchief countless times and kissed his scratches, and as an only child, Edmund often applied to her for advice and instruction on matters he knew nothing about.

As the years passed, Georgina had stayed more often in London with her family. After Edmund departed his home for boarding school, he developed a strong penchant for letter-writing and maintained frequent correspondence with her.

In fact, she regularly received imperative letters asking such things as: 'Does it mean he likes me if he allows me to walk first into a room?' and 'Is it a positive sign if he sends me a note of gratitude in reply to a posy I sent him?' Georgina's fondness for Edmund enabled her to handle these requests with more patience than she typically showed others. She advised him that a smile, a dance, or a leisurely stroll did not always guarantee romance would ensue.

Georgina understood that Edmund's zeal stemmed from an overwhelming desire to form a long and abiding attachment to someone, and while she did not aspire to such an outcome for herself, she respected his ambition.

"I'm in a scrape, George," Edmund announced at last, his eyes downcast.

Georgina, intimately familiar with this opening phrase, registered no surprise. "Oh, yes? What has happened this time?"

He glanced furtively around, as though someone might hear something confidential. "It started a couple of weeks ago," he began. "I felt rather low after Michael Chiswick cleared off to Brighton for a tryst with that new beau of his. Oh, how Michael deceived me." He patted his chest to emphasize his broken heart.

"To brighten my spirits, I passed the hours with my old friend Arthur. Mr. Arthur Coombes, you know the fellow." Edmund rubbed his face as though to wipe away something most distasteful. His flawless peaches-and-cream complexion flushed. "He really is the most amusing, amiable chap."

Georgina arched an enquiring brow at him.

"Good gracious, nothing like that, George. We are merely friends. Arthur is very much attached to a young lady already. But as he often relies on his parents or that silly sister of his to take him out, I felt it was to our mutual benefit to escort him to see the sights and introduce him to some clubs. Well, Solitaires. Mrs. Gardner's establishment in St James's Square, to be precise."

Georgina wrung her hands. Edmund struggled to handle his own fortune and reputation at gaming houses, let alone taking responsibility for someone else's. She doubted this story would end well for anyone.

Arthur was one of the most likeable fellows in London. When Georgina first had the pleasure of meeting him some years ago, he beguiled her with his cheeky smile and affectionate manners. Arthur was an honorian, a person who navigated the world with some measure of assistance. More specifically, he had been born a miris, like Georgina's older brother, Henry. Thus, Arthur possessed a set of physical characteristics and personality traits that Georgina knew well, including a natural sweetness and naivete that meant he needed extra help to govern his affairs.

Georgina's heart sank. She would never leave Henry in Edmund's charge. One might as well ask the fox to guard the henhouse.

"Have you been there before?" Edmund asked.

She shook her head. "Not my sort of venue, frankly." She could think of nothing more tedious than sitting in the gaming room of some social-climbing nobody, whose idea of a good time consisted of a few dull games of faro and whist, while drinking a glass or two of indifferent wine.

"It's all the crack, George, I promise you."

She let out a long sigh. "I'm sure it is."

Edmund turned on the coach seat and placed his hand on Georgina's wrist. "Mrs. Gardner herself sits on the fringe of society. However, that does not stop the cream of the ton from patronizing her rooms, as well as many hardened gamesters. Everyone knows her den is raucous, but the suppers are simply divine. She also runs an amusing betting book, which promotes daily wagers of a most creative and outrageous nature."

Suspecting that the longer Edmund allowed himself to be distracted by irrelevant details, the greater the drama, Georgina's eyes narrowed. "Ah, yes, I recall hearing Mrs. Gardner betting against young Lord Gillingham being able to acquire the corset of a particular damsel within only two hours?"

"That's the one. The odds naturally favored his lordship, as he's quite the rogue. Though, as fortune would have it, a footman spied Lord Gillingham being hurried up the attendants' stairs by the daughter of the house. Instead of returning with her corset, Lord Gillingham found himself at the end of a thrashing and returned with a shiner across his eye." Edmund chortled at the memory. "On another occasion, Mrs. Gardner challenged two rather foxed patrons to race each other around St James's Square, wearing only their shirts. This incident led to a spot of unwanted attention from a passing night watchman, and Mrs. Gardner subsequently restricted her bets to more discreet activities."

Georgina peered desperately out of the carriage window and wondered if he would soon reach the point of his extended narrative. Solitaires had never interested her, and she only entertained this conversation now because of the implication that something nefarious had occurred to poor Arthur.

"Yes, but what about Arth—"

"She started opening a book for the outcome of duels and curricle races," Edmund interrupted, his eyes shining with glee. "Even who could swallow a full glass of wine in the shortest time. Occasionally, some madcap would nominate a risqué bet, but not often."

Georgina lifted an inquisitive brow. Perhaps Mrs. Gardner's gaming den offered some prospect for amusement, after all. "What sort of risqué bet?"

He blushed. "Competitions between patrons racing each other to achieve sexual climax the fastest."

"Scandalous." Georgina endeavored not to roll her eyes. The ridiculous lengths people went to appear interesting astonished her. "Pray, *how* does Arthur fit into all this gaiety?"

The carriage had by now pulled into Mount Street and come to a stop outside a charming residence, which boasted fresh paint, iron railings, and flower boxes brimming with fragrant blooms. She recalled that the Coombes family resided in Mount Street, and a sense of foreboding crept over her again.

Edmund asked her to wait as he sprang down from the carriage. He skipped to the front door, spoke to a grim-faced butler, and rushed back, breathlessly instructing the driver to hold the horses for a moment or two longer.

"Can we discuss this another time, Edmund? I think I should return home. Whatever it is can surely wait."

"No, I must tell you the whole."

"Well, do get on with it!" Georgina snapped. Her head craved for nothing more than her pillow.

"Arthur enjoyed the company at her establishment and took great delight in learning the various card games and discovering new wines so much that he asked to return. Well, he is so droll, one simply *cannot* deny him."

This decision, Georgina could tell, Edmund had already come to regret, and she dreaded the inevitable revelation. If he had promoted Arthur in such circles, Edmund did him a great disservice. She steeled herself for the next chapter of his story.

He lowered his voice to a whisper. "We did this several times, but a few nights ago, we returned, and I lost track of him. I was engaged at the faro table, and he wandered into one of the back rooms where the unsavory folk play deep. When I finally located him . . ." Edmund frowned and grazed a blond curl back from his forehead. "It was all too late. I found him at the Evens and Odds table, happy as you like and with his pockets completely to let. The predators even coaxed him to write promissory notes to prolong his play and create the most damage!" A film covered his pale blue eyes, and he sniffled.

Georgina stared at him gravely. Her desire to retreat had now abandoned her. She did not know Arthur well, though she could clearly envisage the scene that Edmund depicted, including Arthur's merriment and joy at being embraced by a new group, and the subsequent confusion in his eyes when his so-called friends turned out to be false. The world was a cruel place. She had witnessed immoral people lure her brother Henry into thinking they were his friends, only to turn their backs on him once they got what they wanted. Georgina motioned for Edmund to go on.

"EO is *not* the sort of game I would recommend for Arthur. Once I assessed the state of his affairs, I extricated him from the house and took him home."

"Did you settle the score with Mrs. Gardner?"

"I made a push to before we left, but she denied me. Said it was a private arrangement."

Georgina suspected that Mrs. Gardner possessed sinister motives for not allowing Edmund to discharge Arthur's debts right away, above any sense of moral obligation or duty towards the young man.

"Does Arthur have any means of paying her back?"

Edmund shook his head. "He has barely enough to last him to the end of the quarter."

Georgina found her patience for Edmund tested beyond measure. His actions were both foolish and completely negligent. "How could you have let him out of your sight?" She gripped the seat of the hackney, and her knuckles turned white as an unbidden memory stirred within her.

Edmund blushed in disgrace. "I became occupied. I never intended for any of this to happen. You must believe me, George."

Georgina did believe him, of course. Edmund was a kindly man overall, despite his weaknesses. She eyed him seriously.

"Did a fellow distract you?"

"Good grief, no. Once I left the faro table, I accidentally took a tumble over someone's cane that rested on the floor. Some chap called Hobbs accused me of being properly shot in the neck. I denied this, of course, and minutes later I found myself in the book, with everyone betting that I could not prove my sobriety by standing motionless for five minutes with a notebook on my head. I'll have you know, I triumphed." He grinned to himself before remembering to look solemn again. "We have to help him," he pleaded.

Georgina's stomach knotted. She suspected, this time, Edmund did not merely wish for her advice and would require her to undertake a more *active* role in saving their young friend from the clutches of Mrs. Gardner.

"We?"

The door of the Mount Street house swung open, and Arthur emerged, sparing Edmund from replying. With a little difficulty—posed by his short limbs—the young man clambered into the compact carriage space on top of Georgina and Edmund. They made room for his stout frame beside them, as Georgina inwardly wished they had acquired a conveyance large enough to accommodate the three of them more comfortably.

"Good day, M-Miss Pace. Hello, Edmund." Arthur spoke like a gentleman, though his large tongue made it difficult to articulate his words with clarity, and he had an occasional stammer.

Georgina reached across Edmund and shook Arthur's hand. His almond-shaped blue eyes twinkled, and he beamed, pushing his spectacles back up on his nose. He really was a lovely fellow—and reminded her of Henry, whose soul shone like a beacon in the darkness. That someone might take advantage of him cut her deeply.

"Call me George, Arthur."

"I've been telling George about our scrape." Edmund rapped his walking cane on the roof of the carriage, which rumbled forward once more.

The throbbing in Georgina's head intensified. Perhaps she had imbibed too much the night before, paired with the sheer lack of sleep. Either way, she craved a darkened room and perhaps a cup of strong coffee or a large brandy.

"Can we not discuss this indoors somewhere?"

Edmund's eyes bulged. "You are in your cups, George. Too many ears in our homes. Must stay on the move and keep our voices low."

Georgina rubbed one tired eye with the heel of her hand. "You sound rather delusional, Edmund. Unless Mrs. Gardner is involved in some sort of espionage and has entangled Arthur in her criminal dealings, I hardly think this level of secrecy is required."

Arthur's mouth dropped open, and the freckles across his nose became more noticeable against his increasingly pale countenance. "I'm a c-criminal?"

Edmund patted his hand. "No, my dear chap. Of course not. George simply does not understand our need for discretion."

"Oh yes; you said she was indiscreet," Arthur said ingenuously.

Charming.

Georgina shot Edmund a glare, making him blush and hurriedly hush the innocent Arthur.

Georgina decided to press one point. "Technically, you are both criminals. For I do *not* believe Solitaires is a legitimate gaming club. If the Runners decide to raid the place and conduct an audit of Mrs. Gardner's books, I think you'd all find yourselves locked up in Bow Street. They won't care how lofty the clientele is if she has not registered her enterprise and paid taxes. Nothing will prevent you from being imprisoned, regardless of your rank."

Arthur shifted upon the seat.

"And Mem Lavigne's is better?" Edmund demanded.

"Naturally. It's far too expensive not to be legitimate." Georgina grinned.

"That makes this matter even more delicate, George. Not only is it critical that Arthur's father not hear tell of this, but we must reach a discreet resolution as quickly as possible, without the gossips getting hold of the story. That would be dire."

Two pairs of eyes were now trained upon her in a hopeful stare, and the pressure to solve this situation inexplicably mounted. Smothering her face with her hand, hoping to remove her headache, Georgina wished they could expedite this solution so she could return home to bed.

"Do tell, why so dire?"

"We must maintain Arthur's reputation, George. There's a lady at stake."

"She would be f-furious if she heard."

Georgina suffocated an urge to leap from the carriage. She recalled the letter from Prudence, still heavy in her breast pocket. It had already made her question her return to London. Now, Edmund burdened her with the responsibility of rescuing Arthur from a scrape of *his* making, in order to support Arthur's matter of the heart.

Arthur peered at her through his skewed glasses, and despite her frustration at Edmund, her heart ached. She forced a smile, even though her mouth tasted bitter.

"Let me get this straight, Arthur. You have lost all your money to Mrs. Gardner. You have no means of getting your vowels back, but you need to settle your accounts so that you might marry a lady?"

"Yes. But please do not tell my papa," he insisted. "It will v-vex him terribly. He is particularly strict."

"Of course not. Neither of us shall breathe a word to him," Georgina promised.

Edmund gave her a sharp dig in her ribs. He required her to provide more reassurance to Arthur, it appeared.

She gripped the handrail of the carriage to avoid striking Edmund. Had he not been so foolish, she might have been resting in Lottie's embrace at this moment, sleepily sated.

"M-must m-marry M-Maggie," Arthur declared.

His determined stutter softened Georgina's heart. "It sounds like you must. Tell me, why do you like her so much?" she pressed, tilting her head slightly. People in love fascinated her.

Arthur's dewy eyes glistened, and an irrepressible grin exploded onto his face. "She is sweet, makes me laugh all day, loves animals, dances beautifully, paints with me and kisses *so* well." He ended this with a cheeky wink that made Georgina and Edmund chuckle.

"Well, we *need* to put this to rights, do we not? These matters have a way of ruining all one's enjoyment of life, I find," Georgina sympathized.

Arthur nodded, his eyes ever-trusting.

"I am skilled at helping people out of scrapes," Georgina said. "Usually myself, if I'm honest. That said, this is simple to fix. I am willing to supply you with everything you lost at Solitaires, and we can transfer the notes into my name. Then you need never think about it again." Whatever the sum, Georgina was willing to pay—if only to alight from the carriage forthwith.

Arthur's mouth pressed into an unyielding line. "No. My debt. My honor."

A weary sigh escaped Georgina's lips. This would be neither quick nor simple. Why did people insist so much on *integrity*? Damn Arthur's parents for instilling in him such a rigid sense of propriety. Georgina would have to employ a different approach. Both gentlemen were staring at her, unblinking and expectant. She forced a smile. "I have hatched *another* plan to retrieve your money!"

Edmund clapped his hands. "I knew you would, George."

Arthur beamed at her. "You have hatched a plan?"

"Oh yes," Georgina lied. At this point, she would say almost anything to be allowed out of the carriage. "So, while I implement my strategy, I would like to offer you the sum of twenty pounds. Just so that your father does not guess our plot." She wrinkled her nose a little. "He is a delightful fellow, but I suspect he might hinder our success if he learned of it." She retrieved a wad of pound notes from her pocket.

Arthur squinted suspiciously at the bills.

"You will, of course, pay me back at a later stage," Georgina assured him, aware that he might be hesitant to accept a further loan. "But I must ask you to promise me you will *not* gamble further. That never serves to reinstate one's fortune." Georgina extended her hand across Edmund once more to seal the agreement.

After a thoughtful moment, Arthur took her hand in a firm shake and accepted the notes. "Thank you, George. It is *so* kind of you to help me."

Georgina thumped on the roof of the hackney and told the driver to stop. "Now, as much as I would like to linger with you both, I must take myself home."

She climbed out, not minding that she had descended into the center of the bustling road. This was the quickest way to exit the vehicle, and she did not want to delay her departure. She dodged out of the way of an oncoming coach and a pair of riders on horseback, darting between them at an optimistic speed.

After the coach driver hurled a few choice expletives in Georgina's direction, a lovely face peeked out of the carriage window to ascertain what all the fuss was about. Georgina winked at the lady before narrowly missing a gentleman on horseback, who was obliged to tug at his mount sharply to avoid a collision. Georgina chuckled and retreated to the safety of the footpath. She had no idea how she might assist Arthur, but at least she could address her most pressing issue: getting some sleep.

Ten minutes later, Georgina arrived at her house on Half Moon Street, and her butler, Jarvis, greeted her on the threshold. At her request, he settled her in the library with a generous glass of brandy and sent down for a large pot of coffee. Ensuring the drapes were closed, he waited patiently for further direction.

"Is it too soon to return to Yorkshire, Jarvis?" She crossed her feet and stretched back on the sofa with her eyes closed, recalling the series of events that had snatched her from the comforting shadows of Mem Lavigne's and seemingly placed her at the center of Arthur and Edmund's ominous scrape. Even the monotony of Yorkshire seemed favorable by comparison.

3

GEORGINA SPENT THE rest of the day catching up on missed sleep and allowing her headache to subside. By the evening, she had bathed and changed into fresh clothes, restoring herself sufficiently to undertake the first step in assisting Arthur out of his difficulties. Not that she had a firm plan in mind. All Georgina knew was that Arthur had displayed such a high level of confidence in her, she could not let him down. The journey to the establishment of ill-repute would give her ample time to contemplate her options. After dining with her father, she set forth to St James's Square.

Calling to mind Arthur's hopeful eyes watching her keenly from behind his spectacles, Georgina rallied herself as she stepped down onto the street outside the discreet façade of Solitaires. It looked just like every other residential dwelling on the street. She hoped Mrs. Gardner would be receptive if she offered to repay the debt in full, although she anticipated an appeal to this woman's sensibility and morality would prove useless.

In trying to hit upon a solution, Georgina had briefly entertained a range of dramatic methods for settling the issue, including holding up Mrs. Gardner at gunpoint during one of her parties or simply sourcing a dishonorable fiend to invade her home and overturn it in search of the promissory notes. As titillating as it was to consider such measures, Georgina opted for the most straightforward solution.

She paused on the street, surprised at her own sudden passion to protect Arthur. Admittedly, his resemblance to Henry made it difficult to deny him. Nor could she sit by and allow any other like him—whether a miris, honorian, or otherwise vulnerable person who trusted easily or out of necessity—to be put at risk.

Not wanting to alert Mrs. Gardner to her involvement in the matter yet, Georgina decided that a reconnaissance operation would be beneficial. She would seek admittance into Solitaires, promising to gamble, and this would provide her with the chance to monitor some of Mrs. Gardner's tricks and, with any luck, spy where she concealed her promissory notes. If housebreaking became necessary later, this information would serve her well.

Georgina strode up the stairs to the front door. She had to find a way inside. Houses such as these relied on maintaining a low profile to avoid detection by the authorities. This allowed them to avoid paying the appropriate taxes on their revenues and set them apart from the more honest clubs—the type that enjoyed Georgina's patronage.

One could gain admittance into Solitaires via personal invitation from the hostess herself or another club member. Georgina had neither. It was unfortunate that she had not had more notice; she could have commissioned one of her friends, Lord Robert Coulthurst or Mrs. Sarah Fortescue, to attend with her. Their titles would have simplified her entry. Nevertheless, she was certain her own social standing would facilitate her entry. Mrs. Gardner would be a fool to turn away the legendary Miss Pace and her substantial fortune. Georgina counted on this.

However, she also wished to be inconspicuous. Nothing about her, or her friendship circle, denoted discretion.

Georgina had dressed herself appropriately for the evening's entertainment, selecting a pair of beige pantaloons displaying her shapely legs, knee-high black riding boots, a white blouse with a lace cravat and a green coat, tailored and threaded by Weston's expert hands. A ribbon secured her glossy black curls, and a few loose tendrils framed her face.

The young maid who greeted Georgina at the door regarded her dubiously.

"Good evening. My name is Miss Georgina Pace. Might you let me in to Mrs. Gardner's party? Sadly, I do not have an invitation." Georgina cast one of her brightest smiles, calculated to smash down the resistance of even the most cynical person standing in her way.

The maid's cheeks colored deeply. "M-Mrs. Gardner is not having a party."

Georgina knew that the Bow Street Runners would welcome the intelligence of such a prolific, though highly illegal, gambling den. She therefore suspected that Mrs. Gardner had tasked the young woman with evaluating the quality of the arriving guests—to filter out such emissaries, and to only welcome guests with a formal invitation.

"She is not? My good friend, Lord Telford, must have advised me incorrectly. . . . Excuse me, you have something there." Georgina removed one of her gloves and, with her thumb, wiped an invisible smudge off the girl's pink cheek.

The maid's breathing deepened visibly. "Oh!"

Gratified that she had put the young creature off guard, Georgina leaned against the doorway, the tails of her long greatcoat swishing around her. "Now, sweet girl, are you going to turn me away? Surely you might sneak me in somehow?"

The girl gulped. "If I let you in, I will be in a lot of trouble, miss."

"Of course, that won't do. *If* your mistress is displeased by my presence—and I vow she will not be—then I shall say I overthrew you," Georgina said with a laugh, removing her other glove and tucking both into her hat, which she then passed over with her coat to the lass.

Moments later, she was across the threshold and into the house. That had almost been too easy.

The obliging maid ushered her up the stairs and into a gaming room, where she found gentlemen, ladies, and electora of the ton playing piquet, whist, hazard, faro, and EO. A good range of amusements were on offer, Georgina granted. Without prior knowledge of the gambling hall, one would not know it existed. She certainly admitted that Mrs. Gardner did well to maintain discretion and order over her establishment.

The room reminded Georgina of a beehive. Music hummed around the chamber and blended with the buzzing sounds of laughter, dice rolling, and cards being shuffled. Attendants sailed between the tables, topping up the guests' drinks to the brim. This was a most pleasing sight. Georgina did appreciate an establishment with an excellent and abundant cellar.

Unlike the patrons of Mem Lavigne's velvet-draped salon, most of Mrs. Gardner's guests wore full evening attire. Had people worn less, perhaps the room would have entertained her more. Georgina wondered whether she might last the hour here before she succumbed to boredom. She suspected, for all the activity inside this busy little hive, she would find very little honey.

The helpful maid drew Georgina's attention to a small Venetian side table and explained the significance of the betting book. Mrs. Gardner expected all her guests to place a stake on the bet of the night.

Georgina read the lazy scrawl in the book.

Tonight, the house wagered that Mr. Harry Carruthers could not hold his drink without relieving himself before the clock struck midnight. *Of all the ridiculous ways to waste one's time and money,* she thought, annoyed at this arbitrary prerequisite to enter the house.

She scribbled her name in the column supporting Mr. Carruthers to win, dropped a shilling in the purse, and sauntered over to a table that was forming for a game of faro.

Georgina accepted a glass of Burgundy from a passing attendant and cast her eyes around the room. She recognized a few faces but would be hard pressed to name them. In the main, she did not care for social niceties, and she was aware that the ton only tolerated her for the sake of her father and sizeable fortune. Except for her lovers, of course, who tolerated her for a different set of gifts entirely. She wondered which character Mrs. Gardner was. At some point, Georgina would introduce herself and crave forgiveness for intruding on the soiree. For now, however, she wished to gather as much information as she could about the establishment—to ascertain how Mrs. Gardner preyed upon people and whether she used underhanded methods in her approach.

A striking lady sat to her left at the table. Georgina's eyes drifted over her for a moment longer than was socially decorous. Her coiffed light brown hair lay in curls atop her head, with a delicate cluster of flowers pinned over one ear. Her features were well-defined: a straight nose and fine eyes. She appeared to be a velina, a lady who was born male. Her slender arms rested at the edge of the table, half-hidden by the little puff sleeves of her dark-blue taffeta gown.

"I could sit for a portrait if you fetch your paints, should you desire to regard me indefinitely," the lady offered. Her deep, silky voice sliced through the noise of the room, and Georgina gasped, surprised out of her reverie.

"Forgive me," Georgina murmured, lowering her eyes. "However, you cannot blame me for staring. Your forearms are exquisite, madam."

The woman blinked at her. "Forearms?"

Georgina took a slow sip from her glass before answering. "Yes, forearms." In one fluid movement, Georgina traced her fingertip from the lady's elbow down to her wrist, enjoying the velvety soft skin under her touch. She withdrew her hand. "Delightful." Georgina watched the woman to see what would happen next.

"My name is Lady Elizabeth Mortimer."

Georgina straightened up and reached to shake the lady's hand. She noticed a delicious scent as she leaned a little closer. "The *Countess* Mortimer? I'm Georgina Pace."

Curious as to how Mrs. Gardner's shady gambling den had garnered such illustrious patronage, Georgina accepted her hand of cards from the dealer. She cast a sidelong look at the Countess. Her clear gray eyes were pretty, though impenetrable, and she bore an air of both amusement and shrewdness.

"Is your luck in?" Georgina referred to the faro box positioned beside the dealer's elbow. Perhaps Mrs. Gardner did not discriminate in who she victimized at her tables.

"I find it never is when I play here." Lady Mortimer studied her cards and then regarded Georgina from beneath hooded lids.

"And yet you attend here regularly?"

"I come more for the company, Miss Pace. One never knows who might attend." Her voice lilted as she touched the cards in her hands. "I find it is an excellent place to make interesting new friends."

The two ladies locked eyes for a moment, and Georgina felt a thrill. She could not tell if Lady Mortimer was flirting with her or not. She was singularly difficult to interpret.

Georgina swallowed hard. She could not afford to be distracted right now. She placed her bet and returned her eyes to the dealer, watching him as he handed out further cards.

"And what of this bet of the day? Do you suppose Mr. Carruthers shall prevail? I hope so. I am unacquainted with him, so my bet was completely blind."

"I think you might safely consider your wager lost, Miss Pace. Carruthers will probably make use of the privy before the hour is out, and well before the midnight curfew."

"I have so much to learn, it would seem." Georgina extended her already half-empty glass to the attendant to be topped up.

Lady Mortimer's lips twitched. "I'm sure your time will be well-employed learning the bathroom habits of all Mrs. Gardner's guests."

Georgina grinned. Lady Mortimer's dry sense of humor appealed to her . . . along with her finely tapered forearms and the delicious scent of fresh orange blossoms.

Noticing Lady Mortimer's empty glass, the attendant said, "I shall bring your wine at *once*, my lady," and scurried away.

This piqued Georgina's interest. "You must come here often to have established your very own cellar, my lady," she ventured.

Lady Mortimer took her time responding, laying her cards down first. "I favor certain wines, and Mrs. Gardner is kind enough to accommodate me."

Georgina reminded herself that the arrangements Lady Mortimer made with Mrs. Gardner for personal enjoyment had nothing to do with her. Her purpose for being here was to glean information about Mrs. Gardner's more unsavory tactics, and such was her sole interest in getting to know Lady Mortimer. That Georgina found her attractive was merely an extra benefit.

GEORGINA HAD SAT at the table long enough to render her purse significantly lighter when Lady Mortimer rose and led the way to the supper room established in the adjoining parlor.

"I suspect I will be out of pocket soon," Georgina said. "But I would just as soon lose to you as anyone else, my lady."

The Countess lifted her brows. "I think you should not aspire to lose, Miss Pace."

Lady Mortimer was the eldest daughter to the late Earl of Mortimer. She inherited her title at a young age, and while her years advanced beyond forty, she had not settled with a partner. Lady Mortimer apparently devoted her time to philanthropic activities by day and gambling by night, a lifestyle Georgina could only admire.

"It would be my privilege to lose to you." Georgina was accustomed to receiving playful banter in response to her flirtation, yet Lady Mortimer appeared impervious to her charms. "Are you a skilled gambler, my lady?"

"My fortune has not been depleted yet," Lady Mortimer remarked. "I must be doing something correctly."

Georgina handed the Countess a plate of assorted treats she had selected, and together they withdrew to a table at the side of the room. "I trust you can detect a ruse when you see one?"

Lady Mortimer sighed. "Fortunately, Mrs. Gardner no longer takes me for a flat. She ceased trying to fleece me long ago."

Georgina was puzzled. If Mrs. Gardner did not take advantage of the Countess, what could explain Lady Mortimer's repeated losses at the table?

"I must remark that you just lost a substantial sum. Perhaps that is part of an unusual strategy?"

"I have a benevolent spirit, Miss Pace."

Georgina regarded her. "Do you always come *here*, or do you spread your generosity across other gaming establishments throughout London?"

A forkful of ham suspended halfway to Lady Mortimer's mouth. Unconsciously, Georgina's eyes drifted down the smooth surface of her ladyship's arm, noticing the baby-fine hair that covered the creamy skin. "Not *always* here, Miss Pace."

Georgina tore her gaze away. "Does she host parties every night?"

"Most evenings, I believe."

"And when you are here, have you noticed many quite *young* guests?" Georgina realized too late that her tone was more eager than casual.

"A range of ages. I do not think Mrs. Gardner discriminates in who she invites. . . ." Lady Mortimer's voice tapered off, and she leaned back in her chair, her eyes narrowing.

Georgina cleared her throat and summoned up a smile. "Those are such pretty earrings."

Lady Mortimer instinctively touched the jewels dangling from her earlobes, a slight blush to her cheeks. "Thank you."

"They set off the blue tinge of your gray eyes beautifully."

Lady Mortimer tilted her head to one side, like a cautious sparrow eying a new and unfamiliar creature. Was she assessing Georgina as friend or foe? Lady Mortimer was an unusual character herself. She possessed confidence without hauteur. She had height and a voluptuous presence but did not come across as imposing. Her countenance was pleasing, but this was *not* the time to be distracted by a pretty face, Georgina reminded herself.

"It is lovely to see such a diverse range of players. Though I wonder how Solitaires has managed to avoid the scrutiny of Bow Street. Has she ever had trouble with law enforcement?"

"Not to my knowledge." Lady Mortimer's words were quite deliberate now. She paused. "Miss Pace, are you all right? You appear quite agitated."

The Countess's demeanor softened then; her eyes took on a kindly glow. She put her fork down and covered Georgina's hand with her own.

Georgina felt the heat rush to her cheeks. Suddenly self-conscious, she put a finger to the distinct furrow creasing between her brows. She had been frowning deeply. No wonder Lady Mortimer was alarmed. "Goodness me, I ramble on."

Lady Mortimer left the table and returned with a glass of water, which she edged across to Georgina. "Perhaps you had a trifle too much wine."

Georgina shook her head, as if to dislodge a trance that had overtaken her. What an insufferable suggestion. She cast the Countess a withering look. The woman clearly did not know to whom she was talking. No one had ever insinuated that Miss Georgina Pace could not handle her drink.

Lady Mortimer resumed her supper, showing no signs of being perturbed. Georgina begrudgingly took a sip of water, thinking that while Lady Mortimer was rather enchanting, she most certainly was *not* adept at judging someone's tolerance for liquor.

Just then, a woman with an impressive air of confidence interrupted them in a flourish of apricot. She held the kind of poise that might come from commanding a successful gaming house—this had to be Mrs. Gardner.

The woman had an attractiveness about her that stemmed more from self-assurance than traditional beauty. Her malt-brown hair was swept up into a neat style and tied with a pale orange ribbon matching her dress. Her jawline was chiseled, and her piercing dark eyes caught sight of Georgina like a hawk fixating on its prey.

Mrs. Gardner loomed over their table like a shadow, gesturing to a passing attendant to refill the ladies' glasses. "Elizabeth, a delight to see you as always," she said, her syrupy voice turning Georgina's stomach. "And Miss Pace, I believe this is the first time I have had the honor of you at my tables, is it not?"

"Your parties receive the highest praise throughout town, Mrs. Gardner. I could not keep away." Georgina allowed a matching saccharine undertone to seep into her voice. "You will forgive me that I came without an invitation."

"Consider yourself welcome here, Miss Pace." She took Georgina's hand and squeezed it. "Your reputation precedes you, of course. I will be happy to add you to our list of regular invitees. And you know Elizabeth?"

Georgina suspected that Mrs. Gardner's success as a hostess depended on how much tasty gossip she had to pass along to her patrons. If there was a story to derive from Georgina being engrossed in conversation with Lady Mortimer, she would try to wrangle it out of them and then disseminate it widely.

"We met each other only this evening." Lady Mortimer grinned at Georgina across the table. "But I sense we shall become old friends in no time."

"Splendid!" Mrs. Gardner revealed her yellowed teeth in a broad smile. Then, distracted by a young fellow who had risen from the hazard table, she excused herself and disappeared into the crowd in a rustle of taffeta.

Georgina watched her depart, certain she was on her way to prevent the young man's escape and guide him to another game. "What an attentive hostess."

Lady Mortimer smiled grimly. "Quite so. It is often difficult to get away once she has you in her grasp."

Just as Georgina had expected, Mrs. Gardner slid her hand around the young man's shoulders and led him to a table, whispering into his ear, then erupting into a trill of laughter. She pressed a glass into his hand and gestured to the dealer, who promptly dealt a fresh hand of cards.

A knot formed in Georgina's stomach. She raised her glass and took a deep sip from it. Perhaps she would no longer be content to simply get Arthur's vowels back.

Arthur's bespectacled eyes came to her mind, imploring her. She couldn't blame him for falling prey to Mrs. Gardner's cunning tactics, believing himself to have made new friends. This group of vultures had seen him as nothing more than an easy mark. They didn't know what they had in store for them. The fire of a protective older sister burned inside Georgina. She needed to help Arthur, for Henry's sake.

Since childhood, Georgina had seen in Henry the best of humankind. Her older brother was golden-hearted, a jovial child despite early illness related to being a miris, a flirtatious teenager (which made Georgina proud), and a fiercely loyal young man despite his proclivity for teasing his baby sister. There was no one like him. And yet, she saw in Arthur the same exceptional kindness *and* exceptional vulnerabilities that Henry possessed.

She could not, *must* not, stand by and let Arthur be victimized. Georgina needed to act—and act now.

AFTER SUPPER, GEORGINA and Lady Mortimer exchanged calling cards and retired to different tables. Georgina was sorry to part ways with Lady Mortimer, but she knew that Mrs. Gardner would need to consider her impaired to take advantage of her like she had poor Arthur. Therefore, she adopted a careless demeanor. She semi-reclined in her seat and swiveled in her chair so she could cross her legs at the ankles. She kept her cards turned down on the table, referring to them only occasionally, to appear wild and daring.

Georgina's play grew more and more reckless as she dispatched several glasses of Burgundy between hands of cards. She maintained a blank expression and regarded her fellow players from beneath half-closed eyelids, taking the odd sip from her glass. The more she drank, the less calculated her outlays became. She was aware of Lady Mortimer's occasional glance. Perhaps it would prove beneficial that the Countess believed she could not hold her liquor. Georgina doubted that her new friend was complicit in Mrs. Gardner's shady behavior, but Lady Mortimer's concern would not hurt public acceptance of her little performance.

"Lady Gianna, Major Gentry, Peer Ormskirk, Miss Pace!" Mrs. Gardner crooned, sidling up to their table from nowhere. "I trust you are all enjoying yourselves!"

Georgina raised a brow and watched the hostess casually dismiss the dealer from his post holding the bank. "Goodness, you have all been playing for the most paltry stakes! How lily-livered you all are. I thought you were all significantly more hardened than *that*!" she challenged. "Shall we set the stakes at twenty-five pounds?"

Major Gentry made a choking sound. "Oh, my good woman. That puts me out." He vacated his chair.

With those stakes, Georgina was not surprised that no one immediately swept into his empty seat.

Either way, it did not matter. Georgina had successfully lured Mrs. Gardner like a bee to nectar, and she met the wagers without hesitation. She laughed responsively at Mrs. Gardner's jokes, despite loathing the lady to her core. She resented the need to outlay any money in this establishment, and it made her blood boil to watch the others at the table lose the contents of their pockets. No one seemed to mind what was going on.

It would all be worth it to help Arthur and other honorians who might have fallen victim. Georgina smiled valiantly through her disdain and continued to push notes and coins across the table as her losses mounted. When it looked like she had exhausted her funds, she patted the breast pockets of her jacket and extricated a crumpled pound note. She took her time to flatten it out on the table before tossing it carelessly towards Mrs. Gardner.

A minute or two later, Lady Mortimer claimed the free spot in the game.

"This is an unlucky table." Georgina revealed her cards to anyone who happened to be looking.

Lady Mortimer maintained her gravity. "Let us see if we can even the score a little."

Georgina watched, surprised, as Lady Mortimer matched her bets with an equal measure of negligence, only to lose a substantial sum to Georgina. Whilst she could not be certain, Georgina suspected that Lady Mortimer's presence had checked Mrs. Gardner, who had downgraded the stakes. Had Lady Mortimer signaled to her to reduce the bet? Or was her mere presence enough to stop Mrs. Gardner from hunting prey?

Georgina had wanted to appear vulnerable, drunk, and uninhibited, in the hope that Mrs. Gardner might put her guard down and reveal her ploys of deception. Georgina needed to see the predator in action before she could get Arthur's vowels back and then expose Solitaires to the authorities. How could she do this with Lady Mortimer hovering nearby?

To her annoyance—and despite her efforts at the contrary—Georgina started to win hands against both Mrs. Gardner and Lady Mortimer. Her teeth grazed her bottom lip.

"I believe you shall ruin me, Miss Pace," Lady Mortimer said. "Might I persuade you to capitulate so I may keep my dignity?"

Georgina blinked a few times, disoriented at once by Lady Mortimer's piercing gaze and the sudden turn of events. "Of course, Lady Mortimer. I surrender." She extended a conciliatory hand.

In place of a handshake, Lady Mortimer kissed Georgina's hand delicately.

A trill of pleasure fluttered through Georgina. This was in stark contrast to the frustration of her thwarted plans. No one ever kissed her hand. What the devil was going on?

"Now that you have defeated us all, might I escort you home?"

Georgina suffocated a curse. Under different circumstances, she would have relished being escorted out by an attractive woman. Right now, she wished Lady Mortimer would simply go away, stop distracting her with that sweet scent, and leave her to her business.

"I can fend for myself, my lady."

"I do not doubt it, Miss Pace. But I should not rest easy until I have seen my new friend safely settled at home."

Georgina's belly tightened, and she realized that the Countess still held her hand. Lady Mortimer's fingers were narrow and long, free from gaudy rings. Her fair skin was incredibly smooth. Perhaps Georgina could dismantle Solitaires another day. She would benefit from some time reflecting on a strategy—and could even consult her best friend Coulthurst on the matter.

"You would not deprive me of a good night's sleep?" Lady Mortimer's eyes flashed.

"That *would* be a privilege, my lady," Georgina quipped instinctively, enjoying the color that flooded her new friend's cheeks in reply.

After bidding Mrs. Gardner a good night, the two ladies found themselves on the street outside, where Lady Mortimer hailed them a hackney.

Georgina slipped her gloves on, all the signs of her supposed drunkenness dissolving. "Fresh air is quite miraculous. It clears the head *quickly.*"

"I thought you were completely in your cups, my girl."

Georgina shook her head. "It takes a little more than that, my lady. But I appreciate your solicitude."

Lady Mortimer signaled for the passing carriage to stop, then turned to Georgina and regarded her with a stern frown. "Me-thinks *you* are playing a deep game."

"Possibly." Georgina held her hand out and assisted Lady Mortimer inside. She climbed in after her and gave the driver her direction. "Might I restore your losses to you? I have an inkling that you lost to me on purpose."

"Not at all. You won squarely."

"Well, please allow me to apologize for the deception, at least." Georgina flashed Lady Mortimer a bright smile.

"There is nothing to forgive, Miss Pace."

Georgina liked her. Lady Mortimer appeared respectable in every conceivable way. She was honorable, possessed her own title and fortune, and would have nothing to gain from working with the likes of Mrs. Gardner. As the ill-sprung hackney bounced the pair along the streets, Georgina decided the Countess could be trusted with the truth—or some part of it.

"I am trying to assist a friend of mine to remedy a difficult situation. I have it on good authority that Mrs. Gardner has acted rather disgracefully. She needs to be held to account."

Lady Mortimer's hands were folded in her lap, but her thumbs rubbed together. "That is a serious accusation. I wish you every success in correcting the situation, Miss Pace. How do you intend to hold Mrs. Gardner responsible?"

"Never you mind, my lady." Georgina turned away to stare into the night. A misty rain had started to fall, lightly obscuring the lamp-lit street. Hooves made rhythmic clicks upon the slick cobbled stones, as the carriage rocked gently from side to side. "The fewer people who know, the better."

Lady Mortimer sighed. "I do hope you will be prudent."

"Alas, Prudence follows me wherever I go," she returned wryly, speaking more of the person than the adjective. The hackney had stopped outside Georgina's residence. She took a long look at Lady Mortimer, then offered a hand. "Here we are then. I cannot promise an uninterrupted night's sleep, but I vow not to deprive you of anything else."

In the darkness of the carriage, Lady Mortimer stifled a laugh. "Miss Pace!"

"You are not joining me? How disappointing. I thought you wished to see me safely settled at home."

"I trust your doorstep is safe enough for now, Miss Pace."

"Very well. For now, my lady." Georgina took Lady Mortimer's hand and placed a kiss on it. The rain suddenly intensified, and the urge to remain in the carriage indefinitely also grew. However, Georgina would not make the driver suffer. "Thank you for your company this evening. I hope I have proved to be a sufficiently interesting new acquaintance that you might wish to see me again?" She descended onto the street without pausing for an answer.

Almost in a whisper, Lady Mortimer replied, "A most interesting new acquaintance, Miss Pace." The vehicle lurched away into the night.

4

LORD ROBERT COULTHURST inspected his reflection in the full-length gilt mirror. As a noted Corinthian, his attire was fashionable and elegant but lacked the fancy embellishments that denoted dandyism. Just the balance he liked to strike. Colt possessed a powerful athlete's build that gave him a certain advantage in his bearing. With a self-satisfied smile—a smile that had melted the hearts of many—he regarded his presentation with approval. A knock at the door interrupted his appraisal.

His distinguished butler, Scanlan, was a mature woman of around fifty. Attired from head to toe in black—aside from a neat white necktie—she possessed stern features and slicked-back hair. Over the years, she had earned herself a reputation for being diligent and precise. In exchange for her excellent service, he provided her with ample remuneration, full board, and two days off a week that she might enjoy as she wished.

"Mrs. Fortescue is here to see you, my lord. In the library."

Colt raked his hand back through his hair, as the familiar pleasure and torment of Sarah's presence washed over him. He thanked Scanlan and hurried through the final stages of his dressing.

His library was decorated in a masculine style. A pair of crossed

Hussar sabers formed a menacing 'x' above the cluttered mantlepiece that held a tortoise-shelled cigar box, a rustic mantle clock standing proudly upon its four brass feet (yet running ten minutes behind time), and a small container which Colt idly identified as a snuff box he had misplaced some days ago. Two of the four walls boasted ceiling-high shelves overcrowded with old books that exuded an earthy aroma. A fire, lit by an obliging attendant some time earlier, crackled and smelled like burning coals tempered with sandalwood.

Sarah was perched near the fire on the Italian sofa, an elegant piece of furniture with pale, green-striped satin and carved mahogany edging. Her wicker bonnet framed her pretty face, with olive- and black-striped ribbons tied in an oversized bow under her chin. Not a single hair was out of its rightful place. She wore a white muslin gown and a peach spencer coat, which enhanced the richness of her russet skin tone. She glanced up and caught Colt's eager appraisal; her brown eyes kindled as they met his, and she stood up.

"Sarah," he greeted her, bowing over her hand. Glancing down at the fingers touching his, he squeezed them. "Your hands are like ice. Warm them by the fire, dearest, and tell me, to what do I owe this unexpected pleasure?"

Sarah extended her hands to the fire to thaw. "I am glad you are at home, Robert."

"I hardly perceive how I would not be at this early hour. Unless I slept somewhere else, of course." He grinned at his afterthought.

"I have just been at Hatchards. While perusing some novels, young Miss Chen approached me. She is an *exquisite* girl. I daresay she will be married in no time. I wonder who the lucky person shall be?" She stared into the flames, but then her gaze flashed back to him. "That signifies neither way, however. We discussed a few of the latest titles, and I took it upon myself to dissuade her from some books that were *not* suitable for a debutante in her first season."

Colt regarded her with an air of confusion, unclear how Miss Chen's choice of reading material related to him. "I daresay your counsel will have the opposite of its desired effect, Sarah."

She frowned. "Oh, that is true. I did not even consider that."

He continued to smile, waiting for her to proceed with her story.

"*Then*, as I made my purchase, I looked outside and spied none other than Mr. Pace," she said at last.

"Indeed?"

"Mr. *Silas* Pace. Georgina's father."

"He is the only Mr. Pace I know, in fact." He gave an indifferent shrug.

"This means they have returned to London."

Colt made his way to a table cluttered with bottles and crystal glassware. "Can I offer you a drink?" Without waiting for a response, he poured her a large glass of Madeira. "I hate to be the one to inform you of this, my dear, but I already knew they were back in town. Our George returned one or two days ago. I heard whispers in the clubs."

"I wonder why she has not yet called upon either of us." Sarah accepted the drink, eagerly bringing it to her mouth.

"I can think of many reasons, Sarah. Perhaps she is simply busy restoring her town affairs into order . . . or she is becoming reacquainted with a ladylove." He did not take it personally that Georgina failed to notify him the moment she returned to London. He knew her too well.

Sarah pouted. "You don't share my happiness about her return. Surely you missed her. There was no one to compete with you."

"You puzzle me, Sarah. I am not sure to what competition you allude."

Sarah surveyed him over the edge of her glass. "Do not talk such fustian to me, Robert. Perhaps *this* year, you might encounter your ideal match and stop playing your games."

Colt, Sarah, and Georgina had met over a decade ago, at the Derby Stakes in Epsom Downs. All three had backed the winner, Ditto, owned by Sir Hedworth Williamson, but when it came time to claim their winnings, they all realized they had been hobbled by the same bookmaker, who had absconded with both their original bets and winnings. Joining forces, the trio managed to track him down all the way to Hull. While he never paid what he owed them, they did recover their initial outlays, together with a sense of justice, when they handed him over to a local magistrate. Since then, they had never been apart.

Georgina and Colt, in particular, shared a common interest in the petticoat line, and often bantered over who possessed the greatest skill in this area. Whilst Georgina sought more worldly lovers, Colt preferred the thrill of unmarried damsels. He had acquired quite the reputation among social circles for his ability to assist women in learning the scope of pleasure and intimacy available to them before settling into relationships. Naturally, his *services* were not entirely altruistic. He thoroughly enjoyed participating in the process.

Of course, there were instances when this did not unfold the way he intended. At times, it was more like balancing on a razor's edge. One small slip, and he could find himself tethered at the altar. It was a fine art, indeed, to assist someone *without* promising wedlock. But he boasted many short dalliances with ladies who wished to enter their eventual marriages well-versed in their own bodies and desires. As such, he considered himself far superior at the game of seduction than his dear friend George.

Though Sarah did not aspire to become a libertine herself, she witnessed her friends in their respective dalliances with indulgent tolerance. Occasionally, they called upon her to aid them out of a romantic entanglement or to soothe the ruffled feathers of a society patron.

Colt lounged beside Sarah on the sofa, pivoting his body to face her and draping an arm over the couch. He could detect the faintest hint of jasmine. For all his fair conquests, the mere scent of her could still drive him mad with desire.

"Surely you did not call me from my bed merely to tell me that George is back in town?" Colt had no desire to discuss his matrimonial prospects with Sarah.

She beamed at him. "I deemed it highly critical news."

"Perhaps you hoped to discover me still in bed?" he teased.

There was the barest hint of a smile. "Nonsense."

Colt's long fingers traced over the grooves of wood along the rear of the sofa. He averted his gaze from her. "If you wish to find me abed, I recommend calling on me *before* ten o'clock."

"I also visit you for your excellent Madeira."

Colt clasped his hand across his heart. "I thought you came here to see *me*."

"Enough! You are being ridiculous," she reprimanded him. "I want to talk to you about Georgina. What is to be done?"

"In what way? I'm unsure what you want me to do about her return. Send her back to Yorkshire?" Colt put his hands up in defeat.

Sarah must have been mad to think he might prevail upon George to change her ways. That would be like trying to persuade a river to modify its course.

"She acted rashly in Cornwall over Christmas," Sarah went on. "She seduced the Atkins chit and left the house under the cover of darkness. Or so I hear, at least. Her behavior did not go unmarked, and the town gossips have already tattled extensively about her exploits. Miss Atkins's credit almost did not survive the ordeal, and if it were not for Lord Ravenscroft's timely marriage proposal, I struggle to imagine society countenancing her." Sarah fidgeted with her bracelet, twisting it backwards and forwards on her wrist. "Georgina, *whenever* she shows her face in town, will not crawl out of the affair unscathed."

He gave a half-hearted shrug. To fully agree with Sarah felt like a betrayal of his other friend. He shuddered to imagine Sarah's reaction when she heard the whispers circulating that Georgina had already been witnessed skipping down a street half-naked two nights ago, in a state of unabashed glee. *He* would not tell her.

"I am hardly qualified to reproach Georgina. A trifle hypocritical of me, don't you agree?"

"Certainly, but we *must* set her back on the path of propriety." Sarah took another sip of her drink.

"Indeed. We should marry her off and hope her wife can tame her!"

Sarah's countenance lit up, and she clapped her hands in delight. "I know you mock, Colt, but that may be the ultimate answer. It's my belief that, for all her bravado, Georgina maintains her single lifestyle to protect Mr. Pace. After everything he has been through, I know she considers his needs above her own. We must convince her to settle down."

"A romantic and fanciful notion, Sarah, but I cannot see George being so sentimental."

"Georgina has sacrificed her heart so that she might take care of her father. You cannot convince me otherwise. And, whether you meant to, I think you have hit upon the solution."

A sense of foreboding struck him. He frowned and dragged both hands back through his hair. "You are not to meddle, Sarah."

"Of course not. A gentle nudging will not go astray, though. Are you attending the Blakes's ball on Saturday?"

"They have invited me, and if you say I must be there, I would hate to disappoint you."

Sarah laughed. "Be sure to dance with me, then."

"I should like that. But what about you? So keen to have Georgina married off. Do you never find yourself lonely, my dear?" He lowered his voice and held her eyes in a flirtatious gaze.

She regarded him, her mouth set in a firm line. "Sometimes, Colt. Not to the extent where I wish to become someone's fleeting mistress, however. At least, not on *their* terms."

Colt gave her a steady look, unblinking. He had never considered her in that light. He thoroughly adored Sarah and would have leapt at the chance to call her his. Sadly, she had never taken him seriously.

Sarah had become a widow five years ago. Almost twenty years her senior, the late Commander Fortescue had enjoyed a successful military career, most recently earning honors for his bravery at the Battle of Trafalgar. His precarious vocation, however, was not what had seen an end to him. The Commander met his fate following a frivolous evening at his club with a few of his cronies. He had indulged in a few too many libations and, at the close of the evening, drove himself home. During this drive, he sadly miscalculated the speed of his curricle and pair when taking a rather sharp bend, and the resultant collision killed him instantly.

Following the tragic accident, Colt supported Sarah through her year of mourning. She naturally grieved for her husband; though it was not a marriage for love, she had grown fond of him. Soon after dispensing with her mourning blacks, Sarah had settled into the more liberated lifestyle of an attractive young widow, garnering the attention of many eligible gentlemen, including Colt himself. He cast a protective and often jealous eye over gentlemen callers who attempted to woo her and did not hold back pointing out some defect or other whenever she found favor with one of them.

He waited respectfully, wanting to afford her ample time to grieve, before even attempting to fix his interest with her. She dismissed his every attempt. Despite being spurned, he continued to flirt with her over the subsequent years. He suspected he may even have tempted her once or twice. To his ongoing frustration, however, she remained steadfast in her resolve to reject his advances.

Not wishing to make his friend feel uncomfortable by his proximity, Colt stood and crossed the room.

"And how would you like to assist our dearest George?"

A slow smile formed on Sarah's lips. "You will goad her into it, as you always do. Now, let us away to Half Moon Street immediately. We don't have a moment to lose."

WITHIN HALF AN hour, Jarvis had ushered Colt and Sarah into the front parlor of Georgina's residence. Colt assumed a confident pose by the fireplace, leaning his elbow on the solid marble mantlepiece, while Sarah disposed herself on the straw-colored satin sofa. An immense portrait of one of the family's forebears—looking not unlike George, with deep brown curls and mischievous eyes—towered above them, framed in elaborate giltwood. A metal grate stood before the fireplace, protecting the Aubusson floor rug from straying embers.

Colt wished he knew what Sarah had in mind. She had insisted he accompany her, and he obliged, but how she expected him to cajole Miss Georgina Pace into mending her ways, he had no idea. He maintained his position by the fire for some minutes. Just as it grew tiresome, the door finally opened to reveal their friend.

He bowed over her hand. "George." He smiled and placed a light kiss upon her knuckles. "How do you do?"

Seeing his friend after months apart gratified Colt. She wore riding breeches and a black jacket. She knotted her cravat indifferently, though presented an excellent figure overall. It never ceased to amaze Colt how well Georgina looked, whether she wore a resplendent gown at a ball, or mud-specked breeches following a ride. Georgina excelled at executing a natural—if somewhat unpredictable—enigmatic style.

Presently, her long dark hair had been tied back carelessly with a ribbon, and the shadows around her eyes suggested she had not benefitted much from sleep of late. He suspected the gossip he had heard about town may have been accurate. The thought of her frolicking half-naked around the streets of London made him stifle a smile. At least the news had not reached Sarah's ears yet.

Sarah rose and greeted her friend with a warm embrace and a peck on each cheek.

"Sarah. It is good to see you." Georgina yanked on the bell, summoning service for her guests.

"I spotted your charming father this morning passing by Hatchards, and my excitement that you had returned fairly overthrew me," Sarah said, her voice abuzz. "Why did you not write to advise me? Did you enjoy Yorkshire? Will you remain here for the season? I had hoped you would come back now that the Miss Atkins affair is over with."

Colt chuckled. "You're hardly giving George a chance to respond, my love."

"A terrible business," Georgina said. "I did my best to keep you appraised, but you know I am not much of a letter-writer. And, yes, the plan is for us both to stay awhile. My father prefers town life infinitely more than the country, and he has no patience for running the estate. When we are in Yorkshire, he spends most of the hours visiting neighbors or hunting. It falls to me to attend to the tenants, ensure the farms are operating correctly, and negotiate wages." Georgina gave a little yawn, covering her mouth with the back of her hand. "Now that we are back, I have high hopes that Papa's clubs might keep him entertained—"

"We have missed you," Colt interjected. "London is not the same without you. No madcap stories to amuse one over the breakfast table."

Sarah quirked a brow. "And I cannot manage to rein Colt in alone."

"Colt, have you been making inroads with the latest debutantes? I suspect you mean to gloat over all your successes," Georgina teased.

Colt gave a sheepish smile. "What a singularly inappropriate suggestion, George. I would never *gloat* about such matters. However, as you have asked me, I shall only say that a *great* many beauties have graced London so far this season. Do I pick up a tinge of jealousy?"

Georgina rolled her eyes. "Anyone can seduce young ladies, Colt. It requires *much* more skill to entice a woman of the world."

Sarah rolled her eyes. "You are both children."

Choosing to ignore Sarah, Colt gave Georgina an appreciative smile. "Touché, George. I presume you have learned that Miss Atkins recently married?"

Georgina's eyes lowered, and her cheeks colored up. "Indeed, I read about it in *The Times*. A fortunate outcome for all."

Colt raised his brows. So Georgina was not immune to societal opinion, after all.

A maid entered at that moment carrying a tray with a pot, three cups, and a small jug of milk. She served them all steaming coffee before leaving them alone again.

"I *could* remark that *I* have never fled town because of an enthusiastic ladylove." Colt took a spoon and stirred it through his cup. "How foolhardy of you. You are better suited to ladies who will *not* mistake your intentions." He eyed her in amusement.

Throughout their acquaintance, he had witnessed Georgina

commanding many admirers, young and old, of all presentations. She could hardly walk down the street without receiving an invitation. Despite her many options, Georgina was selective with her dalliances, opting for married or widowed ladies who would not require her to come up to scratch.

Colt had no desire to be locked down to one partner. Unless that partner was Sarah.

Georgina occasionally vilified him for his role in corrupting younger, impressionable ladies. She insisted that even the most informed young ladies might see Colt's aversion to marriage as a challenge to overcome, especially given his charm. But George, too, made her share of missteps.

"It was unwise of me to dally with Miss Atkins—or, I should say now, Lady Ravenscroft," Georgina admitted.

"Was it worth it?" he inquired, crossing one booted leg over the other.

"Robert!" Sarah said. She shot Georgina a look and shook her head.

"When I realized Prudence took my attention seriously, I withdrew."

Colt chuckled. "And you retreated to the country. Rather pudding-hearted of you, my girl."

"There was no other option," Georgina responded with a huff of indignation. She replaced her cup on the table beside her. "I am not the marrying sort."

"Georgina, I think you are. Perhaps you have not discovered your lady yet," Sarah said quickly, sitting upright.

Colt nodded. "I agree."

"Neither of you would condemn some poor soul to suffer me."

"She would need to be *very* special," Colt said.

Sarah cleared her throat. "And now that you are back in town, I hope you shall endeavor *not* to fall into a scrape like you did in Cornwall."

Georgina gave her an arch look. "Better a scrape than a mésalliance."

"You sail close to the wind, my girl," Sarah countered. "One of these days, you shall find that doors are closed to you."

Colt noticed Georgina's bright blue eyes flash, and he interjected quickly. "It will take a lot for George to be exiled, Sarah."

"I do not dread that day, in any event. Then I shall at least be spared the monotony of society."

Sarah sighed. "I hope you will not ruin yourself. I wish you might marry, put that great heart of yours to use, and stay out of mischief."

Colt preserved his silence, knowing Sarah's tactic would be futile. He could already see the annoyance building within George. It would be up to him to try to claw back into George's good graces if Sarah continued in this vein.

Georgina moved to sit on the edge of her desk. She folded her arms across her chest.

Colt felt the distance she placed between them.

"Marriage is the last thing on my mind. I am content with my life as it is. I can assist my father whenever he requires. I can go to my clubs when I choose, attend balls, and go wherever I like, without a chaperone. Why would I sacrifice freedom in tying myself to one person?"

"There *are* benefits," Sarah said with a twinkle in her eye. "Particularly if you fall in love."

Georgina frowned. "Let us not speak of this further, Sarah, or I shall become vexed."

Colt drank deeply from his coffee. That answered his question. Georgina responded more readily to his playful banter than Sarah's direct approach. That was clear.

Georgina turned the subject. “Tell me, Sarah, how *you* have been?”

Colt’s posture straightened. Suddenly, he was deeply invested in the conversation.

Sarah faltered for a moment, but the words that hovered on her lips faded away. “All has been well for me. My household runs along like the gears of a clock. Usually reliable and only occasionally needs winding. I am hardly needed for anything. I discovered a marvelous new milliner—which I dare not share with you, lest you try to up-stage my custom.” She raised her brows cheekily.

Colt felt himself relax. This was much safer terrain. He stared down at the coffee in his cup and wondered if the ladies were open to exchanging it for a whiskey.

“Did she create that confection, Sarah?” Georgina gestured to Sarah’s bonnet. “It becomes you well, but would not suit me, I think.”

Sarah’s hand went self-consciously to the olive- and black-striped ribbons under her chin.

“It’s most fetching on you, my dear,” Colt reassured her, inclining his head to one side and regarding her with a smile. As far as he was concerned, Sarah could wear a flat cap or a crown befitting a queen, and she would look adorable.

“And have you found yourself a lover yet?” Georgina asked Sarah.

Colt nearly choked on his coffee. Sometimes he wished their friendship circle did not have to be so intimate.

The color of Sarah’s cheeks deepened. “No, I have not found someone to fill that post.”

Georgina clicked her tongue. “Perhaps you are too discerning?”

With an icy stare, Sarah crossed her arms. “I have standards, at least.”

Georgina laughed. “Put your barbs down, my dear. I merely jest.”

Colt thought it more likely punishment than jest, given the way

Sarah had pressed Georgina on marriage. He kept his thoughts to himself.

"Perhaps it is my misfortune that I do not crave women as lovers; I think there is a shortage of good men," Sarah mused.

"Shall I just take my leave?" Colt demanded, aggrieved.

Sarah reached out and took his hand, squeezing it. "Oh, you know I do not mean you, my love."

Colt ground his teeth. He did not crave Sarah's pity. He met Georgina's gaze, and her eyes twinkled. Damn it, was she laughing at him too? He put his coffee down a touch too hard, rattling the table. He stood and walked to the window, folding his arms over his chest.

"I was meaning to ask, do either of you know anything about Solitaires in St James's Square?" Georgina inquired.

Gaming hell? Now, that was a more enticing conversation. Colt turned back to see Sarah wrinkle her nose.

"Been there once or twice. Nothing noteworthy, except that two rum dogs, Ellis and Montgomery, sponsor it. Why do you ask?" he replied.

Georgina regaled him with the account of her young friends, Lord Edmund Telford and Mr. Arthur Coombes, and explained that she had visited Mrs. Gardner's the previous evening in search of evidence.

"I have every reason to suspect they target susceptible people of means who do not know they are being taken in." The muscle in Georgina's cheek twitched.

It all sounded like a bore. Colt preferred it when Georgina fixed her interest on some damsel or wished to race him in a seduction. Whatever plan she was hatching now did not have the same hedonistic ring to it that he enjoyed, and he recognized the stubborn tilt to her chin.

He turned back to the window to show his disinterest in discussing this further. It occurred to him that he might claim a prior appointment at his tailor and excuse himself immediately, but he could not abandon Sarah to Georgina's mercy. That would sink him in her estimation.

Luckily, a familiar upturned face, floating amidst the crowded street, offered him unexpected respite from the tedium.

"Is that Lady Prudence Ravenscroft standing outside?"

Georgina's cup clattered back in the saucer as she shoved it on the table. "What?" She rushed to the window in alarm, then hid behind Colt's broad physique, peering from behind him. "It is her!"

Colt burst out laughing. "Did you invite her?"

"Of course not. Look, she is passing by. Thank heavens." Georgina gave him a playful slap on his arm. "What a fright you gave me. She already wrote me a letter propositioning me for an affair, now that she is a married woman." Georgina massaged her face with her hand.

"What an impact you must have made in Cornwall," Sarah interjected wryly.

"I think we can safely assume our George makes an impact wherever she goes."

To Colt's annoyance, Sarah redirected the conversation back to Arthur and his lost IOUs. "What is your plan to support Mr. Coombes? Mrs. Gardner's cannot be a straightforward citadel to breach. Not even for your charms."

Georgina rested her head on Colt's shoulder. "I must think of something. There'll be the devil to pay if I don't help Arthur! The last thing I want is to bring Henry's wrath down upon me."

At Georgina's reference to her brother, Colt's heart sank. He exchanged a sidelong look with Sarah.

Georgina did not seem to notice. Instead, she had withdrawn her fob watch from her pocket and was idly rotating it between her fingers. "I will return tonight. I must speak with Mrs. Gardner about the

IOUs, but I am concerned my temper will get the better of me. Come with me, Colt? I need you."

There it is, he thought grimly.

Her bright blue eyes captured his, and she smiled irresistibly.

Attempting to deny George proved futile once again. With a grudging nod, Colt agreed. Now, he really had earned that whiskey.

5

COLT FOLLOWED GEORGINA into Solitaires just after eleven o'clock that evening. They gained admittance without difficulty, and within minutes, had divested themselves of their outer garments and were being ushered into the lively gaming room.

"I wonder what curiosity they have put in the book tonight," Georgina mused.

Colt checked and rolled his eyes. "Some prize snails are set for a race. Do you think Mr. Shelby or Mem Slicker will prevail?"

At that, Georgina erupted into an explosion of whispered profanities. Colt chuckled and scribbled their names, betting his own shillings on Mem Slicker. He put his hand on the small of Georgina's back and moved her away from the offending table before she upended it.

His gaze swept over the room, noticing little out of the ordinary. He had never observed any underhanded methods being employed at Solitaires and had been surprised by Georgina's accusations.

"What's the plan?"

Georgina loosened her neckcloth slightly. "I'm going to see if I can observe the attendants employing any more tricks, aside from simply encouraging people like Arthur to play deeply. Perhaps if we can make our way into the *back* rooms, there might be more to see. Then,

I will ask to talk with Mrs. Gardner and do what I might to *persuade* her to relinquish Arthur's IOUs. I will pay the full price if necessary, including interest."

Colt grinned. From his experience, there certainly would be more to see out the back, though he doubted it would assist George in solving the puzzle.

"Colt, by Jove! You here?" a voice called out from a nearby table.

Colt turned. "Leggy!"

Colt approached the table. Leggy was an enthusiastic gentleman with fair skin, a smattering of freckles, and a wild crop of ginger hair swept roguishly to one side. He rose, his green eyes bright.

"Wonderful to see you, old chap."

Colt shook Leggy's hand. His friend was dressed impeccably as always, with beige pantaloons, shining boots, and a walnut-colored coat that fit him well.

"Join us, will you?" Mr. Samuel Leggett coaxed, gesturing to a chair.

A handful of acquaintances made up Leggy's table, including one Lord Ravenscroft, Prudence's new husband. Colt wondered if Ravenscroft knew his young wife continued to pursue Georgina. Colt glanced at Georgina, who gave him a slight nod and disappeared in the other direction.

Lord Ravenscroft acknowledged Colt frostily as he sat and was dealt a hand of cards. Colt had once enjoyed a brief dalliance with Ravenscroft's younger sister, Hester, much to the disapproval of her older brother. While the affair ended amicably and without associated scandal, Mr. Ravenscroft resented Colt's unabashed lack of shame.

The other players showed no awareness of the tension between them.

Ravenscroft possessed dark, silver-flecked hair and gray eyes that shone in cool contrast to his olive skin, creased from age and many hours spent outdoors. He wore spectacles and required a cane to walk. *A fine-looking man*, Colt thought. And a formidable card player, too, as he relieved his opponents of the contents of their pocketbooks expeditiously.

"Ravenscroft, how is your sister, Hester?" Colt asked, hoping to distract Ravenscroft into an error with his cards.

Ravenscroft's gaze snapped up, and a tell-tale muscle clenched in his jaw. "Mrs. Spalding is well, thank you," he responded in a clipped tone. His eyes focused back on his cards.

"Yes, I spotted her only yesterday, driving through the park. She looks to be quite heavy now," Colt remarked. Hester was soon to be a mother.

"By Jove," Leggy interjected with a frown. "Not good form, you know, Colt."

Ravenscroft looked up in surprise.

"Nothing wrong with a bit of flesh on a woman," Leggy continued. "I, for one, am most partial."

Colt and Ravenscroft regarded Leggy in mutual confusion.

"She is heavy *with child*," Ravenscroft offered.

"Even more reason not to take exception to it. She can't help that." Leggy directed an admonishing glare at Colt. "What have you got against women in the family way? I daresay you've been responsible for a number of them."

Colt was no longer amused. "Oh, be quiet, Leggy."

Colt studied the cards that Ravenscroft laid down. He had hoped to distract Ravenscroft with his remarks about Hester; he did not account for Leggy driving the conversation off on one of his famous tangents. Fortunately, Leggy's intervention yielded the desired outcome.

Colt played his own card and hoped he did not show his eagerness to celebrate Ravenscroft's mistake.

Ravenscroft peered over his glasses at Colt. With a sigh, he dropped his cards in defeat.

"Has Lord Coulthurst ended your run of good luck, dear husband?" a soft voice cooed.

A stunning redhead with piercing gray eyes, wearing a gown of emerald silk with a shimmering beaded overlay, now stood at Lord Ravenscroft's elbow. She placed her hand on his shoulder and beamed at Colt.

He recalled dancing with Miss Prudence Atkins the previous year, at her very successful come out ball. This critical—and often embarrassing—ordeal involved proud parents and guardians coercing their young lady, gentleman, or electora into a social event in their honor, thereby announcing their introduction to London society. Though Miss Prudence was cute, it had seemed she was not susceptible to Colt's charm. Georgina was more her type, it seemed. He rose from his seat and bowed.

"Lady Ravenscroft. Glad to see you! Allow me to congratulate you on your nuptials."

She extended a graceful arm, and he kissed her bejeweled hand. "I am also a mother."

Colt regarded her with an arched brow. The woman had only been married two months. Even Ravenscroft, as athletic as he was, would struggle to sire a legitimate child so efficiently.

Prudence giggled. "Practically a mother, at any rate. To my husband's ward: His name is Mr. Lawrence Dalrymple. At the Blakes's ball, we shall perform an introduction. He has recently completed his studies and is now making his way into town. He would benefit from some new friends."

Colt smiled uneasily. The last thing he wanted was to be saddled with a green cub to escort about town.

It appeared this notion did not sit well with Lord Ravenscroft either. He cleared his throat and tried to redirect Colt's attention back to the table.

"Did you spot Miss Pace, my lady?" Colt said, regaining his seat and taking up the hand of cards the dealer had supplied him. He could not resist stirring trouble. Perhaps next time, Georgina would enlist Sarah to help her instead.

Prudence fixed him with an eager gaze. "Georgina is here?"

He shuffled the cards in his hands from front to back. "I believe she is milling around somewhere."

Prudence cast a look around the room, feigning disinterest. "I might go in search of a port. I cannot abide this Burgundy." She placed her glass on the table and swept away.

Leggy studied his own glass. "Rather fancied it myself. Pass it over here. Waste not."

"Oh, Leggy." Colt released an affectionate sigh.

AFTER TRIUMPHING SEVERAL more times against the good-natured Leggy and the surly Lord Ravenscroft, Colt grew bored and removed himself from the table. Thanks to several glasses of Burgundy, he felt ready to tackle anything.

He ambled through the main gaming rooms, scanning for any sign of Georgina. If she was spying on Mrs. Gardner, she did so most furtively. He reached the back parlor, which exuded a dark and intimate ambience.

In contrast to Mem Lavigne's club, however, this room did not provide a positive, sensual energy. One could not be sure what was going on at the assorted tables. Colt suspected fledglings would struggle to leave such a room unscathed, and he wondered if this was where Arthur had met his misfortune at Mrs. Gardner's hand.

"Colt! You shit-sack!" Georgina's voice hissed. "Where have you been?"

He swung around to find Georgina in a darkened corner, concealing herself from view. He knew laughing at her would only incense her further, so he pressed his lips together to hold back a smile.

She wrinkled her nose. "You reek of wine."

"They held me up at the whist table. Why are you hiding?"

"Someone told Prudence I was here. I overheard her asking for me," Georgina said, keeping a vigilant eye on their surroundings. "I intend to avoid that sort of confrontation tonight."

He hoped the guilt of his betrayal would not creep across his countenance. "What have you uncovered?"

"Aside from the fact that *you* are next to useless? Very little. I must speak with Mrs. Gardner."

Uneasiness gnawed at him. "Not one to interfere, George. But have you quite thought this through?"

It was one thing to try to settle a fellow's debts for him. It was another matter to seek to dismantle a gambling enterprise like Solitaires. Some very influential—even dangerous—business partners sponsored this place. He did not want Georgina becoming entangled in that.

She shrugged. "I don't have a choice, Colt."

"What will you even say to her?"

"I will ask to purchase Arthur's IOUs from her. I shall even offer to pay her interest. My offer will be more than fair. And after that . . . we shall see what is necessary." Georgina looked over her shoulder again. "I also would like to escape without running into Prudence. Particularly if her husband is here. Husbands don't tend to like me."

Colt did not want to alarm Georgina about Mrs. Gardner or her associates, but she had to act cautiously. Prudence needed to be the last thing on her mind. He hoped, however, she would endeavor to be careful. "Mrs. Gardner is an enterprising woman, George. I doubt she has made herself so successful by giving easy concessions to people."

Georgina tossed her hands up in the air. "I must try. Edmund landed Arthur in this mess, and they have applied to me to extract them from it."

"And if she returns the notes to you, that will be the end of it?"

There was a stubborn set to her chin. "No. This has to stop." Georgina gestured about the room with her hand.

Colt frowned. He could foresee little peace in his future while George participated in this self-imposed crusade.

"Now, if you cannot discover how to be more useful, I suggest you take yourself back to Leggy. Or, better still, go and observe the snail race." Georgina strode away and accepted a glass from a passing attendant, pausing to exchange a few words. She tossed her head back, laughing at something the attendant said. Georgina leaned in and whispered a few words near her ear. The woman's cheeks flushed, and she winked in reply before continuing through the room with her tray.

Colt watched his friend. George had petitioned him to join her, ostensibly to keep her temper in check. And yet his headstrong friend had refused to heed his advice. He did not know whether to growl in frustration or smile with pride.

6

MRS. GARDNER PRESIDED over an EO table, where she laughed uproariously and kept her guests distracted with animated chatter. Annoyance surged within Georgina, such that she withdrew from the shadows at the back of the room and approached the table.

"My good woman, please excuse the interruption. I could not stay away." Georgina extended her hand, but Mrs. Gardner ignored the gesture and hauled her into an unceremonious embrace.

"My *dear* Miss Pace," Mrs. Gardner purred. "Two visits in as many days? I am *so* obliged to you. Your presence here is doing so much for my credit."

This notion sickened Georgina. She swallowed the sour taste in her mouth. "You were very kind to grant me unfettered admittance last night." She took a spot at the table, accepted a drink from Mrs. Gardner, and promptly placed a bet.

"Are you here with Elizabeth?"

"Lady Mortimer?" Georgina wondered if Mrs. Gardner intended to distract her from the game by mentioning the enigmatic lady. Briefly, the ploy worked, as Georgina thought about how she would relish the chance to see Lady Mortimer again and even challenge her to a few drinks. But she had a greater purpose for being here this evening and had to keep her eye on the target. "No."

"She is around here somewhere. I saw her a little while ago."

Georgina plunged her free hand into her pocket and located her round fob watch. Holding the heavy, cold silver calmed and refocused her.

After several rounds of EO, winning one and losing two, Georgina had observed nothing particularly underhanded in the operations of the spinning wheel. She supposed the house might conceal a magnetic mechanism beneath, which could move the ball to a preferred number when spinning. Though she dearly wished for evidence to deliver to Bow Street, she would stop short of clambering beneath the tables.

Mrs. Gardner had remained at her side throughout. Georgina finally drained the contents of her glass and turned to her.

"Might I steal a private word with you?"

Mrs. Gardner drummed her long fingernails on the wooden table, making an unnerving clicking sound. "Well, of course you may. I shall have you escorted to my private parlor, and I will join you presently."

A maid—the same blushing woman from the previous evening—led Georgina from the back saloon, out into the musty-smelling hallway, and into another room. The maid paused a beat too long in the doorway, likely hoping Georgina would pay her attention again. Eventually, with a sigh, she instructed Georgina to wait.

Muted sounds from the festivities down the hall created a low hum. A candelabra flickered softly, casting a warm glow on trinkets that adorned every corner of the overcrowded space. The furnishings were cluttered together in a way that was unusual yet oddly pleasing to the eye.

A yellow, thick-satin sofa sat opposite a plush floral print armchair in pink hues. The vibrant colors of a large Persian rug drew Georgina's eye to the floor, where a low Queen Anne coffee table nestled in the center of the room. A stunning blue-and-orange Qianglong vase sat upon a gilded table on one side of the settee. Objects from around the world crammed the mantlepiece above the fireplace. The décor suggested that Mrs. Gardner either enjoyed a well-traveled life, or someone brought her the items from far and wide.

Had it not been for the circumstances of this meeting, Georgina may have liked to inquire after this interesting collection of artifacts and their owner. However, Mrs. Gardner's want of proper conduct meant a closer acquaintance with her would be both inappropriate and undesirable. It was almost a shame.

She wondered how many guests were allowed into this private space. Absently, Georgina wiped a finger along the stained wood of the shelf to reveal a fine layer of dust. How unpleasant. She rubbed her hands together to get rid of the residue. That was when the door behind her creaked, and she turned around.

Mrs. Gardner sailed into the room and guided Georgina towards the sofa, then sat across from her. "Dear Miss Pace. I cannot express how delighted I am that you have decided to become a *regular* at my humble parties. I declare, you shall secure my success as a hostess."

Georgina swallowed the small amount of bile this speech had stimulated. "You are most fortunate to have found such an excellent house. Such convenient and *discreet* locations in the heart of the ton are difficult to come by."

"A dear friend leased the house for me, Miss Pace."

Georgina folded one leg over her knee and draped an arm over it. "You must be *very* lucky in your friendships."

Mrs. Gardner offered a tight-lipped smile, but no warmth reached her eyes. "Pray tell me, how might I be of service to you?"

"It is a rather *sensitive* matter, Mrs. Gardner, but I am optimistic we shall contrive a satisfactory outcome."

"This sounds most intriguing."

Georgina sat forward on the edge of the sofa, her hands now between her knees, fingertips pressed together. "I understand you have lately become acquainted with a friend of mine, Mr. Arthur Coombes."

A curtain dropped over Mrs. Gardner's eyes, yet her stony smile remained in place. She said nothing.

"He is a dear friend of mine, and I am quite *protective* of him." The deliberate serenity of Georgina's expression, meanwhile, contrasted with the crisp tone of her voice.

"Naturally." Mrs. Gardner's fingers fidgeted with the handkerchief she crushed in her hand.

"He is a charming and enthusiastic young man. When he visited here to enjoy your marvelous hospitality, he may have been a trifle dipped, playing beyond his means at your tables."

"A pleasing young man is our Mr. Coombes," Mrs. Gardner said.

Mrs. Gardner had not become the proprietor of a successful gaming den by chance. She must possess some measure of intelligence to have established herself so well. Georgina decided a forthright approach might be most suitable.

"I will get straight to the point. I came here tonight with a business proposal. I should like to purchase Mr. Coombes's vowels from you. Together with a nominal amount to cover any interest owed since you accrued the debt, naturally."

Mrs. Gardner rose from the seat and turned her back, making it difficult for Georgina to interpret her reactions. She stood near the fireplace and tugged on the bellpull.

Georgina crossed her arms, wondering who she might be summoning. An attendant, perhaps? Or a bruiser? She hoped Colt had remained in the vicinity. She might have needed his assistance, after all.

"My dear Miss Pace, I wish I could oblige you, but I fear I cannot." When Mrs. Gardner turned around, her hands were clasped in front of her chest. "When I enter a debt of honor with someone, the terms are absolute. Others cannot exchange or negotiate with them. Suppose I *was* to sell you Mr. Coombes's IOUs. You might then use them to extort even *more* money from the poor fellow. One can never be too careful, you understand."

Georgina clenched her teeth so tightly her jaw throbbed. Her brother's face came to mind, fortifying her. "What an appalling suggestion. We do not *all* possess corrupt motives, madam."

Mrs. Gardner flashed a sweet smile, this time with those hideous teeth. "The agreement is between Mr. Coombes and myself only."

Georgina rose, anger swirling in her chest. Mrs. Gardner was every bit as calculating as she had originally supposed. "Very well. I shall return with Mr. Coombes and assist him to discharge his *own* debts."

Mrs. Gardner sighed. "Alas, that cannot happen, Miss Pace."

"I am sure it can."

"No, I'm afraid not."

Georgina wished that she herself had come with a bruiser. "Do go on," she prompted, her tone sharp. It seemed Mrs. Gardner had contrived a way to force poor Arthur into a corner, like some manipulative alley cat bullying a kitten.

"Did Mr. Coombes not explain to you the terms of our agreement? No, of course he did not, poor fellow. He may not have perfectly understood when I explained the terms to him. We agreed his dear Papa would be rather disappointed to learn of his gaming, and he was most anxious to avoid being sent back to the country to kick his heels until he comes of age . . ."

Georgina suppressed a gasp. *The blackmailing shrew.*

"So, he agreed it was best to wait until he reaches his majority, when he might pay the debt in full, including all interest accrued for that period. It grieves me that I cannot assist you, Miss Pace." Mrs. Gardner stepped forward and extended a hand to Georgina. "I am sorry for your wasted visit. I hope you stay to enjoy supper and play a few games of faro."

So that was how she amassed her wealth: by locking people into contracts beyond their understanding, which benefited only this gambling house and would leave the other party struggling to meet the terms. Rage shook through Georgina, though she did not let it express across her features. She stood up but ignored the proffered hand. "Let me speak plainly."

"I thought we had done so. *I* certainly have."

Georgina took a step towards her. "You will return my friend's IOUs and stop extending such predatory agreements. Or you will suffer some very, *very* unpleasant consequences."

7

FROM A DISTANCE, Colt kept an eye on his friend. After a few games at the EO table, a maid escorted her from the room. Then straight away, Mrs. Gardner forged a path towards Ellis and Montgomery, those scoundrels he knew would be behind all this. After a whispered word, she disappeared in Georgina's wake. His mouth dried up.

Nothing good would come of interfering with these people, he knew. Yet Georgina would only heed so much advice. When she had taken an idea in her head, he knew well how difficult she was to distract from it. Typically, the subject featured nothing sinister or serious—usually questions like where she would flee to at the end of the season, or if she would go against the current mode by supporting a new tailor. Nothing of *significance.*

At the outset, her involvement in this affair had not stirred much apprehension for Colt. However, witnessing the depth of her determination now left him genuinely concerned about the unfolding situation. Arthur's need awoke a zeal within Georgina that Colt had not seen in a long time. He'd assumed she had found peace from those memories that haunted her. On the contrary, they had merely lain idle. It concerned him most that she appeared to be on a mission to avenge wrongs committed against Henry.

Colt presently retreated to the front gaming room in search of Leggy. Colt located him seated on a sofa beside a heavily draped window, emitting a cloud of smoke from a cigar he held between his long fingers. Across from him sat Lady Mortimer, sipping from a glass of red wine.

Colt heaved a sigh. He knew Lady Mortimer from occasional social gatherings, and he did *not* favor her company. He enjoyed passing the time with people who shared his tastes, who enjoyed pleasure and delighted in the chase. From what he could gather, Lady Mortimer usually occupied herself with philanthropic work and other high-brow pursuits. However, her presence at a gaming hell suggested she was quite eccentric, which he reluctantly admitted offered a certain fascination. He approached them, resigned to whatever would happen while he waited for George.

"Any success in the back, Colt?" Leggy quizzed, making space beside him on the sofa.

Colt sat, nodding in greeting to Lady Mortimer, who smiled. "Did not play, Leggy. Just poked my head in to see what was afoot. Are you not watching the snails, my lady? Thought that would be riveting for you." He could not resist goading Lady Mortimer.

"Never fear, my lord. I have a ringside seat reserved, so I shall not miss a single slither later," she replied smoothly.

Colt laughed.

"Lord Coulthurst, I thought you said Georgina was here?" the shrill voice of Lady Prudence Ravenscroft interrupted.

"Georgina?" Lady Mortimer repeated.

"Miss Pace," answered Leggy, helpfully. "Definitely here earlier. Saw her with my own eyes."

"Here again?" Lady Mortimer's brow furrowed.

Prudence planted her hands on her hips. "I don't care where she *has* been. I want to know where she is now."

Colt shrugged. Georgina had attracted a lot of attention to herself. "I am afraid I cannot answer you, Lady Ravenscroft. She wandered off some time ago."

"I need to speak to her." Prudence now tapped her foot on the floor.

"I would not mind having a word as well," Lady Mortimer added.

Colt threw his arms up in the air. "I'm not her damned secretary!"

Leggy grinned. "Don't need a secretary. Here she is."

Sure enough, Georgina had reentered the room, a stormy look about her. Her fair cheeks were a dark shade of pink, and her blue eyes flashed brightly. She strode over to Colt while somehow managing to stay as far from Lady Ravenscroft as possible.

"Georgina," Prudence breathed.

Colt pondered how someone could interpret a situation so poorly. Prudence clearly had no insight into Georgina's mood.

Lady Mortimer gave a subtle nod of greeting but did not make any push to engage Georgina in a conversation. Neither did Leggy. Colt made a mental note to commend him on his astuteness later. There was a first time for everything.

"The whole world has been looking for you, George. I hope your quest with Mrs. Gardner was fruitful?" Colt asked, moving his arm so that Georgina could perch beside him on the arm of the sofa.

To his astonishment, Georgina whipped her head up and looked squarely at Lady Mortimer, perhaps checking to see whether the Countess was listening. As it happened, she was paying close attention to the exchange, and Georgina's cheeks colored further. What was going on between those two?

Colt suspected Prudence had also witnessed this exchange given the stiffening of her body and souring of her expression. "Georgina, why haven't you called since you got back to London?"

Colt's throat tightened. This could go one of two ways. Prudence would receive a withering set down or Georgina would make time for an assignation. Either option could result in a public scene.

Surprisingly, Georgina simply returned a bland smile. "Apologies. I found myself quite absorbed in making new friends." As she spoke these last words, Georgina's eyes were on Lady Mortimer.

The Countess met Georgina's gaze. "Just making friends? In addition, you seemed quite determined to gamble away your fortune, Miss Pace," Lady Mortimer interjected.

"Along with my soul, my lady."

By the King's own corset, what could all this mean? Since when was Lady Mortimer a friend—or foe—of Georgina's? Meanwhile, poor Prudence shifted her weight from one foot to the other. Georgina had responded to her advances with neither flirtation nor contempt, rather with *indifference*. An effective strategy.

With a flush mounting her countenance, Prudence retaliated. "What soul?"

This remark garnered the attention she clearly desired. All eyes fell upon Prudence.

"Now, there is no need for insults," Lady Mortimer scolded, her voice measured. "For all her devil-may-care reputation, I suspect Miss Pace secretly harbors a sensitive side."

"I will happily show you all my sensitive spots, my lady," Georgina countered.

"For my part, I'm quite sensitive to all things dairy," Leggy volunteered.

Colt choked on a sip of wine.

"Mr. Leggett . . . " Prudence began, with a note of exasperation in her tone.

"Yes. It's dashed inconvenient. One of life's pleasures I shall never be able to fully enjoy." He sighed.

Before Leggy had a chance to expound on his digestive track record with cheese, Georgina intervened. "Colt, we're leaving."

He could not protest. He was eager to take his leave and particularly wanted to quiz George about her curious behavior with Lady Mortimer.

The pair murmured a few words of goodnight to those nearby. Colt took Georgina's arm and led her out, past a crimson-faced Lady Ravenscroft.

Once they were in the safety of the carriage on the way back to Half Moon Street, Georgina required no encouragement to unburden herself of all that had transpired during her private conversation with Mrs. Gardner.

Georgina explained that she had first offered to pay off Sir Arthur's losses—including interest—only to be rebuked. Naturally, she threatened Mrs. Gardner with physical repercussions if she did not dissolve the debt forthwith. This tactic had been quite promising, Georgina insisted, as Mrs. Gardner had quaked beneath the intimidation. Until Mrs. Gardner's reinforcements—those two oafs, Lord Ellis and Mr. Montgomery—turned up. Georgina, finding herself outnumbered, had been obliged to disengage. Not that she did not fancy her chances against them, for two more feeble-looking gentlemen she had rarely encountered, but she had no desire for a complete dustup.

Colt listened quietly to this impassioned diatribe, concerned that Georgina had fallen into trouble beyond her means of self-preservation. Ellis and Montgomery were dangerous, and while they might not have looked menacing, their reach extended well beyond Solitaires. Mrs. Gardner was surely just one pawn in their game.

"What do you mean to do now, then?" Colt asked.

"I shall break in and steal his vowels, thus sending Mrs. Gardner a message *and* releasing Arthur from his debt."

He choked on an incredulous laugh. "Are you serious?"

She nodded.

"For goodness's sake, George! You'll end up imprisoned. What will Sarah think of all this?" He gripped her wrist.

"Well, nothing. She cannot know about any of this. It would worry her too much."

He released her wrist and ran a hand through his hair. She clearly did not mind saddling *him* with worry. Why could she not have left him in blissful ignorance?

"What about going to the authorities? Exposing her for who she is?"

"She has Arthur's notes. They will implicate him in any court proceedings, which will notify his father of what he did and surely ruin his plan to propose to Lady Maggie." Georgina clenched her hands into fists at her knees, her face fierce. "And then, once Mrs. Gardner has served her punishment, which will invariably be lenient—half the magistrates patronize these types of houses, you know—she will be back to her old ways within a month."

She had thought this through, Colt understood. But she denied him some details.

"And is part of your strategy to seduce Lady Mortimer? In the hope of undermining the enterprise from within?"

George flashed him a fiery look. "In what way is she involved?"

Colt shrugged. "Another great mystery, my dear, but she's certainly attached to Solitaires, isn't she? Which does not match her prim persona. Personally, I would steer clear of them all."

"I cannot."

"At least take precautions, George."

"What sort of precautions?"

"If you must invade her privacy, choose a night where she will have few to no guests and is expected to close early, such as when there is a large ton party. Make sure everyone *sees* you at said party, so you have an established alibi in case she accuses you. Slip away before the party finishes and ensure no one sees you leave."

This earned him a laugh. "Do you have a secret criminal life, Colt? You surprise me."

"No. I simply don't want to see your pretty neck in the noose."

They remained quiet for a few moments as the carriage tilted them from side to side in the darkness.

"It may be simpler to furnish Arthur with the monetary support until he comes of age and can repay his loan himself," Colt offered.

"I have a sense Arthur is not going to settle for anything less than his actual notes. His honor will prevent him from being satisfied with a substitute. Anyway, should we allow Mrs. Gardner to continue to take advantage of vulnerable ladies, gentlemen, and electora simply because their hearts are kind and trusting? Or because they are in their cups, or sick, or too young to know better?" Georgina's voice was strained, as if holding back tears. "No. Then she will win."

Colt had suspected that Georgina's sudden passion stemmed from more than a need to assist Arthur. Her speech now confirmed this.

"You can't save everyone, George." The carriage had stopped. He covered her hand with his for a moment. "What happened to . . ." he faltered, then decided he must spell it out. "What happened to Henry was not your fault."

"Henry's situation is an entirely different matter. But I am very much to blame for it." Through the darkness, he heard her swallow hard. She snatched her hand out from under his. "Goodnight, Colt." She jumped down from the carriage and hurried up the steps to her house.

8

To the Interesting Miss Pace,

I regret that I did not have much of an opportunity to speak with you last night at Solitaires. You seemed to be in distracted spirits. I hope you had not taken too much wine again. Perhaps we might converse soberly at the Blakes's ball on Saturday.

Sincerely yours,
Lady Elizabeth Mortimer

Georgina held the missive as she sat at her dressing table. She regarded herself in the mirror and watched the color rise unbidden to her cheeks. Surely, Lady Mortimer did not intend to bait her into a seduction. Or perhaps she did. If so, it immediately elevated Lady Mortimer in Georgina's esteem, regardless of Colt's innuendos.

She went to her desk and withdrew a quill and paper.

Dear Lady Mortimer,

I fear you overrate sobriety. However, I look forward to you finding me interesting again at the Blakes's ball. Perhaps you would like to distract me?

Warmest regards,
Miss Georgina Pace

With a satisfied little hum, Georgina sealed the letter and bestowed it on a footman to be delivered to Grosvenor Square.

SATURDAY EVENING BROUGHT the long-awaited Blakes's ball. Georgina had departed from her custom of breeches and instead selected a dress of deep red chiffon. Unadorned with embellishments, lace, or jewels, the delicate fabric, fine stitching, and elegant cut revealed the quality of the gown. Its bold hue leant her an exotic air. *The perfect choice to draw attention to myself*, she thought, as she glided confidently into the room.

As a recognized crush of the season, this ball would serve as the perfect guise for Georgina's plot. She had recently met Lords Lucas and Horace Blake riding through the park, where they bragged about the vast number of invitations they had delivered. "We only hope our ballroom will be sufficient for all the acceptances we have received," Lord Horace had said. Georgina would make her appearance, then sneak away to Solitaires later in the night. Being present this evening would mean half of London could vouch for her whereabouts, should Mrs. Gardner ever accuse her.

The Blakes had decorated their fine ballroom in all that was opulent. Ample candles flickered from the shining brass wall sconces lining the great hall. The sounds of music, chatter, and laughter spilled out into the vestibule. Bunches of white roses clustered in huge vases and added to the sweet aroma of the room. Bright loops of scarlet silk, shipped from Provence, adorned the ceiling, contrasting with the crisp white cloths shrouding long tables arranged along one wall. They had not exaggerated when they insisted they would spare no expense for the enjoyment of their guests.

Each buffet was laden high with refreshments, while attendants circled the room, refilling the wineglasses of the thirstier guests. The Blakes had commissioned a splendid orchestra for dancing and established card tables in an antechamber for those who wished to indulge.

Georgina approached her hosts and congratulated them on the grandeur of their home, thanking them for their kind invitation. The Blakes reassured her she humbled them with her presence and offered to connect her to a suitable dancing partner straight away.

"Thank you, but refining one's dance card for an evening is delicate work," she informed them teasingly. "I should like to take my time."

They furnished her with a glass of gin, and she circled the room, exchanging pleasantries. Through the crowd, she spotted the luscious lady of Albemarle Street, standing with a few of her friends. They made eye contact briefly, and Georgina saluted her with her glass, but she made a mental note to keep an eye out for the woman's husband. Then again, he might not have been able to recognize her—she had not been wearing much when she scrambled out of his marital bed and through the window, and it had been rather dark. Nevertheless, she did not court *that* sort of scene this evening.

Georgina surveyed the dancing couples, looking for Sarah or Colt. Alas, another waltzing figure captured her attention.

Lady Prudence Ravenscroft looked as ravishing as ever. Prudence's charisma was what had originally intrigued Georgina, after all. She watched warily as Prudence smiled up at her own dance partner, dimples appearing in her cheeks. Despite Georgina's rude dismissal of the lady at Solitaires the other evening, Prudence had made it clear—through multiple missives and her occasional presence strolling up and down Georgina's street—that she would welcome further interactions. Georgina remained uninterested.

Prudence glanced up, and her eyes locked upon Georgina. The smile froze on her face. She stopped talking to her companion.

A tightness formed in Georgina's belly as she recollected her own behavior in Cornwall. Even she deemed her actions reckless and deplorable.

The Christmas party she had attended with her father seemed so long ago now. Her dalliance with Prudence was intended only to relieve her boredom during an insipid holiday season. They had shared a few intimate moments together, but Georgina had not grown emotionally attached to the chit. On the fateful night when Prudence murmured words of love and excitement about their future together, Georgina knew she had taken things too far and contrived to leave at once. To her father's astonishment, Georgina required him to quit Cornwall with her the following morning. As their procession trundled away before most of the other guests had emerged for breakfast, Georgina praised herself for making such an artful escape.

However, seeing Prudence now, Georgina could admit her retreat had been cowardly. In fact, she suspected Prudence would be well within her rights to confront her about her contemptible conduct.

Not that a confrontation was likely, Georgina told herself. Prudence was now happily married to Lord Ravenscroft. Yet her unyielding determination to track Georgina down had been noticeable. Drumming her fingers along the crystal of her tumbler, Georgina shifted her weight from one foot to the other. She wished she had never put herself, nor Prudence, in such a position. It was less than ideal.

She turned away from the dance floor and found both Edmund and Arthur approaching her in a determined fashion.

"Gentlemen," she greeted them both, dipping a curtsey.

Both men proffered her an appropriate bow.

"I say, George. You look a treat," Edmund declared, casting a critical eye over her through his quizzing glass.

"I live for your approval, Edmund. How are you, Arthur?"

"Qu-quite well, G-George."

Arthur's features were a little paler than when she had seen him before. Perhaps the stress of the Great Matter was weighing on his mind.

"That's not entirely true, now, is it, Arthur?" Edmund prompted.

Georgina motioned for the pair of them to follow her to the far side of the room so they might converse more freely. This also took her out of Prudence's direct eyesight.

"What is troubling you?"

After a reassuring nudge from Edmund, Arthur said, "I am running short on time. I think Lady Maggie may not wait for me if I do not propose. She wants me to buy her a ring."

"Well, that is rather audacious. Young people have no sense of romance these days," Georgina remarked, offended on Arthur's behalf that he should feel so sewed up. "Perhaps Lady Maggie is not your ideal match if she is this demanding."

Edmund jostled Georgina. Perhaps she *was* being a little too harsh on the poor chap.

The wounded expression on Arthur's countenance softened when Edmund patted him on the back. "Of course she is your ideal match, Arthur. You have loved her this last year at least." Edmund glared at Georgina. "Don't listen to her. She is very negative about love."

Besieged by guilt, Georgina smiled at Arthur. "Edmund is right.

Indeed, Lady Maggie seems like your true love. And you shall be able to purchase an engagement ring for her presently." Seeing an opportunity present itself, Georgina decided to try her luck. "As it happens, I have your money at my house, Arthur." She took his hand and squeezed it, hoping he would not detect her holding her breath. If he accepted the financial assistance, at least that would remove him from the equation.

Arthur's eyes narrowed. "N-no. Not silly, G-George. Need the I-IOUs."

Georgina sighed. "Well, I have not got those back yet. I have *almost* settled the Great Matter, Arthur. I hope to have good news on that front soon."

"By Jove, you are a corker, George," admired Edmund, his face radiant.

The waltz had drawn to a conclusion and Georgina did not wish to stand in the one spot for too long, lest Prudence found her. Besides, she had to be viewed by as many people as possible this evening, should she ever require an alibi.

She gave Arthur a pat on his arm. "Now, if you will excuse me. I believe Sarah is beckoning me over to her. I wish you both a pleasant evening."

GEORGINA LOCATED MRS. Sarah Fortescue standing before a backdrop of white roses. A gown of white with a gold silk net overlay and long white gloves complemented her warm brown skin tone. Her glossy black curls were pinned into a cluster at the crown of her head, and a gold- and emerald-set tiara framed them.

"How stunning you are, Sarah," Georgina said, embracing her with a light kiss on each of her cheeks.

"There you are, George. It's such a squeeze tonight. I can hardly find anyone I want to talk to."

As a much-exalted widow of the town, Sarah could enter the most prestigious of events as she desired. This led to ambitious parents seeking an acquaintance with her for the sole purpose of improving their offspring's chances in the marriage mart. Sadly, for every authentic person seeking to know her better, she dealt with a dozen artificial friends. Georgina sympathized with her plight and did what she could to drive the more spurious people away.

"Here, hold this for me, will you?" Sarah handed Georgina her Champagne glass. "I think I have broken the button on my glove. It won't stay fastened."

Georgina and Sarah became so preoccupied refastening the glove that they did not notice a young lady approach from the side.

"Might I assist you, Mrs. Fortescue?" a sweet voice offered.

Georgina looked up and saw Miss Emily Coombes, Arthur's younger sister. She had recently arrived in London for her first season, though Georgina could recall her as a child, when she was let out of the schoolroom on special occasions to visit with her parents' guests. She always had been precocious.

This evening, she wore a gown of evening-primrose pink that quite matched her cheeks, and her sandy blonde hair was twisted into an elegant knot, nestled with pale pink flowers.

Sarah smiled and extended her slender hand. "Why, thank you, child. It is such a trial to correct with the inferior hand."

"I am delighted to oblige you." With a twitch of her fingers, she buttoned the glove. "Hopefully that will hold."

Georgina passed the wine back to her friend and eyed Emily dubiously.

"It is Miss Emily Coombes, is it not?"

Emily executed a graceful curtsy, fluttering her eyelashes in a beguiling manner.

"Aren't you enjoying the ball?" Sarah asked. "How can it be that such a fetching little thing as you are not dancing?"

Emily cast a longing look at the set forming on the dance floor. "I am not well acquainted with many people. We came to town later in the season than expected, so I fear I may have missed my chance of having a successful debut."

Georgina rolled her eyes. Surely Sarah would not fall for such transparent toad-eating?

But in fact, Sarah's brow wrinkled in sympathy. "I am sure you are not destined for such a tragic outcome, Miss Coombes. Let me see if I can perform a favorable introduction for you."

Emily clapped her hand to her heart. "You are too kind, Mrs. Fortescue. I am not destined to remain a wallflower forever."

Sarah laced her arm with Emily's and began pointing out key figures throughout the room. "Georgina, we simply must assist Miss Coombes in securing some suitable partners."

"Must we?" Georgina returned dryly. Although she held a deep affection for Arthur, Emily's ingratiating ways irked her.

"Naturally, we must. Now, Emily, that is Peer Ormskirk over there. They are one to dance with if you would like to secure an invitation to the best musical soiree of the season. Lady Gianna Moretti is somewhat intimidating, but if you are courageous, it might be worthwhile making her acquaintance. She will be invaluable if you wish to source vouchers for Almack's."

Georgina credited Emily with at least giving her undivided attention to Sarah. That is, until the form of an attractive gentleman came into view.

"And who is *that*?" Emily asked, her words tumbling out in a rush of excitement.

Georgina's eyes narrowed as she turned to follow Emily's gaze. No surprise at who had caught her attention. Colt was slicing his way through the crowd. He cut a dashing figure in a sharply tailored gray coat, a crisp cravat, and tailored knee breeches hugging his muscular legs.

"That, my dear child, is the Earl of Coulthurst. Despite his fortune, nobility, and looks, he ascended to the title young and suffered a lack of guidance from a firm parental figure. Coulthurst has always shown a want of propriety in relation to the ladies. You will find that most parents warn their daughters against becoming familiar with Coulthurst. Even his friends have dubbed him 'Colt' as a nod to his proclivities with women. You would do well to steer clear of him," Sarah declared. She pulled Emily with her as she moved to get a better view of the dance floor.

Georgina agreed with Sarah's cutting—if somewhat passionate—assessment of their dear friend. Emily was exactly Colt's type, and the last thing Georgina wanted was to solve Arthur's difficulties just to stumble into a new misfortune for that family.

"I see Lord and Lady Ravenscroft with Mr. Lawrence Dalrymple. Now, *he* would make a fine dance partner for you," Sarah continued. "Mr. Dalrymple is twenty years of age and has been Lord Ravenscroft's ward for the last ten years. His parents died tragically in a curricle accident, and they left their son in Lord Ravenscroft's care."

Georgina caught Emily's crestfallen expression and read in it: *Mr. Dalrymple is no Coulthurst*. Oblivious, Sarah started through the room towards the Ravenscrofts and Mr. Dalrymple. Georgina fought a desire to flee in the opposite direction.

Sarah went on as they walked, "Lord Ravenscroft, you understand, is a most honorable man, and he accepted the duties of a guardian without hesitation. He covered the entire expense of his ward's education, ensuring he completed his studies at Cambridge.

That's not to say that Mr. Dalrymple is destitute. I understand he will come into a comfortable independence when he comes of age."

Emily mustered a crooked smile as they came to a halt before Mr. Dalrymple, and Sarah performed a pretty introduction. The young man possessed smooth brown skin, tight curly black hair cropped short, and expressive dark eyes that regarded Emily keenly. He bore a lean and athletic figure, though he boasted only a moderate height.

Mr. Dalrymple gazed at Emily intently, but his words failed him.

In response, the young lady sighed and rolled her eyes. Georgina had an urge to slap her. What fault could she truly find with this young gentleman, aside from a moment of flagging confidence? This was likely not the first time Emily had rendered a gentleman speechless.

Georgina stood to one side, acutely aware of the stares of both Lord Ravenscroft and Prudence. She threw the pair a curt smile, then dropped her gaze. She did not wish to hinder the young people from becoming acquainted.

"Miss Coombes . . ." Mr. Dalrymple began. "What a. . . . How. . . . We. . . ."

Emily glanced at Sarah in some alarm. "It is a pleasure to meet you."

Mr. Dalrymple smiled awkwardly.

"Do you enjoy attending balls?" Emily spoke clearly, enunciating every word.

Georgina's eyes narrowed as she observed this exchange. Did Emily think Mr. Dalrymple was of slow wit, perhaps?

When he did not reply, Emily nearly shrieked, "I LOVE to dance!" Her volume had increased to an uncomfortable level.

Apparently, Emily surmised that Mr. Dalrymple had difficulty hearing. Georgina was unsure whether to be amused or thoroughly mortified on Emily's behalf. As far as Georgina understood, Mr. Dalrymple's ears worked perfectly. Besides, her deaf acquaintances got along well, speaking with their hands and reading lips. No shrieking required.

Regardless, Mr. Dalrymple played along. He amplified his voice to match Emily's. "INDEED, Miss Coombes. I enjoy DANCING. Very much, in fact."

"Perhaps we should DANCE?" Emily shouted back at him.

"Indeed, YES," Mr. Dalrymple replied, a note of relief in his voice.

Rows of couples formed on the floor for the cotillion. Mr. Dalrymple led Emily into the set nearest to where they stood.

"Why are they shouting?" Georgina whispered into Sarah's ear.

"It's difficult to say," replied Sarah, looking baffled.

From where the group stood at the periphery of the dance floor, they could pick up fragments of Emily and Mr. Dalrymple's overly loud conversation.

"I understand you live with your guardians, Lord and Lady Ravenscroft?" Emily bellowed as the dance drew them together.

"Indeed, in South Audley Street."

Her face lit up in instant recognition as they moved down the set. "We live near to you, in fact, on Mount Street!"

"You must allow me to accompany you to the park one afternoon, Miss Coombes?"

Emily cleared her throat. Georgina did not wonder at it. All that projection would strain anyone's voice. "Certainly, Mr. Dalrymple. I should be delighted to join you."

Sarah leaned towards Georgina. "There, you see, I have promoted an amiable match."

Georgina scoffed. "If you think that pretty little ninnyhammer will be interested in the likes of Mr. Dalrymple, you need to think again. She has *much* loftier ambitions." Glancing at Prudence and

Lord Ravenscroft, Georgina guided Sarah away from the floor. "I have known the Coombes family for many years now. Even as a youthful girl, Emily identified the type of partner she would seek. She's quite uncreative: He must be a gentleman, masculine and strong, be handsome and fashionable, though *not* a dandy. He must be athletic. And, above all, he *must* have a title."

Sarah wrinkled her little nose. "That is quite an extensive list of qualities for such a young lady."

"And she is a superficial brat, to boot."

"Perhaps you are being uncharitable, Georgina."

Sarah's lenient nature often made her too considerate. "See if you can keep her away from Colt. She is determined to throw herself in his path. More fool her if she does."

Georgina followed her friend's gaze across the crowded room. Colt appeared oblivious to their scrutiny.

Sarah frowned. "One day he will find himself shot at dawn." She drained the rest of her Champagne.

"More likely exiled for murder," Georgina said, also finishing her drink. "He is an excellent shot."

The cotillion had concluded, and they watched Mr. Dalrymple lead Emily back to the safety of her parents across the room.

"Shall we, my love?" Georgina offered, extending her arm.

Sarah accepted, and Georgina led her into the next dance. Dancing with the beautiful Sarah would certainly draw all eyes to her. This would assist in cementing her alibi.

9

COLT SURVEYED THE room for a suitable diversion. The unmarried ladies he preferred to dally with had to exude certain qualities. Foremost, they had to show a willingness to dispense with their chaperones. This was pivotal to anything that came next. Then, they had to look pleasing to him. They did not need to be diamonds of the first water, but a certain prettiness went a long way. Confidence in their manner and carriage also attracted him. Last, the ladies that caught his attention often had a glint of mischief in their eyes. This factor alone usually meant they would be receptive to—even seeking of—his company.

This evening, as he sauntered through the crowds, chatting cheerfully with friends and acquaintances, he struggled to find a lady who met these criteria. He approached a long table and poured a generous glass of whiskey into a crystal tumbler.

From out of nowhere, a young damsel appeared beside him. She peeped up at him sideways as she filled a glass of water from a pitcher.

"Only water, Miss . . . ?"

"Coombes. Miss Emily Coombes." She dropped into a curtsy. "And yes. Only water. My throat is a little sore after my prior dancing partner. I don't believe he could hear well."

Colt executed a confident bow over her hand, wondering what her relation was to Georgina's friend, Arthur Coombes. "Delighted to meet you. Lord Robert Coulthurst, at your service. We are not acquainted, but I have certainly seen you about town and have been quite desperate for an introduction." A small untruth never went astray when it came to flattering ladies. "Might I claim you for the next waltz, if you are not too fatigued?"

A blush spread across her cheeks, and her lips curved into a coy smile. Miss Coombes agreed readily, and as the music began, he swept her onto the dance floor. He was delighted she had not insisted they consult a parent or guardian, who would have certainly curtailed the suggestion. A promising start.

"You dance well, Miss Coombes," he said. "So graceful."

Miss Coombes cast her eyes away demurely.

His gaze rested on the angle of her throat, wondering if she had turned her head deliberately to display her neck to such advantage. She looked back at him, and he became certain that she was watching for his reaction. He smiled in appreciation, then allowed his eyes to sink over the soft swell of her bosom for a moment.

"Such a beautiful creature has no business being so modest." He gave her a slight wink and a mischievous, dimpled grin.

Her eyes lifted to meet his, and her lashes fluttered.

Miss Coombes certainly displayed a penchant for flirtation. He pressed his thumb into her palm, and she did not shrink away, meeting his unspoken challenge. Colt thought this night may just have become interesting.

As one of the most eligible bachelors in the ton, Colt was well accustomed to the glare of envious onlookers. With her chin held high and a confident smile, Miss Coombes exuded happiness.

"It does not sound like you enjoyed your last dance, Miss Coombes?" Colt ventured as they glided through and amongst other couples.

She gave him an arch look. "How inappropriate it would be for me to criticize one gentleman to another. Though I *will* say that I am glad the previous dance is at an end. I am sure Mr. Dalrymple is a pleasant fellow, but his hearing issue makes it more challenging to exchange words."

Colt lifted a brow. "Dalrymple. I met him briefly yesterday in my club, with his guardian. I must say, he seemed perfectly able to hear me."

Miss Coombes's cheeks suffused with color. "He seemed only to respond to me when I spoke loudly."

Dalrymple must have been trying a rather unique method of wooing. "Perhaps he was merely jesting, my dear."

When Miss Coombes's face contorted into a pout, he added quickly, "Or, your beauty nonplussed him, and he struggled with what to say."

Mollified, Miss Coombes sighed. "Indeed, I believe you are right. Mr. Dalrymple barely talks at all, anyway. At least, not about anything interesting."

Colt snickered. "That is not for me to say. Fortunately, no one has ever described *me* as a poor conversationalist, so hopefully we shall rub along nicely." Colt stared serenely into her pretty, upturned face. "And how are you enjoying your first season?"

"I am rather green, I fear, my lord, with so much to learn. For example, I just discovered one should not pay a morning call in the morning. How absurd. Another thing that baffles me is whether it is *ever* respectable to go walking with a suitor without an attendant, or only when one is married or more mature?"

"I daresay that will depend upon whom you ask," Colt sympathized. "I suspect your *mother* would insist that you are never in the company of a suitor without a chaperone. If you asked me, I would encourage you to walk alone with gentlemen at every opportunity. Particularly if I were the suitor."

"Oh, I infinitely prefer your advice, Lord Coulthurst."

He could not believe his luck. The twinkle in her eye practically invited him to dally with her.

"Would you care to try? I am happy to smuggle you away from the ballroom, so we might enjoy a walk together—though I understand if you would rather not. Going against one's matriarch requires rare courage. Dare you?"

"Oh, I certainly dare," she countered.

Joy rippled through Colt as the steps of this all too familiar dance fell into place, not unlike the waltz they presently enjoyed. He waited until a lively conversation occupied Miss Coombes's parents before he grasped the lady's hand and led her out through the doors onto the balcony.

As Colt escorted Miss Coombes across the terrace, he kept his hand on the center of her back, gently propelling her out into the dark evening.

"I believe you know a good friend of mine, Miss Georgina Pace? She is well-acquainted with Mr. Arthur Coombes; is he your brother?" he said conversationally, steering her to the stone railing where they could gaze out across the garden.

Lanterns were strewn throughout the property, allowing glimpses of the yard below. The aroma of rose petals wafted on the evening breeze. One needed a wrap, cloak, or strong arms to stay warm in the cool weather. Hence, the terrace presently remained free of other guests. The perfect spot for a romantic interlude.

"My family has known Miss Pace and her family for many years. I recall her from when I was but a child. She always had more time for Arthur than for me," Miss Coombes replied, with a slight curl of her upper lip.

"Arthur reminds George of her brother," Colt responded, then instantly regretted his utterance. Georgina would not appreciate her private affairs being discussed.

Fortunately, Miss Coombes displayed little interest in the subject. She gave an involuntary shiver and edged closer to him so his broad frame might protect her from the draft. He caught a note of her subtle fragrance on the breeze. *A hint of sweet musk*, he mused.

"How thoughtless of me to draw you outside where you might catch a chill, Miss Coombes," he murmured, his voice husky. "Shall we go in?"

"Please, call me Emily. And I should be an insipid creature indeed if I let the weather stop me from stealing a few moments in your company, my lord."

"Surely you must know what scandal lies ahead of you if someone discovers you alone with me, Emily?"

Her little rosebud lips pouted. "You would not ruin me, would you, my lord?"

Colt tossed his head back and laughed. "I do my best not to ruin young ladies."

"And yet, I know your reputation well," she admitted, her eyes kindling.

"And yet, you still walked with me," he parried. He enjoyed watching the color steal over her cheeks.

"I confess, I had *heard* that you have a remarkable art for. . . ." Emily's words tapered off.

Colt raised a brow and took one step closer. "For . . . ?"

"Opening the eyes of less experienced ladies to the assorted pleasures of the world . . . prior to them settling into matrimony."

Emboldened by her words, Colt slid a hand around her waist.

Emily gasped at this action, and a giggle erupted from her.

"Is that what they say about me? That's quite a testimonial," he growled. "And you find this notion appealing?"

When the pretty creature smirked back up at him in response, a small spark of hesitation glimmered inside him. He disregarded the qualm as quickly as it emerged, however, and drew her closer towards him.

"My lord, what if someone were to happen upon us?" She turned away slightly, scanning their environment.

"Devil take them." Colt waited for her eyes to return to his, then bent down and kissed her neck fiercely.

Emily rubbed her hands up along his chest as a squeal of delight burst from her throat.

"What a sweet taste you have," Colt murmured, his voice muffled by her flesh.

Before he could even start to show her pleasure, however, the lady pushed back from him. "Please, my lord . . . no. We must not. My reputation!" Her voice was trembling.

Colt had barely a moment to register Emily's words when they were interrupted.

"When a lady says 'no,' you really must heed her, Colt," came a familiar voice from behind. It was none other than Mrs. Sarah Fortescue.

Emily gasped, and Colt released her. She stumbled back and thankfully caught the railing for support. Colt straightened his jacket and fixed a pleasant expression on his face. He turned to address his friend.

Beside Sarah stood Lady Elizabeth Mortimer.

Emily, with a red face, stepped forward, though her hands fluttered around her forehead as though she might faint.

Sarah's disapproving brown eyes lingered upon Emily for a moment before sweeping across to Colt. She arched one austere brow.

He flashed a defiant grin and dragged his fingers back through his hair. "Sarah, care to join us?"

Sarah exhibited no signs of amusement. "Elizabeth noted your departure from the room, Colt, and suggested an intervention might be pertinent."

Colt glowered at Lady Mortimer. "Did she?" Apart from being prudish, her ladyship had a habit of meddling in affairs that in no way concerned her.

"I . . . I am very much obliged to you, Lady Mortimer," Emily said in a small, breathless voice.

Colt saw all hopes of a liaison disappear before his eyes. To hell with interfering women. Emily had sought *him* out for her enjoyment.

"Not at all, child. We have all been young," Lady Mortimer replied, offering her a smile.

Sarah, however, gave Emily an unyielding stare that Colt could not readily interpret. "Allow me to return you to your mother, Miss Coombes."

Without waiting for a word of acquiescence, Sarah threaded her arm through Emily's and returned her to the warmth of the ballroom.

Colt cast a scornful look towards Lady Mortimer before he took his leave. He distrusted Lady Mortimer, but his true issue was with his friend, whose disappointment made him feel uneasy. How Sarah perplexed him.

10

WHEN GEORGINA SAW Colt and Emily retreat from the dance floor, she shook her head, marveling at her friend's audacity. Over the years, she had witnessed many imprudent young women become enticed by Colt's playful banter and handsome countenance. She suspected Miss Coombes faced the same fate as many foolish damsels before her. Georgina was confident, at least, that Colt would not consider marrying the young lady.

After her dance with Sarah, Georgina found herself pinned down by Lord Horace Blake, who performed an animated monologue about his interest in purchasing one of her famous chestnut mares. She laughingly told him that he could offer her no price for the horse, as she was not for sale, and he went on to lament the quality of the horseflesh available at Tattersalls.

Upon noticing Colt's return from the terrace with a somewhat flustered appearance, she took it as an opportunity to excuse herself. She made her way straight over to her friend, fetching them both a glass of Burgundy along the way.

Colt readily accepted the glass.

"A rather reckless choice, if I may say," Georgina remarked, linking her arm with Colt's to take a turn around the room.

He followed her lead obediently. “You assume I make everyone the object of my affection, George?”

She scoffed, almost choking on her laughter. “You did not seduce Emily on the terrace? I am surprised.”

He shrugged.

His silence spoke volumes. “Colt, I implore you. Please do not involve yourself with Emily. She is Arthur’s younger sister. We cannot complicate matters for *her*, just when I am trying to extricate *him* from a scrape.”

Colt rolled his eyes like a chastened boy who had a much beloved toy wrested from him.

“Moreover, Emily is calculating. Mark my words. She will entrap you to the altar. And *that* would be a tragedy.”

“It sounds like you have gone all soft, George. Whatever happened to our games?”

She leaned against the wall for a moment. The mere weight of his question tired her. “Romantic entanglements are too difficult to control. As it is, I have Prudence breathing down my neck, literally. Sarah would like to see me married off and out of harm’s way, while *you* would prefer me to make sport of everything.”

He gave her the dimpled grin she always found irresistible. “It makes life less dull, George. You must admit that.”

“Did Sarah interrupt you and Emily? Or did Emily think better of accessing your *services*?”

“Sarah. She was in a most peculiar mood. I’ve rarely seen her so out of sorts.”

Indeed, Georgina had noticed Sarah become distracted when she saw Colt dancing with Emily. It was unlike her to take such a protective interest in a young debutante.

“Of course, Lady Mortimer also made her appearance on the balcony, meddling as usual.”

Georgina's ears pricked up at the mention of her new friend, and an involuntary smile crossed her lips. So, the curious Lady Mortimer *was* here.

"I must dash. Excuse me." She thrust her glass into Colt's hand before stalking off towards the balcony.

GEORGINA SPIED LADY Mortimer leaning casually against the banister, her indigo gown rustling in the breeze as she gazed out at the garden. Her hair was gathered up with diamond pins that glittered in the light afforded by the torches jutting out from the building above them. Georgina felt lightheaded for a moment, drinking in the sight.

"Have you been rescuing fair maidens, Lady Mortimer?" Georgina lifted the hem of her gown as she stepped up onto the elevated terrace to join her ladyship. "You are almost comically chivalrous, you know."

Lady Mortimer glanced over her shoulder, her lips parted on a sharp inhale. The reaction caused Georgina's heart to thud noisily in her chest. Perhaps her dress was capturing attention just as she'd intended. The glint in Lady Mortimer's eyes was unreadable.

"Miss Pace, what a pleasure it is to see you again. And there is no glass of alcohol in sight, I note."

"How droll you are, to be sure." Georgina shook Lady Mortimer's hand in greeting, but also leaned towards her and rose on to her toes to place a light kiss on her cheek. It was a salutation like one might give an old friend. Or a lover.

"You are quite the savior, it seems," she teased.

"We have that in common, Miss Pace, do we not? I recall your efforts to rescue your friend from some trouble with Mrs. Gardner. Are you enjoying the ball?"

"It's delightful. Yet I would much prefer to be at home, drinking wine and reading, or playing chess."

"Not everyone derives enjoyment from the diversions of a large ball like this. Your preferred pursuits are nothing to be ashamed of."

"How do you typically spend your time?" Georgina leaned on the railing so she was facing Lady Mortimer. The woman was striking—tall yet curved, strong yet full of grace, eyes full of mysterious warmth.

"I am fond of many things. I too enjoy reading, playing the pianoforte, riding, dancing, studying art . . . gambling," Lady Mortimer added with a grin. "Occasionally, I dabble in politics. I enjoy learning things and being as useful as I can be."

"Goodness, how dull I must seem in comparison." Georgina corrected one of the seams of her gown to make it fall straight.

"Not at all. It appears you seek to keep your mind active without filling it with social decorum, drama, flirtation, and so forth."

"I never denied liking flirtation," Georgina objected. Could she have been more overt? "I thought that was rather obvious." She winked and discerned the slightest hint of a blush on Lady Mortimer's face. Or perhaps it was merely a trick played by the torchlight. "And I do enjoy going out. But my tastes are more *relaxed* than this."

"Intriguing, Miss Pace."

"Perhaps one day I shall take you to *my* club," Georgina said, a playful tone in her voice.

"How goes your plan to help your friend?" Lady Mortimer asked, toying with one of her earrings.

After their banter about flirtation, Georgina felt a pang of disappointment at the lack of reciprocation. She had been told many times that her charms were impossible to ignore, yet Lady Mortimer seemed impervious.

"Slowly, my lady. I have made no inroads on behalf of my friend."

"Yet, you appeared at Solitaires again, only a few nights ago. Why?"

Georgina stiffened. While she appreciated the directness, she had no desire to discuss what had happened with Mrs. Gardner that night. Lady Mortimer, after all, was still a stranger to her.

"I wished to try my luck at the tables once more. Sadly, I lost a pretty penny." She turned to look back into the garden.

"I presume it is no easy task to hold Mrs. Gardner to account for her behavior?"

Georgina regretted her candid disclosures to Lady Mortimer that first evening in the carriage. Perhaps her judgment *had* been impaired by the wine, or by the charisma of her companion.

"I confess, I have been shamelessly procrastinating."

"It is kind of you to wish to intervene on behalf of your friend. I hope you know you might rely upon me to assist you, if you should wish to share the burden." Lady Mortimer's eyes were sincere and bright. "I have connections in that household."

Georgina wanted to believe her. But although Lady Mortimer appeared trustworthy, her continued interest in the matter made her suspicious. Georgina could not let her guard down just yet.

"I am exceedingly grateful for the offer, but this is my problem to solve. Besides, your services are already engaged in assisting the Miss Coombes of this world. I daresay she will have plenty more ineligible lovers who will need to be sent about their business."

"We can thank Mrs. Fortescue for *that*," Lady Mortimer responded. With a small nod towards the entryway, she indicated they should make their way back inside.

Georgina did not want to surrender their time alone together so quickly, but she could hardly force her ladyship to remain.

"I merely agreed to accompany her. It was she who insisted on intercepting the couple. Not I," Lady Mortimer clarified, turning away.

Georgina, who wanted a chance to drive the conversation back to a more flirtatious direction, stared regretfully towards the door. One hand flexed at her side, resisting the urge to reach out and stop Lady Mortimer from walking away. Instead, she followed her demurely.

"Besides," Lady Mortimer continued. "I would rather help you with your friend's scrape. It sounds in need of a lot more attention."

As they neared the door, both ladies reached for the handle at the same time. Lady Mortimer's fingers brushed over Georgina's for a moment, and whether by accident or design, their eyes locked—Georgina suddenly grew breathless.

"A-After you," she stammered, moving to allow Lady Mortimer to pass by. She could not recall the last time a woman had flustered her. On the contrary, it was most always the other way around. She cursed under her breath. This circumstance thoroughly confused her.

Back inside the room, an attendant approached, and they both accepted a glass of wine.

"You seem to have a devotee, Miss Pace." Lady Mortimer made a gesture towards Prudence across the room, who was surrounded by a group of admirers yet trained her eyes quite obviously upon Georgina. "Lady Ravenscroft looked for you high and low at Solitaires the other evening, if I am not mistaken. She seems most desirous to catch your attention."

Georgina rotated to avoid the direct gaze of her former paramour. "*Not* a devotee, I fear. Only my sins returning to haunt me."

Lady Mortimer lifted one shapely brow. "Indeed? How fascinating."

Georgina's cheeks were warm. "If only it were, my lady. But there is nothing more tiresome than a mulish young lady throwing her cap at you."

Lady Mortimer's face tightened, her expression inscrutable. "Such disdain, Miss Pace. You surprise me."

Georgina experienced a sudden, unexpected tightness in her chest. She was accustomed to society censuring her behavior and rarely let it worry her. This new feeling troubled her.

"It surprises you, my lady, that I have enjoyed liaisons?"

"No, Miss Pace. Only that you regard the young lady with contempt. I should imagine the circumstance of unrequited love to be painful. Particularly when one is in love with *you*." Lady Mortimer's emphasis on that final word was unmistakable.

Georgina's chest gripped still further. Lady Mortimer had a way of complimenting her at a striking depth, yet without overtly flirting. She bit her lip instinctively. "Indeed, how heartless I must seem."

Lady Mortimer examined her with a shrewd eye, but in the softness of the candlelight, she did not seem unkind. "Not heartless. Only very *cautious* when it comes to your own heart, I should say."

Georgina held her breath, waiting to hear what further insights Lady Mortimer might share.

"Sadly, Miss Pace, I think your luck has run out. Your Prudence is heading this way."

A sudden alarm sounded inside Georgina. "Please, dance with me? We must tell her I have already promised the next two dances to you."

Prudence was easy to spot in a crowd, as her stunning red hair flashed in contrast to an elegant gown of dark blue satin. She elbowed her way through and paused in front of Georgina.

"Good evening, Lady Mortimer. Georgina, might I steal you for the next dance?"

Georgina was about to claim her prior commitment when Lady Mortimer spoke over her. "Indeed, Miss Pace was just telling me that she was looking for a partner." She smiled sweetly at Georgina.

Of all the underhanded tricks.

With Prudence radiating obvious joy, Georgina had no choice but to comply. She straightened her gown, fingers sinking into the red fabric, and glared at Lady Mortimer, who returned a placid smile.

Taking Prudence by the hand, Georgina escorted her towards the next set that was forming, all the while considering how to exact revenge against the Countess.

"You have been very elusive, Georgina," Prudence murmured, taking her place in the dance.

"Forgive me. It has been a trifle hectic settling my father back in town and becoming reacquainted with everyone." Georgina hoped their position in the dance, surrounded by other guests, would limit what Prudence might say to her. Out of the corner of her eye, she saw Colt leading Sarah into the dance as well.

"I might almost describe you as rude when I saw you at Solitaires."

Georgina lifted one brow. "I could hardly sweep you up in my arms in greeting, Prue. Your husband was walking around."

Prudence pouted. "Did you receive my letter?"

"I had the pleasure. You have such a pretty way with words, my dear," Georgina remarked, wishing to deflect from the content of the missive as much as possible.

Prudence's keen eyes regarded her without blinking, despite the movements in the dance drawing them away from each other.

"And have you put any thought into my suggestion?" she probed as the dance brought them back together. "I did everything you told me to do in Cornwall."

"Ah." Georgina gave an uncomfortable little laugh. "I am flattered, Prudence. One cannot jump into these things." She noticed Prudence's full bottom lip quiver. "But I shall give it some more consideration."

To her relief, the dance progressed, moving her away from

Prudence and alongside Colt. She smiled at her friend. “Sarah is a much more sensible flirt than Emily.”

Colt regarded her in annoyance. “I daresay you are correct, George. I hope your own love, Lady Mortimer, will not see fit to intervene in my dance with her.”

Heat crept up the back of Georgina’s neck. She gazed through the crowd and observed Lady Mortimer standing off to the side with another small group of guests. Their eyes met for an instant before she turned back to her friend.

“I will never have a love, Colt.”

“We shall see,” he replied as the dance drew him away again.

Prudence returned to Georgina’s side. “When you say ‘consideration,’ what does that mean, exactly?”

This was why Georgina rarely entangled herself with young lovers. They were never content, and she hadn’t more to give.

She thus endured the remainder of the dance, fending off questions, feeling each second drag on, and inwardly cursing Lady Mortimer and her knowing eyes.

11

AFTER SEVERAL MORE dances and a generous supper, Georgina decided nearly everyone at the ball had seen her. Should Mrs. Gardner ever accuse her of housebreaking, she would find herself up against nearly two hundred members of the ton, swearing Miss Pace had been at the ball the entire evening. She slipped away unnoticed, leaving Colt to continue referring to her presence long after her departure.

Whilst her beautiful gown had served the purpose of drawing eyes to her at the ball, this was not the effect she desired when breaking into a house in the middle of the night. She returned home to Half Moon Street to change her raiment.

In her dressing room, she deftly unfastened her gown and laid it on the daybed. She pulled out a pair of riding breeches, a shirt, boots, and a jacket, all in black. Dressed again, she tied her hair back in a simple knot, donned a long black greatcoat to shield her from the chilly air outside, slipped a hairpin into her pocket alongside her trusty fob watch, and crept out of the house, collecting a bag from a cupboard as she went. She intended to find Arthur's IOUs and escape unnoticed. However, if something went wrong, she would have to make the theft look like a regular burglary. She decided rather prudently not to arm herself. If someone caught her, she had no intention of injuring anyone or taking this whole affair to a more sinister level.

Even as morning approached, darkness and fog blanketed London. It was too far to walk on foot, so Georgina set forth for Grosvenor Square, where she located a carriage and was soon dropped off at St James's Square.

A few people still occupied the street. The watchman's voice, calling out the hour, echoed in the distance. He would not pass through here for a while, at least. She waited for the street to clear, and her dark, cat-like figure slipped down the side stairs to the area outside the kitchen and attendants' quarters. Retrieving the hairpin from her pocket, her nimble fingers twisted it into the bolt until it clicked and released.

Georgina learned this skill as a girl. Her father had remained a warm and indulgent man after her mother died, though he employed a rather strict governess to preside over the schoolroom. She used to lock Georgina in her chamber as punishment for any of her misdemeanors, of which there were many. This forced the willful Georgina to use her wits to identify a way out. A strong-minded young lady, she was bright and resourceful. She studied the latch and attempted to pry it open with assorted implements. Though she had success using a variety of wires and rods, she found a hairpin to be the most efficient device.

On entering Mrs. Gardner's unoccupied kitchen, Georgina warily looked around, glad only an eerie silence confronted her. She moved into the attendants' parlor, where a few candles guttered in the darkness. The fireplace showed no hint of glowing embers from the evening before, even though most of the staff would have only just found their beds after a busy night serving and feeding Mrs. Gardner's boisterous guests.

Getting caught housebreaking would surely signify the end of her current existence. She recognized how distraught her father would be if she were locked up in Bow Street. Moreover, if they convicted her of a criminal act, it would irrevocably cut the social connections and freedoms she currently enjoyed.

Georgina's eyes darted in every direction, and she listened for any tiny sound. She eased through the lower level, stepping into the shadows as the waif-like form of a young scullery maid passed, carrying a bucket from one room to another, sloshing water over the floor as she went. Georgina held her breath. If the girl had looked her way, she would have spotted her. Perhaps she had arrived too late in the morning, and the possibility of being discovered was now too great.

Clenching her teeth, Georgina knew she had to take the risk to find Arthur's vowels. Once the girl disappeared, Georgina slipped over to the staircase. The foyer stank of stale smoke and a hint of mildew.

It would be daybreak soon. All the revelers and gamblers would have left the establishment not long ago, many with considerably lighter purses. She did not expect Mrs. Gardner to emerge soon, though Georgina knew the girl with the bucket would be the first of many setting about restoring the residence. She needed to move quickly.

Georgina speculated that Mrs. Gardner would likely keep assets in a desk or perhaps concealed in a locked compartment somewhere. If it proved difficult to find, she would need an alternative plan. She could not turn the house upside down searching.

She opened one door and peeked inside. The shapes of the furniture suggested she had stumbled upon a sitting room; however, it did not boast a bureau.

The second door she tried offered more success. Creeping into the study, she lit the candle on the desk, illuminating the contents of the drawers. Georgina pulled out a pile of papers and leafed through them. They were only bills. Her eyes widened in astonishment at the outstanding amount owed to a fashionable modiste. She enjoyed a comfortable fortune and liked to dress well herself, but even she did not spend so extravagantly on attire.

This knowledge further fueled her determination to assist Arthur and teach Mrs. Gardner not to take advantage of those who could not protect themselves. To her ultimate annoyance, however, she could not find the documents she sought in any of the drawers. She considered that Mrs. Gardner might always keep them close to her.

Bold enough to commit burglary, Georgina did not choose to tempt fate further by breaking into Mrs. Gardner's bedroom while she slept. She blew out the candle and sat in the dark, collecting her thoughts. With every moment she spent in the building, the chance of her being caught and the attendant consequences increased.

She bit her lower lip and smiled as another viable solution suggested itself. It came with its own risks, but she could not leave empty-handed.

Having visited Solitaires earlier that week, Georgina recalled the location of the gaming rooms on the first floor, towards the rear of the dwelling. She navigated there and shut the door behind her.

The smell of cigars, spilled wine, and an unpleasant hint of salmon lingered in the room. During the hours she had feigned being foxed, Georgina had covertly observed the games. She realized she could do little to prevent the proprietor from cheating her patrons through sleight-of-hand tricks, but she suspected Mrs. Gardner used a range of methods to rob her guests. Mrs. Gardner's faro box, for example, made it difficult for the house to lose. If, as Georgina suspected, someone had rigged the device to favor the bank, it would be invaluable to Mrs. Gardner. Luckily, it rested in plain sight on a round mahogany table.

Picking the device up, Georgina studied it for a moment and placed it into her bag. She had not intended to steal a faro box, but Georgina suspected this item would serve as an excellent incentive for Mrs. Gardner to relinquish Arthur's IOUs.

Georgina wandered over to another table laden with clean glasses and a decanter of Burgundy. She poured herself a generous portion and sipped it as she explored. The first rays of dawn peeped between the thick drapes, exposing more of the room, and she could make out assorted shapes around her. A sofa, a trestle table, a candelabra.

"It's very late to be calling," a muffled voice said.

Georgina's eyes shot towards the door. For the briefest moment, she thought Mrs. Gardner had directed those words at her, but then she realized the door remained closed. Panic seized her and squeezed the air from her lungs.

The sound of footsteps stopped just on the other side of the door, and through the dim light, Georgina watched the handle turn slowly. She had to hide.

In a flash of panic, Georgina released the glass of wine, which fell onto the carpet with a muted thump, the contents soaking into the threads of the rug. She mouthed a silent curse and crouched down behind a pair of wing chairs nearest to the window. The darkness that shrouded the room meant her blackened figure remained concealed by the shadows of the chairs—or so she hoped. She lowered her pale face to avoid detection. She was grateful she had taken the time to go home and change out of her bright red gown.

Two pairs of footsteps entered the room as the door swung open. Mrs. Gardner's voice drew closer to her. "What brings you here? I thought you were spending the evening at the Blakes's ball?"

Mrs. Gardner and her companion had brought candlesticks with them. Darkness no longer cascaded about her. Georgina ducked lower, wishing she could dissolve into the rug along with her wine.

"I did. It's practically dawn. But I thought to call in briefly on my way home. Forgive me if I woke you." Lady Mortimer's familiar voice sent ice through Georgina's veins, even as heat rose to her cheeks.

There could be no denying the lady's association with Mrs. Gardner now. But what did it entail?

"To what do I owe the pleasure?" A creaking noise sounded from the sofa, and Georgina presumed Mrs. Gardner had sat down. A knot formed in her throat. Good grief, hopefully this was not the start of an improper rendezvous.

"A curious matter has come to my attention lately, Julia. An acquaintance of mine hinted you have 'acted disgracefully' at your tables. I was confident they must be mistaken, but I wished to check with you. You would tell me if something was going on to make someone develop such a passionate dislike of Solitaires?" Lady Mortimer spoke in a soft voice, such that Georgina could barely hear her.

Georgina pressed her ear against the backrest of the wing chair, as though this might assist her to hear better, but it made a creaking sound when she touched it. Stricken, her mind raced through assorted weak excuses to explain her presence if they turned and located her.

Fortunately, Mrs. Gardner had chosen that same moment to use a tinderbox to light an additional candle. The scratching noise, followed by the sound of the flame igniting, filled Georgina with relief. She exhaled a slow, shaky breath.

"It's unlike you to listen to gossip, Elizabeth," Mrs. Gardner chided. "I wonder who has been filling your head with such nonsense."

"I feel reassured then. It would sadden me to think you have fallen into difficulties or the way you run your business here is not *de rigueur.*"

"Of course not."

The impulse to spring from her hiding place and declare Mrs. Gardner an unconscionable liar came upon Georgina. She erred on the side of discretion for a change and clamped her mouth shut instead.

"As you may recall, I've never approved of your plan to start a gambling den."

The pause that followed this comment suggested Mrs. Gardner was scrambling for a suitable answer. Georgina wished she could see her squirm under Lady Mortimer's interrogation. "Naturally, I am grateful for everything you have done for me," Mrs. Gardner said, "but I needed to find my own way. . . ."

"I scarcely think following the advice of Ellis and Montgomery constitutes finding your own way. Instead of assisting you towards an independent living, my suspicion is they have continued to lead you down a path of roguery." Georgina detected a stern note in Lady Mortimer's voice. So, she knew *something* of the illicit nature of Solitaires, condemned it, and yet patronized the establishment regularly? Georgina's fascination with the Countess deepened.

"Those gentlemen have been most generous to me." Mrs. Gardner sounded feeble.

Lady Mortimer responded with a cynical laugh. "You are not dealing with a babe born yesterday, my dear."

Mrs. Gardner sniffed dramatically. "Perhaps *generous* is not the appropriate word," she conceded.

"We both know that your compliance does not stem from a sense of gratitude. Their hold over you is made of stronger stuff than that."

Georgina longed to be able to read Mrs. Gardner's face. What were they talking about?

"I made mistakes very early in my dealings with them, Elizabeth, yes. And I am still paying the price. Despite all your efforts to help, they seem to be one step ahead, and any effort to escape their control only makes my—*our*—situation worse."

Lady Mortimer sighed. There was a rustle of fabric, which Georgina presumed was Lady Mortimer moving from her position on the sofa. "I shall take my leave of you." There was a significant pause. Georgina stiffened but dared not crane her neck to see if Lady Mortimer was looking in her direction. "Please, see me to the door."

"Very well," Mrs. Gardner replied. She extinguished the candle she had just lit, and the two exited the room, closing the door behind them. Georgina was plunged into relative darkness once more. She released a loud sigh and collapsed from her hiding place in relief. That had been rather too close for comfort.

She went directly to the door and pressed her ear to it. She waited for the sound of Lady Mortimer taking leave, followed by the distinct footfall of Mrs. Gardner making her way back upstairs. Georgina slipped out of the gaming room and back down the stairs to the main hall. That had been close. Too close.

Footsteps sounded on the staircase behind her, and Georgina held her breath again, sinking into the darkness of the walls as much as possible. Her heart raced, thudding so hard she thought she could hear it echo throughout the house. Had Mrs. Gardner heard her coming out into the hall, or was it an attendant getting ready for the day?

Another young maid—this one carrying a large basket overladen with laundry—emerged briefly from the shadows, then disappeared down the attendants' stairwell. Georgina understood she must escape from the house immediately and not risk the same path by which she had gained entry.

As she stepped out of the shadows, however, a young footman emerged from an open doorway to her right. He had been preoccupied dusting some lint off the arm of his livery, but upon seeing movement, he gasped in surprise.

Georgina gauged him to be only nineteen or twenty, and from the expression on his face, she was not sure who suffered the bigger fright.

The lanky young man looked as though he were about to call out, but he hesitated when Georgina beamed up at him.

"Sorry, my dear fellow. Forgive me for alarming you. Fell asleep. Back there in the, ah . . . one of the, ah . . ."

"The private rooms?" he supplied helpfully.

"Indeed. One of the private rooms. Must have shot the cat. Quite unusual for me, you understand. Can't think what came over me."

He eyed her warily for a moment, but at her good humor, he nodded.

She reached into her pocket and retrieved a shilling. Pressing it into his hand, she said warmly, "Apologies for any inconvenience."

"Thank you, Miss . . . ?"

"Ravenscroft." With a smile of self-satisfaction, she strode to the front door, opened it, and disappeared into the dawn.

Feeling invigorated by her thievery, Georgina opted to walk home, even detouring for a brief stroll via Green Park to enjoy its frosty morning beauty. By the time she returned to Half Moon Street, Georgina could think only of her bed. Her eyes stung with fatigue, and her body ached for rest. She hid the spoils of her night's work in the desk in her library before retiring up to her room. In a matter of minutes, she stripped down to her underwear and climbed into her turned-down bed, most content with her efforts.

It would have been most straightforward to discover the young man's promissory notes lying conveniently on a desk, but Georgina felt she made the best of a situation and at least now had a means to coax Mrs. Gardner into relinquishing Arthur's IOUs. No sooner had her head hit her pillow than she fell into a dreamless slumber.

12

Dear Miss Pace,

I regret not accepting your invitation to dance last night. I fear it was rather shabby of me to abandon you in your time of need. I hope my actions did not cause you to leave the Blakes's ball early. Hopefully, after your long and eventful evening, you were able to finally get some sleep.

Sincerely yours,
Lady Elizabeth Mortimer

Georgina read over the missive twice. Could it be that Lady Mortimer had seen her concealed in Mrs. Gardner's parlor and recognized her? Georgina deposited the parchment onto the table and regarded it warily. This seemed unfathomable. Yet Lady Mortimer's message carried a cryptic tone. Perhaps she merely meant to tease her about Prudence.

She remembered the distinct pause before Lady Mortimer had asked Mrs. Gardner to lead her from the house. Was it possible she'd wanted to give Georgina a chance to escape?

Twirling the signet ring on her finger, Georgina reflected on everything that had happened over the last week. She had returned from Cornwall—barely repentant after a minor indiscretion—found herself immediately dragged into a young man's gambling troubles, and ended up a housebreaker. All of this, set in motion over her inability to resist helping Arthur, over the way he tugged at her heart with his smile and thick spectacles. His likeness to her brother meant he appealed to her sympathies in a manner few others could.

Along the way, she had met the curious Lady Mortimer, who appeared immune to Georgina's flirtation, yet showed her care in the most surprising ways. Not to mention her confusing and rather inconvenient connection to the gaming house at the root of all Arthur's difficulties. Lady Mortimer attended there regularly, demonstrated a keen interest in Georgina's claims against Mrs. Gardner, *and* had showed up there in the early hours of the morning to speak to the very same villain. She had queried Mrs. Gardner about her tactics, which suggested an overall innocence in the affair. She was certainly a contradiction. A contradiction who smelled deliciously of orange blossom and possessed the most attractive forearms in all of England.

The combination of Lady Mortimer's imperviousness to flirtatious advances and her puzzling link to Mrs. Gardner added an intriguing layer to an already complicated situation. Perhaps Georgina should avoid her until all was sorted. Was she willing to do that?

Amongst her other correspondence was a summons from Edmund to meet him at Brooks's at once, where he wished to debrief his "long-awaited promenade" with one Mr. Dalrymple. Georgina arched an eyebrow at this, then took a moment to scribble a brief reply to the Countess.

Dear Lady Mortimer,

Your denial left me wounded to my core. Sleep continues to elude me. I would appreciate any advice on how I may achieve nocturnal fulfillment.

Warmest regards,
Miss Georgina Pace

GEORGINA READIED HERSELF to leave for her club, studying her image in the mirror, satisfied she looked well enough. Making a final adjustment to her cravat, she donned her coat and hat, then handed the note to her attendant.

Welcomed inside at Brooks's, she was escorted through the grand mahogany doors into a long gaming room. She wandered past assorted wooden benches and leather chairs, where gentlemen, ladies, and electora read, played hazard, or debated political trends and crises. She ordered a large glass of her favorite Burgundy and found a free chair towards the rear of the room, near Mr. Samuel Leggett.

He appeared to be engrossed in a book which rested on his knees, though he smiled in greeting when she sat down.

"Good afternoon, Miss Pace. A pleasure."

"Hello, Leggy." She crossed one leg over the other and lounged back in the chair.

"So glad Lady Ravenscroft found you. Been thinking about it for days."

Georgina raised a brow.

"Glad she found you at Solitaires. Was searching high and low for you. Reminded me of someone. Read about it once. Wouldn't give up."

Georgina glimpsed longingly across the room at one of the other sofas that had since become vacant. "Reminded you of who, Leggy?"

"A shepherd, I think it was."

"Lady Ravenscroft reminded you of a shepherd?" Georgina repeated, wondering where he was taking her.

"Yes. Ninety-nine sheep, no less. But wouldn't stop until he found the last one." Leggy smiled, eyes beginning to glisten. "A moving story of resilience and determination. Saw that same stubborn dimple in Lady Ravenscroft's chin when she was seeking you out."

Georgina's mouth fell open. "Are you likening Lady Ravenscroft to a character from *the Holy Bible*?"

"That's the book!" Leggy agreed with a cheerful clap. "Aren't you a clever puss to identify it so readily? Picked it up for the first time recently. Quite the tale. Long, though."

Georgina was spared from further comment by Edmund, who waved at her from across the room. Color suffused his cheeks. Georgina wondered whether his suggested walk with Mr. Dalrymple had been a positive one. As he got closer, she detected a glimmer in his eye.

"Telford! Join us, won't you?" Leggy gestured to the chair beside him.

Edmund collapsed onto the seat with a dramatic sigh.

"Did you have a pleasant stroll, Edmund? He has been in Hyde Park with Mr. Lawrence Dalrymple," Georgina added for Leggy's benefit.

"The most blissful walk I have ever enjoyed." Edmund's boyish grin spread from ear to ear.

Georgina doubted whether he could be trusted to interpret any young man's true intentions. "Are you sure that Mr. Dalrymple means to woo you, Edmund?"

He rolled his eyes impatiently and turned to Mr. Leggett. "Leggy, you're a chap."

Mr. Leggett adjusted himself in his chair. "Made no secret of it, Telford. Always have been a man. Nothing against lorians," he added, referring to gentlemen who were born ladies. "But I'm not one. Ask my mother. She'll confirm it."

Georgina suffocated a groan. Edmund should have recognized that Leggy was in a literal mood. Now Edmund was at a crossroads: Would he surrender the subject valiantly or persevere recklessly?

He chose the latter. "If you encouraged another chap to come to the Vauxhall masquerade and said it was 'bound to be an evening full of romance and intrigue'—that would be a pretty obvious invitation, would it not?"

Georgina imagined Mr. Dalrymple talking to Edmund with enthusiasm about Vauxhall, citing the diversions it offered and oblivious to the passion he was kindling within his would-be lover. She remained silent.

Leggy's brow creased. "My dear Telford, I am supremely grateful for the thought, but I have a prior engagement."

"What?"

"Can't get out of it, I'm afraid. My old aunt is holding a small musical soiree, and I pledged to be there. No one enjoys them. I've told her that before. Many times, in fact. But she ignores me. She invites the same group every time, mainly old ladies. Smell like herrings."

"And you do not enjoy these?" Edmund murmured sympathetically.

"No, not at all. Don't like any fish, in fact," Leggy responded, screwing up his nose in distaste.

Georgina rubbed her face with her hand.

"Either way, that doesn't signify. She expects me to be there," he continued. "Must spend the night circling the rooms, being charming to the ladies. It's a dashed dull affair, Telford. But honor-bound to go, you see. Otherwise, I'm sure I might try to accommodate you. Not keen on the romance, though."

"No, no, no. I am not inviting *you*, damn it!" Edmund exclaimed.

Leggy looked relieved. "Well, that *is* good to hear. Very fond of you, Telford, but no wish for you to press me into attending the masquerade for an evening of romance and intrigue. Not something I should like."

"I'm not pressing you into anything," Edmund defended. "If *you* invited a chap for such an evening, would that mean you had taken a shine to him?"

"Well, that *would* be a shabby thing to do, I must say."

This startled Edmund. "Why so?"

Georgina leaned back, resting her arms across her chest. This had all unfolded just as she suspected it would.

"Well, if I had to pick a sex, then I suppose I must prefer ladies, Telford. Wouldn't ask another chap. Stands to reason," Leggy said, his integrity impugned. "I *never* promised such a thing. Never taken a shine to fellows, either. Or electora, if it comes to that."

Georgina had remained quiet throughout this exchange, as she could see no benefit adding further confusion to what had already spun out of hand. However, they appeared to have passed a point of no return.

"Edmund," Georgina pleaded in a firm voice. "Let it be now."

"If *you* were committed to helping me, George, *you* might ask your old friend Lady Ravenscroft about Mr. Dalrymple's inclinations. Then we might know for a certainty," Edmund pouted.

"Ah, the shepherdess herself!" Leggy interjected joyfully.

"What shepherdess?" Edmund asked.

Georgina cursed.

She took her leave, abandoning Edmund and Leggy to their dizzying conversation. She needed to inspect the faro box.

13

AFTER GEORGINA EXTRICATED herself from Brooks's, she returned home and spent the remainder of the afternoon managing her accounts and discussing arrangements with the housekeeper. As evening fell, she sat down to dine with her father.

Ensconced in his chair at the head of the impressive oak dining table, Mr. Silas Pace wore a well-fitting coat of mustard and superfine silk evening breeches. Having consigned his corsets to the fire several years ago, Silas now accepted his stout figure and relished his abundant lifestyle, void of the silly diets propagated by folk who preferred to maintain a leaner frame. His dark hair tended towards gray, and his kind blue eyes displayed creases at the corners from a lifetime of smiling.

He heaped a generous spoonful of mint jelly on top of his roasted lamb, and the attendant served him extra vegetables.

"Are you staying in this evening?" Georgina asked him, pushing the food around on her plate with her fork.

His rosy cheeks brightened. "Ah, no, I shall go to my club or the theater. I have not decided."

"Would you like me to join you?"

"Oh no, you would not enjoy it," he insisted.

Georgina opted not to press him on the subject. She suspected he may have an interest in a lady friend. It would be easy to tease him, but she refrained. He deserved a little joy.

Her parents had loved each other deeply and raised her and her older brother well. Like many honorians, Henry had needed help to get along in the world, which was no problem in itself; their parents found pleasure in looking after him. But the tragic loss of their mother after complications from influenza set in motion a most unfortunate chain of events for their family.

When their mother died, their father lost his way. He struggled to manage their affairs and took little happiness from life. Georgina was only fifteen at the time. She contrived to care for her family and perform the many responsibilities of a house manager, but when they took up lodging in town, Georgina found the new diversions around her rather distracting. She lost some of her levelheadedness and fell into reckless ways. *If Mother was alive, so many things would be different now,* Georgina thought wistfully.

"You are not eating?" Her father paused his meal.

Georgina looked up and saw that his eyes were on her fork, which she had been raking in delicate circles across the plate but had not put near her mouth.

"Are you well?"

Georgina speared some lamb and raised it to her lips. For his benefit only. "Of course."

Yes, he deserved happiness. And she would do all she could to ensure it. She had taken over the management of the estate since she came of age, keeping their fortune in check. She even negotiated some lucrative business transactions to improve their situation. She had done her best. Georgina told herself this, swallowing the knot in her throat.

After dinner, her father referred to his watch and sprang to his feet with a sudden urgency. Georgina gave him an indulgent smile and watched him leave. After so many years without her mother, she hoped he did have a lady friend. The notion warmed her.

Jarvis came into the dining room with a note for her on a tray. She recognized Lady Mortimer's seal and accepted it gingerly.

Dear Miss Pace,

I am bereft to learn you have difficulty attaining nocturnal fulfillment. I do not doubt you will elaborate when we next meet. Hopefully, that will be soon.

Warmest regards,
Lady Elizabeth Mortimer

Georgina inhaled sharply and read the note once more, this time closer to the candlelight, in case she had mistaken the implications. Carelessly, she rubbed her head, paying no mind to the ribbon that held her hair in place. A few curls became dislodged and fell about her face. Georgina stood up and headed for the dining-room door but came back to the table and picked up her glass of port. A swarm of butterflies had taken flight in her stomach.

GEORGINA RETIRED TO the library. At her desk, she glanced at the missive from Lady Mortimer once more and loosened her cravat. Georgina lifted the paper to her nostrils and detected a hint of orange blossom. This really was the most distracting woman alive. She hid the note in the hutch with the others, determined not to let her mind wander.

Reaching into a drawer and retrieving the stolen faro box, she examined it, looking at the hinges and panels to see how a dealer might load it. On initial inspection, she could not see how it might have been modified, so she procured her own deck of cards from a nearby cabinet to test how it functioned.

She placed it on the desk and set the cards into the box, scrutinizing it with a frown.

After some trial and error, Georgina discovered the box had two levels that allowed for dual dealing. Presumably, this permitted the operator to select when to release cards fairly and when to distribute cards that would benefit the dealer and bank.

Georgina sat back and turned the faro box over in her hands, a satisfied smirk playing at the corners of her mouth. She wondered what Mrs. Gardner would think when she discovered it missing and hoped it would cause her at least as much discomfiture as she had caused poor Arthur.

She could use the artifact to ply Mrs. Gardner around to her way of thinking.

Withdrawing some parchment and her quill, she penned a brief letter to the owner of the faro box.

Dear Madam.

The nib scratched along the thick paper.

I happened upon a unique item which, I presume, must be of considerable value to you. I would have the pleasure of giving this back to you if you might see your way clear to returning Mr. Arthur Coombes's promissory notes. You received these notes by mistake, and I am convinced you would wish to rectify this situation promptly and without involving Bow Street. Once he confirms to me that you have restored the notes, I will return your item.

Regards,
Miss Georgina Pace

She folded the paper. Even if she had chosen not to sign the letter, she was confident that Mrs. Gardner would guess who had written it. Georgina picked up a stick of dark red wax and held it to the candle. As it bubbled and melted, she trickled the thick ruby liquid onto the join and, while still soft, pressed down on her stamp, observing with satisfaction the scarlet wax swelled around the signet. She scribbled the direction on the outside and commissioned her footman to deliver the letter to Mrs. Gardner in St James's Square.

Georgina then strode up the staircase, taking the steps two at a time in a rush to get changed. She needed a distraction, something to divert her thoughts from the weight of what she had become involved in.

Within half an hour, she descended the stairs once more, looking elegant in a black velvet evening coat, black breeches, and top hat, her glossy curls tumbling over one shoulder. She collected her gloves and walking cane from Jarvis and advised him she would spend the evening at Mem Lavigne's club in Pall Mall.

14

GEORGINA SAT PARTIALLY reclined on one of two large, pink velvet sofas with smooth mahogany trim, set off to the side of Mem Lavigne's main parlor. She had removed her coat, loosened her cravat, and unbuttoned her black waistcoat. With one leg outstretched, she crossed the other leg up so that her ankle rested upon her thigh. This allowed her to use her knee to support her hand, which held her glass of port.

A robust fire flickered nearby, and one of Mem Lavigne's scantily clad young men plucked at a harp, enhancing the relaxing ambience.

Sarah and Colt sat across from Georgina. They had sought refuge here, following a rather insipid ball they both attended.

"We were certain we might see you at Lady Preston's soiree tonight," Sarah said with a sigh. "Aside from the dancing, they were playing whist for penny stakes. It was rather droll."

Georgina gave an imperceptible shudder. "I have no interest in gambling presently, not even for penny stakes," she replied, thinking back to the damned faro box secreted in her desk at home.

"Mem Lavigne will be disappointed."

"Young Miss *Coombes* was there," Sarah went on. "Declining the offer of dances with many suitors, *just* so that she might be available for Colt."

"And did you dance with her?" Georgina quizzed, with a look of mild interest.

"Good grief, no," Colt replied.

"Indeed, such a move would be far too premature," Georgina teased. "Having offered her a sampling of your services last night, it behooves you to ignore her for at least a week, to pique her interest."

Sarah flashed Colt a disapproving look. "Eventually, Colt, you will find yourself *forced* to marry one of these young women. And I daresay it will serve you right when you find yourself shackled to a pretty little goosecap."

Colt grinned.

"No, he will not," Georgina answered for him. "He will sooner be called out by an enraged parent and bleed to death on a misty heath than relent in such a dull way."

"I always take good care not to be found in compromising situations by parents and the like. And I am *always* open about my intentions. There is never a breach of promise involved, I assure you," Colt said. "You, George, know how important *that* is. How *is* Prudence, by the way?"

"She is none the worse for our encounter in Cornwall and appears to be now happily established with Lord Ravenscroft."

Sarah regarded her serenely. "Although she worked very hard to secure a dance with you last evening. You did your best to avoid her, if I am not mistaken."

Georgina scowled, fiddling with the signet ring on her hand with her thumb. "Lady Mortimer expressed her disapproval of my conduct with Prudence last night, then practically threw me into her arms. So, there is no cause to read me another lecture now."

Colt's brows snapped together. "Lady Mortimer is *extremely* priggish. I should not think she would be to your taste *at all.* And yet—?"

Sarah rolled her eyes.

Georgina had no interest in defending her friendship choices to Colt. "Lady Mortimer amuses me. Just because she supported Sarah in stopping you from ravishing Miss Coombes, I hardly think she is *priggish.*"

Colt and Sarah exchanged meaningful looks. Georgina felt her temperature rise, as it often did when the conversation turned to Lady Mortimer.

"Enough of this nonsense from you both," Georgina chastised them. "I wish you will have a care, Colt. For while you jest about it, dabbling with innocents can have significant implications, and your luck cannot be in forever."

He grinned in self-satisfaction. "I always have a care to avoid, ah . . . *significant implications.*"

Georgina suspected he hinted at the more intimate methods he adopted to avoid illegitimate offspring. "A little conscience would become you, Colt."

He laughed. "Who is reading the lecture *now*? I believe I hear the pot calling the kettle black."

Georgina cast him a withering look.

"Did you steal back those vowels yet, my girl?"

Sarah scowled. "Steal?"

"You lobcock," Georgina muttered.

"You would not steal from Mrs. Gardner?" Sarah demanded.

"She said she would. If she hasn't already. She planned to do so last night," Colt added.

If she did not possess so much respect for Mem Lavigne's establishment, Georgina would have hurled her glass in Colt's direction.

She expected Sarah to round on her in a tirade of reproaches. To her surprise, she glared at Colt instead.

"And you knew about this?"

The smug smile dissipated from Colt's face like smoke in the air. "I—I couldn't *stop* her."

"Did we not agree that Georgina needed to be encouraged towards *settling down*?"

It was Georgina's turn to take umbrage. "What?" She could hear that her voice had risen to a pitch much higher than she normally spoke at.

Both Sarah and Colt had the grace to look guilty but did not respond to the question.

Lottie's buxom figure sauntered over to the group at this moment, offering to refill their glasses. She came to Georgina last and lingered.

Georgina glanced up and beckoned her to accept the seat beside her. At least she could rely on Lottie not to ambush her, unlike her other friends.

Lottie discarded the decanter she held and curled up next to Georgina willingly. It did not seem to bother her that the lime-green, translucent robe she wore left little to the imagination, and that both Sarah and Colt could make out every inch of her well-curved body from where they sat. Just as well—Georgina was not the possessive sort.

Fortunately, both of her friends were discreet.

"You joining me at the Vauxhall masquerade, George?" Colt changed the subject.

"Of course," Georgina agreed, allowing Lottie to take her arm so that she could stroke it up and down with her skilled fingertips. Normally, she might enjoy such physical intimacy. This evening, the touch left her feeling empty. "I should like that very much."

"Pace!" a deep voice bellowed from one of the alcoves as a disheveled man tumbled out. He staggered over to them, pointing an accusing finger towards Georgina.

The three friends looked up at him with varying expressions of curiosity and bewilderment on their faces. Lottie appeared unfazed.

"You!" he shouted. "You have been with my wife, damn you!" His slurred speech suggested he had taken too much wine.

"Very likely, if she has to put up with a husband like you," Georgina replied.

Sarah's eyes widened. "Georgina!" She stood and went to the gentleman to place a calming hand on his shoulder.

Lottie snorted and bit her lip to quell a grin.

"Brazen minx. She's been with my wife."

"Who is he?" Georgina asked Colt quietly, wrinkling her nose.

"Lord Phillip Dawson. Resides in Albemarle Street," he replied.

Georgina returned a knowing nod, confirming the fellow had not mistaken the matter.

Sarah directed a long-suffering look at Georgina. "A misunderstanding, Georgina. Surely? You and Lady Dawson are simply very good friends, are you not?"

"Hmm? Oh, yes. She is a *very* good friend of mine," Georgina agreed.

Fortunately, thanks to Sarah's sensitive and diplomatic nature, Lord Dawson stumbled away from Georgina without further fuss. Sarah bestowed him into Mem Lavigne's tender care for further attention.

Georgina watched her friend's return, marveling at how easily she managed to deescalate irate partners. "It's a wonder, as you never fall into such scrapes yourself. But you are so *skilled* at managing these things."

Sarah sighed. "I have spent many years talking both you and Robert out of difficulties. I am quite used to it now."

With a grin, Georgina reached over and squeezed her friend's hand. "I am sorry we are such a burden to you." If only Sarah would find happiness for herself. Then perhaps she would not feel so responsible for the two of them.

"We could do with you working here, Mrs. F," Lottie chimed in. "The scuffles you might help us avoid with that syrupy tongue of yours." She added a cheeky wink.

Georgina gave Lottie's behind a playful little smack. "Never you mind her syrupy tongue!"

SOMETIME LATER, GEORGINA spied an attendant murmuring something to Mem Lavigne, who came over and excused the interruption. "Forgive me, Miss Pace, but I have a visitor for you, waiting below. She is unknown to me but craves admittance to speak with you."

"Curious. Who is it?"

"The Countess Mortimer, Miss Pace. Shall I tell her ladyship that you are not receiving?"

Colt made an exaggerated grimace. "Yes, damn it."

Georgina cast him an annoyed look while her own heart rate accelerated. What would make Lady Mortimer track her down *here*, of all places?

"No, thank you. I will vouch for her. Please, show her up directly, Lavigne."

Sarah's brow lifted in apparent surprise.

"*Priggish*," Colt hissed at Georgina.

"Be damned, Colt."

Some minutes later, Lady Mortimer, having divested herself of her cloak downstairs, came into the parlor with Mem Lavigne. She wore an elegant, rich blue satin gown with black beading. A regal black plume pinned her stylish coiffure into place. She scanned the room, and when her gaze rested upon Georgina with her companions, she hesitated.

Georgina had not tried to disengage Lottie, who draped herself over her arm and curled one knee over Georgina's lap.

"Forgive the intrusion, Miss Pace," Lady Mortimer said, dipping her head in a dignified nod. "I see I have interrupted you at an inconvenient time. Perhaps I should call upon you tomorrow at your home?"

"I suspect you must have *some* pressing need to speak to me if you would seek me out here, Lady Mortimer. Stay a while. Sarah and Colt were about to take their leave." She directed a significant look at them both.

Colt did not move, but Sarah agreed. She smiled at Lady Mortimer and held her arm out to Colt.

Grudgingly, Colt drained his glass and stood up. He hooked his arm through Sarah's, shook his head, and escorted Sarah through the maze of tables and chairs out of the chamber.

Lady Mortimer assumed a spot on the vacated sofa.

Georgina studied her and decided she did have a rather prim air, particularly for a setting such as this. "Lottie, please fetch my dear friend something to drink."

Lottie, her mouth set in a tight line, obliged Georgina's request. She fetched a glass, thumped it down onto the table, filled it with wine, and slammed the flagon down beside it with enough force that its contents shuddered. She shoved the glass towards Lady Mortimer with a fierce glare.

Georgina grinned as Lady Mortimer accepted the glass with a tentative hand. Had Lottie possessed a poisonous tincture conveniently to hand, Georgina thought she would have slipped it into Lady Mortimer's drink, such was her evident annoyance at her interruption.

"Thank you, Lottie. Give us the room, will you?"

With an audible huff, the damsel swept away from them, a cascade of apricot-colored hair trailing behind her.

"I have the impression you may find yourself severely berated once I take my leave," Lady Mortimer mused.

"She will not see me again today. I will be held in contempt for at least a day or two. How may I help you? Your presence tonight puzzles me."

"Your most amiable butler Jarvis provided me with your destination. I went to call upon you after I visited Solitaires," Lady Mortimer began, her voice slow and pointed.

Georgina stiffened and took a sip, but continued to watch Lady Mortimer over her glass. "You are a frequent visitor there, my lady."

Lady Mortimer's expression was inscrutable. "I might remark the same about yourself, Miss Pace. I have seen you there almost as often as I have been there, of late. You might imagine my surprise when I overheard the proprietor describing you in some rather *colorful* terms this evening."

Georgina put her glass down and leaned forward confidentially. "Is that so? Tell me more. Have I caused a scandal?"

A smile hovered around Lady Mortimer's mouth. "I am not sure I would call it a scandal *yet*. Though it seems you have been up to some mischief. Can it be you have turned into a thief, my dear?"

A knot formed in her throat, mortified at what Lady Mortimer must think of her. However, she quashed it immediately and mustered a lighthearted tone.

"Lud, yes! You have discovered my secret. I am nothing better than a common housebreaker."

Lady Mortimer traced the fine carvings of her crystal tumbler. Her gray eyes glinted in the firelight. A delicate muscle in her forearm tensed, then released. "There is nothing common about *you*, Miss Pace."

"I am a thief."

"So I gathered following the Blakes's ball."

"You *did* see me."

"I did. We have all been young and headstrong." Lady Mortimer's mouth quivered. "No, no need to bristle at me, girl. You are yet young, compared to me. Arguably, you should be past petty crime at your age, though I commend you on your passion for assisting others. Though I am curious about why you have resorted to theft. You do not strike me as impoverished."

Georgina, tempted to take umbrage, found herself full of mirth instead. It was difficult to be annoyed when Lady Mortimer had a point and was so deliberate in making it. She did not seem put out that Georgina had committed a crime. Nor that it involved Mrs. Gardner. Plus, there was the intriguing question of age—an older woman? The Countess was going up in Georgina's estimation once more.

At this moment, two naked bodies partially emerged from a nearby alcove. Apparently, in the fervor of their lovemaking, the couple had slipped to the floor. Their entwined bodies moved together unbridled, and their moans heightened as they approached their climax.

Mem Lavigne appeared from nowhere and pulled the curtain around the sweating bodies, lost in their ecstasy. Groans and cries signaling their peak echoed from behind the drapes. Mem Lavigne cast a smile towards Lady Mortimer, who remained composed throughout.

Indeed, her ladyship was full of surprises. Georgina had half-expected her to flee the room. She was tempted to ask the Countess what she made of the show, but instead she cleared her throat.

Georgina ignored her question. "Please tell me what Mrs. Gardner's colorful words were. Is *everyone* talking about it?"

"I am loath to disappoint you, my little thief, but no. Mrs. Gardner was in a rare form after receiving your letter. Fortunately for your reputation, I chanced to be nearby, and she confided her grievances to me rather than all her other guests."

Georgina sat back against the couch again. "I was not worried about my reputation. She can say what she likes. I do not care a jot for her opinion or anyone else's."

"Indeed, of course not. Though I think you'll find that there is a vast difference between your *current* reputation and being branded a thief. That would be . . . *regrettable*."

Georgina lifted her chin in defiance. What did it matter to Lady Mortimer what the world thought of her?

"And do you care so much about my reputation?" Georgina prompted.

"Not really."

Georgina struggled to understand why she could not provoke a more explicit response from Lady Mortimer.

"Fear not. I shall cease my thieving ways."

"And will you give me the spoils of your thievery?" Lady Mortimer prompted.

"You *are* priggish," Georgina exclaimed, sympathizing with Colt.

Lady Mortimer's brow furrowed, and Georgina clapped a hand over her mouth.

"I mean, *no*. I shall return Mrs. Gardner's possessions *once* Arthur's vowels are safely back in his hands."

Lady Mortimer's lips parted. "So, Julia has the vowels of a friend of yours?"

Georgina nodded. "The vowels belong to Mr. Arthur Coombes. It happens he is a miris, and a charmingly naïve fellow. She should not have permitted him to write IOUs, let alone encouraged him, and under predatory terms. Solitaires is extremely disreputable. The faro box is merely an example of the many tricks they employ. I offered to pay for the value of the vowels, including interest, and yet she would not relinquish them. I can only deduce that there are unknown factors at play preventing her from doing so. But who is behind it, I cannot say."

Lady Mortimer's expression had hardened, her lips forming a tight line. "Only say the word, and I promise to have them restored to your hands."

Georgina frowned, recalling the night of the Blakes's ball, when she had overheard the two women talking. She did not want to be responsible for complicating this matter further. "I appreciate the offer, but this is my undertaking." They sat in silence for a moment. "Are you so familiar with Mrs. Gardner that you would become invested in this matter?"

"I have been acquainted with her for many years and would merely like to avoid unnecessary conflict."

Something about Lady Mortimer's calm dignity both troubled and intrigued Georgina. She demonstrated strong views, and yet she never displayed outright censure. Her mild temperament suggested both wisdom and worldliness. She exercised impeccable restraint over her emotions, never displaying anger. Though for all this arcadian gentility, Lady Mortimer also had a level of playfulness about her. At times, she presented a serious demeanor and yet remained composed in the face of a couple fucking on the floor beside her. She was an original. And *what* was she doing calling on Mrs. Gardner at that time of the night? Really, for Georgina to understand what she was up to, she would have to get to know her better.

Standing, Georgina went to the decanter and refilled her glass. She sauntered back over to Lady Mortimer and topped up her drink.

She replaced the bottle and returned, this time sitting on the sofa beside Lady Mortimer.

"You don't mind if I call you Elizabeth, do you?" Georgina said, swiveling on the seat so they could see each other better.

Elizabeth's brows rose in surprise. "I do not mind."

"Now, pray tell me, how do you mean to reform me?" Georgina quizzed. "I sense that is your intention. Not only am I insufferably cavalier about the feelings of my young admirers as you told me last night, but my character is sadly unsteady and reckless. And I am a thief. *Something* must be done. I look forward to you reining me in."

"It is not my place to reproach or correct you."

Elizabeth's expression continued to be difficult to read.

"Then you might *guide* me. You shall lead by example," Georgina told her in a level voice. "Shall we begin tomorrow?"

With a laugh, Elizabeth replied, "Sadly, I have plans already for tomorrow. I must attend a meeting at Somerset House with the Royal Academy."

"I note you have not invited me to join you."

Elizabeth's cheeks colored a little. "You might come, though I suspect you would be entirely bored."

"I should not be at all bored," Georgina promised. "Let me join you?"

"If you wish," Elizabeth capitulated, looking a trifle harried. "I shall collect you on my way to the Strand at eleven o'clock."

"Eleven. Goodness, you are scarcely leaving me time to sleep."

"I cannot change my plans, Miss Pace. Perhaps we can attend to your nocturnal fulfillment another night."

A thrill of anticipation bubbled inside Georgina at her reference to their playful missives. Elizabeth had finally flirted with her.

Elizabeth rose, ready to take her leave.

"Where are you going?"

"Home. . . ."

Once again, Elizabeth retreated the moment things were getting interesting.

"Very well." Georgina also stood up and collected her coat, draping it over her arm. "Allow me to see you safely there."

"That is unnecessary," Elizabeth assured her, but Georgina placed her hand on the small of her back and propelled her towards the exit.

"Unnecessary, perhaps. But I would not sleep easy unless I knew you were settled safely at home. You would not deprive me of a good night's sleep?" Georgina grinned, parroting Elizabeth's words from the first night they met. "And besides that, I must be up in time to make our appointment."

Georgina bade Mem Lavigne a pleasant evening and looked around for Lottie, an apologetic smile ready on her lips. But the young woman seemed unbothered. She lounged in a most luxurious high-backed velvet armchair while a handsome lorian with sinewy arms knelt in front of her, happily massaging her feet. Lottie simpered at Georgina, who gave a small wave and escorted Elizabeth downstairs.

15

HAVING STRETCHED PROPRIETY to its limits in demanding to accompany Elizabeth home, Georgina was astonished to find herself invited inside for a drink.

As Elizabeth procured her a port, Georgina stole covert glances at her. One beautifully tapered arm reached across the tray as the Countess distilled the liquid into each glass. The fine muscles beneath the smooth skin of her hand contracted as she placed the decanter back onto the table. Georgina could imagine what it would feel like to be beneath that hand. A pulse throbbed deep inside her.

Elizabeth stood over Georgina, holding a glass out to her. "Are you well?"

"Yes." Georgina grabbed the tumbler and took a generous sip. As Elizabeth assumed the seat beside her, her divine scent once again intoxicated Georgina. Forevermore, she would associate the delicate fragrance of orange blossoms with the racing of her heart and the sudden moistening between her legs.

Georgina cleared her throat. She needed to collect herself. "Did Mrs. Gardner send you to find me tonight, or did you come of your own volition?"

"I sought you out of my own accord. I was curious to hear your side of the story, else I would conclude you must have committed all manner of sins to have garnered such ire."

Georgina detected amusement in Elizabeth's eyes. "Aside from my thievery, what did she say?"

"I am far too well-bred to repeat her particular phrasing." Elizabeth winked. "It was quite a task to convince her you did not intend on murdering her in her sleep when you broke into her home."

Georgina flinched. "That is not in my style. If I ever decide someone is worth murdering, they will *certainly* see it coming."

"Now *that* I do believe." Elizabeth paused to sip her port. "I took the opportunity to educate her about the impropriety of using fixed devices and other tricks to ensnare vulnerable patrons at her tables. *Again*."

Georgina shifted slightly on the sofa so she could study Elizabeth better. "I hope that she heeds your advice, for if she continues in her current fashion, she will force my hand. I will not be as gentle as you."

Elizabeth rotated her bracelet around her wrist and kept her eyes lowered. "Some of her associates may make her compliance with your requests difficult. In fact, you should have a care about how you interact with that set. I have known them to . . . make problems disappear. I do not want them to consider you a problem, Georgina."

A familiar indignation gripped Georgina's chest. First Colt and now Elizabeth. Why were good, respectable people suggesting she look the other way in the face of significant victimization of honorians and vulnerable people? Surely, the more dangerous and disreputable the villains, the greater the need to disband their business regardless of any personal risk.

"It is a shame no one provided such a warning to Arthur Coombes *before* he lost his fortune to Mrs. Gardner and her friends," Georgina countered.

A blush formed on Elizabeth's cheeks. "I once went to great lengths to help Mrs. Gardner find her way, but I never encouraged her to open Solitaires. Without consulting me, she accepted financial backing from Ellis and Montgomery, and they advised her to keep the establishment off the books. To someone with minimal business acumen, this seemed like a reasonable strategy, as she wished to make an income without delay. However, Mrs. Gardner quickly learned that they would use this knowledge, amongst other things, to compel her obedience. Whether she feared being imprisoned by the Runners for tax evasion and illegal gambling, or more perilous outcomes, she dared not deny them."

Georgina regarded her from beneath hooded lids, her lips compressed. "My heart truly bleeds for her."

"She is not evil. I have known her for a long time, and she has only recently traveled off course. I try to assist her by patronizing Solitaires. Even losing. But I do not agree with her recent conduct," Elizabeth explained.

Georgina, who could be very black-and-white in her thinking, struggled to see how someone as upstanding as Elizabeth could still sympathize with Mrs. Gardner, given her dastardly behavior. "Well, perhaps she will develop some compassion and a conscience, and my intervention will not be necessary."

Elizabeth sighed. "Why are you so set upon bringing about Mrs. Gardner's complete downfall?"

Georgina's eyes narrowed. "Why are you so set upon protecting her?"

Elizabeth drummed her fingertips over her glass. "Can we not assume I am trying to protect everyone?"

As her breathing quickened, Georgina endeavored to control her temper. She did not want to quarrel with Elizabeth. "Everyone except Arthur?" But not only Arthur. Henry's tremendous smile flashed before her. “Arthur and other honorians like him are the real victims here.”

“I hope to protect Arthur too. You are right, no one should be victimized.” Elizabeth put her hand on top of Georgina’s. It covered hers almost entirely. “Or hurt.”

Georgina’s heart thrummed in her chest.

“I know this must be difficult for you, especially . . .” Elizabeth’s tone was as soft as cobwebs, yet it ripped through Georgina without mercy. “Especially given how your brother died.”

The loud, rhythmic beat of Georgina’s heart seemed to suspend in time with Elizabeth’s words. Had her heart stopped entirely? She swallowed hard, hoping to dissolve the lump that blocked her throat, making it difficult to breathe.

“That was a long time ago,” Georgina said eventually. “But I certainly wish to spare others his fate.” In a fluid movement, she drained the rest of her glass and stood. “Thank you for the drink, Elizabeth. I look forward to seeing you at eleven tomorrow.”

Georgina looked down into Elizabeth’s sympathetic gaze. She would *not* be pitied. Without waiting for the Countess to bid her goodnight, she departed.

On the street, Georgina hailed the next passing hackney and directed it to her home.

As she stared out the carriage window blankly, emotion welled in her throat. She attempted to suck back the tears, but they were determined to escape tonight.

It still felt strange to cry about Henry, when all he brought in life was joy. She recalled his delight in making his darling little sister giggle. And giggle she did when he was around. He may not have been the most sensible brother, but he brought her comfort. And he taught her the importance of always saying sorry when she made the wrong choice—an area where she could still use improvement.

As the hackney jolted her from side to side, Georgina remembered the moment their lives changed forever. Eight grueling years ago. In contrast to the quiet passing of her mother, characterized by the inevitable peace that came at the conclusion of an extended period of terrible sickness, the loss of Henry had been brutal and unexpected.

Georgina had only just gone to bed after a particularly late night out when she heard the distant clang of the doorbell downstairs. As she fumbled for her dressing gown, wondering who could be calling at such an hour, she heard the haunting echo of her father's primal sob. Even sitting in this musty carriage so many years later, Georgina could relive the visceral sensation of dread as she raced from her room and stopped at the top of the stairwell.

Her father, Silas, pale and broken, thrashed in the arms of a stranger. "*Henry*," he kept saying. But Henry was not there. Others stood around him, glancing at each other helplessly. Georgina had clenched her eyes shut tightly and covered her ears with balled fists, trying to block out his guttural keening. Her fingernails had dug into her palms until they bled. Nothing could have prepared her for the subsequent chaos that descended upon their lives as grief in its truest form ripped through them.

Even with the assistance of Bow Street and some of Henry's repentant cronies, they pieced together little of what happened. As with Arthur, people who feigned friendship with Henry had taken advantage of his unsuspecting nature. With neither father nor sister there to protect him, these "friends" lured him away from safety, and he fell victim to a band of evil marauders. He would have willingly given the shirt off his back to anyone who needed it, though this did not prevent a brutal assault from taking place, merely for the sake of his pocketbook and ring. Henry's frail body had not survived the attack.

Georgina and her father had yet to find peace after his death. In fact, Georgina could not always believe Henry was gone. How could it be true?

In the speed and savagery of the assault, the aggressors had overlooked Henry's fob watch. Once this item had been restored to the family with a few other personal effects, Georgina carried it with her always. Henry would never leave her side.

She pushed a tear from her cheek, resenting Elizabeth for making her confront memories she preferred to leave dormant. *Difficult* did not begin to describe Georgina's feelings. Once the carriage stopped and she paid the driver, Georgina hurried into her home—a sanctuary, yes, but also where all her hidden ghosts dwelled.

16

DEPARTING MEM LAVIGNE'S, Sarah and Colt retreated to the street, where they hailed a hackney to deliver them to Sarah's residence on Curzon Street. Since leaving the club, Colt could slice the tension in the air with a knife. By choosing to disclose George's secret to Sarah, he had intended to draw her closer, assuming she'd want the truth. He'd had no way of predicting that she would somehow turn it on to him and hold him accountable for leading Georgina astray.

The two climbed down from the carriage, and Colt supplied the driver with a coin. Silently, he followed Sarah inside.

"We need to discuss Georgina," she said abruptly. "Let's have a drink."

Colt nodded, but a sense of foreboding gnawed at him. He wanted to enjoy a casual drink with Sarah. He did *not* relish a lecture, not even from her.

A maid scurried over from her chair where she had sat reading a book in comfort.

"Good evening, Mrs. Fortescue, I trust you had a pleasant outing," she ventured, accepting Sarah's velvet cloak and gloves, and extending her hands for Colt's greatcoat and hat. She smiled over the top of the pile of articles she held for them.

"Thank you, Rachael. It was most enjoyable. Please leave those things on the hall stand so that Lord Coulthurst can find them on his way out later. Goodnight."

Sarah led the way into her parlor and sat down as Colt fetched them both some port. She accepted the glass from him, and he sat down beside her, closer than a casual onlooker might deem appropriate. Damn it, if she was going to be cross with him, he was at least going to make himself at home.

Sarah straightened the folds of her gown around her legs. "How did she come to break into Mrs. Gardner's?"

He shrugged. "How does George always land into these dashed scrapes? She went along, resolved to pay her off. The woman confounded the matter by saying no. George got a bee in her bonnet and won't back down." He sighed. "It's not about the vowels, Sarah. It's about Henry."

Sarah's fine lips formed into a silent *O* shape.

Colt pushed his hair back with his hand. Supporting Georgina had not always been a straightforward matter.

"Hence why I have tried to be gentle with her."

"*Gentle* does not seem to be effective with Georgina," Sarah said. She tilted her head to one side as she regarded him, dark eyes curious. "What is it?"

Colt frowned. "There are times when she talks as though he's still alive."

Sarah inhaled sharply.

"Rationally, she must know he is gone, but she is not accepting it," Colt continued.

"I see. That might explain her need . . . her *compulsion* to help Mr. Coombes."

He nodded slowly. "I do not want to be too blunt with her."

"We have *all* been sympathetic, allowing her to grieve in her own way."

"Truly," Colt agreed. "Even Mem Lavigne and their attendants placate Georgina's idiosyncrasies. They cater to her addictions and give her free rein to do as she pleases."

Sarah lowered her eyes. "Perhaps we have been lenient for too long and not encouraged her to confront the pain."

Colt appreciated why Georgina would not wish to face such misery. "I have done my best to distract her instead."

"I would much rather she focus her attention on *settling* herself than seeking distraction or trying to solve the problems of the downtrodden."

This drew a sudden laugh from him. "George never seeks to be involved in these matters, Sarah. They have a way of finding her."

"Lady Mortimer seems rather attentive to George," Sarah remarked. "Do you imagine they might be developing a *tendre* for one another?"

Colt scowled. "Damn, I should hope not. Can you imagine *George* shackled to someone as upstanding and dull as Lady Mortimer?"

"We agreed that Georgina would do well to find herself a wife. I do not think it would be such a poor match. I quite like her."

"I cannot imagine why."

"You do not like her because you cannot gain from her—she is neither interested in a dalliance with you, nor in the pursuit of young debutantes for amusement. Perhaps you are jealous that she steals your friend's attention."

Sarah was right, of course, and he loved her for it. Colt draped his arm along the sofa and allowed his hand to toy with one of the ebony curls at the base of her neck.

"You gave Rachael the impression I would not be staying long?"

Colt observed, changing the subject. "Though I daresay you could not well tell her I would join you upstairs tonight." He could see Sarah's skin prickle under his soft caress.

"When have I ever permitted you to stay?"

"I am persistent," he answered.

"I shall not change my mind."

The firelight made her eyes flash almost black, and her skin glowed a warm shade of bronze. Her gown of jade-colored Belgium silk created a sublime contrast. She tilted her head to one side so that it rested companionably upon his shoulder.

"Do not seek to ruin our friendship, Robert," she murmured, staring into the fire.

Colt's arm tightened around her, and he gathered her a little closer so that she leaned against his broad chest.

"I am not seeking to ruin anything. I would like to strengthen it."

She relaxed against him, and he rested his chin against the side of her forehead. He inhaled the jasmine scent of her hair deeply as her head rose and fell with the movement of his chest.

With his glass still resting between the fingers of his right hand, he allowed his left hand to stroke her arm.

Sarah shifted so that her ear pressed against the lapel of his coat. She smiled. "Your heart beats quickly, Colt."

"You have that effect on me, amongst others."

She had her arm draped along his thigh. So close to the hardness within his breeches that now pushed against her. "You should go home."

He groaned. "Must I?"

She nodded and sat up, disentangling herself.

Colt finished his drink and bowed his head, clasping his hands around the glass as he took a sharp breath. Once he composed both his mind and body so that he might walk unhindered and with dignity, he stood. Gazing down at her, he tilted her chin up with one of his fingers, inspecting her countenance one more time before departing.

Colt smiled. “Goodnight, my dear.”

“Goodnight, Robert.”

At the door, he hesitated for a moment. The weight of unspoken words chained him to the room. If he declared his love for her, would she let him stay? It would not be a lie. Yet it would not solve the problem of her inability to have faith in him. He could not demand her trust. That had to be bestowed freely. Without a backward look, he stalked out of the room.

17

GEORGINA WOKE IN more elevated spirits. As usual, she had taken quite a lot of brandy before she went to sleep, so her memories of the previous evening were on the hazy side. She wished to keep it that way. As she sat up in bed, she reached for the decanter on her dressing table and poured herself a large glass.

It was a fortunate circumstance that Georgina did not employ an abigail, for she took longer than usual over her dressing. Had someone been there to witness this deviation from routine, it would have led to a good deal of speculation below stairs. She would ordinarily dress in haste and not pay any particular attention to her choice of boots or jacket; today, Georgina tried on not one, not two, but *three* of her fine coats until she found one that met her satisfaction. Moreover, she discarded several neckcloths in her attempts to create an elegant barrel knot.

Georgina stared at her reflection in the gilded Venetian mirror while she attached some sapphire drop earrings to her ears. Her hair was already fastened up, and she affixed her black hat in place on top of her shining curls with a cabochon sapphire hatpin. Stepping back from the mirror to assess her attire, she was satisfied that the tight breeches and gleaming boots flattered her figure well.

Glancing at her fob watch at precisely eleven o'clock, Georgina went down to the hall so that she might be waiting when Elizabeth arrived.

One of her footmen was busily arranging a large vase of flowers in the vestibule, and she greeted him cheerfully. "How is your mother, Toby?"

"Her hip has been playing up again, Miss Pace. But otherwise, no complaints," he replied, clipping the stems of some foliage.

"Did you see they passed a bill supporting greater entitlements for attendants?" She winked at him. "You'll be able to visit her even more regularly and go for that holiday sojourn."

As the hand of the clock clicked to ten minutes past, Georgina's expression sank to disappointment. It seemed unlike Elizabeth to be tardy. Perhaps she had decided not to come, after their squabble the previous evening.

Hearing hooves finally coming to a stop outside, a wave of relief washed over Georgina, and a wicked idea struck her. She plucked one of the white roses from the vessel on the table and snapped the bulb from its stem. She apologized to Toby for interrupting his careful design and donned her gloves before leaving the house.

Elizabeth's phaeton was pulled up outside her house. A groom had already sprung down and held the reins at the horses' heads. Elizabeth, wearing a well-fitting driving habit of gray muslin with a matching cropped jacket and pleated skirt, stepped onto the curb. A black top hat, with a little mesh veil that scooped coquettishly over part of her face, completed her attire.

Skipping down the couple of steps to the road, Georgina greeted Elizabeth and put her hand out to assist her ladyship back into the carriage.

Once seated in the phaeton, Georgina revealed the rose-head

clasped in her hand. She inspected the flower, noting the tiny cracks and blemishes on the velvet petals.

Elizabeth regarded her uncertainly.

"I had meant to give this to you," Georgina said and sighed. "But then you were late, so I cannot think you deserve it." She exhaled again and tossed it onto the street.

The gesture surprised a laugh out of Elizabeth. "Forgive me, Miss Pace."

"Georgina," she corrected her.

"Forgive me then, Georgina," Elizabeth amended. "I was waylaid this morning. I apologize for my lateness."

Georgina bestowed her most charming smile upon her. "You must seek a way to atone."

Elizabeth chuckled. "You, my little thief, are very adept at cajolery," she remarked, signaling the groom to step back from the horses' heads.

They quickly traversed the distance from Half Moon Street to the Royal Academy on the Strand without incident. Georgina had trepidations that Elizabeth might draw the conversation back to Henry and was relieved when she made no such attempt. That would have made for a very awkward outing. While she did not believe Elizabeth had intended any malice in bringing up the subject of her brother the previous evening, Georgina did not wish to discuss it again.

The groom deposited both ladies on the sidewalk and took over the control of the phaeton to deliver it around to the mews.

Elizabeth extended her arm, her glinting eyes revealing her pleasure.

Georgina tucked her hand in the crook of her ladyship's arm and allowed her to lead the way towards the impressive façade of the Royal Academy. She had passed by here many times but never had cause to stop. The building was an exquisite piece of Palladian design, with large columns stretching from the ground to the domed ceiling. Arched windows flanked the sides of the quadrangle, and symmetrical brickwork followed the length of the building.

"What *are* we doing here?" Georgina quizzed as they made their way across the expansive courtyard.

"I wondered when you might ask that," Elizabeth replied. "I sponsor several of their budding artists, and my fellow board members and I are coordinating the purchase of some nearby properties to serve as their accommodation," she explained.

This surprised Georgina. "How exceedingly benevolent of you." She stopped walking in her tracks, her hold on Elizabeth's arm inducing her companion to stop as well. "Is there *no* end to your goodness? Defender of the virtuous, champion of the fallen, and now supporter of the creative. You put us mere mortals to shame."

Elizabeth's lips twitched. "I will gladly confess to being a supporter of the creative. But the others are titles only *you* have given to me. I was pleased to assist Miss Coombes, though I have never had to do that before. Besides, Sarah was the real savior there. Had it not been for your friend, Coulthurst, our intervention would not have been necessary." A hint of disapproval laced her tone. "And *you* are hardly fallen," she added. "Merely somewhat wayward."

"Well, I would like it known that *if* you continue to be so abominably virtuous, I will have no option but to compromise you."

"You might *try*, Georgina," Elizabeth replied.

Was that a second instance of flirtation from the countess? Thrilled, Georgina chuckled and gave her arm a squeeze. They strolled towards the entrance, Elizabeth pointing out various features of the building as they approached. Georgina listened, wondering how Elizabeth could retain and impart so much information. A few times, the pair shared a glance. When this happened, Georgina found herself losing track of the conversation, and this disconcerted her immeasurably.

Her developing interest in Elizabeth continued to puzzle her. In nature, they were vastly different. Georgina believed that her character flaws could not be acceptable to someone as wholesome as Elizabeth. Yet for some reason, the Countess seemed to accept—if not welcome—her interest. Georgina regularly made amusing or outrageous remarks contrived to make her smile, and she enjoyed the flutter of excitement inside her when the lady reacted. This dynamic perplexed Georgina, who had always been on the receiving end of such efforts, and she struggled to reconcile herself to these new feelings.

AFTER ELIZABETH'S MEETING with the many trustees of the board, where they discussed and settled upon several business transactions needed to secure the new artist's lodgings, Elizabeth invited Georgina to explore the house where the artists busily worked on their assorted projects.

Georgina had no intimate appreciation of art, but she did not want to offend Elizabeth and agreed to this with a warm smile. She'd created this situation herself, after all, and could hardly abandon the outing now.

Side-by-side, they crossed the marble tiled floors and followed a procession of like-minded visitors from one salon to the next. Countless flickering wall sconces lit the building. Large, polished oak tables and clusters of brocade chairs and sofas were arranged at random around each room.

A vast range of people crowded the workrooms. Individuals of rank, resplendent in their finery, mingled with painters and sculptors, shrouded in stained smocks. Some sat for portraits, others strolled, enjoying the modish new painting styles and effects.

Elizabeth led Georgina into a room where a mature lady perched on a stool, engrossed in her oil painting. A female model with golden-tan skin and black hair sat unclothed on the chaise in the middle of the room, partially covered by a sheet that draped across her body. The artist's eyes were trained upon her as she captured each of the model's exquisite lines with her brush. A few other onlookers stood in a semi-circle around the artist, observing the masterpiece in progress. She did not seem to be aware of the surrounding company. Her grotty, paint-smudged hand held a narrow brush as though it were a feather. She dipped it into blobs of paint on her palette, mixed it together in a seamless movement as she went, then dabbed it onto the canvas with precision.

Georgina watched, quite fascinated by how the artist's brush moved in such a fluid motion to capture every tiny detail of the model's body. The overpowering smell of the paint was intoxicating, and so transfixed was she by the sensual beauty of the model, Georgina did not hear Elizabeth speak to her.

"I'm sorry?" she said, reluctantly dragging her gaze away.

"This is Lady Maria Bell. She is a very talented painter," Elizabeth repeated. She appeared completely indifferent to the model's nudity.

Georgina blushed. "Indeed, she is."

Elizabeth smiled and led her to a section of the room where other artists were tutoring aspiring painters in technique and method. After spending a moment taking in the scene, Georgina observed a familiar, spectacled face peeping out from behind an easel, balancing precariously on a stool that was a little too tall for him.

"It's Arthur," Georgina called in delight, taking Elizabeth's hand and pulling her over. She introduced the two, watching their exchange closely. If Elizabeth became acquainted with Arthur, perhaps she would rethink her alliance with Mrs. Gardner.

"It's a pleasure to meet you, Mr. Coombes," Elizabeth said, bestowing a curtsy. "I am encouraged to see so many people are here enjoying the facilities we offer."

Arthur nodded. "I was a g-good painter b-before. But now I am e-excellent."

Georgina stepped back to inspect his artwork. He was recreating a still life painting of a vase with some beautiful flowers. He should be truly proud of his talent. "Indeed, Arthur. This is wonderful. Perhaps you will paint a picture for me one day."

"You must buy it, G-George."

His candor always made her laugh. "Of course, Arthur." She leant towards him and embraced him warmly. "We must continue on. I will see you again soon."

With pink cheeks, he bade them both goodbye and resumed his painting.

Georgina locked her arm onto Elizabeth's. "Arthur is a breath of fresh air."

"I can readily understand why he has such a firm place in your heart. Perhaps I should inquire of him as to how one goes about achieving that."

Georgina flashed Elizabeth an arch look. She felt heat rush to her cheeks.

In silence, they moved into another large hall hung with various paintings of different sizes and styles. Beautiful frames completed several of the paintings that styled the walls, while unfinished canvases were displayed on easels around the room.

Distracting Georgina from her embarrassment and restoring comfort, Elizabeth commenced describing the histories of the many pieces they inspected as they strolled through the room.

"What do you think of this one?" she asked, referring to a landscape painting with rolling hills and impressive storm clouds.

"I prefer Lady Bell's," Georgina replied, giving it the barest of appraisals. "This one is quite insipid. The colors are not vibrant, and all the lines are blurred."

Elizabeth looked at her with piercing eyes, her eyebrows knitted in thought. "Do you not *enjoy* art, Georgina?"

Having no wish to prevaricate, Georgina gave a little shrug. "Not particularly. Though I appreciate many other people do, so I suppose there is a purpose to it all."

"It seems I have brought a sympathetic philistine to the Royal Academy," Elizabeth commented.

This made Georgina laugh. It was indeed the truth. However, even though she did not take great delight in the artwork herself, she felt increasingly fond of her guide. Elizabeth's instruction throughout kept her amused, and she liked peeling back the layers of the mysterious Countess.

"Do you like this piece at all?" Elizabeth asked, moving Georgina on to the next painting.

"No," she replied without hesitation.

Elizabeth's lips twitched. "Can you see the skill in the brushwork used to achieve the effect of distance?"

Georgina crinkled her nose and squinted, leaning closer to the canvas. "No."

A gentleman standing beside her made a loud scoffing sound and strode off, jostling Georgina as he went.

"Well, really," Georgina remarked, shocked. "How rude."

Again, Elizabeth teetered on the brink of mirth. "That was the artist."

Georgina bit her lip and suspected she might be blacklisted from here forever.

"Come, let us leave now before you bring further condemnation down upon us. I'll take you for tea at Gunter's."

She placed her hand on Georgina's back and ushered her through the hall.

Once they had retrieved the phaeton, Elizabeth navigated the crowded streets with light hands on the reins, and they soon pulled up in Berkeley Square.

18

GUNTER'S WAS A popular venue at all times of the day, and members of the ton flocked there to enjoy their famous ices, tea, and cream cakes. One might see nurses and tutors alongside their respective young charges, or courting couples who wanted to steal a moment alone without the prying eyes of their chaperones. Large windows at the front of the shop, together with ample candle sconces, kept the room bright.

Several glass cabinets brimming with an appetizing array of cake and sweetmeats lined the space. Despite the crowds coming and going from the shop, it did not feel oppressive, owing to the cool room at the rear that kept the ices from melting and swept regular bursts of chilled air into the main hall.

Elizabeth and Georgina established themselves at a small table in the corner, and an attendant provided them with a large pot of aromatic tea and a tiered plate containing assorted sandwiches and some small cakes.

This was as good a time as any to intensify her attempt to seduce the impenetrable Elizabeth. If she gleaned any additional information about Solitaires along the way, then so be it. Georgina sipped her milky tea, eyeing Elizabeth over the rim of the cup.

"Shall we discuss how I might compromise you?" Georgina asked in a low voice.

Sharing the cut sandwich squares across both of their plates, Elizabeth replied, "I thought we might discuss how I am to reform your character instead."

"Alas, I can think of nothing that will save me. I am beyond redemption."

"I disagree. You need a project. Something to occupy that intelligent head of yours and keep you out of trouble. When your mind is not engaged in something worthwhile, you seem prone to roguishness."

Georgina swelled, gratified that a scholarly person such as Elizabeth found her intelligent. She considered her point.

"What manner of project do you have in mind?" she asked, taking a bite of her sandwich.

"Well, as we have established today, it should have nothing to do with art." Elizabeth steepled her fingertips together. "But that need not limit you. There are many aspiring musicians who would benefit from a patroness. You might approach the Theater's Guild regarding the support of their actors. If that does not interest you, what about animal welfare? They are often seeking volunteers to assist with homing stray and injured animals. Or you might raise funds for the community gardens?"

Georgina stared at her, her teacup frozen midway to her mouth. Elizabeth baffled her.

"Is it exhausting being so passionate about so many things?" She smiled and put her hand on top of Elizabeth's as it rested on the edge of the table. "Your goodness does you credit. To my shame, I have given none of these matters much thought. And you are quite correct that, given my position and means, I *should* make myself more useful."

Elizabeth's expression softened into a smile. "Perhaps once you have secured a project to amend your ways, I might allow you to compromise me. A little."

Georgina grinned, and she reclined in her chair, crossing her arms over her chest. "In principle, I already agreed with you. But *now* I have a most significant incentive to find a project at once."

"Have I just unleashed a beast of epic proportions?"

Georgina swiped her tongue lightly over her upper lip. "From the moment I observed your forearms, I'm afraid."

Elizabeth rested her elbow on the table and cupped her chin in her hand. "You intrigue me, Georgina."

It occurred to her that perhaps Elizabeth did not welcome her flirtation and merely entertained her dalliance out of politeness. Georgina was far too forthright to want her to do that.

"In a pleasant way?"

Elizabeth nodded and sipped her tea. Georgina waited for her to elaborate. Unfortunately, she did not.

THE LADIES MAINTAINED a light-hearted conversation as they finished their tea, and after making payment, they returned to the street to await Elizabeth's carriage. As they lingered on the sidewalk, edging towards Bruton Street, Elizabeth became distracted by a commotion occurring on the corner. She led the way into the fray, and Georgina followed casually.

A young boy with scruffy hair and a dirt-smudged face was being held by the collar of his shirt by an enraged man. His captor, a street vendor, stood beside a large cart set up with baskets of fresh-smelling bread, bags of grain and flour, and a few sweet buns. He gave the child a harsh shake when he tried to free himself.

The crowd thickened around them as curious onlookers gathered, keen to witness the disturbance.

Georgina cast a quizzical look at Elizabeth, who made a gesture for her to be quiet. Now, what was she going to do?

The man growled at the fearful young boy, reciting every punishment from both Bible and law that would come his way for succumbing to the vice of stealing.

Georgina knew that many children who resorted to thievery stole out of necessity and were unlikely to be reformed through punitive measures.

A stout gentleman of kind disposition edged into the dispute, offering the tradesperson some coins in payment for the boy's misdemeanor.

"Please, my good man! Take the money and let him go," the gentleman urged. "No harm done, after all."

Georgina liked him. He was sensible. Sadly, the tradesperson had a different sentiment.

"We need a constable!" the man shouted, tightening his grip on the boy. "He needs to be taken to the watch."

"That's quite unnecessary," the gentleman insisted. "I can settle this matter in an instant if you would but take payment. There is no need to trouble the authorities, I assure you."

"And have him free to steal from me again tomorrow?" He puffed up his chest, as though to emphasize the seriousness of his claim. "He deserves a thrashing, at least!"

Georgina felt her pulse rise. If he raised a whip to that child, he would be on the end of her cane before he could blink.

Elizabeth edged her way past the gathering crowd. "Indeed, sir," she agreed with the vendor. "Allow me to dispatch this child to the nearest constable. If I were you, I would accept this gentleman's payment and lose no time in continuing your work; every moment without earnings is a moment wasted, don't you agree?"

With a bewildered frown, Georgina looked between Elizabeth and the man. At least thrashings seemed to be off the table for the moment.

The tradesperson seemed to appreciate Elizabeth's argument. His greedy eyes fixated on the pocketbook of the kind stranger. He accepted a generous amount well beyond the value of the misdemeanor and stepped back.

"Ah, my carriage." Elizabeth waved to her groom, who pulled the phaeton up beside them. "Georgina, if I might prevail upon you to climb up first. This little fellow is tiny. I daresay he will fit between us easily."

Georgina complied and stepped nimbly up into the carriage before reaching down for the boy's hand. His small face contorted with worry, but he did not object to going with them. He weighed little, and lifting him up required minimal strength. As he settled on the seat beside her, his feet did not even brush the floor.

Could Elizabeth really mean to surrender this poor child to the authorities? Georgina thought that a rather callous outcome for such a trifling matter. Over his head, she gave Elizabeth a stern look. "He's a child. I won't let you!" she hissed.

Elizabeth appeared rather unimpressed by this pronouncement. She rolled her eyes but said nothing.

Georgina gave the little fellow's arm a reassuring squeeze. No matter what Elizabeth had in mind, he would not be going to a constable.

Elizabeth climbed up next and took the reins, oblivious to her groom's startled glance. The crowd disbursed from around them, and Elizabeth jogged the horses along.

Once around the corner, Elizabeth stared down at the boy. He wore a grubby tunic, hole-ridden breeches, and no shoes. His baggy clothing drooped over his emaciated little frame.

"Where are your parents, my boy?"

"Nah, I ain't got parents," he replied, revealing a thick cockney accent. "I'm an horphan," he added helpfully.

"I see. And where do you live?"

"Down by the docks. Me mate brung me up West yesterday. Said *all* the toffs live here. Right he was, too. I could have me dinner off these here streets."

His naïve words gripped at Georgina's heart. She pressed her lips together and stared away.

Elizabeth continued to drive in silence for a while. "My name is Lady Mortimer, and the lady beside you is Miss Pace."

He nodded to them both. "You swells ain't taking me to the watch?" He eyed them with no little suspicion.

"No, we will not do that," Elizabeth reassured him. "What is your name?"

The tightness in Georgina's belly relaxed. Her sense of charity towards Elizabeth restored.

"Joshwa," he answered, settling into the seat, reassured that they were not en route to a local constable.

"A pleasure to meet you, Joshua," replied Elizabeth. "There is no pride in taking something that is not yours to take, but perhaps you would like to *earn* a wage in a respectable household." Joshua's pansy brown eyes widened in disbelief. "I know of just such a job, running errands and so forth for a kind and obliging mistress?"

Georgina found herself wondering, not for the first time that day, if there were any bounds to Elizabeth's goodness. She truly helped everyone who crossed her path. An unbidden smile crept onto her face.

"You kidding, Missus? A proper wage?"

"A handsome wage, a warm bed to sleep in at night, plenty of food and time off to play," Elizabeth confirmed, tugging the team to a halt outside Georgina's abode in Half Moon Street. "Even toys."

Georgina found herself again astonished by Elizabeth's generosity of spirit.

Joshua beamed up at Elizabeth and agreed most readily to her proposal, thanking his stars that he came across such fine ladies.

Georgina could not help but smile at the pure relief on his little face. He had likely never been given such an opportunity, and extending kindness to him now had the potential to change his life. She looked over his head at Elizabeth, her eyes twinkling in appreciation.

Elizabeth gazed serenely back at her.

Climbing down from the carriage, Georgina opened her mouth to say 'goodbye,' when Elizabeth instructed Joshua, "Down you hop, my boy. This is your new home. Miss Pace shall take care of your needs from now on."

Georgina's mouth dropped open. She glared up at Elizabeth, who smiled at her.

"Consider this your first project, Georgina. Rather apt that he is a thief."

Georgina's breath hitched in her throat, and she made a slight choking sound, perhaps a laugh combined with a yelp.

By now, Joshua had clambered down to Georgina's side. He raised his eyes to meet hers.

Georgina hesitated. Elizabeth could not fathom what she was asking of her. Georgina was *no* fit guardian for a child. Or anyone. That had been proven eight years ago. She took a nervous step backwards and plunged her hands into her pockets, feeling for her fob watch. "Most comical, my lady. Though I do believe *your* track record of supporting those in need is much better than mine." Georgina now fixed an imploring gaze on Elizabeth.

Elizabeth regarded her with a kind smile. She was no longer teasing. "Give yourself a chance. You will do well."

Georgina reluctantly nodded and hoped her friend was right. She did not want to let this little fellow down. She glanced at him again and met his stare of complete trust. The poetry of the situation was perfect. *Damn Elizabeth.*

A moment later, the phaeton lurched forward, leaving the unlikely pair standing in the street.

"Come along then, Joshua," Georgina said in a crisp tone. "I shall introduce you to my butler and housekeeper. They will be in charge. Do you understand?"

Jarvis accepted the new arrival with surprising affability. Georgina could not discern any censure in his haughty countenance.

"He needs something to eat. Some milk or lemonade. And then a bath." She paused, realizing how poorly equipped she was to understand the needs of a young child. "Perhaps a maid or footman can get him some clothes as well. A black livery for when he is working. And extra shirts, breeches, shoes, undergarments, some toys. . . ." Her voice tapered off. "I'll leave it to your excellent judgment. I suppose he will also need some instruction. Perhaps advertise for a tutor?"

Without a further word, Georgina hurried to her library and closed the door behind her. This day had not turned out as she had thought it would.

THE MUSTY SMELL of old paper hung in the air as rows of cloth- and leather-bound volumes crowded the shelves. Heavy damask curtains, held open by gold cord, framed the window that overlooked the street below. As the rain held off, Georgina opted to leave the window open to enjoy some fresh air and the gentle bustling noise from the road.

Removing her hat and gloves and tossing them on the sofa, Georgina poured herself a large brandy and collapsed back on an armchair set closest to the flickering fireplace.

Elizabeth had much to answer for. It was unacceptable to impose a new charge upon a household in such an overbearing manner. She had given no consideration for the potential inconvenience it would have on Georgina or her father. Georgina took a sip and savored the liquid in her mouth, enjoying the tickle of the alcohol on her palette before she swallowed.

The warmth of the drink spread through Georgina's body as she took another slow sip and considered her other project, that of Arthur's IOUs. Elizabeth, whatever her role turned out to be in this affair at Solitaires, complicated matters. She now knew Georgina had stolen the faro box from Mrs. Gardner and yet had not recoiled from her. If anything, their bond had only strengthened. Elizabeth intrigued her, like a tantalizing book she simply could not put down. Georgina felt compelled to turn the page, wanting to know more about her, though dreading the inevitable moment when she must lay the book aside.

She held another warm swallow in her mouth for a moment, her mind going in many directions. A book. With a burst of energy, Georgina leapt up from the chair and hurried over to the shelves. Within moments, she spotted what she was searching for. It was called *The Maidens' Tryst* by Mrs. Jane Goodchild. Not a thick volume; its worn cover suggested someone had read it often.

Georgina took it to her bureau and sat down to craft a carefully worded letter.

Dear Elizabeth,

Thank you for the educational trip to the Royal Academy

today. I am also grateful for the opportunity to better myself by accepting Joshua into my household.

Though we established I am no lover of art, I do greatly appreciate reading. I have enclosed one of my favorite novels, which I think you might enjoy.

Also, would you do me the honor of joining me at the Vauxhall masquerade at the end of the week? An excellent opportunity to compromise you, I think.

Yours, etc.
Georgina

She dispatched this message and the book to Grosvenor Square and settled down to wait for the reply.

Elizabeth did not make her linger for a response. A return messenger arrived just before dinner.

Georgina, who was about to lead her father into the dining-room, snatched the missive off the tray with fervor.

Her father regarded her with an inquisitive look. "Are you expecting some urgent correspondence, Georgina?"

Not wishing to draw undue attention, Georgina stuffed the unopened letter into her pocket and determined to wait until after dinner to read it.

"How are Lord Coulthurst and Mrs. Fortescue? They have not been loitering about the place as much as they used to," Silas asked, as they enjoyed a delicious repast laid out before them.

"They are unchanged. Sarah continues to pine for love, while Colt is a rogue towards every young lady in his path." Georgina shrugged.

"And have you heard from that young lady who caused you a headache in Cornwall?" He was paying a lot of attention to his dinner plate.

Georgina grinned at his attempts at discretion. "I appreciate your delicate phrasing. Indeed, I have heard from her several times. She has sent me messages, left me her card, attempted to find me at assorted clubs, and we have danced at a ball."

The fork slipped from Silas's fingers with a clatter. He picked it up quickly. "A most eager girl."

"She would benefit from a little discretion, yes."

He resumed eating. "And how is Edmund?"

This drew a sigh from her. "Lovelorn, of course. And extremely careless."

"Keep an eye on him, my love. His parents will expect you to."

Georgina clenched the serviette on her lap. "I am doing my best, Papa," she assured him. Had Edmund's parents perhaps performed their duty more thoroughly and educated him in the ways of the world, she would not presently be in this untenable situation.

"So, tell me about this little fellow we have downstairs? James, is it?"

"Joshua. He is our new . . . page—house boy. Whatever we need him to be, really."

Silas scratched his chin. "Did we need him?"

"Well, naturally we did, Papa," Georgina replied. "Or he would not be here." Explaining Joshua's arrival was difficult enough without bringing up Elizabeth.

He shrugged and chatted about other members of the ton he had seen since returning to town at the start of the week, and Georgina's thoughts drifted back to the letter concealed in her pocket.

Finally, when Silas departed for his evening's engagement at the theater and Georgina retired to her library, she had a moment alone.

She pulled the note from her pocket, snapped the wafer open, and her eyes tracked the handful of words on the page.

Dear Georgina,

Thank you for the novel. I shall be sure to read it. Also, I would be honored to join you at Vauxhall. I shall meet you there.

Warmest regards,
Elizabeth

Georgina released an audible sigh. After building up such anticipation throughout the evening, this brief letter proved rather deflating. At least she had secured Elizabeth's pledge to join her at the masquerade.

She thought back to the book she had sent Elizabeth, and a roguish smile grew across her face. The tale captured a modern love story about two star-crossed damsels. The passionate and rather descriptive language and imagery used to depict intimacy would make even the most open-minded reader blush. Georgina had handpicked a novel intended to arouse the reader—one almost impossible to set aside. Let Lady Mortimer try to resist her now.

AS GEORGINA LAY in her own bed that night, her room dark aside from the glowing embers that flickered in the fireplace, her thoughts drifted again to Elizabeth. Georgina prided herself on her independent spirit and her ability to detach emotionally from those she dallied with. Yet, she struggled to displace Elizabeth from her consciousness.

Georgina could not deny her growing attraction. As a velina, Elizabeth possessed many feminine traits, without being typically female. Aside from her comely countenance and bright eyes that twinkled responsively when Georgina teased her, Elizabeth exuded knowledge, wisdom, and intelligence. She displayed a fierce sense of honor, along with vast interests and charitable pursuits. It made no sense for Georgina to like someone so terribly worthy.

Georgina rolled onto her side. To find herself seeking opportunities to flirt with Elizabeth came as quite a surprise to her. Elizabeth was a woman of the world, but she also showed a level of reserve in her dealings. She indulged Georgina's dalliance but did not initiate flirtation herself. Elizabeth did not shy away from Georgina, nor did she pursue her. She was impenetrable.

Naturally, Georgina mused, her own intentions were playful, and she had no desire to become *seriously* entangled with Elizabeth. Though, she admitted the notion of becoming physically involved with Elizabeth grew more appealing with every day.

She had been deliberately provocative in sending Elizabeth the book. Georgina wanted to convey her interest explicitly and wondered how far she would have to go before Elizabeth laid her own cards down.

Georgina rolled on to her back and stared up at the canopy of her four-poster bed. With a sigh, she slid her nightdress up to her hips and moved one hand beneath the covers, down the curves of her body. She began stroking herself, slowly at first, then rhythmically, dipping inside.

Memories of Elizabeth's arms, strong but slender, flashed in Georgina's mind.

It was not just the shape of those arms—though heaven knew that had been enough to unravel her—it was the way they moved. The way Elizabeth's forearms tensed subtly when she reached for something, a hint of power beneath their elegance. The way her fingers drummed absently on a tabletop or twisted a lock of hair while she thought. Or the way the early afternoon sun had caught on the fine down of her pale skin, turning it to gold, when they had driven away from Gunter's that afternoon.

Georgina could still remember the restraint it took not to reach out that day, not to run her hand along the curve of the woman's arm. It had been a passing moment, on an ordinary afternoon, but she had not been able to shake it from her memory.

Now, thanks to Elizabeth, the intoxicating smell of orange blossom would forever drive her to distraction. Georgina clenched her eyes tightly shut. She imagined Elizabeth with her, touching her, tasting her, and she could feel her pleasure build. Picturing their bodies intertwined, Georgina writhed on the bed, her movements faster and more urgent. Her free hand gripped the cool sheets desperately, and she arched her back, crying out as waves of ecstasy washed over her and her body pulsed around her fingers.

For some minutes, every breath quivered as her satisfaction rippled through her. This was the first time she had pleasured herself while holding the enigmatic Elizabeth in her thoughts. She smiled sleepily and wondered again what Elizabeth would think of the novel she had sent. Then, at last, she slept.

19

ON THE NIGHT of the Vauxhall masquerade, with darkness falling over London and the air mild, the Pleasure Garden was already a hive of activity. Hundreds of masked visitors filled the Chinese Pavilion and supper boxes. Thousands of lanterns illuminated the maze of pathways, while many secret alcoves and walks remained in deliberate darkness to encourage more discreet assignations. The masquerade was Colt's favorite activity of the season by far, and he had enjoyed many romantic trysts here over the years. Musicians played throughout the garden, so no matter where one strolled, the hum of cheerful music echoed nearby.

Colt and Georgina commissioned one of the many small boats crossing the Thames for their arrival. It contributed to the overall magic and glamor of the evening, except Colt could not rid himself of the desire to have Sarah with him instead. Although, given her mood of late, he suspected she would only reproach him.

He glanced over at Georgina. A shadow hung over her dark blue eyes, and her typical playfulness had all but disappeared. When he asked her if she wished to find herself a light-o'-love for a jaunt down one of the dark walks, she dismissed him out of turn and scolded him for being a reprobate. He found himself lost for words. Recent matters were obviously playing on her mind.

As vessels ferried patrons over the inky black water, lanterns swayed at their bows to guide the way like fireflies in the night. The echo of music and people in the garden grew louder as they approached. Colt wondered what lay in store for him tonight.

When they arrived, a dazzling array of costumes and masks crowded around them. The gardens offered entertainment to appeal to many tastes. There were ample opportunities for dancing should one feel so inclined, and the tightrope performers amused those seeking a little excitement. Those who stayed late would be treated to a thrilling fireworks display. Colt often missed this part of the evening. It was when guardians were most often distracted and did not notice their debutantes slipping away for a quick assignation with a notorious rake.

"Ah, look, it's the Coombes family. Let us say hello." Colt could think of nothing better than renewing his acquaintance with the pretty Emily.

Georgina glared at him. "I warned you away from Emily, Colt. She will have you wed by the conclusion of the season."

Surely, that was a challenge. Georgina may not have been her usual self tonight, but she was no prig. Colt gave his old friend a wink and sidled his way through the crowd with Georgina close on his heels. He wore an indistinct black domino and matching mask, but no one could mistake his impressive form.

Colt greeted Mr. and Mrs. Coombes with a warm smile. "That orange domino you wear is most striking, Mrs. Coombes," he said, referring to her bright cloak. "You might be the most beautiful woman here."

Mrs. Coombes tried to suffocate a giggle. "What fustian! Good evening, Miss Pace."

Georgina responded to her politely and turned her attention at once to Arthur, who gushingly introduced her to Lady Maggie Marchwood. The young couple pulled Georgina aside to engage her in a most earnest conversation, through which Georgina nodded and smiled while keeping one eye on Arthur's parents.

Colt suspected they were discussing Mr. Coombe's desires to propose, so he did his best to keep both Mr. and Mrs. Coombes distracted. And what better way to do this than by launching into an overt flirtation with their daughter? Had she not, after all, indicated that she wished to get to know him better?

"How lovely you look this evening, Miss Coombes."

"You cannot see my face, Lord Coulthurst," Emily pointed out pertly.

"You exude beauty, Miss Coombes."

Her mother cleared her throat as he teetered on the boundary of respectable dialogue. "And do you seek a bride this season, Lord Coulthurst? You are infamous, are you not, for remaining a bachelor?"

Clearly, Mrs. Coombes did not beat about the bush, and of course he understood he had a reputation. Some young ladies came to him having heard about him at university, or perhaps from older siblings or cousins who had spent some transformative time learning the art of pleasure with Colt during their first season. When ambitious mothers sought him out on behalf of their daughters, it was for a different set of reasons—he was a single, attractive, wealthy earl. With Mrs. Coombes's eyes piercing through him, he bestowed what he knew to be one of his most adorable, dimpled smiles upon the matriarch. "One never knows."

As Georgina, Arthur and Lady Maggie drew near again, Colt decided he had discharged his duty, and it was time to press his luck.

"Miss Coombes, do you like mimes? I spotted a most amusing one over there. Allow me to escort you to look at her," he urged.

Emily glanced at her mother, with both dire threat and appeal in her expression. Colt recognized this mute exchange. It signaled that any objection from the parent would lead to a tantrum of epic proportions.

"I shall ensure her safety, of course," Colt added.

Mrs. Coombes was guarded in her response, remarking her daughter's eagerness, but agreed, insisting they stay within eyesight.

Colt promised he would take excellent care and vowed to meet Georgina at their box later in the evening. For a moment, he had thought Mrs. Coombes would not agree, so he had a little extra spring in his step as he escorted Miss Coombes along the path.

"It is so charming here," Emily chatted, wide eyes peeping out from behind her handheld mask of pale blue silk, silver thread and diamantés, which matched her evening gown. "I have never seen so many people in one place. And everyone is wearing such bright, colorful masks!"

Colt smiled and created a space for her in the crowd that gathered around a gold- and red-painted mime. The mime enacted an elaborate tea party with a blushing fellow she selected from the onlookers. She seated him at an imaginary table with her and served him invisible tea and cake in complete silence. The crowds laughed as she prompted him to reciprocate, and he complied ineptly. The mime caught some non-existent cups that he 'dropped' and gave him a stern look, waggling her finger at him, causing more uproarious laughter from the growing audience.

Colt took the opportunity of the crowd thickening around them to step closer behind Emily. He slid his hands onto her waist.

Emily gasped. Her alabaster skin reddened, and she glanced over her shoulder at him before returning her eyes to the mime.

"Shall I stop?" he asked beside her ear.

"No," she whispered, leaning back against his body, inviting him to touch her further.

Colt smiled and slid one hand from her waist, down over the front of her hip. He trusted that the crush of people would shield them from the prying eyes of her mother. "Is this what you want from me? To help you discover what you need?"

"Yes." Emily's voice was breathless, and she squirmed as his hand slid between her legs. Her body tensed in anticipation. A tiny sound escaped her lips, and she gasped in pleasure. His hand clasped over a most sensitive spot for a long moment, then rubbed back and forward between her legs, his fingers quickening.

She made frantic movements against him as she enjoyed the sensation of his hand between her thighs. He stilled his movements and withdrew.

She stared at him over her shoulder, her eyes dark with hunger behind her mask.

"Did you like that, Miss Coombes?"

She panted. "Indeed, your hands are quite magical. They create the most *agreeable* feelings."

"Would you like more?" he asked, his voice low and husky. "I can offer you a wealth of exquisite fulfillment, Miss Coombes, but it is rather scandalous for a young, unwed lady."

She swallowed. "I would like more."

"Even without an offer of marriage?" he asked in a deliberate tone.

Emily hesitated, her eyes flicking to the side where her mother stood in the distance. "Yes," she breathed.

Colt wondered, given the mischievous spark in her eye, if Emily might envisage him as someone she could wrap around her finger. Perhaps she had indeed convinced herself that she could make him fall in love with her. Surely, she might blame her own vanity for that. He had done his part to narrow her expectations. "If you are sure, then you should escape from your family and meet me in a little while."

"Where should I meet you?"

"Down there." He gestured towards a pathway that branched off into the darkness. "In half an hour? I'll find you," he promised.

Once she agreed, he led her back to her family, satisfying Mrs. Coombes that no harm came to Emily during their little walk.

AFTER RETURNING EMILY, Colt bought himself a large drink and took a slow sip from it. He looked forward to dallying further with her. She was ready and receptive. And though he did not offer marriage, Colt believed his unique part in Emily's journey to be rather noble. He sincerely hoped his service would lead to more contented lives, each lady's eyes newly open to pleasure.

He checked his watch for the time and, as he began towards the designated pathway, he became distracted by a figure slicing her way through the crowd towards him.

A gown of deep scarlet with a low-cut bodice revealed a significant amount of her impressive bosom. Her black hair was pinned up, and she wore a mask of black lace over her bright eyes.

He would know Sarah anywhere, and she had never looked so ravishing.

When she reached him, she stopped and gave a slight curtsy. Colt knew she recognized him just as easily; as if by some tacit agreement, they both decided it was much more interesting to play strangers. Her lips were stained crimson, and she moistened them with the tip of her tongue.

"What a lovely evening," she murmured, giving his figure a slow, sweeping look as though deciding whether she approved of him.

"Most beautiful," he agreed, talking about the evening as much as the vision standing before him.

She took the glass from his hand and finished his drink. She set it down on the tray of a passing attendant.

"What do you enjoy most about Vauxhall, sir?" she asked with an unusual level of formality.

This amused Colt. "The anonymity, madam. And the excitement in the air. What is most diverting to *you*?"

Sarah's hand rested lightly at the base of her throat. Her hand drifted down, her fingers traveling across her exposed chest and over the curve of her breasts. "The sense of liberty to do whatever one wants, with *whomever* one wants. . . ."

Colt had enjoyed years of bantering with Sarah, but she had never flirted with him so overtly before. His chest tightened. Did she finally mean to acquiesce to their mutual desire?

"The gardens of Vauxhall boast so many secrets and mysteries," he remarked in a low voice.

"Not to mention pleasures," Sarah added, giving him a sultry wink through her mask.

"Shall we?" he said, extending his arm to her.

She took it, and he led her away from the crowds and down a darkened pathway.

They walked in silence for some way, occasionally hearing laughter from dark pockets of the gardens. The deeper they ventured, the more moans and grunts sounded from unseen alcoves and in amongst the trees.

Colt noticed his body reacting in anticipation. He had spent years yearning for this.

They ventured off the main path towards a small, vacant arbor. He had wanted for so many years to taste her mouth and feel her soft lips against his own. He could not hold back another instant. Without awaiting an invitation, Colt pressed Sarah up against a stone pillar and kissed her savagely.

She received his kiss most willingly, opening her mouth to his demanding tongue, digging her fingers into his back, pulling him towards her. Colt grew hard against his breeches, and Sarah rocked her hips against him as he pressed to her stomach.

He gripped her bodice and pulled it as far down as it would allow, one breast now spilling from the top. He took her nipple between his lips, and she cried out in desire. She pushed him back towards the stone bench and sat him down. Within a moment, he released his cock from his breeches and groaned when she sank to the floor on her knees, resting between his thighs.

For all the years he had spent assisting maidens towards their sexual awakening, their innocence usually meant an absence of skill or confidence when it came to this sort of thing. Sarah bent down, taking his hard flesh in her mouth, sucking him with abandon. She gripped his corded shaft in one hand and rubbed the skin up and down in time with her mouth.

"Fuck!" he growled between his teeth, as all control deserted him. "Sarah, please," he hissed urgently, holding both her shoulders between his hands, trying to slow her movements before he came prematurely.

She released him from her mouth, and her dark eyes held him through her mask. Her glistening red lips parted.

He beckoned her with one hand.

Sarah rose from the ground and in a swift movement climbed astride him with her skirts hitched up high.

Colt reached between her thighs with his hand. She wore no undergarments, and her own sticky moisture seeped from her core. He cursed under his breath as the mere touch of her almost cast him over the edge again.

His erection grew thick and long as he eased his way into her tight body, shallow at first and then deeper. They both groaned with pleasure as he filled her, their mouths still locked as their bodies established a brisk rhythm.

He braced her with one arm, and she leaned against him, arching her back while grinding herself down, taking him to the hilt.

"You will finish me quickly, Sarah," he warned her between gasps. He tried to guide her movements to a slower rhythm, but Sarah refused to allow him to dictate the pace.

"Then finish quickly," she murmured near his ear, gripping his shoulders and bouncing herself on him frantically.

Colt then caught her mouth in a kiss and, as her body clenched around him, growled as his load spilled inside her.

Sarah threw her head back and cried out. They shuddered together, both panting.

Colt swallowed, his breaths shaking.

They remained joined, cradling each other, thus catching their breath. Sarah had collapsed against his chest, clutching him as the waves slowly subsided. He held her in his arms, her body precious and revered. He did not want to move lest he lose her forever. He savored every throb and inhaled the sweet scent of her hair.

Eventually, she clambered off him, and he reluctantly let her go.

She at once became preoccupied with smoothing out her gown and restoring her bodice to order, keeping her eyes away from him.

Colt watched her in silence. Did he read sadness on her face? Still breathless, he stuffed the remains of his erection back into his breeches along with his shirttails. He corrected his own attire and refastened his domino, which had fallen to the ground in their lovemaking.

She cleared her throat. "Do not get any ideas from this, Robert."

A pang of disappointment shot through Colt. He forced a laugh and tucked a straying tendril of her hair back behind her ear. He extended his arm to her.

"Of course not," he agreed, taking her the long way back to the main festivities. "But I have never . . . that was magnificent."

As a mature lady, Sarah had the confidence to seize what she wanted, however whimsical. Colt adored this about her. Her decision to make love to him tonight had taken him completely off guard. If only she did not come to regret it.

She threw him a smile and a nod of agreement. "It was."

Without a further word, he escorted her back to the crowds where they located the box Georgina had hired for the occasion, though she herself was nowhere to be seen. He wondered briefly where she had taken off to. Perhaps she had followed his advice and found someone with whom to frolic down the dark walk.

He procured Sarah a glass of Champagne and sat down beside her, keen to attend to her every need.

She accepted his courtesies graciously but did not meet his searching gaze.

The mystery of her thoughts unsettled him.

He also recalled his planned assignation with Miss Emily Coombes. Never mind, no harm done there. She would find another beau, and this evening could not have turned out better.

20

AFTER SHE EXCUSED herself from the Coombes family, Georgina meandered away in search of her hired box. By now, the festivities were well underway. She accepted a glass of Champagne from a passing attendant and scrutinized her surroundings. There was yet no sign of Elizabeth.

Georgina had spent a significant amount of time perfecting her appearance for this occasion and hoped it would not be wasted. She wore a gown of lazuli-blue silk, which she understood drew out the color of her eyes. This would be her first meeting with Elizabeth since sharing the scandalous novel with her, and Georgina wished to look appealing. As Vauxhall was a sensual affair, she had no qualms that her bodice was cut a little low, and she'd dampened the fabric of her gown so that it clung more precisely to her curves. She donned a matching mask, tied at the back with a satin ribbon. Georgina often kept her hair fastened back, but tonight she allowed her lustrous curls to tumble down her back. One long tendril rested over her shoulder.

"All alone, my little thief?" Elizabeth's voice murmured as she entered the box.

A gown of black satin with a shimmering silver overlay shrouded her tall frame. The dress had little gossamer puff sleeves with silver threading, and she wore long black gloves that extended above her elbows, revealing only a glimpse of the smooth, pale skin beneath. Diamond-clustered pins that glinted in the lantern light fastened her hair into place, and she wore a simple black mask.

"Not anymore," Georgina replied, taking Elizabeth's gloved hand and kissing it. She poured her a glass of Champagne and filled her own to the top again. "You look exquisite."

"As do you," Elizabeth responded. She glanced at the assorted activities happening nearby. "Allow me to thank you for the novel."

Georgina endeavored not to choke on her Champagne. She had not expected Elizabeth to mention the gift so swiftly.

"My pleasure," she answered. "It is a tale that is close to my heart."

"I was not previously familiar with the work of Mrs. Goodchild. You have opened my eyes," Elizabeth responded with gravity.

"That pleases me."

"Yes, I thought it might," Elizabeth retorted. "Perhaps not quite as eye-opening as Mem Lavigne's club, nevertheless."

"Few things can rival Mem Lavigne's establishment in that regard. Would you care to borrow another book?" suggested Georgina.

Elizabeth, sipping her drink at this moment, nearly choked as laughter overcame her.

Georgina grinned. "Control yourself, Elizabeth. You are making people stare."

Elizabeth smoothed out her expression. "*You*, my dear girl, are uncommonly provocative."

"I am?" Georgina asked with wide-eyed innocence. "Would you prefer me to be *commonly* provocative?"

"Heaven, help me," Elizabeth uttered under her breath, a smile breaking through. "I would *prefer* you to behave."

"I always behave. Sometimes even well!"

Elizabeth gave her a pointed look as she took a sip. "Indeed. And where is your escort presently?"

"Coulthurst disappeared in search of amusements beyond what I could offer him. He dislikes you immensely, by the way."

Elizabeth's eyes glinted. "I am crestfallen," she returned in a dry tone.

"He thinks you judge him, and it makes him uncomfortable. I'm sure he would like you if he knew you better."

"You alarm me. Please do not encourage him to pursue our closer acquaintance."

This made Georgina laugh. "Alas, it is beyond my power to promote a friendship between the pair of you, so I vow not to attempt it."

"A great relief," Elizabeth replied. "And how is young Joshua? I trust he has settled in?"

Georgina detected a teasing glint in Elizabeth's cool gray eyes, but she responded earnestly. "Joshua is quite at home. He is already a firm favorite of my housekeeper, who has a maternal partiality for him. My butler, Jarvis, seems to be reserving his judgment. Aside from running errands, his primary duties include walking the dogs and helping in the stables. I've never encountered such a vivid imagination before. Every chance he gets, he tells me some gruesome story or other. He shocks my father regularly with his bloodthirsty tales. Also, he has adopted the role of quality management in the kitchens. And he feels the need to sample *everything* that is prepared." Georgina grinned. "I cannot blame him for that. He was part-starved when we found him. When *you* found him," she corrected.

"Ah yes, I apologize for the underhanded stratagem," Elizabeth said with apparent contrition. "A necessary evil."

"Necessary?" Georgina repeated. Something about watching

Elizabeth's face behind a mask was especially intriguing. Mysteries behind mysteries.

Elizabeth took a long sip of her wine and eventually raised her eyes to peep coyly at Georgina through the slits in her mask. "I knew I could not rely on you to find yourself a project. But *now* you are entitled to compromise me." Georgina's lips parted in surprise as she noticed Elizabeth swell to her full height, as though ready to accept the challenge. "What *is* your plan to do so? I suspect you have something in mind. You always seem to."

Elizabeth's sudden candor made Georgina also stand upright. "I confess, Elizabeth, I have no such plan. To date, you have proven singularly difficult to engage in such caprice. I always feared you would not submit to the attempt."

"How very unlike you to indulge such fears," Elizabeth remarked. "Let us see about submission, shall we?" She extended her arm, and Georgina linked her own through it.

As they abandoned the box, Georgina marveled that Elizabeth had a destination in mind, threading a way through the abundant revelers around them. She brought them to a clearing in front of an archway shrouded in ivy, the entrance to a dark walk.

Georgina's heart raced in her chest. She had enjoyed many pleasurable walks through the darkened gardens of Vauxhall, and yet a strange shyness presently overcame her. That Elizabeth would, in fact, entertain her flirtation *tonight* had never crossed her mind.

Georgina walked with Elizabeth through the archway and down the lane that led them deeper into the gardens. Few lanterns hung along these walks, offering only minimal illumination. A knot of exhilaration developed inside her, and her breathing quickened.

They took one path that led to a small circle of rose bushes edged with stone benches. The aroma of dew-covered flowers encompassed them. At the heart of the clearing towered a solid Grecian statue.

Elizabeth released Georgina's arm and turned to face her. In silence, she stood so close that the hems of their gowns brushed against each other. Being much taller than Georgina, Elizabeth's figure loomed over her. Their eyes locked.

Georgina's cheeks warmed beneath her mask. Her back rested against the stone idol behind her, and her pulse leapt as Elizabeth extended an arm over her shoulder to lean on the statue. A feeling of both surprise and wonder flooded Georgina as she gazed up at Elizabeth.

"You requested to compromise me, did you not?" Elizabeth murmured in a husky voice, leaning towards her.

The hint of lamplight behind Elizabeth cast a silver glow around her, and her figure seemed to hover over Georgina like a masked and luminous specter.

Georgina inhaled the faint citrus aroma of Elizabeth's perfume. The warmth of her body, standing inches from hers, excited her. Exquisite anticipation left Georgina bereft of speech.

Words were unnecessary, as the next moment Elizabeth drew her closer, meeting her lips in a kiss.

Georgina's mouth matched Elizabeth's desperate need as they tasted each other for the first time. The fervency of their kisses revealed their mutual desire at last. Yet there was familiarity, as though they had been kissing forever. Beyond today, everything between them would be different.

Georgina's hand reached instinctively for Elizabeth's arm, the glove a frustrating barrier. She clawed the glove down to Elizabeth's wrist and trailed a finger back up her forearm, delighting in the softness of her skin. She continued this movement along Elizabeth's chiseled jaw and into her hair, before reaching an arm around her slender neck. Georgina's fingers dipped beneath the silken collar of Elizabeth's gown, trying to touch more of her intoxicating skin.

A groan rose in Georgina's throat as Elizabeth's own hand drifted to the middle of her back and pulled her even closer. Far from withdrawing, her hold on Georgina tightened.

Instinctively grasping Elizabeth's face to deepen their kiss, Georgina's thumb traced the corners of their lips. She leaned towards her, her fingertips digging into the skin of Elizabeth's shoulders, her breasts crushing against Elizabeth's chest. She pulled her mouth away from Elizabeth's and trailed a line of kisses down her throat and across the edge of her bodice.

Elizabeth's head fell back in response, her chest heaving with each ragged breath. She allowed one hand to stray past Georgina's waist. She squeezed Georgina's behind through the fabric of her gown, her muscles tensing in response, and pulled her even closer.

Georgina would have happily continued kissing Elizabeth indefinitely. The world was suddenly timeless.

The noise of shoes crunching along the gravel path nearby, together with some muffled giggles, brought Elizabeth, at least, back to her senses. She released Georgina and regarded her with a longing gaze before stepping backwards. Raising her hands to restore a few curls to her original coiffure, Elizabeth cleared her throat. To Georgina's surprise, she withdrew a clean handkerchief from the reticule at her wrist and used it to address Georgina's smudged lipstick for her. She then traced around her own mouth, wiping away evidence of their interlude as best she could in the low lantern light.

Elizabeth tugged her long glove back into place. "Now, allow me to escort you back to your box."

Entirely flushed, Georgina adjusted her gown. She placed a tentative hand on Elizabeth's arm and walked alongside her, back down the path. Confusion and desire thickened the silence between them.

Back at Georgina's box, Elizabeth's lighthearted mood seemed to have evaporated into dry indifference. She barely made eye contact and declined the drink that Georgina offered her.

"I beg your pardon, Georgina, but I believe I will retire for the evening. Thank you for the pleasure of your company."

"Will you not stay for the fireworks?" Georgina struggled to fend off the disappointment that threatened to flood her.

Elizabeth shook her head. "Another time, perhaps." She took Georgina's hand in hers and drew it to her lips, kissing her knuckles softly. "Goodnight."

Georgina, conscious of a lump in her throat, watched Elizabeth disappear into the crowd. She poured more Champagne and drank from it deeply, confounded. She had never been kissed so desperately before, and yet Elizabeth could not wait to get out of her sight. She should not care, anyway. This was meant to be fun. Georgina blinked and sniffed, but this did not stop a determined tear that escaped from the corner of her eye and ran down her cheek. She brushed it away.

WITH HER GLASS in hand, Georgina abandoned her box once more. If she was going to suffer an attack of emotion, she would be damned if all of society saw. Her mask would only serve to conceal her sadness so much. She returned promptly to the dark walk, ignoring the pairs and small groups of lovers engaged in romantic trysts about her.

Georgina walked silently, trying to collect her thoughts, until she rounded a bend and almost collided with the unmistakable silhouette of Miss Emily Coombes.

"Emily, what are you doing walking down here without a chaperone?"

The maiden clutched her mask to her face as though it might protect her from recognition, despite it clearly being too late. "I—I must have wandered off."

Georgina's eyes narrowed. She did not believe her for a moment. Emily always acted by design. She had plotted a rendezvous with some chap or other, Georgina wagered.

Hearing footsteps behind her on the walk, Georgina glimpsed over her shoulder a figure making a determined approach. He wore immaculate evening attire and a black mask painted with gold. From his average height, dark skin, athletic stature, and bright smile, Georgina recognized Mr. Dalrymple.

His arrival piqued Georgina's curiosity. Not only had she been convinced that Emily had no interest in the likes of Mr. Dalrymple, but if Edmund were to be believed, Mr. Dalrymple was also well on his way to being head over heels in love with *him*.

"Good evening, ladies," he murmured with a bow. "Might I have the pleasure of escorting this fair maiden for a stroll?"

Emily met Georgina's eyes with a look urgently begging rescue. No, she certainly had not consented to meet Mr. Dalrymple, Georgina decided, wondering who Emily had hoped to encounter. Oh, no. Could it have been Colt? Of course—who else?

"I do not think the fair maiden should be strolling with a gentleman at this hour," Georgina interjected charitably. "Nor should you, sir. Where is one of your guardians to chaperone you?"

Mr. Dalrymple's shoulders slumped. His attempts to exude a confident coup de main faltered at the first signs of resistance.

"I should like. . . ." Mr. Dalrymple began with a stutter, but was interrupted by yet another merrymaker emerging from the darkness.

An individual wearing a well-cut turquoise coat, knee breeches, stockings, and glossy black shoes approached. His generous cravat billowed in an intricate style from his throat. His mask, adorned with diamond studs, matched his coat, and boasted a rather unexpected peacock plume sticking from the top.

"There you are," Edmund cooed.

Emily gripped her mask tightly, and Mr. Dalrymple spun around on his back foot, his mouth open in astonishment.

"I am most keen for that stroll you promised me, Mr. Dalrymple," Edmund said with a coquettish smile.

Mr. Dalrymple's eyes widened. "Ah. . . ." Now *he* looked at Georgina for support.

Georgina's eyes flicked between the two gentlemen. This was an utter mess. "Oh, for goodness's sake. None of you should be here!" She linked her arm through Emily's. "Let us all walk together."

Edmund extended his arm to Mr. Dalrymple, his chest swelling with pride.

Mr. Dalrymple's eyes darted from side to side, but he reluctantly placed his hand on the proffered arm.

"This is my first masquerade at Vauxhall," Edmund began, leading the way. Georgina and Emily followed a short way behind. "I'm most excited about what the evening might hold. The hour advances."

"I was diverted by the tightrope walker," Mr. Dalrymple remarked, his voice breaking, as they went farther along the darkened path.

"I like the dancing. Nothing as romantic as waltzing with a handsome chap in your arms," Edmund said, giving Mr. Dalrymple a coy smile.

"Take me back to Mother," Emily hissed, tugging at Georgina's arm.

Georgina cast her a quelling look. "Do as you're told, brat. I'll return you to your mother shortly. We cannot abandon Mr. Dalrymple now."

It was clear Edmund had mistaken this young man's affections, just as Mr. Dalrymple had misjudged Emily's, and this whole scene was likely to end awkwardly. She wished to save Edmund from embarrassing himself if she could. Besides, the impropriety of the younger folk on the dark walks without a chaperone would be scandalous. At least Georgina's escort, however dubious her own reputation was, might spare them some censure.

Georgina saw that Edmund had tried to place a hand on Mr. Dalrymple's back, but Mr. Dalrymple had swiftly turned and hurried to the end of the path, gesturing into the distance.

"I wonder what it looks like during the day," he squeaked, beads of sweat glistening on his brow.

Edmund, Georgina, and Emily joined him and squinted through the darkness. The distinct outlines of a couple making love against a tree near to them emerged from the shadows. They did little to conceal their activities.

Georgina dragged the innocent Emily in the opposite direction.

Mr. Dalrymple's eyes widened. "Good God!"

Edmund blushed. "Oh! You like to be a spectator? Well, I can be quite open-minded."

Wiping the sweat from his brow, Mr. Dalrymple turned his back on the amorous couple. "Oh, no. I did not mean. . . ."

Georgina was about to insist they all return to the festivities when another voice startled her.

"I'm here," Leggy declared in a joyful tone.

"Leggy," Edmund said, looking astonished.

"Evening." Leggy acknowledged everyone else. "Came after all, old chap," he said to Edmund. "Cried off from the aunt's soiree. Said I had a headache. Couldn't well leave you deserted in the garden, all alone. Decided to join you. Not promising anything, though. Just a brisk evening walk to clear the mind is all I need. Still no head for romance."

Mr. Dalrymple blinked through his mask. "I—I must find my guardian," he stammered. "I bid you a good night." With that, he fled back down the path.

Georgina sighed. At least there was one less person she needed to worry about.

"Oh, Leggy," Edmund cried out in dismay as Mr. Dalrymple scurried away. "I never meant for *you* to join me."

"Well, of all that is *ungrateful*!" Mr. Leggett's indignation suffused his voice. "I should be listening to Mozart presently, and instead I'm down this dashed dark path, encountering all manner of unsavory types along the way, and you do not even thank me. *And* it cost a shilling for admittance! Had I known I would be lining the coffers of that George Barrett fellow, I might have thought twice about it." He seemed quite disgusted and misused. "I was not keen on the romance side of things, but I'm not the sort to leave a man stranded."

Emily tugged meaningfully on Georgina's arm and received a sharp dig to her ribs in response.

"You *are* a good chap, Leggy," Edmund mumbled. "I did not mean to mislead you. Here, I'll give you that shilling back." He groped in his pocket for a coin.

This small gesture mollified Leggy. "No need for that, Telford. Plenty of blunt."

"Was your aunt distressed by your absence?" Georgina asked, guiding them along the winding path towards the Pavilion.

"I should say she was. No one to circulate through her friends."

"Are you not concerned that she will discover you have deceived her?"

"Why on earth should I? I have a mask. No one will be able to tell her I was not laid up in bed with a headache."

Georgina glanced up at Leggy's striking crop of ginger hair. No, she would not point out that the best mask in London could do little to conceal him once someone caught sight of that. Better he discover this by himself.

21

AFTER GEORGINA RESTORED Emily to her family, she returned to her box to find Sarah and Colt. They had brought with them some additional Champagne and cake, but Georgina had no appetite and soon grew bored with them both.

"Was the pleasure garden too risqué for your priggish friend, Lady Mortimer?" Colt teased.

Sarah gave him a sharp look.

"Evidently," Georgina agreed.

Despite Sarah's urging her to stay for the fireworks, Georgina soon bade her companions a good evening and left Vauxhall in a carriage bound for home. Her mind raced over everything that had transpired. Her longing for Elizabeth, the sensation of pleasure that surged through her when they finally kissed, and the dejection she felt when Elizabeth had withdrawn so quickly after their exchange.

Georgina sat in the darkened carriage and scowled. She had never thought herself an *indifferent* lover, and it wounded her pride to think Elizabeth withdrew from her physically.

The hackney pulled up outside her house; gathering the folds of her blue gown, she climbed down to the pavement with care. She reached up and paid the driver, and the coach creaked off down the street.

Georgina mounted the first step, but found her wrist seized from behind and jerked down, forcing her back off the stair. She gasped and tried to wrench her arm free as she whirled around to face her assailant, all the while trying to regain her footing.

A burly man had her in his unyielding grip, and despite her dexterity in movement, her strength did not match his and she could not jerk free. My god, he meant to mug her!

Georgina tried to tell him he might take her reticule with the money inside, but she found herself unable to find the words. She waved her arm up, hoping he would take notice of it and flee with his contraband, but he seemed disinterested in her belongings. Could he be here for her?

She fixed her eyes on his face but did not recognize him, and those features she could see were difficult to discern in the dim streetlight. He had a short, unkempt beard. His gray hat, pulled low over his eyes, cast a shadow over his face.

He took her shoulder in his other hand and dug his fingers into her collar. The small beads hemming the bodice of her dress pinched against her skin, stinging her. Georgina knew the more she fought against him, the faster her reserves of energy would deplete. Yet she could not simply give in.

His other hand released her wrist, and he wrapped his grubby fingers around her throat. He tightened his grip, cutting off her airways and her hope. As Georgina struggled to breathe, fear ripped through her. How far would he take this? Her movements became more frantic.

When he finally released her neck, she coughed violently, but he quickly covered her mouth with his fingers, pressing her cheeks together.

Georgina glared at him. She tried to move her head, but he held her fast, breathing into her face. He reeked of pickles and cheap whiskey.

"I've heard you have something that belongs to a friend of mine," he whispered beside her ear. "Mrs. Gardner would like her trinket back, along with some ready that you owe her."

Mrs. Gardner. The fiend.

The scent of him made her want to vomit. She wished her legs were not presently tangled in silk, or that she had her cane with her. She certainly had not dressed for a brawl tonight.

Georgina endeavored not to panic, but the odds of getting out of this situation unscathed were quickly narrowing. She had trained as a Corinthian and enjoyed being recognized as a member of that set. As such, Georgina benefited from some of the best schools of pugilism in London, including Gentleman Jackson's very own Boxing Academy. No amount of training prepared one for combat such as this, where one's life was in actual danger. No one mentioned the terror.

Nor did this man move or skirmish in the same way a boxer would. Little of his behavior resembled anything she experienced while studying under the masters. Mrs. Gardner's friends did not hail from the same circles.

She eyed her front door. Even if she could break free of this man, she doubted whether she could cover the distance to the safety of her house without him catching up with her. Such an attempt would be foolish indeed. This coward clearly hoped for a reason to inflict more than just a warning.

His breath made the wisps of hair near her face quiver, and his fingers were sticky against her flesh. Georgina's nostrils flared as he continued to hold her mouth closed. Her eyes locked with his. If she kept looking at him, at least she would be ready for his next move.

"Happen I've been here before," he breathed into her face. "'Twas years ago now, but I never forget a door."

The realization of what he insinuated hit her hard. *Henry.* Georgina jerked instinctively. His grip on her only tightened. "Shhh. Listen up. Bad things happen to people who don't pay up, see, missy. This debt is not meant to be reckoned for years, but seeing as you have kicked up a dust about it, my employers have agreed to negotiate with you. They want Mrs. Gardner's card box back, along with the settlement of the young man's vowels, with two years' interest. Happen they said you could have until Sunday, but I suspect a governor like you would have all that blunt inside." He wet his lips. "I think they'd give me a tasty reward if I delivered it all early. What's about we go inside, and you give me what I need now." His eyes raked down over her clinging gown. "And maybe a nice little thank-you for being so gentle-like. I'll even put in a good word that you cooperated."

Georgina tried to keep her thoughts straight, despite an overwhelming urge to vomit. No, she would not give him such satisfaction. He released her mouth slightly but kept a biting grip on her chin. She ground her teeth together.

When she did not respond, he continued, "And if you disagree with these terms. . . . Well, the other young man may end up discovered on the banks of the Thames, just like that brother of yours. You wouldn't want to be responsible for that now, would you?" A sneer twisted the man's face. "Not after last time."

Rage and grief competed to overwhelm Georgina in equal measure. She would not survive another death on her conscience. She needed to spare Arthur.

The man tugged her roughly against him. "Now, what's it to be?"

Whether from fate or simple good fortune, the door of her house opened at this moment, a sliver of light spilling out over them and distracting the footpad momentarily.

Georgina took advantage swiftly. Balling her free hand into a fist, she aimed it with great force toward the man's fleshy groin.

He bellowed in pain and released his grip on her face and arm as he hunched over.

Now unrestricted, Georgina dealt him an additional right hook to his nose and pushed him off balance as she lurched past him.

The door opened wider, but she made out no silhouette. No butler or attendant came to her aid. Convinced she had only disabled this man a moment or two, Georgina scurried up the stairs but slipped on the silk of her skirt as it tangled underfoot. She cursed as her knees hit the stone steps and wasted no time scrambling back to her feet to cover the final distance across the threshold, slamming the door closed behind her.

The man's voice echoed outside, and Georgina's hands shook as she fumbled with the bolt. She slid it across the door, and it locked with a loud clunk.

PANTING, GEORGINA COLLAPSED against the door. Feeling a rustle beside her, she glanced down to see Joshua's pale face watching her with a deep frown.

"Friend of yours, Missus?"

The man outside punctuated his shouts with his fist, hammering hard behind them.

"I think not, Joshua." Georgina appreciated his irony. "Thank you, by the way. How did you know to open the door?"

His cheeks colored, and he gestured to the small window embrasure. On the windowsill sat a half-eaten pork pie and a yet untouched jam tart.

Georgina had interrupted Joshua's supper feast. The banging subsided, and she suspected the villain outside had finally given up. She was not about to unlock the door to check, however.

"Do you enjoy looking out on to the street?" Georgina asked, distracting them both.

"Yeah. It's boring looking at the back end of the house all the time."

She nodded. "We shall see about moving your room, so you have more to look at."

Joshua scratched his nose. "That cove were right rough with you, Missus. I don't like that."

"I didn't much enjoy it, either, Joshua," Georgina agreed.

"I've a mind to plant him a facer!"

"I already did," she reassured her bloodthirsty champion.

"I reckon you's in a hobble. You's need some *protection* while it's sorted."

Georgina's eyes narrowed. "What do you mean?"

He rubbed his face and yawned, then cast a longing look over at the remains of his supper. "Someone to keep their blinkers on you, is all I mean. Or maybe someone who can help you with these people what are bothering you."

"Do you know such people who might help me?" Georgina inquired, going over to the window. She peered behind the curtain and saw no sign of the burly man. Perhaps Joshua had an answer to at least some of her current problems.

"'Course, Missus. I can fix you up, good and proper."

Georgina gave his head a little pat. "Then we may have an errand to run tomorrow," she declared.

"As I were listening through the open crack in the window, I hears him say that your brother ended up on the banks of the Thames. Is that true, Miss Pace?"

She really did not wish to indulge Joshua's highly morbid and bloodthirsty imagination with the details of her brother's tragic demise. Not now. Possibly not ever. His earnest eyes regarded her without blinking. She sighed. "Yes, Joshua. It appears I just met my brother's murderer."

"We could have clobbered him, tied him up, and eaten the jelly from his eyeballs." Joshua's tone was almost gleeful.

"You are disturbed, Joshua. And I'm alarmed at how fond I am becoming of you," Georgina declared, nursing her sore throat. She picked up Joshua's food and handed it to him. "Goodnight, Joshua. And thank you."

She watched him scamper up the stairs and hoped he would not be too distressed to enjoy his snack. She suspected his young eyes had seen plenty of violence during his short life. He would take this in stride, like everything else, and sleep easily in his warm bed. Georgina hoped so, at any rate.

Retreating to her library, she roughly poured herself a brandy, careless that her shaking hand spilled several drops on the table. She sat down beside the dying embers of the fire and sipped the fortifying liquid, cradling the glass between both hands.

What exactly had she got herself into? In stealing the faro box, she had hoped to taunt Mrs. Gardner into returning Arthur's vowels. She had expected it would resolve matters quickly. Arthur could then propose to Lady Maggie, and his father would be none the wiser about his indiscretions.

Moreover, Mrs. Gardner would have learned not to exploit the vulnerability of young people like Arthur. She should have been thanking Georgina for showing her the error of her ways and teaching her some morals.

Instead, Georgina found herself stuck in the devil's own scrape, with no clear way out. Georgina reached up and touched the sensitive part of her throat where the fiend's fingers had gripped her. She suspected a bruise might already be forming.

Perhaps she should have been more focused from the beginning. Elizabeth had distracted her along the way, but Georgina could not truly blame her. She sniffled and took a slow sip of brandy. In any case, that dalliance had concluded before it began.

Despite all she had encountered thus far, she could not afford to surrender. Colt, with all his insinuations, was correct. Her desire to assist Arthur stemmed from more than mere benevolence. She was fighting for Arthur because the person she truly wanted to protect was no longer alive.

Not only was Henry gone, but she was more convinced now than ever that his death was her fault.

She gazed into her glass, tears blurring her vision. The night he died, Henry had asked her to join him at a new underground gaming hell he had been frequenting of late. He had mentioned he needed her help with something. However, Georgina had arranged an assignation that evening from which she had no intention of crying off.

Georgina remembered the slump of his rounded shoulders and the little worried frown that marred his face when she'd declined him. She had quickly reassured him that they might go together another night. Unusually pensive, he'd pushed his glasses up on his nose, referred to the time on his fob watch and wandered upstairs to his room.

Georgina would give anything to go back in time and agree to accompany Henry. Her stupidity, her selfishness, and her utter negligence had been the cause of his death. For all these years, she blanketed herself in blame, never able to acquit herself of the crime of not being there to protect him, but neither able to look directly at the truth. For eight years, she'd hid behind her life of alcohol and hedonism—anything to numb the pain. This had suited her well until Edmund dragged her into this matter with dear Arthur. And then Elizabeth had dredged up the subject of Henry. And tonight. . . .

Georgina swallowed hard and allowed the tears to flow. She would keep Arthur safe. Giving up was simply not an option.

22

BEFORE SETTING FORTH with Joshua the following day, Georgina took a few moments to pen a hasty note to Edmund. Given he had initiated this whole drama, he damn well could make a small effort to ensure the wellbeing of their friend, Arthur.

In clear and precise terms, she instructed him to proceed immediately to Mount Street and insist that Arthur pack some belongings and remove to Edmund's own lodgings for a few days. If anyone inquired, they were to announce a stay with friends in the country and provide no further advice. While there, Arthur was to remain discreet and preferably indoors, until at least Monday. It would fall to Edmund to keep him amused, and she suggested he might procure some art supplies to facilitate this.

Anticipating a plethora of objections, Georgina also warned Edmund that this was a matter of life and death, and that any obstacles he might create would be unacceptable. This had to override any existing plans, romantic or otherwise.

She sealed the missive and sent it off with a messenger before calling for Joshua and her carriage.

Within half an hour, Georgina was driving her curricle through some of the lesser-known and more dangerous streets of London.

With Joshua perched up beside her, she experienced her first pangs of doubt about his scheme.

In the initial fright afforded by the stranger assaulting her in the street, the boy's plan had offered a level of merit. Yet, in the stark light of day, after a restless night's sleep and a general sense of foreboding, Georgina started to question Joshua's judgment on the matter.

These scoundrels coming after her were dangerous. While Mrs. Gardner must have been involved, Georgina understood that Montgomery and Ellis were at the heart of it. Thanks to the waggling tongue of the brute last night, she understood their much darker connection to Henry's murder. If they were capable of such a despicable crime, what would prevent them from repeating it—or worse? The prospect made her shudder.

At breakfast that morning, Georgina had drunk only her coffee and declined all offers of sustenance. She had entertained penning a letter to Elizabeth to seek her counsel on the matter, but recalled her abrupt withdrawal from the masquerade and decided her upstanding friend would not appreciate such an appeal for assistance. Moreover, Georgina was haunted by a new question—did Mrs. Gardner know about Henry's death? Further, did Elizabeth realize her "friend" was connected to such people?

She could not be distracted now. Georgina therefore did her best to push Elizabeth from her mind, as they drove into Holborn, an area known for its criminal underworld.

Joshua gestured for Georgina to pull into Hatton Garden; after proceeding down this bustling road a little way, he pointed her to a narrow laneway to be taken on foot.

Georgina pulled the curricle over to the side.

Buckby, seated behind, leaned forward and murmured something about nothing good coming from meddling with these sorts.

Georgina jumped onto the street. “Your optimism is relentless, Buckby.” She rolled her eyes at him. “Meet us back here in half an hour.”

He nodded and jogged the horses forward.

A confident Joshua led the way down Ely Court, a narrow lane barely wide enough for two people to walk abreast.

Nestled at the end of a constricted lane, she could not see the public house from the street. She would never have known of its existence without Joshua’s direction.

Once they reached the cobblestoned courtyard, Georgina took the lead and went towards the door of the tavern. She hoped the relatively early hour of the day meant they might avoid unsavory characters.

She pushed the door open with a creak and walked inside with Joshua close on her heels.

A landlady stood behind the bar, drying a glass with a questionable-looking dishcloth. Everything about her was wiry and narrow, and her eyes tracked the newcomers with suspicion as they came in.

A handful of other patrons were present: a gentleman sitting nearest the front window with a large tankard of beer, looking a little worse for wear; another gentleman in quite genteel attire having some lunch; as well as two ladies chatting in undertones to themselves over glasses of clear liquid, which Georgina suspected was gin. She once again questioned her trust in Joshua’s scheme.

Joshua winked at her and set forth to the bar. He scrambled up onto the stool, beckoned to the landlady, and leaned across the bar to whisper something to her.

The landlady put the glass down and wiped her hands on her apron before coming out from behind the bar to lead the way over to the gentleman finishing his lunch.

“Might have some business for you,” she murmured, clearing

away his plate. She pulled an extra chair over to accommodate both Joshua and Georgina at the gentleman's table.

The gentleman settled back in his chair. "How may I be of service?"

Georgina, confronted with the irregularity of her situation and trying to explain it in words, hesitated. "I find myself in danger. Yesterday, an unsavory sort of person set upon me and physically threatened me."

The man steepled his hands together. "And was this a random attack? What makes you think that danger remains?"

"It was not random. I have something that the knave wants, and I suspect they will make the attempt again until it is back in their possession."

He studied her intently as she spoke, taking in her every feature. "*Back* in their possession? So the item belongs to them. How does it come to be in *your* custody?"

Georgina blushed.

"She took it. So we's want to protect the Missus. And we's also want to wallop 'em." Joshua's overexcited voice drew gawks from the other patrons.

Georgina's eyes widened, and she glared at her impulsive charge.

"Miss Pace wants the Thames to run red with their claret." His large brown eyes were wide, expressive, and Georgina feared, wholly convincing.

"Miss Pace does, does she?" the mystery gentleman said, highlighting Georgina's sudden loss of protective anonymity.

She opened her mouth to protest that this was, of course, a young boy indulging in fantasy. But the child leaned on the table with his elbows and continued with zeal, "She wants their bloody heads on spikes! No one will want to cross the likes of her."

"Joshua!" Georgina hissed.

The gentleman, taking everything in, folded his serviette and placed it down. "Well, Miss Pace, I'm afraid I cannot provide you the type of help you require. . . ." He paused and called out, "Harrison!"

The beer-drinking man from the front window stood up, scraping the legs of his chair along the wooden floorboards. He came and stood at Georgina's elbow, his shadow stretching over her. Was this a referral of services?

The gentleman rose. "My name is Gibbs. I am a law enforcement officer from the Bow Street Magistrates' Court. This is not your lucky day, Miss Pace."

GEORGINA GASPED, THE color draining from her face. She had questioned her good fortune from the day Edmund had thrust her into this whole matter. She was now convinced that Lady Luck had not only turned but was conspiring to bring about her complete downfall. Joshua, for all his good intentions, had led her completely astray with a catastrophic impact on her family, particularly her father.

"Blast me eyes, it's a Bow Street Runner," Joshua proclaimed in an awed tone.

Georgina's own eyes widened as she tried to land on an explanation the officer would find plausible. "There has been a misunderstanding."

"That's what they all say," the man behind her said in a gruff voice. "You'll have your chance to tell the Magistrate *all* about it, I'm sure."

He gripped Georgina by the arm, and she stared down at his hand. "That is unnecessary, sir. I won't be resisting." She stood up, plunged her hands in her pockets and followed the rougher of the two men out of the public house and into the courtyard.

The more well-favored gentleman followed, holding Joshua by the wrist.

As they assembled in the courtyard, Georgina asked Gibbs whether it might be possible to convey a message to her groom, who would soon be waiting in Hatton Garden.

Harrison laughed. "Oh, the fine lady wants us to wait on her."

Gibbs sneered and shook his head.

As they jeered at her high-handedness, Georgina gestured with her head to Joshua and used her eyes to direct him down the laneway.

Go! she mouthed silently.

He shook his head fervently.

Now! she mouthed.

His eyes implored hers, the little fellow clearly honor-bound to remain with her in trouble. She nodded firmly towards the street once more.

In a moment, his tiny wrist slithered out of Gibbs's grasp. Though the officers reacted quickly, his small and nimble frame ducked and weaved outside their clutching hands. Their efforts were futile. Joshua jumped out of their reach and ran in the opposite direction, down the far side of Ely Court, and decamped out of sight.

"Slippery little bugger," Harrison snarled.

"Isn't he?" Georgina agreed, repressing a smile of satisfaction. At least Joshua would suffer no ill consequences from their outing.

As though anticipating Georgina would make a similar break for it, he grasped her by the arm again and yanked her down the laneway.

23

GEORGINA SAT ON the cold stone bench, her head resting against the wall as she stared into the darkness and huddled her cloak around her. The basement holding cell in which they had confined her offered no warmth and minimal light from two guttering candles on the guard's table down the hall. The cell stank of urine; unsurprising, given that it lacked facilities or even a useful commode for the detainees. She opted not to think too much about the occasional scurrying movements in the darkness but shifted intermittently, lest she become the target of an inquisitive rodent.

The officers had removed all her effects, so she soon lost track of the hours without her fob watch. She felt bereft without it, her one piece of Henry, and had even begged them to allow her to keep it. Her entreaties—first whispered, then shouted—were met only with the cold silence of indifference.

Clearly the Magistrate had other matters of importance to deal with today, as the wait seemed interminable. Her stomach grumbled audibly, but she supposed she should be grateful for the cup of pale, lukewarm tea Harrison had brought her in a chipped, stained cup sometime earlier. It had been something, at least.

Georgina was glad Joshua had managed to escape. She suspected most of the London Magistrates would know him already from his prior life on the streets, and obtaining a fortunate outcome for him may have proven difficult. She wondered where he had run off to and hoped that he had not been so alarmed by the Runners that he would disappear completely.

The irony of the entire situation struck her. Her friend Edmund, who had been responsible for Arthur's downfall by introducing him to Solitaires in the first place, had lost interest in the affair. He was completely distracted, having decided he was in love with Mr. Dalrymple, a young man she was *convinced* favored ladies. She could only have faith that he would follow through with her directions. At present, there was no way to find out. And here she was, in jail after being pursued to her doorstep by a nasty footpad, with a bruised neck and aching shoulder for her trouble.

She regretted having managed matters clumsily. Arthur still did not have his IOUs, he could not propose to Lady Maggie, and his situation grew more dire with every day that lapsed. She rubbed her hands together. The sooner she extricated herself from this scrape, the sooner she could return home to rectify matters.

Maybe, if she could rescue Arthur, the crushing weight of her guilt over Henry would finally fade. And perhaps Georgina would somehow find peace without the eternal assistance of alcohol and debauchery. Her mind flashed again to Joshua, and her heart gave a tender squeeze.

Georgina sat in silent reflection until, at last, the sound of rattling keys and clanking doors suggested something might be about to happen. She heard the distinct accent of Harrison, the less engaging of the Runners who had brought her in, together with a softer, feminine voice.

She sat forward, puzzled at which female of her acquaintance might come to her aid at such a time. While Georgina could certainly rely upon Sarah to assist her, how would she possibly have learned of her plight? It had not occurred to Georgina to send Sarah or Colt a message begging for assistance. Now that she found herself detained in Bow Street, Georgina wished to spare her dearest friends the indignity of finding her thus imprisoned.

The answer to Georgina's question arrived quickly. Harrison shepherded none other than Mrs. Gardner into the hall outside her prison cell. She wore a floral print day dress and a simple straw bonnet tied under her chin with a ribbon.

Mrs. Gardner smiled at Harrison and asked him for a few moments' privacy.

As he complied, Georgina contemplated insisting that he remain but had no intention of providing Mrs. Gardner with any sense of satisfaction beyond what her present indignity already afforded.

Mrs. Gardner turned back to Georgina and peered inquisitively between the bars, much like a child would look at a curiosity behind a circus cage.

"Goodness me, how difficult this must be for you, Miss Pace. For one so used to the *finer things* in life. And to liberty."

"What do you want?"

"A social call, my dear. To check on your wellbeing."

Georgina stood up from the bench and walked over to the bars. She curled her fingers around them. "Forgive me, I had the impression from last night that my *wellbeing* was not of paramount importance to you."

Mrs. Gardner gave a stiff little smile. "You seem *determined* to meddle in affairs that do not pertain to you, Miss Pace."

"I will meddle in affairs that require meddling, and you will not stop me."

Closing the gap between them, Mrs. Gardner's gaze sharpened and did not waver. Georgina recognized the burning determination. What spark drove this fire? Her purpose was personal.

Mrs. Gardner lowered her voice. "This is beyond the both of us, Miss Pace. I beseech you, most earnestly, to let well enough alone. Do as you have been asked and allow that to be the end of it."

Georgina detected a tremble in Mrs. Gardner's breath. So, she too was afraid.

"I think we both know that it will not be. I suspect I only know a little of what is really going on, and it sickens me." She paused, holding Mrs. Gardner's gaze. "Did you know about Henry?"

As the color drained from Mrs. Gardner's face, she failed to supply an answer.

The muscle clenched in Georgina's cheek as she glared in disgust. "I've a mind to inform that Runner Harrison about your little soirees when he comes to escort you out and be done with it."

"That would not be wise," Mrs. Gardner said quickly. "I *hope* you will not remain incarcerated for too long, my dear. If something happens to me, I suspect your troubles will escalate. Not only do you have to worry about poor Mr. Coombes, but think about your dear Papa. He will surely miss you not being there to look after him."

Rage coursed through Georgina, and she slammed both hands against the bars, making the steel rattle. "If either of them is harmed. . . ." she growled. Arthur might have been safe for now, but her father had no one to protect him while she was locked up.

Mrs. Gardner stepped back, and the door swung open as Harrison tumbled back into the room with a curse. "What the blazes is going on?"

"My guest is leaving."

To Georgina's relief, Harrison bundled Mrs. Gardner out of the room. She paced up and down the cell. When would this damned

Magistrate see her? Mrs. Gardner's associates clearly had no issue with resorting to violence, and Georgina feared for the safety of both Arthur and her father. Where she had been content to sit patiently before, she now did not want to risk being away from her house a moment longer than necessary. She needed to resolve the matter, once and for all.

AFTER WALKING WHAT felt like several miles inside her rather confined space, Georgina collapsed back onto the bench again. She curled over on the cool stone and closed her eyes.

She awoke sometime later to the sound of keys unbolting the door once more. Two voices speaking in hushed tones echoed down the stone stairs. Finally, Harrison and Gibbs came into view between the cell bars.

Harrison placed the key in the lock, turning it. The door swung open, and he stood back, gesturing for Georgina to exit.

She stood up and stretched, giving a little yawn. "Should I expect a Hanging Magistrate?" she asked whimsically, following them out into the hall.

"As it happens, Miss Pace, you *are* in luck. Someone of consequence has intervened on your behalf, and you are free to go."

"Ah, nepotism at its best!" Georgina approved. "That must be rather irritating for you," she sympathized. "Should I decline whatever favor has been called in and face my due punishment?"

Harrison gave her a puzzled look, but Gibbs almost smiled.

"Your benefactress is awaiting you in a carriage out the front," Gibbs informed, as they reached the top of the stairs.

Harrison handed her a small bundle of her belongings.

Another mystery lady. Almost certainly Sarah, this time. Georgina took the items, holding the fob watch tenderly for a moment before restoring everything to her pockets. She extended her hand to Gibbs. "It really *was* a misunderstanding," she said, bestowing one of her rarer smiles on him. "I favor gibbets to spikes."

With a glint in his eyes, he shook her hand and allowed her to walk past him and out of the building.

AN ENCLOSED CARRIAGE with a grand crest emblazoned on the side panel awaited her. Four beautifully matched black horses marked time, steadied by a liveried coachman. A groom held the door open for Georgina. Of all the people to come to her rescue, it had to have been Elizabeth. She wavered for a moment before climbing in.

"Still only 'somewhat wayward'?" Georgina asked with a grim little smile, as she positioned herself on the bench seat opposite to Elizabeth.

Elizabeth stared out into the road. Her expression conveyed no amusement.

"I believe I have fallen from grace, after all," Georgina went on. "I did warn you." The carriage swayed as it moved off down the street.

"Do you think I enjoy coming to places such as this?" Elizabeth demanded, finally looking at her. Her gray eyes pierced Georgina. "I have rarely been obliged to use my position and consequence for something so appalling."

Georgina shrank into the seat, quelled by the weight of Elizabeth's disappointed gaze. She resisted the urge to point out she had not begged for help in the matter.

"Most degrading for you, I agree."

Elizabeth's eyes flashed. "Heads on spikes?"

Again, a sense of injustice washed over Georgina. She directed her attention out of the window now. "Yes. A spike, spear, lance. I did not specify which sharp weapon to use," she lied. If Elizabeth was going to think the worst of her, then she was not going to correct her. "But preferably mounted outside my house for all to see."

The carriage rocked from side to side. The clatter of hooves on the cobbles and the general hum of the streets outside filled the rich silence between them.

"Joshua?" Elizabeth murmured.

Georgina nodded, unable to resist dragging her eyes back to meet Elizabeth's gaze.

She was staring at her earnestly now, her frown softened. "What happened to your neck?" Elizabeth shuffled forward on the carriage seat. "Did the officers do that to you?"

Georgina touched her throat. She had neglected to replace her cravat when she walked out of the jail. She shook her head.

"An accident that happened a while ago."

Elizabeth eyed her with disappointment. "Why are you lying to me, Georgina? Have you forgotten that I had *very* close proximity to you only last night and saw no such injury?"

Georgina clenched and released her teeth. "Someone set upon me. They mugged me, after the masquerade."

In a rustle of fabric, Elizabeth moved to sit beside Georgina. "I should have taken you home."

"That would not have prevented what happened, believe me."

"And is this how you came to find yourself in such a place? Were you looking for the person who accosted you?" A furrow had formed in Elizabeth's brow. "Or is this to do with Mr. Coombes? Georgina, please tell me. I want to help you. I *can* help you."

How could she explain what occurred in a manner that would not be absurd to someone as discerning as Elizabeth? *She* would never have found herself in such a scrape. And while she sounded earnest,

Georgina could not forget she had been alongside Mrs. Gardner throughout so much of this. To trust Elizabeth now would have felt like sacrificing a part of her soul.

Exhaustion overcame Georgina. Every limb grew heavy with fatigue.

"It was just a footpad."

The carriage pulled up outside her residence, and Georgina flung the door open before the groom had a chance to even climb from his chair.

"Thank you, Elizabeth, for assisting me out of my difficulties. I apologize for any embarrassment I may have caused you. I shall endeavor not to trouble you again." She snapped the carriage door shut and strode up the stairs to her front door.

SEATED AT HER desk, Georgina frowned. Rays of sunlight stretched into the room from the open window behind her, casting gentle warmth onto her back and a golden glow over her rich furniture and carefully arranged books. It was a stark contrast to the dank jail cell.

She summoned her father to join her and prepared to deliver the news that would signal yet another change in her father's routine, one he would likely resist.

He came into the room with a jaunty spring in his step and his newspaper folded under one arm. He greeted her affectionately, and once he had settled down on the other side of her desk, she commenced her prepared request.

"Papa, I need to ask a favor."

"Oh, yes? You name it, my dear."

"I need you to return to Yorkshire for me." She braced herself for the inevitable resistance. He could not dislike the country more, and it would particularly disgruntle him if he were to miss any of the amusements of the season.

The pallor of Silas's face darkened to an unattractive tone of beetroot. "What? Damn and blast it all, George. We only just got back here. You can't make me trek the whole way back up to the estate again!"

"I do not ask it of you lightly, love."

"Fudge. What silly notion have you taken into that brainbox of yours now?"

Georgina considered telling him the truth, but she wished to spare her father any unnecessary aggravation. She therefore settled upon a harmless fabrication.

"I received a letter from Miss Nelson advising the situation between our steward and cook has descended into utter disarray, and they require immediate oversight."

"What?" he roared.

She picked up a blank sheet of paper and recited fluently, "'If Mr. Pace does not come at once, I fear we shall lose Cook to the Telfords, who are presently in search of a new cook.'"

Silas's eyes almost popped from his head. "After everything we have done for that family. They should not be so treacherous."

"We cannot well stop the cook from leaving our employment if they are experiencing poor treatment at the hands of our steward," Georgina reasoned. "The onus is on *us* to rectify it. And I doubt you will find someone as skilled at making such a sumptuous caper sauce as Darcy." She hoped the tantalizing memory of his favorite meal would melt his apoplexy. She folded the paper quickly and stowed it in her desk, before her father asked to read the evidence for himself.

"Can *you* not go? I am not skilled in these affairs, after all. I think you would handle it much more efficiently, my dear."

She reached across the desk and squeezed her father's hand. "I wish I could go, Papa. I do. But I am currently tending to several time-consuming matters here that I cannot think you would prefer." She slid a random ledger to him, as well as a pile of bills. "There is the financial situation to tend to, but also Joshua to induct, and some civil unrest of our own." She lowered her voice to a whisper. "I heard a rumor that Jarvis has been considering a position elsewhere." This was a complete work of fiction. However, she needed to act drastically to convince her father that Yorkshire might be the easier burden of the two. "I fear I may need to placate him a little."

Silas wrinkled his nose. "Good grief. I had no idea."

Georgina shrugged. "That is why it is so important to stay abreast of these things."

"Indeed, yes. Right, well, I daresay I can go to Yorkshire, though not directly. Allow me at least another day or two. I have a few matters to resolve myself before I rush off again." His color had risen once more, and Georgina suspected these matters had something to do with his secret romantic entanglement. As long as he left by Sunday, he *should* remain safe.

Georgina wanted to whisk him away immediately, but she knew this would be an unreasonable expectation to put on her father. She undertook to commence making the arrangements for his departure.

He removed his glasses and tilted his head to one side. "There's something else amiss, isn't there, George? What scrape are you in? Tell your Papa. I can't bear to think of you shouldering whatever burden this is on your own. I have noticed you acting rather *odd* lately," he went on. "Going to art galleries, staying out at all hours, introducing little boys to the staff."

"Only *one* little boy," Georgina insisted. "And he is a dear little soul. I am glad to have him, for all his meddlesome ways."

Silas chuckled. "Indeed, he frequently sidles into my book room to ask me the most remarkable questions. Today he asked me if I ever dreamed of moving to the Americas. He volunteered to plan the trek for me, so long as he might come along for the ride. Quite the adventurer, I think."

"He does not lack spirit. You can take him to Yorkshire with you if you like."

He winced. "Good grief, no. I think I could do with fewer tales of blood and gore. I suspect he enjoys shocking me."

Georgina laughed, but until she had dispelled the shadow cast by Ellis and Montgomery over Arthur and her father, her tone lacked true gaiety. She would feel much more content when Silas was safe in Yorkshire, Arthur's vowels were back in his hands, and the criminals were stripped of all power.

AFTER GEORGINA REASSURED herself that no harm had befallen her household during the hours she spent at his Majesty's pleasure, she retired to her room to freshen herself with a bath and a light repast on a tray. Once Mr. Walker, her father's valet, had removed the remains of her food, Buckby and Joshua joined her.

"I'm relieved you both made it home," Georgina said, allowing them into her dressing room and bidding them to sit. "Whatever happened to you, Joshua?"

Buckby shook his head ominously.

"First, I hid behind the newspaper stand. When you was carried off, I watched Mr. Buckby circle by twice. I was being careful-like because them Runners oft keep a lookout around the streets. So, when he goes by a third time, I jumped in behind him and told him to get a move on."

Georgina's lips twitched. She could imagine her faithful retainer fearing the worst and his reluctance to follow any instructions from the young fellow.

"He pulled on the reins," Buckby informed, his face twisting in utter distaste at such poor horsemanship. "I tried to get him to tell me what was amiss, and where he had lost you, Miss Georgina, but he would say nothing until we left the area."

Georgina nodded. "And right he was too."

"Finally, when we was well out of danger, I tells Mr. Buckby everything that happened. Including that bit about you wanting to spill their claret."

Buckby rubbed his chin.

"I said they have took the Missus to Bow Street, and Mr. Buckby clipped the street post with the carriage."

"My curricle?" Georgina demanded.

Buckby blushed. "'Twas a shock, Miss Georgina. Told the little scamp that I knew his rum dealings would land you into trouble, and that it'd likely be the death of Mr. Pace when he learned of it."

"And *I* told Mr. Buckby that we couldn't snitch to the guv'nor. It's not the way," he imparted wisely.

"Very correct, Joshua," Georgina affirmed. She rubbed his head. "I am so proud of you. Really, Buckby, you of all people should know not to upset my Papa."

Buckby looked aggrieved.

Joshua swelled up at this. "I then hatched a plan to rescue you."

Georgina sat down on the sofa and crossed her legs at the ankles. "Indeed, I am interested to hear how Lady Mortimer became involved in this escapade."

"I remember the fine Lady M from when you both rescued *me*, Miss Pace. Knew she was a good sort, and a chum of yours. Also, reckoned she'd be able to spring you from Bow Street, right and tight. Also, looked mighty plump in the pocket, so if she had to drop some blunt to get you out, she'd be good for that."

Buckby's eyes bulged.

"You supported this plan?" Georgina asked him.

He shrugged. "He did not use those words exactly."

Georgina chuckled, despite herself. Knowing Joshua, she could believe that. If there was one positive to have come from this frightful mess, it was making the acquaintance of this boy.

24

COLT SPENT A day between appointments with his tailor and his favorite wine merchants, Berry Brothers and Rudd, stocking up his cellars. He toyed with the notion of attending Peer Ormskirk's rout party that evening, but frankly, recent days had left him exhausted.

He endeavored to enjoy a quiet night at home; however, a persistent nagging feeling prevented him from settling. He could not simply ignore the matter of Sarah. Although she had moved on from the events that occurred at Vauxhall, he could not shelve the incident so easily.

Despite having a history of enjoyable flirtation and banter with his friend, Sarah always resisted his many attempts to develop a liaison. Therefore, the boldness she displayed on the night of the masquerade had caught him off guard.

In contrast to Miss Coombes's expectation that he show her the ways of physical intimacy, Sarah knew what pleasures awaited her and had sought *him* out for a reciprocal exchange. Afterwards, he had lingered close to her, curious about her behavior, and what it meant for them. He grudgingly admitted that he also hoped she might invite him to escort her home, so that they might discuss what had transpired. Or perhaps make love until dawn.

Instead, once the fireworks concluded, she bade him a curt goodnight and entered a hackney carriage by herself, leaving him to make his way to his own home alone.

Since then, Sarah had not contacted him. In the past, she would descend on his house without notice most days, to take a glass of Madeira or share a spot of gossip, but she had not visited him. This bothered him more than he cared to admit.

With these thoughts in mind, Colt found himself headed towards Curzon Street following supper that evening to call upon his friend.

Fortuitously, Sarah had also declined to attend Peer Ormskirk's rout, and Colt found her engaged in some delicate needlework by the fireside in her front parlor. She looked up from her sewing frame but did not immediately smile.

Colt hesitated in the threshold. He had hoped Sarah would agree to see him. It would be devastating to have the butler cast him out onto the street.

To his relief, she thanked her butler and requested refreshments for her guest.

When he closed the door, she stood up and placed her hands on her hips, quirking a brow. "I do not believe we had an appointment, Robert?"

"I have never needed to make an appointment before, Sarah." He watched her dispose of the embroidery on a nearby table and resume her seat, settling the folds of her amber gown around her. In the firelight, she looked like a goddess.

"Did you recover from the masquerade?" she asked.

Colt raked a hand back through his hair. "A few things that occurred have left me rather distracted."

"How reckless of you to allow such distraction." Sarah's tone remained stiff and difficult to read.

Colt retreated into silence as the butler reappeared with a tray laden with sweetmeats, as well as a decanter of cognac, tea, and of course, Madeira.

Sarah thanked him and he disappeared once again.

"Very reckless of me," he agreed, as he provided them both a small glass of cognac.

"Not as reckless as forgetting one's engagements, however."

He looked up to find her dark eyes fixed on him. "What do you mean?"

"Today, while I was in Hyde Park, I ran into Miss Coombes."

A sinking sensation at once gripped his stomach.

"She was most keen to unburden herself about Vauxhall. About how she had enjoyed the entertainment, but how someone had left her stranded down a dark walk." Sarah lifted her chin.

Colt fingered the lace at his cuff. "I did say the evening distracted me."

"You are incorrigible, Robert."

"I presume no harm came to the chit?"

"Of course not. Georgina happened upon her and saw she came to no grief. Fortunate on all counts, really, for had you not been otherwise distracted who knows what you would have done to her?"

"I would not have done a thing *to* her, Sarah. *With* her, perhaps. . . ."

She pushed her glass back onto the table and stood, turning away from him and folding her arms across her chest.

Colt also rose. Sarah's indifference was a pretense, after all. She was jealous.

"I want you," he said, almost in a growl beside her ear. For a moment, she didn't pull away, leaning back just slightly so he could feel her warmth. His arousal pressed against her bottom, his body demanding to be noticed.

She whipped around to face him. "I will not be your distraction, Colt. Run along and find one of the dozens of willing maidens fawning after you and leave me be."

Colt took her hand in his. He kissed her fingers, closing his eyes, pressing her palm against his cheek. "I do not want a maiden. Or anyone else. I only want you, Sarah. Can you not see that? You make me feel ... desperate," he whispered.

He drew her towards him and kissed her, and he could feel her reluctance slip away as she took a handful of his hair in her hand, pulling him towards her. Their passion intensified as quickly as it had done the previous night.

Sarah pulled out of his embrace. "Not here," she murmured.

She took his hand and led him out of the parlor and straight upstairs to her bedroom.

SARAH PUSHED COLT into her room, towards the immense bed that dominated the far wall. Draped in heavy damask curtains, it towered above them. An Indian silk quilt of maroon and gold covered the bed, along with a plethora of pillows. Her bedroom boasted a fire, well-tended for when the lady of the house wished to retire to bed.

Colt sat to pull off his boots before standing again.

She liberated him of his jacket and used his cravat to pull him towards her, kissing him as he unfastened his shirt. She pushed it from his shoulders, revealing smooth, pale skin firm with muscles, which tightened beneath her touch.

He caught her against him, wrapping his steely arms around her and kissing her deeply while she tugged at his breeches. The novelty of being undressed by a lady, with such aplomb, intrigued him. Piece by piece, she shed his layers until he stood completely naked before her. Sarah remained fully clothed, admiring what she saw.

As her unabashed, hungry gaze swept over his body, Colt became disorientated. He desperately wished to shield his own eyes—or in some way conceal himself—to avoid feeling so exposed. Did she notice the way his fingers were twitching at his sides? Or perhaps the unevenness of his breath? He was accustomed to giving women what they wanted, but this never involved presenting them with himself. They never took time to *observe* him. Sarah's burning look drove him wild. He knew his member had grown thick and reached towards her, without so much as a touch.

She splayed her hand across the middle of his chest. The pressure allowed him to detect the rapid thudding of his heart. From the smile that curved her lips, she could feel it too.

Colt reached around her and unclasped the back of her gown, kissing every part of her flesh as it became exposed.

She shrugged out of her dress, and the silken fabric pooled at their feet.

Colt set about peeling away her undergarments. He took off each article of clothing, exploring her curves, and when she finally stood nude before him, he caught his breath. Her dark skin was radiant, and her lines were proportioned, feminine, and impeccable. Most of all, she was *her.*

"Sarah. You are so beautiful," he murmured and guided her to the bed.

He laid her back against the pillows and hovered over her, kissing her mouth, his tongue impatient. He needed her with an intensity he could not describe, but he would not rush, determined to savor every moment. His hand cupped her breast, and he watched her reaction, her mouth opening in pleasure. He slid down the line of her stomach and across her hip, lingering at the apex of her legs, before he allowed his fingers to submerge in the soft folds at her center.

Sarah's thighs dropped apart instinctively, and her flushed body arched against his hand as she moved against his fingers. She closed her eyes with pleasure, a moan escaping her lips.

With true fervor, Colt lowered his mouth, placing tantalizing kisses in delicate circles below her beautiful triangle of dense black curls. Sarah uttered a small cry and squirmed beneath him, burrowing her hands into his hair and pulling him towards her.

Confident his maneuvers were on course, Colt increased the strokes of his tongue, tasting and gliding with confidence. She would explode soon, he knew.

Just when he thought Sarah was about to peak, he caught her eyes. Her gaze seemed to darken, and she gave his hair a small tug, signaling he should stop.

Surprised, Colt sat up, wiping his mouth with the back of his hand.

"I'm not just one of your women to pleasure, Robert. This is about *us*. Make love to me."

So many years he had adored this woman, and she finally wanted this. If only she knew how close his heart came to bursting in that moment.

He kissed her in response and, keeping his face near to hers, lowered his body between her legs, his hardness pressing rigidly against her thigh as her legs curled around his waist.

Colt remained still for a moment, in part to assemble his composure, so he did not humiliate himself by finishing too early for this gorgeous woman. He took the opportunity to study the image of perfection that gazed up at him. He traced along the curve of her cheeks and jaw with his thumb. Her eyelashes were astonishingly long, and she had a tiny freckle beside her left eye.

He inhaled deeply and placed the tip of his cock against her, moving just slightly against the slick creases that shielded her core, lingering there as she writhed beneath him.

"For heaven's sake, Robert. Fuck me!" she cursed in desperation.

Her sudden expletive made Colt laugh. He suspended himself above her with one arm, the cords of his muscles flexing under the strain. He held his prick rigid for one moment longer, then released it as he plunged inside her. He covered her mouth with his, suffocating her cry of delight. She gripped him like a vice, and he struggled to contain himself, especially when her moans grew louder. As their rhythm quickened, Colt lifted his upper body and gently coaxed her legs upwards, facilitating even deeper access.

Sarah stretched her hand up to his chest and let it graze down over his muscles. "You're lovely, Robert," she panted. She hooked one leg over his shoulder, then the other, her eyes twinkling.

He cursed inwardly as his pleasure increased, all rational thought leaving his head. How did one woman have the ability to make him lose all control?

As he thrust into her, frantic now, Sarah hardly made any sound. Her eyes fluttered and lips parted, as though their movements together were driving her to greater heights of ecstasy, beyond the capacity to even cry out.

Suddenly, Sarah opened her eyes and lifted her head off the pillow. She gripped his shoulder with one hand and caught his bottom with the other, digging her nails into his skin as she pulled him closer.

This movement, along with the ardent look in her eye, was too much for Colt to bear. He plummeted over the edge, his entire body jerking in rapture. In the same moment, he felt Sarah begin to pulse around him. Time stopped there for a while, with nothing but Sarah's trembling, and then she grew still and soft beneath him.

They lay together for some time, their limbs entangled, waiting for their breath to be restored.

Colt, who always prided himself on taking appropriate precautions to avoid siring a child, questioned how Sarah had distracted him so totally from sensible thought. That had also been the case at the masquerade, and yet he felt strangely unconcerned.

Sarah smiled up at him; he studied her intently.

"You smell glorious," he announced, inhaling her hair.

"This cannot happen, Robert." She rolled to lie on her stomach beside him.

He traced the taut skin on her back with his fingertips, making her flesh prickle under his touch. "I think we have proved that it very much *can* happen, my dear."

"And I shall never forget it, but this nonsense must stop. I will not take you as a lover."

Her words wounded him. "I never knew you to be cruel, Sarah. You have allowed me to glimpse ecstasy, and then you want to take it away?"

"It is not yours to keep, Robert."

"But I want it to be mine. I want *you*, Sarah."

"No, you don't, Colt. And I could not live like that. The only way I might sustain your interest is to deny you mine. The moment I revealed feelings, I would lose you. How fatiguing and unfair for both of us."

Words eluded him. Whilst she had awakened in him a powerful new category of desire, he could not dispute that his behavior to date confirmed her theory.

"I can change," he pleaded, snaking an arm around her and pulling her against him.

"I do not believe you, Robert."

He pressed his face into her hair, kissing the top of her head and bundling her against his chest. "Let me try."

He wanted to try.

Sarah said nothing.

They remained thus for some time, exchanging no further words, until a discreet tap at the door interrupted their silent reverie.

"What is it?" Sarah called, scrambling off the bed and reaching for a sheet to cover her naked body.

Colt similarly plucked through the tangle of bedding to try to find his garments.

"Miss Pace has called for you, Mrs. Fortescue. She is awaiting you in the front parlor." The voice of Sarah's maid sounded neutral and without judgment.

Sarah cursed. "Thank you. Please get her something to drink and tell her I shall be with her presently."

A fit of laughter seized Colt. Sarah shot him a disapproving glare, which served only to exacerbate his mirth. How mortified his dignified darling would be trying to explain to Georgina what had just transpired between them.

TEN MINUTES LATER, Sarah, pink-cheeked and hair unkempt, entered the parlor with Colt following languidly at her heels. His own attire left little mystery as to what had transpired. His shirt, now creased, would have made his fastidious valet wince, and he had barely bothered to fashion a knot out of his neckcloth.

"Georgina," Sarah said, saluting her friend with a kiss on each cheek.

"You are both here, excellent," Georgina said, greeting Colt as well, shaking his hand and sitting down.

She did not seem set to query either their appearance or their entry together. In fact, she did not really look at either of them.

Colt picked up the glass he had been drinking before and settled himself on the sofa once more. The dark circles under Georgina's eyes were more pronounced than ever. She appeared tired and worn down. This was becoming the norm for her. He sat forward and regarded her closely.

"How have you progressed with Mr. Coombes and those infernal vowels of his?" Sarah inquired. "Surely Mrs. Gardner has relented and returned them to you? Or did you steal them after all?"

Georgina shook her head. "I stole a faro box, though."

"I thought Colt was jesting!" Sarah admonished.

Colt rubbed his face. "Damn it all, George. How is a faro box meant to help anything?"

Sinking back onto the sofa, Georgina launched into her story, starting with her impulsive decision to steal Mrs. Gardner's faro box, and her subsequent discovery that the box was as corrupt as Mrs. Gardner herself. Her tale peaked when she described how a brute assaulted her on her doorstep following the masquerade, making vulgar reference to Henry and posing further threats, yet giving her a reprieve until Sunday to come up with a plan. She concluded the story with the final extraordinary anecdote of her spending the day in a Bow Street prison, together with a visit from Mrs. Gardner herself.

Colt felt a sharp pang as he realized his friend had fallen into trouble of this magnitude. Violent attacks? Threats of death? Ellis and Montgomery, in their ruthless pursuit of control, had increased the stakes.

"For now, Arthur is safe, as I have sent him to stay with Edmund. No, Colt, don't grimace so. As long as they are discreet, no one should suspect he is there." She yawned, desperate for sleep. "My father, on the other hand, is another matter. While I was imprisoned, Mrs. Gardner made a thinly veiled threat towards him. I am trying to induce him to leave town, but he is being the most stubborn wretch about it."

"Between us, I am sure we can furnish Arthur with the funds he needs to pay off the debt and interest, and perhaps even leave him with some left over to set up his household. That would allow him to marry this lady of his and be done with the whole affair. I don't want you involved with this anymore, George," Colt declared.

"I fear it is too late for that. To be sure, Arthur might have whatever sum of money he needs, but he wants the vowels, Colt. He understands what they mean. And besides that, I must bring them all to justice."

Colt recognized the glint in her fierce blue eyes. Trying to reason with her was futile.

"But to risk yourself, and even your father. . . ." Sarah ventured slowly.

"Papa will return to Yorkshire directly. And I will not stop until I have destroyed their enterprise."

A tightness formed in Colt's stomach. Georgina thought to protect her father, yet she seemed not to consider the danger she was in herself.

"By attempting to bring down Solitaires, you will be waging war with some very powerful people, George."

A muscle twitched in Georgina's cheek. "Yes. Those 'people' killed Henry, Colt. Are you suggesting I sit by and do nothing?"

"Only that you exercise caution. The benefactors financing Solitaires will be insisting that Mrs. Gardner prey upon people like Arthur. You cannot truly know who else is behind this, beyond Ellis and

Montgomery and their hired muscle." Colt paused. "What do you know of Lady Mortimer's involvement, for example?"

He could see Georgina shift in her chair.

Sarah leaned in and held Georgina's hand. "This may have *nothing* to do with Elizabeth."

They both glared at Colt. He wondered why they always cast him as the villain when he only meant to help.

"I did not say she *was* to blame for all this. Only that you may be dealing with some very rum customers, my girl. It's time for you to take this seriously."

"You have no idea how seriously I am taking this, Colt."

This only worried him more.

25

HAVING REFRESHED HERSELF at home and changed into breeches, a smart evening coat, and a loosely tied cravat, Georgina soon pushed through the unwelcoming doors of Solitaires. This place, once a bothersome inconvenience to her, now offered a sense of foreboding so thick in the air, she struggled to breathe upon entering. She bestowed her hat and cane on the blushing maid, who could not pull a wink from Georgina. She placed the arbitrary bet in Mrs. Gardner's book, paying no heed to the wager at all.

She spotted Elizabeth, who appeared to be the bank for her table and would therefore not be able to interfere in Georgina's business this time. *Good.* Georgina promptly progressed to the back rooms. Smoky haze and raucous laughter encompassed her as she stepped further into the netherworld of Solitaires.

Mrs. Gardner, evidently keeping a sharp eye on the arrivals, spotted her and wasted no time rushing to her side. Unlike previous visits, she gave little pretense that Georgina's presence afforded her any pleasure.

"What are you doing here?" Mrs. Gardner hissed through gritted teeth. "For your sake, I hope you have the faro box with you and the money to acquit the vowels." Her eyes scanned Georgina's frame, but there was neither a satchel nor the outline of an object in her pockets. There was nothing of note to see.

"No. I wish to speak to your *business partners*, if you could call them that. Ellis and Montgomery. I believe my business is with them."

Mrs. Gardner's eyes pierced her, as if she could not say aloud what she wished to. For a moment, Georgina experienced a quiver of doubt.

"You're a fool, my girl," Mrs. Gardner murmured, her voice cracking slightly.

"So I am told. Summon them." Withdrawing was no longer feasible.

Georgina allowed Mrs. Gardner to navigate her through the tables, in the direction of the private parlor. Mrs. Gardner opened the door and allowed her inside. Then, with a shake of her head, she closed the door behind her.

GEORGINA STOOD BY the fireplace, resisting the urge to make patterns in the dust with her fingertip. She could feel her palms growing clammy. It would be difficult to predict how this meeting might unfold. She had clearly antagonized these gentlemen sufficiently for them to threaten her family and friends with violence, and if the rogue who attacked her was to be believed, they may well have been responsible for Henry's murder. It would take a lot for her to contain her anger.

As the door opened, Georgina swallowed thickly. She had met the two gentlemen here before. Their simpering alone would have been enough to draw her temper to the surface. She must play this game correctly.

Mr. Montgomery, tall and long-limbed, led the way into the room, followed by Lord Ellis. The latter possessed a more moderate build and height, and his skin was so fair and devoid of freckle or pigment, he may never have seen a moment of sunlight in his life. They both stood before Georgina and offered her a polite bow. She did not reciprocate the salutation. The pair, true members of the dandy set, exhibited ostentatious evening attire that Edmund would have undoubtedly appreciated. The rich silks and bright colors hinted at a life of leisure, likely funded by the spoils of their immoral activities.

"Good evening, Miss Pace. How delightful to receive a . . . ah . . . *summons* to see you," Lord Ellis said. "You have come to discuss some business?"

"After a fashion."

"Monty, get Miss Pace a drink, will you?" Ellis instructed, sitting on one of the sofas and gesturing for Georgina to sit opposite, while Montgomery went across the room to the drinks tray.

Georgina sat down, her eyes moving from Montgomery to Ellis—who took some snuff while he waited—then back to Montgomery as he supplied them all with generous glasses of brandy.

"We are very understanding businesspeople, Miss Pace. And we were most *touched* to hear that you had stepped in on behalf of young Mr. Coombes, were we not?" Ellis turned to Montgomery for support.

"Oh, deeply moved!" Montgomery confirmed, placing a hand on his heart.

Georgina took a large sip. With these theatrics, she would need a second glass just to survive the discussion.

"Though, when we learned that your passive interest progressed to a more active *interference*, well, sadly, that is when we had to take measures to keep the order. We simply cannot allow people to jeopardize how we run things."

Montgomery interjected with a loud sigh.

Georgina's pulse throbbed, but she maintained her silence and merely took another long sip.

"So, we hope you have followed the instructions and brought the faro box," Ellis said.

"And the full payment for Mr. Coombes's account, including two years' compound interest," added Montgomery. "If you can do this without a fuss, there is no reason why he should be harmed."

Georgina snorted a laugh at their gall. "Your audacity is exceeded only by your absurdity. You truly think you will get away with this?" She blinked then, the room shifting around her. Was her vision a little blurry? She forced her mind to focus, even if her eyes could not. The fiends had dosed her drink. She drew her glass to her lips, and this time pretended to take another deep sip, placing the glass down on the table at her elbow. She could use their antics to her advantage.

"It is merely business, Miss Pace," Ellis replied gently, tilting his head to one side.

Georgina tugged at her neckcloth to loosen it from her throat. "I have not got the faro box or the money with me. A couple of shillings for a hackney ride." She foraged in her pockets and withdrew the coins, together with her fob watch, making a show of her clumsy movements. "See?"

Montgomery produced a monocle from his own pocket and eyed the fob watch through it. "That looks like a charming piece. Let me look at it."

Georgina recoiled.

Ellis smiled. "Ooh. Methinks we have identified *treasure*, Monty."

"No, no." Georgina slurred her words on purpose, drawing out each syllable. She wanted the men to think they had her in a corner. "It is not that valuable."

Montgomery approached and unhooked the fob watch from her

coat before she could protest. He inspected it closely. "Ah! An engraving. 'Beloved Henry, from George.' 'Tis a sentimental trinket, Miss Pace? Your late brother, I collect?"

Georgina untied her cravat completely now and unfastened a few buttons on her waistcoat. "The heat of this room stifles me." She gave Montgomery an imploring look. "And yes, it has *only* sentimental value. Please return it."

"Gladly!" He made as if to give it back to her, but then snapped his hand shut around it. "But I have a better idea! How about a friendly wager?"

Georgina's lips compressed into a thin line, and she ran her hand back through her hair. "Go on."

"Given you have so little on you to bet—aside from this token—I am proposing one short game of hazard. You stake your watch, and we stake these." Montgomery withdrew a little bundle of papers.

Georgina caught a glimpse of Arthur's clumsy handwriting upon them. The IOUs that had been so ruthlessly obtained. She glanced over at Ellis, whose snake-eyes were regarding her keenly. They were playing with her. And she was playing a different game entirely. Her limbs started to feel quite relaxed. Even though she did not ingest the entire drink, Georgina noted the effect; she lacked the capacity to present any physical defense. "Very well," she agreed.

"Excellent!" Ellis said. "Get the dice, Monty. Join me at the small table, Miss Pace."

As Georgina rose to her feet, she stumbled slightly, and Ellis took her arm, escorting her towards the table on the far side of the room.

At this moment, the door swung open, and Mrs. Gardner swept in with Elizabeth close on her heels.

Even through her drugged haze, Georgina could see Elizabeth's mind working. Her elegant eyebrows furrowed as she speedily assessed the scene. "What have you done to her?"

Elizabeth moved swiftly to Georgina and took her free arm, so that she now supported her.

Ellis clapped a hand to his chest in feigned confusion. "I? Why, I have done nothing at all, Countess! Everyone knows Miss Pace enjoys her wine. She and I are just about to settle a few matters over a game of hazard." He sat down, and Montgomery provided him with the dice. On the table, he placed the promissory notes and watch.

"She is in no state to play," Elizabeth spoke firmly, a stormy look on her face.

"Miss Pace has committed to play and agreed to the wager, Lady Mortimer. You cannot interfere," Montgomery announced.

Georgina looked up into Elizabeth's face and smiled admiringly. "It's all right. I will win back Arthur's vowels. I am staking my brother's watch on it."

The color drained from Elizabeth's face. "Georgina, no! You're not thinking correctly. Do not do this. They do not lose."

Georgina felt Elizabeth press her hand and wished she could assuage her fears. At this moment, she felt invincible. "*I* do not lose. *Trust* me."

Elizabeth sighed heavily. She helped Georgina to sit down and stepped back, folding her arms across herself tightly.

"Choose your main?" Ellis prompted.

"Seven," Georgina replied.

Monty gave her the dice with an unpleasant curl of his lips.

She held the two cool dice in her hand for a moment, breathing deeply, and rolled. They numbered eight. Ultimately, Henry would not let her lose his watch. It was her only comfort.

"Chance," called Ellis with a raise of his brows. "To win, you need another eight, Miss Pace."

Georgina released a quivering breath. When she extended a hand to retrieve the dice, it shook visibly.

Elizabeth covered her face with her own hand.

Georgina tossed the dice again. Ten. And another roll. Three. And another. Seven.

"Oh dear," Montgomery said, clicking his tongue loudly.

Elizabeth choked on a sob.

Even Mrs. Gardner turned her back on the table, covering her mouth, unable to witness the rest unfold.

"You lost, my dear," Ellis drawled. He withdrew his snuffbox from his pocket and enjoyed a pinch, as Montgomery removed both the bundle of promissory notes and Henry's fob watch from the table.

Georgina continued to stare absently at the dice in front of her, even when Elizabeth placed a comforting hand on her shoulder.

"You have until Sunday to rectify the other matters we discussed, Miss Pace. You understand *all* the terms," Ellis said.

Despite the plan she'd set in place, Georgina felt a weight crush down on her heart as Montgomery pocketed Henry's watch. She swallowed hard.

Without further words, Ellis and Montgomery sauntered from the room.

THE THREE LADIES remained in an uncomfortable silence, the only sounds being the rhythmic ticking of a nearby clock and the gentle crackle of the fire. The calm of the room contrasted the speed of Georgina's thoughts, which again clashed with the slow-motion blur of her vision.

Mrs. Gardner was the first to speak. "I apologize for their behavior, Miss Pace. I wish you had heeded me."

Georgina finally glanced up from the table. "Hmm? Oh, yes. I believe you should rethink your choice of associates."

This earned a slightly cynical laugh from Elizabeth, who had remained close to Georgina. "I too wonder what it will take for you to realize this, Julia. For now, Georgina, let me take you home."

WHEN THEY ARRIVED at Half Moon Street, Georgina made a half-hearted effort to dissuade Elizabeth from accompanying her inside, though she had never spoken with less sincerity.

Elizabeth insisted she would personally see Georgina safely settled. They both went inside without further fuss.

In the hall, Georgina yawned. Her head had started to pound. "They drugged me. Less than they thought, but enough."

"I could tell. Now, lead the way to your room."

"How I have longed to hear you say that, but I fear tonight my skills may be compromised."

Elizabeth laughed. "It does not seem to matter what befalls you; you continue to be incorrigible."

Georgina leaned on her and smiled. She wondered how long she would feel the effects of whatever drug it was those men had used on her.

"I want to assist you to bed." Elizabeth paused. "There is plenty of time to enjoy your room in other ways at a more suitable time."

A sense of warmth invaded Georgina's belly. She took Elizabeth's hand and drew her up the staircase.

As they walked down the hall, Georgina stretched out her arm and reverently traced her fingertips along one door that they passed by. "Henry's room," she explained to Elizabeth.

When they were safely in Georgina's bedchamber, Georgina removed her jacket and unfastened the remainder of the buttons of her waistcoat. She inhaled sharply when she remembered the absence of

Henry's fob watch. It had been a consistent part of her for so many years. To lose it was to lose the last part of Henry she had. Her eyes filled with tears.

Elizabeth was beside her in an instant and gathered Georgina's comparably small frame into her arms, catching her as she crumbled under the weight of her grief. Elizabeth allowed Georgina to sob and supported her in a strong embrace, giving her the strength to confront her sadness.

"They killed Henry," Georgina choked softly.

Elizabeth cursed under her breath and rocked Georgina gently in her arms. "You poor girl."

"I have to save Arthur."

"Hush," Elizabeth murmured against her hair. "Nothing more tonight, Georgina. You must rest." She released her and slowly removed Georgina's raiment to her undergarments, sighing when she saw the full extent of the bruises and scratches the thug had imparted. She pulled a nightdress from the wardrobe and slid it over her charge. She unfastened Georgina's hair from its ribbon and brushed it gently, before leading her to the bed.

Elizabeth pushed back the covers, and Georgina climbed in, amused at Elizabeth's overall efficiency. They regarded each other in silence for a moment before Elizabeth leaned down and placed a soft kiss on Georgina's lips.

Georgina's heart beat wildly while they exchanged a few words of goodnight. How long had it been since someone had cared for her like this? Had she ever felt quite so safe to fall apart? As she watched Elizabeth leave, Georgina ached to tell her everything about the night Henry died. She wanted to confess to her that she could have prevented it, had she only changed her plans. However, she knew Elizabeth, so perfect and kind, would never look at her in the same light again. Surely Elizabeth could never love someone whose selfishness led to the death of her own brother.

Georgina reached for the decanter on her bedside table, then reconsidered. Instead, she snuggled down into the cool sheets, content to dream of being encircled safely in Elizabeth's beautiful arms.

26

THE LONDON SEASON provided a vast number of galas and balls from which to choose every night. Card parties, soirees and ridottos amused some, while many more were drawn to the ballet, opera and theater offerings of Covent Garden. Tonight, in need of distraction, Georgina opted to join a special gala hosted by Lord Byron at his home in Piccadilly. Everyone of high fashion—together with a good number from the fringes of society—would be there.

Since marrying his husband, Mr. John Edleston, several years before, Lord Byron had produced some of his best works, a testament to his happy and contented life. While Georgina did not care for the fine art that hung on gallery walls, she could appreciate a good poem. Lord Byron was an accomplished poet, as well as a profound and powerful orator in the House of Peers. He was, therefore, highly popular, while his charming husband delighted their friends with his musical ability and witty banter. Lord Byron had a twisted foot, which prevented him from being a graceful dancer in the conventional sense. However, he moved with his own grace; further, as an attentive host, he ensured everyone's dance cards were full.

As Georgina wandered across the marble tiles into Lord Byron's grand entrance hall, her eyes were drawn up, past the many levels towards a vast skylight that revealed the darkening sky outside. She followed the other guests, traipsing up a monumental gilt staircase and into a magnificent ballroom decorated tastefully with ornate furnishings. There was plenty of space for dancing, chatting on sofas and mingling over the refreshment tables. The wide variety of guests ensured the evening would be lively and eventful. As the suite filled up with a jovial crowd, the music began, and couples took to the dance floor to form the opening set.

Georgina wore black trousers, a coat of dark blue superfine, a crisp white shirt, and a neat cravat tied at her throat, concealing the bruises left by Mrs. Gardner's thug. The rub of the cravat served as a painful reminder of the precariousness of her situation.

Georgina exchanged greetings with Mr. Edleston and Lord Byron, her eyes sweeping across the room. Her gaze involuntarily hooked when she spied Elizabeth standing off to the side, engaged in animated conversation with Miss Mei Chen and her mother.

Elizabeth, attired in a striking gown of white with a shimmering silver overlay and a beautiful diamond necklace, turned in her direction, her own expression softening as their eyes locked. She smiled serenely at Georgina. Vivid recollections of the night in Vauxhall flashed in Georgina's memory, and she sensed her cheeks heat.

Her pulse leapt, that trill of butterflies released in her belly once more. Georgina considered throwing caution to the wind and striding across the room toward the Countess, but an arm slipped unceremoniously through hers, preventing her from moving.

"What is the latest in your dramatic escapade, George?" Colt quizzed, turning her away from Elizabeth and moving her in the opposite direction.

"I am not sure where to begin. I heeded no one's advice and went and confronted Ellis and Montgomery. They drugged me with some substance or other and then lured me into a wager."

Colt regarded her with his mouth agape.

"They pitted Arthur's promissory notes against Henry's watch. I lost." Georgina ground her teeth together, braced for the censure destined to fly in her direction.

Colt stepped back as though she had struck him. "The watch?" His good-looking countenance had contorted in horror.

Georgina nodded. "I was not in my right mind, I suppose. My only consolation is that they seem to like causing pain, and so I doubt they will damage the watch. Not while they might use it to taunt me."

"And what about your father? How do you plan to ensure his protection? They have shown themselves capable of violence."

"Ellis and Montgomery have given me until Sunday to settle the debts and return the faro box. By that time, my father will be safely on his way to Yorkshire. I am confident their evil clutches do not extend that far." Georgina accepted a glass of wine from a passing attendant. She looked over at Elizabeth, who had resumed talking with Miss Chen. Georgina wondered for a moment if she should be jealous, then concluded just as swiftly that Miss Chen would not be Lady Mortimer's type. Far too docile. "How is Sarah? You were both acting rather odd last night."

"We were?" Colt's pitch made his voice crack unexpectedly.

Georgina flashed him a suspicious look. "A little distracted."

He laughed. "Naturally, we were distracted. We have been anxious about you, George. Sarah would like to see you settled, you know."

Georgina sipped her wine and glanced around the room. "Not much chance of that."

"Has Prudence continued to haunt you about town? Or has she finally reconciled that your little romance in Cornwall was the end of it?"

"It's difficult to say. I noticed her earlier, with Lord Ravenscroft and Mr. Dalrymple. But she has not made an approach. The evening is young." She sighed.

"And are you convinced that your priggish lover is innocent in the Mrs. Gardner affair?" Colt challenged her.

"Elizabeth is not my lover."

"Not for want of trying. Your calf-eyes are rather fetching."

Georgina glared at him. She had allowed her guard to slip and done little to conceal her feelings of late.

"You should have a care, though, George. If she is not the angel she claims to be, I suspect your heart would not recover."

"What sentimental nonsense," Georgina feigned. She excused herself and hurried away from her best friend's concern.

"DANCE WITH ME?" Elizabeth said from Georgina's elbow, surprising her out of her musings.

A wave of affection swept over Georgina, followed by an unnatural reticence. She faltered, temporarily speechless, then nodded her agreement.

Georgina accepted Elizabeth's hand, and they walked to the dance floor where couples converged for the next waltz. As the music began, Georgina slid her hand around Elizabeth's waist and took her wrist in the other.

Elizabeth's smile held both warmth and welcome.

"Are you all right, Georgina?"

A frisson of nerves, desire, and dread surged through her. In truth, Georgina was overwhelmed.

"It has been a long week." Her clasp on Elizabeth's hand, relaxed.

Elizabeth gave a wry laugh. "You *have* been rather busy. I hope you were able to get some sleep last night."

The mere mention of sleep instigated a yawn. "Joshua is quite a lively addition to my household. I was awoken at dawn this morning, when he hurried into my room with a basket containing three kittens."

Elizabeth blinked as the waltz spun them in rhythmic spirals through the room. "Kittens?"

"Yes. He was evading Jarvis and Buckby and wished for special dispensation to keep them."

"That was not his word," Elizabeth stated.

"No. But now that he knows it, he has been asking for 'dispenation' all over the place. It's quite amusing."

Both ladies burst into laughter. "Was it unfair of me to foist dear Joshua on to you?" Elizabeth asked, her hand stroking Georgina's back gently as they relaxed into the swaying motion of the dance.

"At the time, it seemed important to saddle me with a project, if I recall correctly."

Elizabeth nodded and pressed Georgina's hand. "Precisely. And I should apologize. I overlooked what was in front of me. You were never in need of redemption. You already *were* helping someone. Mr. Coombes."

Georgina's stomach sank. Elizabeth meant to comfort her, but she would never know how desperately in need of deliverance Georgina was. No project or act of charity could ever repair the harm she had caused. She could not reverse Henry's death.

"I daresay Joshua is grateful for the opportunity to improve his circumstances," Georgina granted, averting her eyes. "And while I have tried to help Arthur, I have done much in my life to warrant needing redemption. I could have a house full of the likes of Joshua and still be beyond repair."

Elizabeth's lips twitched. "I quiver to imagine a house full of Joshuas."

This earned another laugh from Georgina.

"It . . . it is good to see your smile," Elizabeth finally said.

Georgina could not swear to it, but she felt the distance between their bodies close slightly as they waltzed. For a vulnerable moment, she allowed the warmth of Elizabeth's gaze to melt through her.

"We should perhaps *talk*. Soon," Elizabeth nearly whispered.

Georgina nodded. The tension between them had built to a point where they could ignore it no longer.

The orchestra played the final notes of the waltz, and both ladies stopped dancing. "We should—" Elizabeth began again, but a shrill voice interrupted her.

"Georgina, allow me to steal you for the next country dance." Lady Prudence Ravenscroft cut in and left no room for dissent.

Georgina cast an apologetic smile at Elizabeth before extending her hand to Prudence. "I will happily oblige you."

As she danced with Prudence, Georgina's heart felt lighter than it had in days. Confusion had dissolved into exhilaration, and this had nothing to do with the lovely redhead smiling across from her in the current dance set. She could not deny that Elizabeth's sweet words and demeanor had ignited a flame of hope within.

"Your thoughts seem miles away," Prudence scolded her as the dance brought them together.

"On the contrary, I assure you," Georgina sighed softly. "How is your ward, Mr. Dalrymple? He is becoming quite familiar with a dear friend of mine, Lord Edmund Telford. I happened upon Mr. Dalrymple wandering around the dark walks of Vauxhall the other evening."

Prudence lifted her finely arched brows. "Lawrence? You surprise me. Was he alone?"

"That's not for me to say."

"How cryptic of you. It's not becoming."

Georgina smiled as the dance separated them for a few moments. "Nevertheless, a gentleman should have some secrets from his guardians," she said as they came together again. "I will say, you or Lord Ravenscroft may wish to have a discreet word with him about enhancing his craft when it comes to wooing ladies . . . presuming his inclinations fall exclusively into that territory?"

Prudence could not hide the dismay that twisted her pretty face. "How very awkward for him. And yes. He—like you—prefers ladies exclusively."

Edmund would be crestfallen when he learned the truth about Mr. Dalrymple. His hopes of a romantic connection would be dashed yet again.

"Perhaps you could provide him with some direction. You are very skilled in that area, if I recall correctly," Prudence quipped.

"Touché. There's the hint of fire I remember." Georgina circled around Prudence and took her hand, leading her away from the dance as the set ended. "Sadly, I do not feel qualified to instruct anyone in such matters. I am rather losing my touch."

"I hope not. I liked your touch very much."

Georgina sighed. If only she had declined to spend Christmas with her father in Cornwall.

27

THE ROOMS NOW overflowed with guests, and through the expanding crowd, Colt caught the chiming sound of Sarah's laughter. He edged his way through the throng of people to her side, where he found her conversing with Mr. Edleston.

Sarah gave him a tight-lipped smile. "Colt, what a becoming coat," she remarked of his well-fitted gray garment.

Colt greeted Mr. Edleston and invited Sarah to dance.

She thanked him and declined the honor as she wished to rest.

He remained awkwardly at her elbow for a few more moments before draining his glass and moving away again, disconcerted. Why was she making him suffer? He crossed the room, hoping to find a card table established in one of the adjoining rooms. Just then, a handful of young people detained him, Miss Coombes numbered among them.

With a level of confidence rare in debutantes, Miss Coombes greeted him. "I hope you mean to ask me to dance, Lord Coulthurst. We are all at a loss here."

Dancing with Miss Coombes was the last thing he wanted to do at that moment. However, the gaggle of hopefuls blocked his escape as they whispered to each other and watched him intently. He could not refuse such a direct request without overt rudeness. He smiled uneasily.

"Of course, Miss Coombes. I would naturally offer to dance with all of you at once, but I fear that would challenge the propriety in even Lord Byron's house," he said, giving the others an apologetic smile, which sufficed to send them all off into a peal of giggles.

In a dark mood, Colt moved through the steps of the dance mechanically, smiling only in response to Miss Coombes when she beamed at him, her eyes almost bulging with enthusiasm. Unlike their prior encounters, he did not seize every opportunity to brush against her or touch her soft skin.

Miss Coombes draped her hand against her brow. "The room is too crowded," she whispered. "I might swoon. Would you be so good as to find me somewhere quiet where I might sit for a moment?"

Colt now regretted each of his previous attempts to engage in a playful dalliance with Miss Coombes. She sought time alone with him with bold determination, and this forced him into an awkward position of needing to deny her. She was a harmless creature and did not deserve to be wounded or embarrassed, but he no longer wished to provide his assistance to her.

Unwilling to let the lady swoon and cause a scene, Colt supported her off the dance floor and out into the hall. He wished to set Miss Coombes away from any curious onlookers as quickly as possible. He tried an adjacent door, and it opened, to his relief. He shuffled her into a modest sitting room, dark except for the light offered by a fire already reduced to embers.

"I hope my mother did not witness our departure," Miss Coombes said. "She would surely pursue me."

"Perhaps your mother should keep a closer eye on you at all times," Colt replied, gesturing to the couch. "You may wish to sit down while you compose yourself?"

She gave him a coy smile and walked over to the window. The curtains were drawn, and this allowed her to gaze down over the street below while she remained in the shadows. Moonlight spilled over her pretty face.

"I believe I should apologize for the other night at Vauxhall. I let myself get carried away. I should not have laid my hands on you as I did," Colt explained, joining her by the window.

"I enjoyed it very much, Lord Coulthurst."

"That may well be, but it was ill-considered of me. Allow me to reassure you that I shall never lay a hand on you again," he promised.

"But what if I would like you to?"

"Then I would be obliged to disappoint you, Miss Coombes."

"But I *liked* it." She spoke with a growing sense of urgency.

"Yes," he stated. "And I wish you success in your pursuit of pleasure with *other* partners, Miss Coombes."

She flushed. "Oh, my goodness," she said in a weak voice, and her knees gave way.

Realizing every gentleman's worst nightmare, Colt leapt forward to catch her.

It was immediately clear, however, that she had feigned the swoon. She blinked at him soulfully from beneath her long lashes, reached around his neck, and pulled him down, trying to kiss him.

Georgina was right. She *was* a brat!

He pulled his face away from hers, but she had a grip on his neck.

Suddenly, light streamed into the sitting room as the door flung open. "For God's sake, you're an animal," Mr. Dalrymple growled. He crossed the room in a few strides.

Colt released Miss Coombes in surprise, and she stumbled back against the window, clutching at the curtains to prevent herself from falling into an undignified heap on the floor.

Colt raised his hands placatingly, hoping to explain the misunderstanding. Before he could speak, however, Mr. Dalrymple landed him a generous right hook to the face.

Despite Colt's excellent boxing skills, this assault took him unawares and left his head rattling. He tottered backwards, off balance.

Mr. Dalrymple took Miss Coombes's hand and moved her out of the way. "Put your affairs in order tomorrow, sir. I will see you at dawn on Sunday morning."

Without pausing for a response, Mr. Dalrymple propelled Miss Coombes out of the room.

Colt reeled in wonder that his first attempt at being honorable had resulted in being challenged to a duel.

28

NESTLED BACK IN the comfort of her library, Georgina gazed at the glowing embers, memories of Byron's ball playing in her mind, much like the shadows cast by the small dancing flames.

She leaned forward and stoked the fire. She knew she should be making strides in her mission to topple Solitaires, as the stakes were drastic, and time was ticking down. Yet her thoughts turned back to Elizabeth. In the beginning, Georgina had only intended a flirtation with the Countess, yet she had developed tender feelings despite herself. Feelings she refused to examine, but ones she equally did not want to displace.

She jumped when she heard the sharp rap of the door knocker echo through the hall. She feared for a moment Ellis and Montgomery had sent a mob around to raid her home in search of the faro box, Sunday deadline be damned. Her stomach tightened in anticipation. She clenched and unclenched her hands.

The library door opened to Jarvis. "Lady Mortimer is here to see you, Miss Pace."

Relief flooded Georgina, followed by trepidation. Why had Elizabeth called so late in the evening? Perhaps she was there as an envoy for Mrs. Gardner and her colleagues, and Colt's suspicions had been correct.

Georgina asked Jarvis to escort Lady Mortimer in. She straightened her evening wear and quickly pinched her lips, trying to draw some color to the surface.

A moment later, Jarvis returned with Elizabeth.

"Would you care for anything else, Miss Pace?" the butler asked in supercilious tones.

Georgina, her eyes transfixed on Elizabeth, replied, "No thank you. You might retire, Jarvis."

He gave a dignified bow and withdrew from the room.

"I was not expecting you," Georgina said, gesturing for her to come in. "I did not realize you meant we should talk tonight."

"Forgive the interruption."

"You are always welcome."

"I wanted to return your book," Elizabeth explained, handing it to her. "You indicated it was important to you."

"Indeed. Thank you." Georgina accepted the novel, returning it to the shelf. "You enjoyed it?"

Elizabeth folded her hands in front of her. "It . . . it gave me much to think about."

"All a part of my greater quest to compromise you. Did you recover from our adventures at the masquerade, by the way?"

"It seems like so much has happened since that night. But yes, I have recovered admirably. Thank you, Georgina. I gather you have also?"

Georgina gave a flippant laugh, but she did not feel amused. "All forgotten. That is what you desired, is it not? To forget?"

Elizabeth's gray eyes darkened, as though a cloud had passed in the way of the sun. Her chest rose and fell as she breathed. "That would be the *wisest* course," she said at last, though her voice lacked conviction. "Would it not?"

"Most certainly," Georgina agreed, distracted by Elizabeth's sweet scent the longer they stood opposite each other. She bit her lip. "Though I never professed to be wise."

Without a word, Elizabeth took a purposeful step closer.

Georgina raised one hand, her fingers approaching the edge of Elizabeth's bodice, near her shoulder. In a fluid movement, she clutched the fabric in her hand and pulled, drawing Elizabeth towards her.

Their lips joined, and where Elizabeth had been motionless a moment before, she now gathered Georgina into her arms, crushing them together as they kissed.

Georgina urged Elizabeth backwards, making her stumble and sit on the sofa behind her. Her breeches allowed her to straddle Elizabeth's lap with ease.

"Georgina!" Elizabeth's protest was only a whisper against her lips.

Georgina gazed directly into Elizabeth's eyes, pleased to have rectified the difference in their heights. Hearing no further demur, Georgina kissed her again, curling a hand behind her head as she deepened the kiss, plundering Elizabeth's mouth with her tongue.

Elizabeth's hands slid up Georgina's back and beneath her coat. Only the thin fabric of a shirt stood between Elizabeth's eager fingers and Georgina's skin.

Georgina arched her back responsively, and her hips pivoted against Elizabeth, making her groan. Georgina found this reaction favorable. She repeated the movement, her eyes alight with mischief.

Elizabeth's delicate appearance belied her strength. Suddenly, she lifted Georgina by her hips and reversed their positions, so that Georgina sat on the couch. Elizabeth kneeled on the floor before her.

Georgina made a move to regain dominance over the situation, reaching to draw Elizabeth into another kiss, but found both of her own slender wrists suddenly seized in one of Elizabeth's large hands.

The sudden strength and dominance that Elizabeth revealed did not scare Georgina. It excited her. Elizabeth's long fingers tightened in a vice-like grip.

Their gaze met, each inciting the other with a challenge. An unspoken dare to go further.

Elizabeth, with a determined glint in her eye, rose to the challenge. Still holding Georgina's wrists in one hand, with the other she deftly parted Georgina's legs, then settled between them. Their locked gaze was alive with tenderness and hunger.

Elizabeth delivered a maddeningly soft kiss. The tip of her tongue teased Georgina's lips.

Georgina, fiery and impulsive, made a movement to kiss Elizabeth properly. Elizabeth, still on her knees, only held her a little tighter, making her wait. Tantalizing her.

Georgina wrapped one slender leg around Elizabeth's shoulders, trying to pull her closer this way.

"Patience, my little thief," Elizabeth instructed her. She gently released Georgina's wrists and stroked the side of her jaw.

Georgina pressed her cheek against Elizabeth's fingers, closing her eyes briefly. When she opened her eyes again, Elizabeth was regarding her intensely.

"We are not all equipped with your virtues, especially *patience*," Georgina said, exasperated.

"Then I must teach you," Elizabeth replied.

"Please don't," Georgina beseeched.

Elizabeth smiled and unfastened the front of Georgina's breeches.

Georgina lifted her bottom as Elizabeth pulled them down over her hips and past her knees.

Elizabeth stroked up the outside length of Georgina's legs, from her ankles, across her knees, and then lingered on the soft flesh of her exposed thighs.

Instinctively, Georgina raised her hips again, trying to get closer to Elizabeth's hands.

Elizabeth clicked her tongue, avoiding the only spot that would ultimately fulfill the ache growing inside Georgina.

Georgina made a little growl of frustration and collapsed into the cushions.

Lowering her face, Elizabeth placed a pathway of kisses up each of Georgina's milky thighs, hovering near the apex of her legs and the neat triangle of dark hair there. With painful deliberation, Elizabeth rubbed one finger along her seam.

Georgina's body jerked in response to this soft touch, and a cry caught in her throat. She stared unblinkingly at Elizabeth.

As Elizabeth's fingers stroked her up and down, Georgina's head fell back, her lips parting in mounting desire. Elizabeth's long fingers moved firmly over her bud, then dipped inside her wetness. The pace intensified, and finally, as Georgina's body convulsed, Elizabeth's fingers sank deeply into her.

Georgina cried out.

Elizabeth groaned as Georgina throbbed tightly around her fingers.

Once the waves of pleasure subsided, Elizabeth slowly withdrew her fingers from the warmth of Georgina's body. They glistened, filmy white.

Georgina retrieved a clean handkerchief from her pocket. She used it to wipe Elizabeth's hand. Then she raised her head and saw Elizabeth's face, expression soft, loving.

A shy smile emerged on Georgina's flushed countenance. "I believe you have just irrevocably complicated things, Elizabeth," she remarked, with more flippancy than she felt. She found herself being soundly kissed.

They withdrew from the kiss, both laughing.

Elizabeth took Georgina's hands in hers and drew them to her mouth. "Things have certainly become more interesting. You have an unaccountable way of making me act impulsively."

"I hope you do not regret it," Georgina replied, her voice soft.

"Never," Elizabeth answered.

She pulled Georgina's breeches back-up, methodical in her movements, then crawled up onto the sofa and drew her against her chest possessively.

Georgina draped an arm around Elizabeth's neck and rested her head on her shoulder, enjoying the scent of her skin and the heady sensation that flooded her body as she returned to reality. In time, her breathing became more controlled. A sigh of contentment escaped her, as she relaxed against Elizabeth, feeling safe, comfortable, and ever-so-warm. She slipped into a kind of somnolence, easily losing track of time.

"Are you sure I cannot persuade you to borrow another book? I should like you to return books to me often."

"Indeed. I am going away for a few days, so a book might be useful for the journey."

Georgina sat up, very much awake. "Going away?"

Elizabeth grazed her hand over Georgina's back. "I must return to my estate."

"Would you like me to accompany you?"

Elizabeth's eyes kindled. "A tempting prospect, Georgina. But an offer I must nevertheless decline."

Georgina could not conceal a frown. "How wretched of you to abandon me."

"There has been an outbreak of illness across the farms, and I wish to ensure that medical treatment has been dispensed to all in need."

"Well, I cannot fault you for that, but I daresay I wish you did not have to go."

Elizabeth smiled down at her. "And why is that?"

Georgina blushed, feeling caught out in her feelings. "I suspect I might miss you," she conceded.

"And I you," Elizabeth replied, her voice filled with affection. She sighed. "I should probably take myself home."

"Please stay."

Elizabeth held Georgina's gaze and shook her head. "I cannot. This is not the time, my dear." She carefully disengaged herself and rose to take her leave. "I shall see you soon," she pledged.

29

AS SATURDAY ARRIVED, Georgina found herself in no mood to confront the flurry and bustle of her regular London haunts. Her father invited her to accompany him to Jackson's Boxing Academy, but she declined and reminded him curtly he was meant to be readying himself for Yorkshire. Despite the ruffian's assurance she had until Sunday to settle the issue with Mrs. Gardner, she remained gripped by an unshakeable fear that if she did not get Silas to safety, he would be in imminent danger.

Silas reassured her of his intent to leave quite early the next day and then set forth to meet his cronies for a robust round of boxing.

Georgina paced the length of the library several times, fixating on the sofa where Elizabeth had brought her to climax with such tenderness the night before. A yearning built in her loins. She had lost all sense when it came to Elizabeth.

Restless and preoccupied, Georgina found remaining at home unbearable, so she called for her carriage and headed to the sanctuary of Mem Lavigne's. At least there, she might think better. Or perhaps not at all.

"GEORGE, THE WORLD is over!" cried Edmund, slumping into a chair opposite her.

What the devil was he doing here? He must have tracked her down here, as he rarely frequented Mem Lavigne's. A frown creased her face.

"You have left your post, Edmund. I told you to stay with Arthur. Are you singularly incapable of following a simple direction?" She did not particularly care if she wounded his feelings.

Edmund grasped her hand imperatively. His own hand was shaking.

This made her stare up at him, and she observed the faintest sheen of sweat on his normally impeccable countenance. The rapid rise and fall of his chest also hinted at recent exertion.

"Edmund, have you been *running*? How extraordinary."

"Had to get here quickly. No hackneys to be had," he panted.

"What is it? Something has happened to Arthur?" she demanded. Her own heart raced as a hundred devastating possibilities presented themselves in her vivid imagination.

"Oh no, he's fine. Painting portraits of all my attendants as we speak."

The wave of nausea abated, and Georgina extracted her hand from his moist grip. The sensation of a sweaty palm always made her wince. "If you have dropped any more striplings into trouble, I am telling your mother."

He shook his head. "No. It is Mr. Lawrence Dalrymple. My love. He is going to die. You must stop it from happening."

Georgina's booted foot slid off the edge of the chair it was resting on. "What are you talking about?"

"Coulthurst. *Your* friend. They are going to duel in the morning." Edmund fumbled in his pocket and withdrew a lace-trimmed handkerchief.

His words were nonsensical. How had Colt found himself forced into a duel? With the sweet and gentle Mr. Dalrymple, no less. A sinking sensation dragged her to reality. Miss Coombes must certainly have some role in the matter.

"Coulthurst's reputation is well-deserved. Dalrymple shall not come out alive. You have surely made some mistake?" Even saying so, Georgina lacked conviction.

"Do something, George. You must save Lawrence."

Georgina swore. It angered her that responsibility so frequently fell upon her shoulders to provide solutions to matters that were not related to her. She smiled grimly.

"What do you expect me to do about it? Tomorrow is Sunday. Could they possibly reschedule?"

He looked baffled by this request. "Don't be absurd. You must talk to Coulthurst. Persuade him to back out of the duel. Marry the girl?"

She wanted to slap Colt. "If it is a duel, Edmund, you should know that Colt cannot simply back out of it. It becomes a matter of honor. Did you see what happened?"

Edmund shook his head, his pale eyes filling with tears. "No, but I called upon Lawrence, and he informed me of it. Lord Ravenscroft is not happy about it, naturally, but has agreed to be his second."

"A sensible choice, at least. I wonder who Colt has asked."

Edmund tugged at her sleeve. "Make him marry Miss Coombes."

Georgina winced. "What a disagreeable outcome for him. Besides, while that might keep Mr. Dalrymple alive, I fear it will not make him love *you*, Edmund. He favors ladies. Prudence told me." Georgina could not beat about the bush any longer with Edmund. If Mr. Dalrymple did not mean to quash Edmund's affections, she would have to do so on his behalf.

Edmund stiffened visibly but maintained a neutral expression. "Whatever the case, Georgina, I should like him to live."

She propped her chin on her hand. “I will try. But this timing is terrible.”

He blew his nose and jammed his handkerchief back in his pocket. “I knew I could rely on you.”

Georgina took inventory. Presently, she must prevent Arthur from being dispatched in the same fashion as her brother, continue to badger her father to depart town without alarming him, and bring down an illicit gambling den, all while preventing Colt from killing Mr. Dalrymple at a duel tomorrow morning. If she could also prevail upon Elizabeth to forgive the evils of her past, then she would be doing well indeed. She suddenly longed for the days of lying in uninterrupted, intoxicated bliss at Mem Lavigne’s. Georgina wished for sleep.

30

COLT'S EYES SNAPPED open, and he saw Sarah standing over him.

"What the devil . . . ?"

He tried to sit up. His duvet had fallen in a crumpled heap off the end of the bed during the night, and only a white sheet remained, covering the lower parts of his body. He valiantly tried to assemble his thoughts. This was certainly his bed. Whilst he welcomed Sarah's presence in his room, he could not account for it. The stab of pain in his left eye reminded him that he had indeed sustained a painful bruise at Lord Byron's ball.

Rather unexpectedly, Sarah slapped him across the face.

"Sarah!" He dodged out of the way of a second blow to his cheek. "What are you doing?" he asked, gripping both her wrists in his hand to avoid her striking him again.

"A duel, Robert? Really?"

"Oh, that," Colt replied in a sheepish tone, the corners of his mouth twitching.

"And over Miss Coombes, of all people. She is a fortune-hunter and a minx!" Sarah hissed. "You could have at least dueled over someone worthwhile."

"Are you jealous?"

Sarah jerked her wrists, trying to break free of him.

"I'm sorry," he answered with a little chuckle, tightening his grip. "It was not my doing. That young cub Dalrymple is at fault! I am blameless in the whole affair."

"I suppose you are not to blame for accosting Miss Coombes in the first place?"

Colt shrugged in response. "Some things are not as they seem."

"Do you love her?"

"What? No!"

"Release me. I will not beat you," she instructed, her voice frosty.

He complied, withdrawing back into the mess of his sheets.

"You say you do not love her, but you will risk your life for her?" Sarah rubbed her wrist where his fingers had been.

He compressed his lips together tightly. The notion that Dalrymple would best him in a duel was absurd. "There is hardly a risk of that, Sarah. And I mean it; this is not how it appears. It's a matter of honor now. I cannot withdraw. Would you have me look like a coward?"

"And is it not cowardly to duel with someone whose ability is vastly inferior to yours?"

"You think I'm superior?"

"You will not enjoy a life on the continent should you have to flee," she said in a soft, low voice. "Nor would you relish being hanged for murder."

Colt glanced at her lips. He yearned to kiss her. "Does that mean you would rather I die?"

"You know I would not. Ravenscroft has vowed to ensure your safety on that score."

"Ravenscroft?"

"Yes. He wrote to me this morning, advising me of all this nonsense. He is Dalrymple's second and will ensure his ward does not have a loaded gun. So, *you* must assure me that you will not take his life."

"I will not kill him, Sarah. What do you take me for?" Colt leaned back on one elbow, aware he had exposed his broad, bare chest. Maybe all this intense emotion could play out nicely for both of them. "And Ravenscroft came to you for help because—"

The color of Sarah's cheeks darkened prettily, and she faltered over her words. "I suppose he knows we are friends, and that you hold me in high regard."

"That I do."

His body responded intuitively to their proximity, and she glanced down at the moving sheet.

"Apologies," he said, abashed at the mound that stood beneath the linen covering.

"Send me a message tomorrow, after your duel," she instructed. "I must go."

"Would you care to stay awhile?" he asked, flashing his dimples.

"*Nothing* has changed, Colt. I fear that you simply do not know how," she murmured, her words barely audible, before leaving the room.

DAWN APPROACHED, AND the ghostly silhouettes of trees emerged through the early morning fog. The dim light revealed the shape of two enclosed carriages as they pulled up on the heath. From behind one, the figure of Colt emerged. He wore a greatcoat with many capes, and a top hat sat at a jaunty angle on his head.

Leggy followed close on his heels, uttering a few words of complaint about the blasted cold.

Colt already questioned his choice of second. He should have petitioned Georgina, but he did not wish to implicate her in any more illegal activities. In his view, further brushes with Bow Street might see her in significant trouble.

They bade the surgeon to wait for them in the carriage, assuring him that he would be called if someone required medical assistance. This proposition suited the mature gentleman, who snuggled back into the carriage with a hot brick at his feet and a small bottle of spirits clutched in his gloved hand.

Colt took a large swig from his own silver flask and offered it to Leggy, who drank from it readily. They waited patiently as Mr. Dalrymple and Lord Ravenscroft alighted from their own carriage.

Displaying an expression of grave dignity, Mr. Dalrymple lifted his chin and joined Colt and Leggy.

Lord Ravenscroft walked behind them. One hand leaned heavily upon his cane, while the other carried a heavy wooden case containing the pistols.

Lord Ravenscroft's eyes rested upon Colt, a glint of silent appeal within them.

Colt gave a slight nod of acknowledgement. Sarah had executed her task satisfactorily. Colt turned to Mr. Dalrymple. "Do you wish to apologize, whelp?"

Bristling at once, Mr. Dalrymple threw him a disgusted glare. "Never. You are depraved."

Colt shrugged. "So be it," he said and removed his coat.

The sound of hooves approaching through the mist made everyone suspend what they were doing. If the authorities came upon them now, it would be difficult to explain away their presence. They exchanged uneasy glances.

"Only one horse," Colt muttered to Leggy.

Through the mist, a sole rider became visible.

"George!" Colt exclaimed.

"Morning, chaps," she chirped, springing down from her horse. "Spot of hunting? Unusual location and weather for it, I must say."

Mr. Dalrymple swelled. "I beseech you not to interfere, Miss Pace. This is a matter between Coulthurst and myself."

"I wouldn't dream of it, my dear fellow." Georgina approached Colt and linked her arm through his. "But a word with my friend."

Unsure what peculiar nonsense she had taken into her head, Colt followed her away from the others.

"I cannot let you do this, Colt. Think of Sarah. I have a pistol. If necessary, I will abduct you."

His eyes widened. "The devil take you. You are not carrying me off, George! Of all the indignities you would subject me to. I am thinking of Sarah too."

Her blue eyes scanned him piercingly, even through the murky gray dawn. "But this appears to be about Miss Coombes."

"And one day you will hear the full story, but not now." He hushed his voice further still. "Believe me when I say that all is in hand. No one shall be shot today."

Georgina digested this assurance for a moment and finally nodded. She returned with him to the group. "And Leggy is your second?"

"I am. You can't elbow in, Miss Pace. Not the thing," he admonished. "Not when I came all this way. If you intended on doing that, you should have told me before I got out of bed this morning."

Colt clapped his indignant friend on the back. "No one is stopping you from being my second, Leggy."

It drizzled now, and Leggy went over to Lord Ravenscroft to inspect the pistols.

Lord Ravenscroft opened the boxes, at first allowing Leggy only a quick glimpse inside.

Leggy, taking the role of second seriously, insisted on retrieving both pistols from the box, one after the other. He even crouched down on the ground so that he could inspect the barrels and triggers of each, to ensure perfect uniformity.

Colt met Lord Ravenscroft's eyes once more and took an additional swig from his flask. Georgina watched on with a critical eye.

After examining the dueling pistols to his ultimate satisfaction and identifying nothing amiss, Leggy stood up, returned them to the box and randomly selected one for Colt. He did not see the slight jerking movement from Lord Ravenscroft behind him, who attempted to direct him to the loaded one. But it was too late.

Leggy had already grasped the gilt-engraved handle of what must have been the unloaded pistol and placed it confidently into his friend's hand.

Colt, who *had* noticed Lord Ravenscroft's slight look of alarm, accepted the underweight gun warily.

Instead of coming to his immediate aid, Lord Ravenscroft hurried over to his ward, who retrieved the remaining pistol from the box with a shaking hand. Mr. Dalrymple forced a timid smile up at his guardian. Lord Ravenscroft murmured something to him and patted him on the back.

Colt threw one final, accusatory glare at Lord Ravenscroft before moving to his position with his back to Mr. Dalrymple.

Georgina cast her eyes between Colt and Mr. Dalrymple.

As Leggy signaled for the duel to commence, Colt cursed and paced forward.

The distance increased between the opponents, and the mist rose in a merciful shield, somewhat obscuring Colt's figure from view.

When they turned to face each other, he leveled his pistol in futility, not even bothering to cock it, knowing it to be completely empty of bullets.

Through the fog, a piercing crack sounded as Mr. Dalrymple fired his pistol in the direction of his adversary.

Colt dropped his gun to the ground as pain shot up his forearm. The blasted young cub had struck him. Blood oozed through his white shirt, turning it a bright shade of crimson, and he clutched his arm near the elbow to stem blood loss as much as possible.

He heard Georgina's voice—in a much higher pitch than normal—scream his name. She was the first to reach him and supported his arm as he crumpled to the ground.

The other parties rushed to them.

Leggy released a small cry of despair, followed by a little gagging cough, then lurched off towards a nearby pile of rocks to cast up his accounts.

Lord Ravenscroft crouched down with a wince and unfurled his neckcloth to use it as a tourniquet, knotting it tightly around Colt's arm.

With an open mouth and unblinking eyes, Mr. Dalrymple watched on in shock. He stepped backwards, distancing himself in horror.

"Get the doctor," Lord Ravenscroft instructed his ward.

Colt watched as Mr. Dalrymple dropped the gun at his feet and bolted towards the carriages. He felt close to passing out.

Georgina ripped Colt's waistcoat open and removed his cravat. She bunched it up and compressed it over the wound firmly. He gritted his teeth as pain coursed through his body.

The only sounds now came from Colt, who panted gently, and Leggy, whose heaving noises continued from behind the boulders.

"I did not intend for this to happen," Ravenscroft murmured.

"A fine punishment for dallying with your sister, Hester, I thought," Colt gasped.

"I should not be so ignoble, Coulthurst. Not even to you. That damned fool Leggett gave you the wrong gun for a start, and that's the first time Lawrence has ever hit something. Mighty bad luck, is all."

"Get me patched up, then take your honorable ward and go away," Colt growled. "He's lucky it's only my arm."

Lord Ravenscroft nodded.

Dalrymple returned with the surgeon, who first set about making Colt comfortable. He administered a laudanum remedy at once and assessed the wound. The surgeon advised immediate treatment to remove any bullet fragments and suggested if he could make Colt comfortable, he would optimally transfer him to a more discreet location, such as his home, to conduct the procedure.

The doctor's voice tapered off and panic once again stilled the group as the distinct rumble of a carriage drawing closer interrupted them once more. There could be no explaining away their presence to the authorities, not with a man injured from a bullet wound.

Colt threw a desperate look up into Georgina's face. "Ride away."

"I'm not leaving," she said through her teeth.

Everyone stood motionless. No one moved to abandon Colt.

The dark carriage emerged through the mist and rocked to a halt.

Excellent. Now he would be arrested for illegal dueling.

GEORGINA PULLED COLT up to support him on her knees, and he winced from the pain. The blood from the wound at least was starting to subside, though he did not like his chances of survival if the authorities carried him off.

A petite figure shrouded in a heavy black cloak tumbled out of the newly arrived carriage.

The mysterious figure floated across the damp grass, her hood obscuring her features until she reached them and pushed it back to reveal fair hair, a pale complexion, and blue eyes stretched wide in the drizzling rain. The group let out a communal sigh of relief.

"Miss Coombes!" Her name tumbled out of Mr. Dalrymple's mouth.

The young lady moved towards them, wringing her hands. As she came closer, she released a strangled sob. "Lord Coulthurst!"

Colt flinched, wishing the doctor had carried him away from the scene with greater alacrity. All of London would descend upon them before too long.

"This is not the place for you, Emily. You must go home," Georgina insisted, continuing to hold the cloth to Colt's wound.

"Lord Coulthurst should never have been called out. This was all a terrible mistake. Everything occurred so quickly." She plucked a handkerchief from her reticule and dabbed her nose. "I feel as though I have been swept up in the relentless winds of a battering storm."

Colt cursed. If she meant to wax lyrical about her emotions, he wished for someone to dispatch him properly. "Kill me now, George," he begged. "Get the gun now. Or use yours. I don't care."

"Would you like to return to town with my guardian and me?" Mr. Dalrymple offered Miss Coombes.

She shot him a severe stare. "I hope you have learned your lesson, Mr. Dalrymple."

His longing expression faded to one of bewilderment.

"You have no business meddling in other people's affairs. Had I wanted you to duel his lordship, I would have asked you to. It was extremely presumptuous of you. If my brother was more athletically inclined, I would instruct him to thrash you for your impertinence," she snapped.

Mr. Dalrymple's mouth dropped open, nonplussed. "I—I meant to be chivalrous."

"Your chivalry is unwanted and entirely misplaced."

The hue of Mr. Dalrymple's dark brown skin reddened in his cheeks. "Then, might I deduce, Miss Coombes, that you have no feelings for me?"

She gave a derisive laugh. "You? Naturally, I do not have feelings for you. My heart belongs to another!"

Colt's breathing grew labored. Despite the pressure Georgina had applied to the wound, he began to feel quite giddy. And he could not mistake that Miss Coombes was gazing at him wistfully. Her smile scattered his already disordered thoughts.

Miss Coombes had not finished berating Mr. Dalrymple, however. "How could you entertain such a notion, anyway? And what about poor Lord Telford? You have allowed him to believe he had hopes with you, and now you propose to cast him aside! I have a good mind to tell *him* of your underhanded ways."

"I understand I have made a terrible mistake, Miss Coombes."

"Yes, I believe you have. It is therefore fortunate that no one was seriously injured today."

"Indeed, you are right, Miss Coombes. I shall trouble you with my suit no further," said Mr. Dalrymple, casting a brooding look down at Colt, cradled on the ground by Georgina.

"For goodness's sake, Ravenscroft, take that petulant boy away. We have no further need of either of you," Colt snapped.

Lord Ravenscroft nodded and led his ward off towards his carriage.

The doctor had secured a temporary bandage over the wound, though from the dizziness he experienced when trying to sit up, Colt suspected he had already lost quite a lot of blood.

Miss Coombes crouched near him and tried to take his hand. "Please, Lord Coulthurst, allow me to express my appreciation to you for coming here today to defend my honor," she breathed, her tongue peeping out to moisten her lips.

Of all the misguided moments to make overtures to someone. Colt grimaced. "That is unnecessary, Miss Coombes. We should all feel fortunate that it settled as it has, and no one ended up fatally injured. So far, anyway."

She gave him a reassuring smile. "I know you must wish to be more *discreet* in the future. Duels at dawn are not the thing. I would like to spend more time with you . . . *alone*. So I can express my gratitude."

Colt saw Georgina roll her eyes.

"Miss Coombes, there is no future for the two of us, and I have no intention of being alone with you. I need you to understand that you should not pursue the matter further."

"But . . . I thought you loved me?" she asked, a little more desperately, her cheeks coloring. She regarded him imploringly.

He frowned. "I said nothing of the sort."

"You dueled for me! How can you *not* love me?" Her shrill voice echoed across the stillness of the cold and rainy heath.

"I dueled *because* of you, Miss Coombes. Not *for* you. One of your beaus forced a quarrel upon me, and we are all fortunate in how it turned out. Or I hope I will be." He winced as the doctor tried to readjust how he was sitting. "I happily admit that I have behaved inappropriately in the past. Given I have been called to account for compromising you and have spilled my blood for it, I see the matter as concluded."

Miss Coombes opened her mouth to argue further, but Georgina interjected in a firm tone. "Emily, go home now, or I will tell your mother everything you have been up to, and she will send you back to the country."

With a wail of despair, Miss Coombes clutched her cloak around her and swept back to her carriage, which trundled away soon after.

Leggy emerged from the rocks, the smattering of freckles on his nose standing out against his unusually white cheeks. He kept his eyes averted, and Colt was sure he could not manage the sight of blood without vomiting. Georgina reluctantly agreed to let Leggy ride her own horse back to town, while she accompanied Colt and the doctor in the carriage to Jermyn Street.

Once stored in the safety of his coach, with the doctor administering additional laudanum and Georgina providing moral support and comfort, Colt drifted into sedated sleep, satisfied he had discharged the debt of honor.

31

ONCE GEORGINA CONFIRMED that Colt was no longer in danger of losing his life, she rushed home, hoping this near-miss would help him realize how dangerous his games could be. For now, *her* time was running out.

When she arrived home, she delivered her mare, Artemis, into the hands of the trusty Buckby, and strode into her house, clutching her gloves and whip in one hand. She had made it through the entryway when she heard an imperative "Psst!" coming from the hall cupboard.

After their recent escapade landed her in prison, Georgina did not wish to provide Joshua with further opportunities to embroil her in any more scrapes. An immediate sense of foreboding overcame her at his unexpected summons from the wardrobe.

"Yes, Joshua?"

"The bleedin' crooks came back. Saw the guv'nor. Gave him a right fright, they did. Him having no clue about what happened this last week!"

She was too late. They were wasting no time following through on their promise. "Where is my father? Is he hurt?"

He gestured to the parlor with his thumb.

"Joshua, run and fetch a doctor at once. Ask the footman where best to find her," she instructed him.

Without removing her coat, Georgina dashed across the hall, her legs starting to feel numb beneath her. Her stomach churned. She should not have heeded her father's trivial complaints about leaving town. Had she only bundled him into the carriage yesterday, they could have avoided this.

Georgina entered the parlor and saw her father hunched over on the couch. Jarvis hovered nearby with a grim frown, and a maid was stoking the fire.

Georgina rushed to him and as she got nearer, memories of Henry flooded her mind. Her heart pounded with each step.

Silas's normally rosy face was pale, and he jumped when the door behind her hit the wall with a loud thud. He had a glass of brandy in his hand, which was trembling.

Georgina crouched at his feet. "Are you all right? What happened?"

When he did not speak, she looked up at Jarvis, who shrugged. "We attempted to keep them out, Miss, but they pushed their way in."

She swallowed hard. "Are you injured? I've sent for a doctor."

"I am not harmed, just a little shaken up." His voice quivered.

"Who came here, Papa?" she asked, deliberately controlling her tone and keeping it as level as possible. She did not want him to see her wrath.

He scratched his head. "There were four of them. Two gentlemen—Montgomery and Ellis, I believe they were. And then another two distasteful types."

Georgina clutched the armrest of the sofa, her knuckles turning milky white. "And what did they want?"

"I can't say any of it made sense. Something about a faro box. I told them we have nothing like that here."

The knot in her belly tightened. In her stubborn efforts to hold them to account, she had put her father in harm's way.

"Is that all they said?" Her voice did not sound like it belonged to her.

"They hoped to see you soon."

"I bet they did," Georgina murmured under her breath. She looked up into her father's eyes and read disappointment and fear within them. She had failed him. "Are you sure they did not harm you?"

He cleared his throat. "Well, I'm not as young as I used to be, George, or I might have taken my chances against them." He looked down at his shaking hands. "Fact is, they knocked me off balance, and I fell and hit my head. Not a fair fight, mind you."

Watching him try to preserve his dignity pulled at her heart like an anchor. "I want the doctor to examine you, nevertheless." She fought back tears of rage. "This was never meant to happen." She took his free hand and pressed it.

"What trouble have you brought upon yourself? I fear for you, George. Your ways. The running about town. And now it appears you are in difficulties beyond anything I thought possible." He shuddered. "One of them had Henry's watch, George."

She kissed his knuckles, squeezing his hand tightly. "The situation is complicated. It should never, *ever* have involved you. I am deeply sorry that I allowed this to happen." She released his hand, stood up, and went to pour herself some whiskey. One hand balled into a fist at her side as her thoughts rushed to vengeance.

Silas's eyes widened as he watched her guzzle the glass of liquid in one go.

"I shall make amends and ensure this nonsense stops." Georgina turned to Jarvis. "Stay with him until the doctor comes. I will be home in a while." She set down the glass and, without another look, marched out of the room, riding crop still in hand. She made a quick detour via her library before heading for the front door.

"Oi, Missus, do you need me? I'm small, but I'm as good in a mill as the next man!" Joshua piped up behind her.

"Not this time, Joshua," Georgina yelled over her shoulder as she rushed out. His solidarity in matters of potential bloodshed endeared him further, but she would not put him in danger.

In the street, she hailed the first passing hackney and climbed inside. "St James's Square."

A NOW-FAMILIAR ATTENDANT—NOT the pretty one, unfortunately—opened the door to Georgina and regarded her warily. She smiled broadly and assured him she had a gift for Mrs. Gardner and her friends and wished to surprise them with it. He stepped aside and allowed Georgina to enter, guiding her to a sitting room.

Georgina strode across the threshold, her footsteps echoing off the walls as she shut the door behind her with a heavy thud. Mrs. Gardner, in a gown of mauve cotton, sat placidly in a thick satin chair, and Ellis and Montgomery lounged side by side on a sofa across from her.

Georgina's stomach lurched when she saw Elizabeth seated opposite them. Attired in a muslin walking dress and gray spencer coat, the Countess cut an elegant shape as she held a cup of tea delicately in her lap.

"How cozy," Georgina murmured. She remembered her father's trembling hand holding his tumbler, and how his glasses sat skewed on the bridge of his nose. He had become an unwilling pawn in this vicious game, which amplified her need for retribution. Yet, here sat Elizabeth, taking tea with the very people behind her father's suffering. *Indeed, the very people behind my brother's death.* Just how complicit was she? Warmth flooded Georgina's face.

Elizabeth inclined her head, brow furrowed.

Ellis rubbed his hands together, as though he had successfully snared some prey in a trap. "Well, well, well, Miss Pace. What a pleasure. We missed you this morning when we called. I am so glad you have joined us. *Have* you decided to return Mrs. Gardner's faro box?"

Georgina's eyes flashed. Her fingers tightened around her whip, but her left hand reached across her and withdrew the faro box from the deep pocket of her long greatcoat. "This? Indeed, yes. You can have it back."

She walked slowly in Elizabeth's direction, almost enjoying the glint of dismay in her bright gray eyes as she tracked the hand holding the whip. At least something rattled her. Did she expect Georgina to strike her after everything they shared?

Very gently, Georgina placed the faro box down on the table beside Elizabeth, tilting her head slightly to one side. The calmer she remained, the more Elizabeth's discomfort appeared to grow.

Georgina turned back to Ellis and Montgomery. "Now, I would like Mr. Coombes's vowels."

Montgomery lifted his brows in surprise. "You have not yet supplied what is owed. We stipulated *today*, Miss Pace."

Georgina shrugged. "The vowels are invalid, procured using illegitimate means."

"You will struggle to prove that, Miss Pace," Montgomery continued. "This affair need never have become such a spectacle, had *you* not made it so. Mr. Coombes would have learned his lesson, paid his debts in due course, and all would have been forgotten."

"Unless the accrued interest proved beyond *his* means, in which case he would have found himself at the bottom of the Thames," Georgina murmured.

"If you are so concerned about that outcome, then I would encourage you to settle his score—and the future interest—today," Ellis added, his tone so saccharine-sweet it made Georgina sick.

"No. I am done with helping." Georgina ensured her voice remained level and devoid of emotion. "I am washing my hands of it all now."

"After all of this?" Montgomery demanded, a confused crease in his brow.

"There you go again, failing to protect people, Miss Pace," Ellis remarked. "It's rather pitiful."

Elizabeth interjected. "Ellis! On the contrary—"

"With due respect, Countess, it's only that Miss Pace's track record is . . . poor. After all, the night Henry tragically died, he'd pledged to bring his sister with him to help settle his accounts."

"*Beloved Henry*," Montgomery corrected, maligning the inscription on Georgina's fob watch. He withdrew it from his pocket as if to check the time.

Georgina knew what was coming next. She wanted to beg them to stop, but she held firm, unwilling to give them another such victory over her.

"Don't." Elizabeth spoke firmly, but they did not heed her.

"Sadly, Miss Pace had cried off. *Une affaire de cœur*, I believe it was," Montgomery added.

Georgina inhaled sharply and felt her reliable Manton's boxlock pistol sway in her pocket. She had packed it for the duel that morning, ostensibly to abduct Colt if necessary. It might yet become useful.

She thought she caught a pitying look from Elizabeth and could not abide. "It was not even that. Just a fuck. And not even a particularly good one."

This remark caught the group off guard. Mrs. Gardner uttered a tiny cry, Elizabeth brought a hand to her mouth, and Ellis and Montgomery exchanged a bemused glance. Seeing the men smile, Georgina's fury overtook her. She raised her riding crop in her right hand and thrashed it hard across Montgomery's unsuspecting face.

Before either shocked gentleman could respond, Georgina raised her booted right foot and ground it down onto Montgomery's lap, pinning him to the sofa, while deftly pulling the pistol from her left pocket. She cocked it the required two times with her thumb and pointed it at Ellis's head. Her whip hovered in the air, poised to strike again at Montgomery.

"Speaking of family, how *dare* you harm my father? Your quarrel is with *me*, you *filthy* vultures!"

The whites of Ellis's eyes bulged, fixed upon the pistol, while Montgomery recoiled from the whip, tiny drops of sweat forming along his brow. His mouth hung open.

"You are pathetic. I wager you *always* task others to do the dirty jobs for you. Keeping your soft hands clean." The sound of her own quick pulse throbbed in Georgina's ears, urging her to release her wrath. She saw Arthur, her father, and Henry all muddied together in her mind's eye, and the room went red. She wanted to punish these quivering men.

"Don't be like them, Georgina," Elizabeth said quietly behind her. "Do not make a mistake you will come to regret."

Of all the things to say at this moment. "Have you not just heard the truth of what I did to Henry? I *only* make mistakes. I told you I am beyond redemption." Georgina hated that her voice cracked, wishing to feel only anger.

"And I still don't believe that." Elizabeth moved closer now until she was standing alongside Georgina.

Georgina glanced up, blinking back tears, pistol still pointed at Ellis. "Your words mean nothing to me."

Elizabeth's lips trembled, but she maintained her composure. "I will ensure the vowels are returned to you, and none of this need ever be discussed again. Correct, gentlemen?"

Both Ellis and Montgomery nodded in agreement.

Georgina struggled to reconcile the Elizabeth who had held her, cared for her, with the lady who was now protecting these fiends. She labored to breathe, her lungs full of ice.

Elizabeth put a hand on top of Georgina's that held the pistol, and the radiating warmth from her skin gave Georgina a shock. It wasn't the first time this hand had covered hers.

"You are defending these people?" Georgina said softly, maintaining her hold on the gun.

"I need to protect people too," Elizabeth responded. She uncocked the pistol and lowered Georgina's hand, yet did not try to wrest the gun from her.

A new pang of hurt struck Georgina. It was true; Elizabeth was protecting Mrs. Gardner. Georgina took a step back from Elizabeth and looked at Mrs. Gardner, her thoughts racing to piece together the connection between the pair. Were they lovers? Or worse, co-conspirators? Had Colt's insinuations been correct all along, and she had been so blinded by her own feelings that she failed to see?

"Get that woman out of here!" Mrs. Gardner's shrieking voice broke through Georgina's thoughts.

"Hold your tongue," Elizabeth growled.

"Is that really how you want to talk to your whore?" Georgina demanded.

Mrs. Gardner shot her a satisfied smile, folding her arms across her chest. "Elizabeth might talk to me however she wants to. Our bond is unbreakable, and the likes of *you* will never stand between us—"

"Hush, woman!" Elizabeth interrupted.

"Countess, what is to be done about Mr. Coombes's debts?" Ellis asked, emboldened now that a pistol was not leveled at his face.

Georgina made an abrupt movement towards him, threatening him with the crop.

He whimpered and put his hands up in front of his face.

"We *agreed* it would be resolved by the end of the day!" Elizabeth replied curtly through gritted teeth. "Georgina, did they harm your father?"

It took a moment for Georgina to trust her voice enough to speak. "He is alive, but they have shaken him up badly. Luckily, they took a gentler approach to my father than they used against me."

"You told me a footpad had set upon you."

Georgina shrugged. She doubted telling Elizabeth the truth back then would have changed this outcome.

"I know vengeance feels like the answer, Georgina, but this is not *you*."

"Stop pretending to know me, Elizabeth. You do not know who I am, just as I am realizing how little I truly know you. I thought you had integrity, for example."

Georgina knew she would not shoot Lord Ellis. She was no murderer. But she'd had enough of Elizabeth's moral high ground.

"Georgina, please go before you do something you might come to regret." Elizabeth's calm voice barely registered through the loud thrumming noise in Georgina's head. "Go now."

Georgina stared at Elizabeth. "I came to trust you. I believed you were honorable. *This* is your choice?"

Elizabeth sighed. "There is no choice to be made, Georgina. I wish you would see that." With a gentle palm on her back, she propelled Georgina towards the door and flung it open.

Georgina wished to resist, but all the energy had evaporated from her body. She allowed Elizabeth to guide her to the front exit, then glanced back over her shoulder towards the parlor.

"You cannot mean that you have washed your hands of Arthur?" Elizabeth asked, as they arrived at the front door. The attendants discreetly made themselves scarce.

"Why not? I could have returned the money to Arthur many times over. Or paid Mrs. Gardner if that would have settled it. This is not about the money. It's about justice. I have proven myself incapable of getting those notes back in Arthur's hands, the one thing that would have brought him comfort and satisfaction. I cannot help him anymore, and I will not lose anything else." Georgina paused, an unbidden tear creeping into her eye. "If something happens to him, I hope you will consider the part you have played in it."

Elizabeth regarded her in the thoughtful way that usually filled Georgina with warmth and desire. Today, she felt crushed. "Nothing will happen to Arthur. And I will ensure his notes are returned, as I always said I would, if you wanted me to. I wish you had been able to see the whole truth. Perhaps then you would not assume the worst of me."

The muscle twitched in Georgina's cheek. "After everything you profess to stand for, I am stunned that you would let them get away with this behavior." She gave Elizabeth a measured look. "And *you* continue to underestimate me, Elizabeth. I am not done here. Again, I tell you: I do not lose. I recommend getting yourself home."

Georgina marched out of the front door, slamming it behind her. She hailed herself the first hackney she could find. Then, in the privacy of the solitary conveyance, Georgina wept. Indeed, Elizabeth had made a choice.

32

BY THE TIME her cab arrived at Bow Street, Georgina had wiped her face and nose and collected herself enough to present a dignified front. It had only been four days since she found herself confined in the filthy prison cells below. No thanks to her young friend Joshua. She smiled at the thought of him and wished to be able to give the child a firm, comforting cuddle right at this moment.

Dismissing this curious impulse, Georgina made her way inside and asked the duty administrator to speak with Mr. Gibbs. They gave her a doubtful look and said it may not be possible, as Mr. Gibbs was particularly busy at the moment. Not wishing to be dismissed out of hand, Georgina asked for them to please tell Mr. Gibbs that if he did not attend to her immediately, the Thames might soon run red with claret, and it would be entirely his fault.

The summons proved most effective, and a grinning Mr. Gibbs soon emerged from a nearby office, greeting Georgina almost as a friend, not a former inmate. Georgina keenly felt the privilege of her social standing.

"Please, Mr. Gibbs, I need to speak with you privately on a matter of grave importance and urgency."

He escorted her into his office, a room sparsely furnished with a large, scratched desk covered in paperwork, two wooden chairs that suggested practicality over comfort, and a sad potted plant withering away in the corner.

"You do not have your small accomplice with you today?"

"No, I *hope* he is safe at home, stealing only muffins from the cook."

Once they settled opposite each other at the desk, Mr. Gibbs steepled his fingers together and prompted her to tell him how he might assist.

She inhaled. This could sound like one of Joshua's tales, so she had to do her best to lay out the details in a believable manner. "There is an illegal gaming house on St James's Square. It is called 'Solitaires.'"

Mr. Gibbs leaned in. "I know of it, but it is a fortress we have not yet managed to breach. Tell me more."

"A young friend of mine, born a miris, was lately taken there and exploited out of a huge sum of money—tricked into writing promissory notes with outrageous terms. Despite my best attempts to settle the debt and avoid the exorbitant costs of those terms, the house would not allow it. I then uncovered other deviant practices they employ, including devices doctored to favor the house, and so forth." Georgina wrung her hands. "I confess, I *did* steal one such item, a faro box, to inspect it and prove its trick. I hoped my possession of the box would persuade the proprietors to return my friend's notes."

Mr. Gibbs rested his elbow on the desk, rapt.

"It was only then I discovered that the enterprise was much more sinister and far-reaching than I imagined. The individuals behind the gaming house sent someone to rough me up. I'm sure Joshua would have a much more colorful description for it if he were here. The henchman did this to me." She revealed what remained of the bruises on her neck. "And that is where you came into the story.

Convinced that I needed protection, my little champion Joshua encouraged me to seek out someone of equally dubious character, hence our meeting and my subsequent arrest that day."

"Do you still have the faro box?"

"No."

Mr. Gibbs returned a dramatic sigh. "That would have been useful evidence! How can I track these people?"

"Mr. Gibbs, I have not finished," Georgina said breathlessly. "The people you are looking for are Lord Ellis and Mr. Montgomery, and potentially one Mrs. Gardner. She is the hostess of Solitaires, but frankly, I think she just does their bidding. I have good reason to believe that these men and their menials were also responsible for the murder of my brother, Mr. Henry Pace, eight years ago."

Mr. Gibbs sat back in his chair and puffed air out through his lips. "Come now, Miss Pace. This is becoming quite the tale. What makes you believe the crimes are connected?"

"The brute who accosted me confessed that he participated in the act. I could identify him, without a doubt, and both Montgomery and Ellis gloated about their role in his death."

His brows were arched high, quite stunned. "Why would they suddenly do that, Miss Pace? And is there proof?"

"Henry's watch. They admitted everything after I saw Montgomery with Henry's fob watch. It went missing the night he died. If *that* is not sufficient evidence, I believe Mrs. Gardner might provide a witness statement confirming the nature of their activities, including confessions made in her earshot during the time she worked for them—in exchange for your protection, of course." Georgina covered her mouth with her hand, concealing a slight smile. She sniffled dramatically, wondering fleetingly if she'd missed a calling as an actress. Then she sobered. "Finally, they violently threatened my father, only this morning. So, with lives at stake, I returned the faro box to them less than an hour ago."

As she spoke, Mr. Gibbs nodded passionately. "If we can recover the faro box and the watch, and gather witness testimony, there may be enough evidence, Miss Pace."

Georgina felt hope rise within her. "I wish for justice for Henry. Whatever I can do to bring my father peace." She stood up and shook his hand across the table.

He walked with her to the door and paused with his hand on the handle. "Miss Pace, I admire your persistence. You've taken on a great risk to yourself."

A tense pause followed, and Georgina moistened her lips. "They killed him, Mr. Gibbs. And there will be others if someone does not stop them."

He nodded. "Then they shall be stopped."

"Good man." Georgina clapped his arm and left the room.

Georgina's scheme, hatched well before the night she played hazard with those odious men, was finally about to unfold. While she hated to be away from Henry's watch, she thought her brother would be proud. He always did love a gambit.

BY THE TIME Georgina returned home, dark clouds cast a morose shadow over London, and a heavy rain poured down from above. She joined her father in the parlor, still resting where she had left him. Regardless of the faith she had placed in Mr. Gibbs, she still had a duty to send him away to Yorkshire to guarantee his safety.

Silas had composed himself while she had been out, and the color had returned to his cheeks. He had patted down his wispy hair, and a restorative glass of brandy had seen him feeling a lot better.

It surprised her to learn he had already instructed Mr. Walker to prepare his belongings, ready to embark on the first leg of the journey that very afternoon. The weather did not promote favorable travelling conditions, but they might have made some inroads on the long trip ahead of them.

At least now there was no duplicity between them. He took her in his arms and held her close. "Might you not come with me, George?" he begged.

She pressed her cheek against his broad chest, feeling for a moment like a child again. The fabric of his waistcoat brushed softly against her ear. "I cannot, Papa. There are things I must settle in town." When she looked up at him, tears glistened on the ends of his eyelashes.

He sniffled. "It's only that. . . . Well. Henry. Oh, George, I cannot lose you too."

Georgina grabbed him against her in a fierce hug. "Nothing is going to happen to me, my darling. I promise you. But before you leave town, there is one thing I need you to do. Stop in at the Bow Street Magistrate on your way and make an official statement about what happened here this morning. Ask for Mr. Gibbs. Ensure that you describe Ellis and Montgomery and the attacker, in every detail, including all that they said about me, that they had your deceased son's watch, everything." She bit her lip. "Just don't mention that I have had possession of Henry's fob these last eight years; that bit of information is *unnecessary* to the case. Understand? You do this, Papa, and this will help settle the matter once and for all. Finally, we will have justice for Henry."

Silas pledged to do so faithfully and kissed his daughter's forehead. She was grateful for his trust.

Within an hour, Georgina watched her father's traveling carriage disappear along Half Moon Street with a smile of grim relief. At least she did not have to fear for him anymore. He would be safely out of London soon, away from anyone's reach.

Georgina hurried upstairs to change. She had been away from Mem Lavigne's for too long. There she could at least rest her crusade against Ellis's and Montgomery's corrupt empire and perhaps find solace from the heartache caused by Elizabeth's betrayal.

Her fascination with Elizabeth had clouded her perception. If she was honest, it was more than fascination—she had cared deeply for the woman. But the evidence of her involvement with Mrs. Gardner was indisputable, and she had made her allegiance clear.

While she hoped Elizabeth had heeded her warning to leave the establishment with haste so as not to end up at Bow Street, Georgina must forget about Lady Mortimer from this point forward. Amidst the familiar surroundings at Mem Lavigne's, Georgina hoped to seek refuge from her troubled heart.

33

ONCE THE INITIAL doses of laudanum had worn off, Colt scribbled Sarah the note she had requested, confirming that he still lived and so too did his opponent. With the help of a sizeable glass of whiskey, he fell into a disturbed slumber.

Colt had expected Sarah to call the following day, but she did not. She failed to send him a response at all. As another day went by, he grew disconsolate, as doubt cast a shadow over their once cherished friendship. Did she not care for him at all? Was her judgment of him harsh enough to keep her away?

Miss Coombes had hounded him after the duel until he was forced to be uncivil. At least it had brought the matter to a head, however uncomfortable it proved to be for them both. Despite his years assisting young ladies with their sexual awakenings, it still surprised him when one was conceited enough to believe she would be the one to tame him. Miss Coombes had proved the most coercive of them all. In the end, Colt felt he'd walked away with his honor intact.

After several days of convalescing in bed, the doctor confirmed that his wound was healing nicely, and he showed no signs of having developed an infection. Colt therefore arrived at Sarah's residence in

Curzon Street that evening, shoulders back and head held high, determined to discuss where he stood with her. He had an important question to ask her. One he should have asked a long time ago.

The night brought with it heavy rain and gusty wind. As he hurried from his carriage, Colt became rather wet, having left his umbrella at home. Upon entering Sarah's house, a footman relieved him of his belongings and led him into Sarah's inviting sitting room.

When Colt sauntered in, Sarah gasped in surprise. She sat at a small desk off to the side of the room, close to the crackling fire, apparently writing some letters. Not prepared to receive visitors, she wore a plain dress of dove gray and a lace shawl draped over her arms. She stood up and adjusted her skirt about her. "Good evening, Robert. Your Madeira is vastly superior. I cannot think you are here to sample mine?"

"I would most willingly share your Madeira, Sarah," he said, playing along.

She poured them both wine, but her hands quivered, and a few drops spilled onto the table.

Colt waited for her to be seated before he sat down across from her.

"You survived the duel, I collect?" she remarked. "I am sure everyone is grateful for your restraint in not murdering Mr. Dalrymple."

Colt was relieved she had some feeling about it. "Restraint seems an ironic term. I had every intention of doing what was requested, but as luck would have it, that damned fool Leggy gave *me* the empty pistol, so I was denied the opportunity. Dalrymple shot me instead."

Sarah stiffened. "Are you all right?"

"Thankfully, he is not a good marksperson. I shall mend soon enough." He took a large sip and refocused on his objective. "I wanted to talk to you about a few things."

"I'm listening."

He wished she would show some emotion. That would make this conversation much easier. "It will please you to know that I have ended the dalliance with Miss Coombes."

Sarah's stony expression did not change. "Indeed? I daresay that is in everyone's best interests. Are you able to cope with the disappointment?"

Colt regarded her closely. Did she really suspect that he had a sincere attachment to Miss Coombes? "It may surprise you to learn that I had no feelings vested in the matter, so I shall endure admirably."

Her eyes flashed, then met his with a hard look. "I am not at all surprised, Robert. You are the only person I know who lives to indulge respectable young ladies and risk ruining them with no compunction, if given half the chance."

An unexpected shiver of shame swept over him. "I cannot deny this. I have been a wretch. But I wish to make amends."

"To *all* of them?"

"To you, Sarah. I have been insufferable to you. At every chance, you have given me your wise counsel, yet I have acted foolishly. I have used the affections and reputations of these ladies to make myself feel alive. Never was there a more selfish soul than I."

She looked surprised. "And this admission should be enough to absolve you, by your reckoning?"

He paused, unsure of what he might say to convince her of his earnestness. "I recognize I am not worthy of absolution. But a chance, Sarah, to prove myself to you. . . ."

Sarah swallowed. "Are you hoping to continue our friendship?"

He sank to his knees at her feet. "I hope to marry you, Sarah. *And* continue our friendship."

She gasped and clapped a hand across her mouth. "Colt, don't!"

"Will you marry me?" he pushed, his eyes locked with hers.

She shook her head. "You cannot bully me, Robert."

"I do not wish to do that. But you are not listening to me," he insisted.

"I am listening to you, Robert. But I am saying *no*."

Colt stared at her, crestfallen, before rising to his feet. He turned his back to her and stood by the fire. He dragged his hand through his hair. What else could he do to persuade her that they were meant to be together?

"You cannot deny the passion between us, Sarah. I have thought of little else since that night at Vauxhall. Since we met, damn it."

"Except for those moments when Miss Coombes was in your arms at Byron's."

He spun around to her again. "You and everyone else seem so quick to condemn me on that head. For the record, I did not take her in my arms that night. I understand that might be difficult to believe. In fact, my past behavior aligns with the accusations leveled against me. But upon my life, what happened in that room was a misunderstanding." He moved to sit beside her, taking her hand.

"She appeared to faint, and when I came to help her, she attempted to kiss me. I was trying to extricate myself from *her* arms, but it was at that unfortunate moment that her scorned beau intervened." Just saying the words, Colt had to admit, it sounded like hogwash. "There was no way of escaping the challenge without impugning her reputation further. I could not well tell him that she was endeavoring to kiss *me*."

He sighed. "Had I not already somewhat dallied with her on prior occasions, I should have been more persistent in denying the allegation. But I simply could not bring myself to blame her. It was entirely my fault for allowing her to entertain hopes about me. So, I accepted the punishment."

Sarah considered him. "Why should I believe you?"

"Because I have never lied to you, Sarah. And I never will."

"You crave novelty and excitement, Robert. While I might seem special now, you would quickly realize how dull I am. Then you would seek someone new to play with."

"I am inclined to disagree with you. I will be devoted to you."

"Why? Because I fucked you?"

Colt smiled, his cheeks warming at her frank words. He knew in every fiber of his being that her assessment was incorrect. Over the years, she had become his closest companion. He spent so many hours walking the parks with her, teasing her with playful banter, and shocking her with his latest exploits. They attended house parties in the country and enjoyed nights where they stayed up until the small hours, long after the other guests retired. There were the many mornings she called upon him when he was still abed, unwell from the excessive diversions of the previous night, and she made him feel better with hot coffee and a cold compress.

He recalled the Christmas they enjoyed together when they found themselves snowed in on their way back to town from a shooting party in Scotland. They stopped at an inn and cultivated Christmas cheer using some spruce branches and a few candles, then shared a cozy meal and innumerable glasses of aromatic mulled wine. They sang traditional Christmas carols with their indifferent voices and exchanged one soft, lingering kiss. He had wanted to make love to her that night, but she had hastily withdrawn. Everything they had ever done together culminated in this moment.

"Because you are my best friend, Sarah. You have tolerated me, looked after me, scolded me when I deserved it, and made me want to better myself. Being intimate not only showed me how well-matched we are, but it also allowed me to hope. Please listen to me,

Sarah. I will do whatever is needed to prove to you that I have changed." He kissed her knuckles. "I will be attentive and loyal and patient. I am yours."

As he spoke, a smile slowly formed on Sarah's lips, like a curtain pulled to unveil a masterpiece. Tears glistened on the tips of her eyelashes. "I suspect patience is not something you have in abundance, Robert."

"And yet, I will wait forever if I have to."

"You will wait?"

He nodded and kissed her lightly on the lips. "As long as you need," he promised. "My love is not going anywhere."

Sarah's cheeks colored prettily. She kissed him back.

Yes, he had hope.

AS COLT STRETCHED out on the sofa in front of the flickering fire, Sarah encircled in his good arm, he decided to raise another subject that had been plaguing him from the confines of his sickbed.

"Have you heard from George?"

She shook her head. "No, though that is not unusual." She absently stroked the length of each of his fingers, unaware how distracting that was to him.

"Then you have not seen the developments in the newspapers about Solitaires?"

"Robert, no. I am not as obsessed with gossip as you think me," Sarah answered, exasperated with his line of questioning. "What development do you speak of?"

Colt scoffed. "Only that the Bow Street Runners conducted a strike on St James's Square on Sunday afternoon. Solitaires was finally unmasked, and both Ellis and Montgomery were arrested."

Sarah swiveled to face him, finally impressed, her face a blend of delight and awe. “That is marvelous,” she cried, embracing him. “Arthur will be saved. Georgina’s troubles will be at an end.”

“Except she has gone to ground,” Colt murmured, stealing the opportunity to kiss Sarah on the nose.

She grinned. “I think you might be able to guess where she is, don’t you?”

34

OUTSIDE MEM LAVIGNE'S establishment in Pall Mall, Colt climbed down from his high-perch phaeton and stopped for a moment to hand the reins over to his groom. Despite Sarah's intuition that Georgina could be found at her club, Colt took a brief detour via Half Moon Street, where Jarvis confirmed that Miss Pace had not been at home in at least two days. Leaning towards his lordship confidentially, Jarvis suggested he might try his luck at Miss Pace's regular club, noting it would be good to have the mistress back, as she had a small mountain of important correspondence awaiting her.

Colt thanked him for the guidance and set forth at once.

A maid escorted him up the narrow stairwell, parting the heavy brocade drapes that shrouded the main parlor, and allowed him to enter. Colt's keen eyes scanned the room. During evening hours, Mem Lavigne's patrons usually spilled from the chamber; however, as it was before noon, the parlor was sparsely occupied.

A young man perched on a velvet stool on a small stage strummed lazily on his lute, while he gazed without too much interest in his surroundings. A feminine voice giggled from within one of the curtained-off alcoves, while a young lorian played whist with a scantily dressed lady. Mem Lavigne themself was nowhere to be seen. Neither was Georgina.

An attendant with a brawny physique revealed by the loose robe that opened over his breeches approached him with a reverent bow. "Lord Coulthurst, is it not? We are honored to have you. How might we pleasure you today? Do you come for gaming, sustenance, or company?" he asked in a low, drawling voice. "We have someone for every taste, although *I* should very much like to take care of your needs."

"Very charming of you, I am sure. But I am seeking my friend, Miss Pace. Is she here?"

Recognition flooded his countenance, together with a curious twist of his mouth. "Ah, indeed, Miss Pace. Yes, she is *here*, somewhere." He peered over his shoulder. "Might I prevail upon my lord to enjoy some refreshments while I ascertain her location?"

Colt's eyes narrowed. "You needn't fob me off, lad. Is she disguised?" He wondered how drunk his friend might be after one or two days lost within the murky halls of Mem Lavigne's den.

"After a fashion." He threaded his way through the tables to the back of the parlor. He pushed aside the curtain and allowed Colt to step past him.

Georgina, clad in a white shirt and taut gray-colored breeches, lay sprawled face-down on the daybed. A tangle of black curls clustered about her head, and one arm fell lifelessly off the side, her fingertips grazing the Aubusson rug.

A girl with strawberry-blonde locks, whom Colt knew from prior visits to be called Lottie, sat nearby, eating a ripe peach.

"How long has she been like this?" Colt inquired, crouching down beside Georgina.

Lottie wiped peach juice from her chin with the back of her wrist. "On and off for a day or so. She's been peevish since she got here. In a right surly mood, if you ask me. Not fancying anything, except her wine. Not even a cuddle!" Lottie took another bite of her peach. She leaned towards Colt and said in an undertone, "Mem said they haven't seen her like this since Mr. Henry died."

Colt's frown deepened. He looked towards the attendant who had stayed nearby, keen to offer service. "Can you please fetch me some coffee and fresh water? And if we might also have some bread and butter. Thank you."

The attendant bowed and disappeared back through the curtains.

Pushing back a black tendril that had fallen across Georgina's face, Colt shook her shoulder gently. "Good morning, my friend. It's time to wake up."

Georgina stirred, fluttering her eyes open. They rolled backwards almost instantly.

"Come now, George. This will not do," he said, more firmly this time.

With a large breath, Georgina pried open her eyes and took a moment to focus on his face. She groaned, and with Colt supporting one elbow, clambered up. One side of her pale face had the clear imprint of the ribbing from the cushion that she had lain on. Georgina rubbed her cheek.

The coffee soon arrived, and Colt dismissed both Lottie and the young attendant, reassuring them that he would restore Miss Pace to her former glory in no time.

"Is this how you have spent all of your time since the duel?" he demanded, after Georgina had ingested two steaming cups of coffee and a glass of water and grudgingly swallowed a slice of bread.

She shrugged. "Only some of it. I am afraid I am simply not the best company at present, Colt."

"Only Leggy came to check on me during my convalescence, damn it."

She dropped her head on his shoulder. "I'm sorry. I have been an unworthy friend."

"Not unworthy." He softened, patting her leg affectionately. "Merely broken. Tell me, did you closet yourself away here *before* the news of Solitaires broke or after?"

"News? I presume the Runners invaded their citadel at last?"

He nodded.

"I only want to know one thing. What of Ellis and Montgomery?"

Colt smiled. "Locked away." At last, he might deliver some happy tidings to her. "And amongst many other things, they have been indicted for the historical murder of one Mr. Henry Pace."

Oh, he was wrong to think she'd like to hear this in her state. Georgina's lips quivered, and her face contorted. She burst into tears, throwing her arms around him and weeping without restraint into his chest. He had never known her to let it out this way, not even at Henry's funeral.

Grateful for the relative privacy of their enclosure, Colt stroked over her back and made soft hushing noises. He should have brought Sarah. She would know what to say.

"I am proud of you, George. Throughout it all, I became scared for you, that something terrible might happen, and I kept counselling you to be conservative. But I misjudged you. You single-handedly toppled this enterprise *and* obtained justice for your brother. You are inspiring, George."

Colt had hoped his small acknowledgement might serve to soothe her sobs, but it only seemed to exacerbate the situation. He sighed.

After a significant time had lapsed—after Georgina's tears had dried, and she managed to engage again in conversation—Colt decided it was time to bring her further news.

He inhaled deeply, assembling the courage. Aside from Sarah, George was his closest companion, and her opinion mattered to him.

They had never discussed his affection for Sarah. It was understood but never explicitly mentioned.

"I proposed to Sarah."

Georgina almost choked on a sip of coffee. Her third cup. She dabbed at her mouth with a serviette. "You proposed?"

"Rather unfathomable, I grant."

"Only that you would propose to anyone. You have always been in love with Sarah."

"She seems to be the last one to know that."

Georgina grabbed his hand. "And how did she respond?"

"She said she needed time." His shoulders slumped. The longer Sarah made him wait, the less hopeful he felt.

Georgina sat back and stretched out her legs. Someone had removed her shoes and placed them out of sight, so she stared at her stockinged feet. "I am both surprised and delighted by this news. But I confess I am, in equal measure, perturbed by it."

Colt frowned. He suspected Georgina might censure him. Lottie was right; she was surly.

"You see, if she marries you, and everything progresses well, then we shall all be happy. If, however, you have not reformed, and you break her heart, I shall invariably lose a friendship."

"She would not require you to disown me as a friend."

Georgina's bright blue gaze flashed. "But I would. You cannot hurt her, Colt."

He accepted this with a calm resolution he had not previously known. "I understand this is what you would have to do. You are the very best of friends. But I will not hurt her." Sarah had become his priority.

They retreated to silence, and he watched her stare vacantly across the table.

"What of your priggish Lady Mortimer? I saw her name in the

newspaper, associated with Solitaires. She cannot have enjoyed that." He noticed Georgina stiffen. "For your sake, I hope she was *not* involved in the enterprise."

"She was not arrested too?"

He shook his head and saw Georgina relax.

"There is nothing more to tell you. I failed in securing Arthur's *actual* IOUs—debt or no debt, the young man wanted nothing more than his papers back in his hands. He must be thoroughly beside himself, still wanting for proof that the ordeal has ended. As for Elizabeth, she vowed to set all to rights, yet I have heard nothing."

"But George, you have hidden yourself away here. How would you know? Jarvis told me you had a pile of correspondence awaiting you at home. Now that your father has set forth to Yorkshire, Jarvis does not know what to do with all the messages."

Georgina peeked up at him from beneath hooded lids. Colt sighed, recognizing the stubborn dimple in her chin that suggested a disinclination to discuss the subject further. He nudged the coffee cup towards her and navigated the subject back to how he intended on persuading Sarah to trust him. Georgina's troubles were far beyond his abilities.

35

GEORGINA LEFT MEM Lavigne's later that afternoon, assuring Colt that she would return straight home and work towards setting her affairs in order. When she arrived at Half Moon Street, however, she found Sarah waiting for her.

A concerned Jarvis greeted her at the front door and advised her that Mrs. Fortescue had sequestered herself in the library for the last hour, refusing to leave until Miss Pace had seen her.

Georgina received this information calmly, familiar with Sarah's strong-willed requests. She hastened upstairs and took a few moments to clean herself up—changing her shirt and breeches for fresh ones—before hurrying back down to Sarah.

"Georgina, you do not look well. What ails you?" Sarah remarked, rising as Georgina came in.

"Apologies for the delay. I have been at Mem Lavigne's. You understand I lose track of time there."

Sarah nodded knowingly and sat back down as Georgina poured them both a hefty glass of port and nestled on the sofa beside Sarah.

"What has happened, my dear?"

One of Georgina's hands flopped by her side, while the other clung to her glass as though it gave her life. "Everything simply went wrong."

Sarah draped a protective arm around her friend's shoulder. "It cannot be as bad as you think."

"Sarah, tell me, what is the relationship between Elizabeth Mortimer and Mrs. Gardner? Is it romantic?"

Sarah gave Georgina a curious look. "I could not tell you if it is *romantic* or not, though I know Elizabeth supplies her with the house in St James's Square. Oh, my dear, I didn't realize you were in earnest about Elizabeth. I thought you were only dallying with her, like all the others. In the past, you have never minded whether people have had other arrangements in place."

Georgina swallowed a knot in her throat.

"Have you felt this way about her for a long time?"

Georgina stared at the fireplace. The unpredictable flickering of the flames afforded her comfort. "I met her just before the Blakes's ball. Not a long time at all . . . and yet it feels like an age." She sipped her drink.

Sarah gave her a sympathetic smile. "She may well have feelings for you. And if Mrs. Gardner is as rotten as I've heard of late, Elizabeth's arrangement—if romantic—might have concluded. I would presume nothing. Perhaps you should ask her?"

Georgina shuddered, recalling her final hour with Elizabeth. The Countess had stood between Georgina and the vultures of Solitaires, trying to protect *them*. The force that had brought them together after Byron's soiree propelled them in opposite directions that day, creating a distance she could not bridge.

Georgina sighed. There was no use dwelling on it. "I hear you have had an exciting time. A proposal?"

Sarah's cheeks darkened with instant effect, and she shrank her shoulders closer together. "We have always bantered together. You know that. But it was never physical until lately." Sarah shrugged. "I told him he must stop pursuing me, but he does not listen."

Georgina knew Colt well enough to recognize this truth.

"It was all a terrible mistake."

"Did he please you?" Georgina asked in a hushed voice, her tone lightly teasing.

"Very, *very* much," Sarah broke into a smile. "I have not known the equal of him. And the pleasure was mutual."

"In that case, it cannot be a mistake."

"But after that, he proposed. I have told him I think the whole idea nonsensical."

Georgina shrugged. "I know you love him."

Sarah looked aghast for a moment, then threw her hands up in the air. "I do. But you see why I have entertained scruples about the matter—and why I should not accept him."

"Naturally," Georgina agreed, adding mischievously, "and moreover, he is so conceited, it will do him good for you to make him wait, if only a day or two."

Sarah giggled.

"I hope he proves worthy of you," Georgina said.

"My expectations are not entirely high on that score, but he has vowed to try." Sarah smiled to herself. "And I do think he may have fallen in love with me. It is strange to see him so smitten."

"He has always adored you, my dear. Everyone knows that. Do you intend on making him linger a significant amount of time to test his commitment?"

"I find that notion distasteful. I told him he might need to wait indefinitely, but the truth, Georgina, is that I *want* to be with him. I miss him when we are not together. Perhaps I *am* trying to prove a point by making him wait. But it's at my expense, it seems."

"I know you will gamble much by throwing in your lot with Colt, but in recent times, I've come to realize that being separated from someone you care about can be pure torment. If you love him, why delay? Be with him."

Tears of joy pricked the inner corners of Sarah's eyes. "You are such a good friend to me. I do love you dearly." She crushed her friend against her bosom in a warm embrace, releasing her only when Georgina coughed, gasping for air. "I'm sorry!"

GEORGINA AND SARAH were deep in conversation when Jarvis entered the library carrying a tray. He brought it over to Georgina and presented her with a thick, sealed letter.

"Miss Pace, I am loath to interrupt, but this letter has been waiting for your attention for some days. The messenger indicated it was quite important. I was not sure when you might return from your club. . . ." The usually unflappable Jarvis appeared unsure whether he had followed the right course.

Georgina recognized the familiar monogram. Her heart pounded in her chest as she snatched the letter from the tray and dismissed Jarvis with thanks.

Sarah watched her over the rim of her glass.

When Georgina broke the seal, a bundle of handwritten pieces of paper within tumbled into her lap.

Despite the fall of Solitaires, Elizabeth had restored Arthur's promissory notes.

A small gasp escaped Georgina's lips, and she clapped her hand across her mouth, fighting an urge to burst into tears.

"Mr. Coombes will be pleased," Sarah remarked, though her dark eyes remained fixed upon her friend's countenance.

Georgina set the notes down and read the letter to herself.

Dear Georgina,

Please find enclosed the vowels belonging to Mr. Coombes. He may safely consider his debts discharged. I regret that you had to go to so much inconvenience to obtain these, and I can only wish you had seen fit to entrust me with the task of resolving the matter at the outset. Even though my own name has now been publicly maligned, something I also regret, I have only ever wanted to help and protect you and those you care about.

It appears I may have been mistaken, after all. Not everyone is capable of redemption. I hope these notes bring comfort to Mr. Coombes and allow him to pursue his future happiness with his intended.

Warm regards,
Elizabeth

Georgina folded the note and forced a smile upon her face. "Arthur will be thrilled. Finally, he can propose to Lady Maggie unencumbered. What a splendid outcome."

Before reading the words, a small hope had kindled inside her heart. She was glad for Arthur, of course, but this letter left her hollow. A tightness gripped her chest, and she breathed through the pain, not wishing to reveal her inner turmoil to Sarah.

"And what about *you* and Elizabeth?"

Georgina gave a look of feigned confusion. "We are not lovers, Sarah. A mere dalliance, as you said." She waved her hand fleetingly. "I shall enjoy finding a new flirt directly."

Sarah gave a hesitant nod.

"Now, tell me what you are going to do about Colt." Georgina swept the topic away from Elizabeth. She did not want to cry again today.

AFTER SARAH TOOK her leave, Georgina set forth from her home once more in the direction of Mount Street, to the residence of Mr. Arthur Coombes. She did not know exactly when Elizabeth had sent the vowels, but given she had been lost in the stronghold of Mem Lavigne's for at least a couple of days, it would be remiss of her to further delay this delivery.

With the news of the demise of Solitaires being liberally brandished across the newspapers, Georgina hoped Edmund might have deduced it was safe for Arthur to return home.

The Coombes's austere butler greeted her. She apologized for the unfashionably late hour of her afternoon call but expressed she craved an audience with Arthur, if he was there. With a disdainful scowl, the butler delivered her into the front parlor, already occupied by Emily.

The butler withdrew, promising to fetch Arthur presently.

Emily sat in a chair close to the fire, a fashion template open in her lap. She wore a white muslin dress with a sky-blue floral print. Upon seeing Georgina, she shrank back into her chair and glanced towards the door.

"Are you here to talk to Mama?"

A puzzled frown formed between Georgina's brows before she remembered Emily's dramatic escapade on the heath following the duel. "No. Though I think some time back in the schoolroom might serve you well, you silly girl."

Emily's pale cheeks turned a rosy pink. "How ungracious you are. I have done nothing wrong."

"You endeavored to entrap a gentleman into marrying you." Georgina's voice lacked sensitivity; though as she looked at Emily's pale face, it dawned on her that Emily, too, may have suffered a broken heart throughout all of this. "Did you love him? Or was it the idea of marrying a rake?"

Emily pouted. "He made me feel *things*."

Georgina grinned. "Yes, and I do not doubt many others will make you feel many wonderful things again. But not Coulthurst." She sat down opposite Emily and clasped her hands together. "You are young and, if you will forgive me for saying it, not so wise yet. You do not need someone like Coulthurst crooning over you. And you certainly do not need to part with your virtue to make someone love you. By all means, take your pleasure, but do so for *yourself*, not from some misguided hope of trying to trick a man into marriage." She paused. "And whatever you do, do *not* shout your words at the next gentleman who asks you to dance—even if he *is* hard of hearing."

Emily's big blue eyes welled up with tears.

Fortunately, the door opened, sparing Georgina an emotional outburst from Emily.

Arthur shuffled into the room, squinting at Georgina through his spectacles. He wore an art smock over his daywear, on which he roughly wiped paint-stained fingers in readiness to shake her hand.

"Go now, Emily. I need to have a private word with your brother," Georgina instructed. To her surprise, Emily complied with her request.

Once the door had closed behind her, Georgina greeted Arthur, a knot of anticipation tightening in her belly, fanning her need to share the uplifting news with him. On the short carriage ride over, she had already envisaged his reaction, and she could scarcely wait to bring his worries to an end.

Georgina urged him to sit down, and, without further ado, she retrieved the slips of paper from her pocket and displayed them to him. Such tiny pieces of paper that had caused such a weight on both of their minds for the last long weeks.

She watched as recognition flooded his face. He clapped his hand across his breast and sighed loudly. "G-George, you have my vowels!"

Georgina pressed them into his hand. "*You* have them. Destroy them and let no one convince you to write one ever again, my dear friend."

"How did you get them back?"

Georgina hesitated. She had no simple explanation for this. She certainly did not mean to bother him with tales of housebreakings, muggings, prison, blackmail, and indictments. "I am not entirely sure. But we have them now."

A beam filled his face, and his joy infected her. Georgina smiled back. She handed him a generous wad of banknotes from her pocket. "These are from Mrs. Gardner. For what you lost at her tables. She is sorry for the inconvenience." Before she handed them to him, though, Georgina took twenty pounds from the bundle. "But you owe me this back. Now, we are completely settled."

"Yes. *Now*, I can ask Lady Maggie to m-marry me, unencumbered."

"She is a lucky woman, Arthur. I don't doubt you will be very happy together."

"Thank you, G-Georgina. I am lucky you are my f-friend."

Her eyes filled with tears. "I'm happy I could help you, Arthur. You are a good friend to me as well."

She swallowed, glad that she had managed to help him, even if it had not been as straightforward as she initially imagined. Despite the disturbances along the way, her intentions had only been honorable. Maybe she was not completely irredeemable, after all.

Georgina wished Henry had been able to find love, get married, and enjoy a life like Arthur. But they'd cut his life short. She hoped her actions in looking after Arthur, including her efforts to bring those villains to justice, had in some way atoned for letting Henry down when he had most needed her.

Georgina left Arthur to his raptures and took herself home. At last, the weight of those damned vowels was off her shoulders, and he was safe. If she ever saw Elizabeth again, she would thank her.

At the thought of Elizabeth, she ached. This entire experience had justified her conviction to never become romantically attached to others. She was delighted that it had worked out for Arthur. Sarah and Colt were about to start their own journey together, and they both valued their friendship with her. She loved each of them and hoped they would bring each other happiness.

For herself, the empty pocket in her chest grew wider with every breath. She was grateful she knew how to shield herself from further pain. Now, to find her next transient romance.

36

THE FOLLOWING MORNING, Georgina glimpsed herself in the mirror while she prepared for the day. Her complexion lacked its typical vibrancy and pink cheeks, and her blue eyes and black lashes stood out against her translucent skin. She pursed her lips, deciding she would benefit from some fresh air.

She sent word to have her horse brought around, and donned her riding breeches, coat, and knee boots. At the front door, she slid on a pair of gloves and sat a top hat on dark curls tied recklessly back with a ribbon.

She left the house to find her beautiful black Arabian mare being walked up and down the street by Buckby.

"She's a sweet goer today," he remarked, holding the glossy beast by her bridle.

"Hello, Artemis," Georgina said in a caressing tone, petting her silken head. She thanked Buckby and, with the freedom afforded by her breeches, sprang up. The horse whinnied and bucked in a restless circle while Georgina settled into the saddle. She took the reins and urged Artemis forward.

Georgina turned to the park, for the open spaces would be less distressing for her mare than the bustling streets. The crisp morning air bit her face, and a few soft rays of sunlight filtered through trees that glinted a vibrant green after a recent downpour. She rode at an unfashionable hour, hoping to enjoy a relatively solitary experience uninterrupted by social pleasantries. But as she turned to recover the ground towards her home, Georgina noticed two other riders coming her way.

Lady Prudence Ravenscroft rode alongside her groom. She murmured something to him, and he advanced forward with his horse, while she proceeded towards Georgina.

Georgina glanced over her shoulder but realized there was no way to retreat without being completely uncivil. She mustered a smile.

Prudence rode side-saddle and wore a bright blue riding gown and matching blue hat with a lace veil that shrouded her eyes. The color magnified the deep red of her hair and her fair skin. They exchanged polite morning greetings. She turned her horse to ride alongside Georgina's.

"Have you settled well into married life?" Georgina inquired.

Prudence sighed. "I am not *unhappily* married," she admitted. "Lord Ravenscroft is kind and patient, just like he was when I first met him in Cornwall, in fact."

Georgina gave her a sidelong look. "However?"

"He is not passionate," she confided impulsively. "I hoped to have a child, but when we make love, I feel no particular desire for him."

Georgina stared off into the distance. She was not inclined to hear about Lord Ravenscroft's sexual deficits at this hour of the morning. "Perhaps you might . . . I do not know . . . explain to him how you want him to touch you?"

Prudence pouted. "*You* did not need me to explain that to you."

Georgina gave a little laugh. "But I am not a man."

"I hoped you might call upon me." Prudence stroked the mane of her horse.

"You have made your hopes quite clear."

"I thought that . . . well, you might like to call upon me so that we can spend some time together . . . when my husband is not at home," she said with a meaningful wink. "In fact, Alfred left a few days ago with Lawrence. They have gone to Bath to take the waters. After that terrible duel, Lawrence was in the most awful despair about his lost love. I persuaded him that the waters would be just the thing to restore him. I do not expect them back until next week. You might visit me without fear of tiresome interruptions."

Georgina gave a reluctant laugh, not wishing to be cold, but she did not reply. Here, Prudence offered her a discreet opportunity to revitalize herself. Yet, an uneasiness crept over her.

Prudence rode her horse closer to Georgina's, so that their legs grazed against each other. She slid her hand up along Georgina's thigh. "Spend the night with me, Georgina. All night," she purred in a soft, seductive voice. "Like the night we almost spent together in Cornwall."

Artemis flung her head down and whinnied loudly, separating the two riders for a moment. This provided Georgina with a reprieve from answering. Her chaotic thoughts raced. Bitterness, hurt, and sadness blended, leaving her in a jumble. Her instinct urged her to decline at once because her feelings were utterly and completely engaged elsewhere.

Georgina clenched her teeth together. Elizabeth did not return her regard. The brief glimpses of emotion detected within her had either been feigned or shared with another, and her entanglement with the hideous Mrs. Gardner was unforgivable.

Georgina settled her mount by stroking her neck gently. "Very well," she agreed.

AS GEORGINA ARRIVED home, Buckby emerged from the mews to take Artemis, and a voice calling her name caught her attention. She turned to find Mrs. Gardner herself standing outside her house, a serene smile on her face.

"Rather daring of you to present yourself on my doorstep without someone to protect you," Georgina remarked, removing her gloves. "Or should I assume you have a burly retainer waiting out of sight?"

"Oh, Miss Pace. There's no need to be hostile."

Georgina scoffed. "Perhaps you lost all your protection when the authorities imprisoned your friends."

"Shall you invite me inside?"

"I would sooner have my man decapitate me and feed my corpse to my dogs, Mrs. Gardner." Joshua would approve of that rejoinder. Georgina's expression remained stony, though inside her heart raced. She wished to deliver a right hook to this woman's face.

"Very well. I can conduct my business on the street."

Georgina folded her arms across her chest.

"I thought, given you had such a *pivotal* role in the closure of my house, my *home*, you might see yourself to assisting me." Mrs. Gardner peeped up at her from beneath the rim of her bonnet, to see if her appeal was meeting with any favor.

Georgina could feel her eyes widen at the woman's effrontery. "Are you mad?"

"Elizabeth would *want* you to help me." Mrs. Gardner was wrapped in an older woolen shawl, which she tightened around her. Her fingers were knotting the fringe, releasing a nervous energy.

"Why is Elizabeth not helping you, then? She has been supporting you this far," Georgina demanded.

"Business took her away. And the manner in which Solitaires closed left our relationship somewhat strained."

Georgina raised a brow. "So, you are applying to *me*?" A gurgle of laughter caught in her throat. The irony was irresistible.

"If you cannot see a clear way to helping me, I see no reason why I shouldn't make life difficult for you, Miss Pace."

Georgina's mouth dropped open at this woman's ability to switch tactics so swiftly. Indeed, she must be desperate. "More than you have already? Goodness, do tell me what you might do now?"

"Well, Mr. Leggett told me all about Lord Coulthurst's duel the other day. How shocking."

Georgina blinked, unsure what devilry she was attempting now. "Mr. Leggett is not known for his discretion. I daresay all of London has heard of it. Why you think I should care has me in a puzzle."

"Oh, Miss Pace, you mistake me. He also mentioned that *you* were there. How irksome to *yet again* find yourself in the center of a scandal." She clicked her tongue. Her tone was sweet, but Georgina read the threat beneath her words. "I understand that Elizabeth has held you in high esteem until now. Sadly, I believe it is my duty to provide her with any information that I have about your behavior."

This was almost comical. "What *do* you want?"

Mrs. Gardner lowered her voice to a whisper. "I could be discreet, for a price."

Clarity broke, like warm light illuminating the dark, making everything suddenly comprehensible. And utterly absurd. Georgina tossed her head back with genuine laughter. "So, with your income stream severed, you wish to try to blackmail me? Oh, Mrs. Gardner, go to the devil, with my love. She and I are good friends."

"I will tell Elizabeth all your scandals! I know everything!" Her voice rose in volume.

Georgina plunged her hand into her vest pocket, withdrew the crumpled-up twenty-pound note she'd pulled from Arthur's stack, and dropped it in Mrs. Gardner's direction, not caring if she caught it. "This is for the amusement you have given me this morning." It was more generosity than she deserved. Georgina's fingers clenched around her riding crop. "As for your threats, you must do as you see fit."

Mrs. Gardner snatched the note and, as her eyes drifted down to the crop, she took a small step back.

With a firm grasp on the whip, Georgina strode up the steps to her front door and let it swing shut with a bang behind her.

37

AT TEN O'CLOCK that evening, Georgina found herself seated at the Marchioness of Ravenscroft's opulent dining table, enjoying a fine repast with her young hostess.

Prudence sat at the head of the elongated table, her petite figure glittering in an emerald-green gown with silver overlay. She wore a large, shimmering necklace that drew the eyes to her neatly defined chest and matching drop earrings that dangled down the narrow column of her neck. Her red curls were gathered high atop her head, exposing her shoulders to their fullest advantage.

She watched Georgina over the top of the glass, her eyes kindling. "How came you to leave Cornwall in such a rush?"

Well, this was inevitable, Georgina thought with exasperation. She set her glass down.

"Prudence. . . ."

"How wry." Prudence scooped the last of her baked custard onto her spoon. "You are rather difficult to predict. One cannot tell if you favor *prudence* or shy away from it." She quirked a brow.

"One must yield to what is right," Georgina replied, choosing her words carefully.

Once Prudence finished her dessert, an attendant cleared away the final covers and replenished Georgina's glass of Burgundy.

Receiving a meaningful nod from Lady Ravenscroft, the attendant withdrew, closing the door softly behind her and leaving them alone.

"You mentioned this morning that you hope to have children?"

Prudence gave a little pout. "We have not yet conceived, sadly."

"Your marriage only took place a few months ago. I am sure there is plenty of time."

"Alfred is everything that is sweet, but he lacks spontaneity and excitement. Something I crave." Under the table, Prudence extended her foot and rubbed it up Georgina's calf.

Georgina leaned back in her chair and took another sip of her wine. She made no move to reciprocate.

"You are much changed since Cornwall, Georgina."

"Perhaps I experience more scruples in London."

"What a bounder. We both know your reputation speaks for itself."

Georgina twirled the stem of her glass between her fingers. Prudence's attempt at teasing her fell flat. "Yes, but one can change," she murmured. "We are all capable of redemption." As the words tumbled from her, it was as if a vice unclamped from around her heart.

Elizabeth may have given up on her when she learned the terrible truth of her past, but Georgina was not the same person she'd been eight years ago. Even Prudence saw it—she was not even the same as she was in Cornwall months back. The tiny muscle at the bridge of her nose stung, and she clenched her teeth, repressing what was either a sob or a scream. The sudden sensation surprised her.

Meanwhile, Georgina's earnest words had elicited a giggle from

Prudence, who reached across the table and covered Georgina's hand with hers. "Well, *I* have not changed, and now that I am married, you need not have any qualms about *my* reputation. You may be as naughty as you please. Whilst Alfred would like me to remain discreet, he does not expect me to deny myself pleasure."

"You have reached an understanding?" Georgina asked absently. She found herself wanting to leave.

"A most satisfactory one. Alfred does not mind what I do. In fact, I think he rather likes knowing I engage in mischief behind his back."

"An ideal husband for you, it would seem."

Prudence stood up and pushed her chair back. It creaked along the floorboards.

Georgina grimaced at the high-pitched scraping noise. She swallowed and drew her hand up to her cravat to loosen it. She felt breathless—and not in a pleasing way.

Prudence loomed over her.

"S-someone might come in." Georgina hardly recognized her own timidity.

"I have very discreet staff," Prudence breathed, leaning over Georgina's chair. She attempted to massage her shoulders. "No one will appear again tonight without me summoning them."

"Ah. Excellent," Georgina managed.

"Your shoulders are so tight." Prudence's small hands rubbed the rigid muscles in Georgina's neck with difficulty. "You can remove your jacket if you like."

"I am cold," Georgina rushed to say.

What was wrong with her? Prudence was a beautiful woman and would surely help her forget her difficulties.

Prudence leaned forward, so that her bosom pushed against the back of Georgina's head, and whispered beside her ear, "I would like to warm you, George."

Prudence slid her hands down the front of Georgina's jacket and cupped one firm breast in each hand.

A visceral wave of nausea washed over her, catching her off guard. Georgina wished she had never agreed to come. She stood up and moved away from Prudence and the dining table.

"Do you wish to go upstairs?"

"No!" Georgina turned to face her. "I . . . I would prefer to remain down here."

Prudence cast a nebulous eye at the dining table. "If you wish. . . ."

"I am opening a home for children," Georgina blurted out.

Prudence's mouth dropped open.

"A safe and warm establishment for orphaned children of all ages to be housed, looked after, educated, and connected to parents seeking to build and extend their families."

It made sense. Georgina did not know how it had not occurred to her before.

"That is . . . surprising," Prudence said politely. "I did not think such matters would be important to you."

Georgina smiled, feeling the weight lifted from her chest. "But they are. In fact, I must attend to that right now."

"What?" Prudence blinked.

Georgina leaned towards her and planted a kiss on her cheek. "Sorry, Prue. I must go. Thank you for dinner."

BACK IN HER library, Georgina sat at her desk. She opened the drawer for some parchment and noticed the letter from Elizabeth tucked neatly on top. This caused a needle prick to her heart, quick and sharp. She may have lost her chance with Elizabeth—whoever Elizabeth was—but this did not need to stop her from being the person Elizabeth hoped her to be. The person *she* now wanted to be.

Georgina had changed for the better, and that was worth something.

Despite the acrimony that tarnished their brief relationship, Elizabeth *had* transformed her. Whether or not she liked it, Georgina now heeded her conscience and took a genuine interest in others beyond her immediate family and friends. Her decision to commission a home for children, while spontaneous, now developed momentum in her mind.

Georgina withdrew the paper from her desk and commenced writing notes regarding how the project would be planned, funded, and implemented. Children like Joshua could access a stable and comfortable home, education, and nourishing food, together with caregivers to provide them with warmth and affection. She wished for Elizabeth's knowledge on how to set up trusts. No, she could not ask her. Perhaps Sarah could prove useful in raising funds for such a venture. She would need to inspire a board of leaders to drive the project and ensure its success. Once she had captured her initial thoughts, she finally took herself to bed, satisfied that it made some sense, at least. As her head hit the pillow, she wondered briefly where Elizabeth was, who she was with, and whether she would approve of her plan.

38

COLT WANDERED INTO Brooks's Club and scanned the room for a chair. He had recovered from his injury well enough, though he tired easily; thus, he did not care to stand idle for long periods without a place to sit when he felt like it. A few chairs were available, and across the room, he observed young Arthur and Edmund engaged in a lively conversation by the distant fire.

From the grin of delight on Arthur's countenance, Colt imagined he finally had those infernal vowels of his back in his possession. He weaved his way through the tables and chairs.

"Good evening, gentlemen. Mind if I join you?" He had already lowered himself into the stiff leather wing chair beside them.

Arthur greeted him cheerfully, and Edmund nodded.

"Do I detect a note of relief in the air this evening? Can it be you have solved the issue of Mrs. Gardner and the IOUs?" Colt bestowed one of his dimpled smiles on them. "George shares everything with me. I hope you do not object."

"George indeed returned them to me," Arthur confided. "I am very fortunate."

Edmund extended a fond smile towards his friend. "And he has just proposed to Lady Maggie, and she consented to be his wife."

Arthur beamed, happiness radiating a sheen in his rosy cheeks.

"Congratulations. That is excellent news." Colt shook his hand warmly.

Edmund sniffled.

If Edmund was in an emotional mood, perhaps Colt had erred in joining these two. He poured them all liberal glasses of wine from the decanter resting on the table between them.

"Cards anyone? Penny stakes only," he added quickly, mindful of Arthur's recent misadventures.

Edmund and Arthur agreed.

"This is infinitely b-better than Mrs. Gardner's," Arthur declared, making himself comfortable as Colt arranged for cards from a passing attendant.

"I should say so. And safer, for you know we will not try to swindle you," Edmund murmured.

Colt dealt the cards.

"I should never have taken you there. Much better to introduce you to games here without the scavengers around," Edmund said.

"Indeed. I do not wager against anyone other than family and friends anymore," Arthur announced with pride.

"Very glad to hear it, old chap," Colt said.

As they played, it became increasingly difficult to ignore Edmund's despondent sighs.

"Why so unhappy?" Arthur ventured after a while.

Colt noted Arthur's sensitivity to others, so aware and responsive when someone labored with a fit of the doldrums. Colt would have rather ignored Edmund's sullen mood, but he supposed he could learn a thing from young Mr. Coombes.

Edmund stretched back in his chair. He took his glass and studied the deep red liquid swirling around the glass. "I am a bit of a fool," he admitted.

"Ah yes," Arthur returned knowingly. "As is my sister, Emily. Both fools for love."

Colt placed his cards face-down on the table. By the looks of things, they would be pausing the game to attend to Edmund's romantic sensibilities.

"I fancied myself in love with the wrong person."

"You do that often," Arthur pointed out. "Luckily, you only feel sad for a day or two and then find someone else."

Edmund inclined his head back and blinked quickly to avoid tears. "You are correct, of course. I *have* made an unfortunate habit of it."

Colt noticed Leggy enter the club and take a seat at the far side of the room, where there were plenty of vacant seats. Colt found himself gazing longingly in that direction, wishing to be far away from Edmund's romantic dilemmas.

"Was I so wrong to believe that Mr. Dalrymple returned my affections? He favored me with several dances. We went for a promenade at the fashionable hour, for all to see, *and* he agreed to walk with me in Vauxhall."

"Did you give him a choice? I have seen you browbeat people," Arthur added, as only a loyal friend might.

Colt made a slight snorting noise at Arthur's candor.

Edmund clapped his hand to his chest, appalled by the notion. "Nonsense! I merely ask and invite. Of course, he could have declined if he wished to," he said, in a voice now lacking in conviction. He poured them more wine, and Colt could see he was turning events over in his mind. "Heavens, I think you might be correct."

Arthur gave another knowing grin. "Yes." They continued the hand in silence for a while longer. "You are good at teaching me cards," Arthur volunteered. "Sh-shall I teach you something?"

Edmund could not repress a smile. "Of course."

"You do not need to be in love *all* the time to be happy, Edmund.

In fact, it is not good for you. I think you should stop looking for a person to love and marry." He let Edmund digest his words. "You are handsome, fashionable, clever, and kind. You will find someone when the time is right."

Colt regarded Arthur with new appreciation.

"And it is far easier to love someone who likes you. D-do not look for him. He will find you. Try painting. That is how I met M-Maggie."

Colt cleared his throat and found both young gentlemen gazing at him, their eyes brimming with expectation. "I am no expert in matters of the heart, but I would say your friend here offers very sage advice."

He frowned. He had managed to get to his age with no significant romantic entanglement. His history was peppered with fleeting affairs, and he had left many broken hearts in his wake. And now, the love of his life refused to trust him. He could only look back with regret at many of the choices he had made.

Edmund shifted his body, so he almost entirely faced Colt. "Forgive me, but that is rather different from how *you* appear to live. You almost died in a duel over *his* sister, at the hand of the man *I* love."

Colt nearly choked on his wine. "I did not almost die! Steady on. Someone has blown that matter out of all proportion, I assure you. Is that what you heard?" Heat rushed to his cheeks. "In truth, I am prepared to change my ways. But a lifetime of inappropriate behavior is coming up against me." He exhaled slowly and stood up. "You are right. I am not one to give advice."

He couldn't even get the woman he loved to marry him.

LEAVING THE YOUNG gentlemen to their game, Colt wandered over to Leggy and collapsed on the sofa beside him with a sigh. At least Leggy would not trap him in morose conversation.

Leggy cast him a dubious look. "What's the matter with you, then?"

Colt considered Sarah. He had seen her only yesterday, and he already missed her. Not only her beautiful countenance, but her warm laugh that set him alight and her easy banter.

"Only that I've done my best to untangle a knot and seem to have only made it worse. At least Georgina had managed to resolve Mr. Coombes's affairs."

A frown descended upon Leggy's features. "Any particular knot in mind? I'm quite good with a bowline. A cousin of mine became a commander in the Royal Navy a few years back. Always fascinated by rope. I am delighted to make an endeavor, if you have some handy."

Colt recognized immediately that his flowery language had been a mistake.

"No, I don't—" He stopped himself as he observed Sarah herself enter the club. His breath hitched in his throat. She snaked through the small clusters of assembled patrons and as she approached, his attention narrowed onto her alone, with Leggy fading into the background along with everyone else.

"Sarah?"

"Hello, Mrs. F," Leggy said, his cheerful voice piercing Colt's trance. "Fancy a claret?"

She acknowledged Leggy but set her eyes on Colt. "This will not do," she announced.

Leggy eyed his glass askance. "You think not? I thought it was quite a fine drop." He sniffed the wine in irritation.

"Leggy . . ." Colt checked him in a menacing tone. "Not now."

"Easy for you to say. You haven't been drinking it! They've been allowing Prinny to select the wine again, I'll wager," he said with disdain.

"The Prince Regent has not been selecting the wine, Leggy," Colt reassured him. "Oh, look, there is Carruthers over there. Did you not wish to talk to him about purchasing those match bays you saw him with the other day?"

"By Jove, yes! Excuse me, Mrs. F. Important matter of business!" Leggy discarded what remained of his inferior glass of wine on the nearby table and rushed across the room in pursuit of Mr. Carruthers.

"Thank you for distracting him. He does tend to go on."

"Indeed, one never knows when or where one of his diatribes will end," Colt agreed. "Might I procure you a drink? Perhaps not the claret." He did not wish to distract her from her purpose, yet his own pulse raced. Perhaps she had concluded they could not maintain their friendship. He fought a sinking sensation.

"No, thank you," she said.

"You seem distracted. Is something amiss?"

Sarah paused, looking unsure. "I am worried about Georgina. She is not happy."

"Indeed, I plucked her from Mem Lavigne's yesterday morning. She had been there for some days. I had not seen her so intoxicated since. . . . Well. Henry."

Sarah nodded. "She told me you helped her. I saw her yesterday afternoon."

He rubbed the back of his head. "And what do you make of her state?"

"She is in love, of course."

"George?" He had never known her to fall in love. Besides, she had been far too preoccupied with the business of Arthur and his vowels to have lost her heart along the way.

"And she is heartbroken."

"Over whom?"

A defiant twinkle flashed in Sarah's eyes.

"Not Lady Mortimer!"

"It does not need to make sense to you, Robert," Sarah countered. The corners of her mouth twitched. "Georgina also told me of her surprise to learn that you proposed to me."

Colt stood suddenly and took a step towards her, a dimpled smile peeping through his cheeks. "You discussed that with her?"

She became visibly flustered as he closed the gap between them.

"What will not do, Sarah?" he asked gently, drawing her back to her purpose.

"What?"

"When you arrived, just now, you said, 'This will not do.' I suspect you are not here to talk about Georgina, after all."

Sarah paused, fingertips pressed against her temples, and took a slow, deep breath. "I would be most obliged if you might consider offering for me again," she declared finally, her tone low to avoid curious spectators. "If you still want to," she added hastily.

His gaze softened upon her, and time slowed. "Sarah, will you marry me?"

"Yes, Robert, I will," she answered, and a smile broke out across her face.

All at once, and completely heedless of their surroundings, Colt swept Sarah up into his arms and off her feet. He twirled her around easily, much to the surprise of the other club patrons.

"How would you feel if I obtained a special license?"

"That would suit me very well," Sarah replied, her eyes kindling.

He took both her hands in his and kissed her knuckles. "Then there is not a moment to lose."

39

THE FOLLOWING MORNING, Georgina awoke early and invigorated. Whilst she yearned for Elizabeth, the previous evening with Prudence had opened her eyes. She thought it would be easy to bed Prudence from a sense of retaliation, using the lady as a balm for her anger. Yet, she had recoiled from Prudence's touches. She had even struggled not to be physically ill in the aftermath. She only wanted Elizabeth. And if she could not have Elizabeth, she wanted her dignity.

After some breakfast, Georgina made her way to Brooks's. She usually ventured to this fashionable private club when she wished to avoid the incessant gossip circulating through the local tearooms, or when she meant to remain sober. She delighted in conversing with the Lords, Ladies, and Peers of the House and did not cower from political debates. Spying her old acquaintance, Frederica, Duchess of York, and her friend, Mr. Beau Brummell, engaged in laughing conversation, she approached them and gave a slight bow.

"This is rather early for you to be abroad, Mr. Brummell," Georgina teased.

"I could not agree more, Miss Pace. I was obliged to curtail my dressing this morning. This damnable woman urged me to meet her here with all haste. I feared a national emergency," he declared with a sigh.

The Duchess grinned. "And in truth, I merely wished his opinion on my latest hat."

"A national emergency," Georgina agreed. She excused herself when she spotted Edmund beckoning her over to him. Georgina joined him with an affectionate smile.

"How can you talk to him so easily, George?" He looked over at Brummell in awe and wonderment. "He is the most admired man in town."

Georgina knew Mr. Brummell to be an interesting fellow, though she also understood he was rather rude when he wanted to be. She owned he looked well and always presented himself to an exceptional standard, but she did not think he merited special reverence.

She gave a shrug. "I cannot tell what all the fuss is about, Edmund. He is, after all, just a man."

He pouted. "One can tell *you* do not hold to dandyism!"

"That is true," Georgina agreed, unhurt. They sat down opposite each other in two oversized leather wing chairs. "How have you been? Have you discovered a new beau yet?"

"I mean to avoid romantic intrigues for a time. I must heal."

Georgina, unaccustomed to Edmund making sensible statements, blinked in surprise, and agreed this was a welcome decision.

"Arthur thinks so too. Says I make life unnecessarily difficult."

"Arthur is wise," Georgina replied. She immediately warmed as she thought about Arthur. "How does he go on?"

"Much better, now that he is no longer in the clutches of Mrs. Gardner. Lady Maggie accepted his proposal. He is excessively happy. All thanks to you. Mighty sorry for involving you, my dear," Edmund said with heartfelt remorse. “Hopefully, they will not reinstate those parties anytime soon.”

Georgina stiffened. “Mrs. Gardner is a fiend. I wish they imprisoned her as well,” she expostulated, with a little more feeling than she intended to show.

Edmund arched an eyebrow at her. “That might be doing it a bit too brown, old girl. I believe she provided vital testimonial evidence against Ellis and Montgomery, allowing all the charges to be secured.”

This took the wind out of Georgina’s sails somewhat. “Generous of her, I am sure. Though she continues to try to make her way in the world corruptly. She attempted to blackmail me yesterday.”

“I daresay it must be challenging for her to get by, now that Lady Mortimer closed the house.”

Georgina frowned. “You have known about their relationship?”

“Well, yes,” Edmund replied. “There was no secret in that, George.”

In annoyance, Georgina sat back in the chair and locked her arms across her chest. Clearly, she was the only one oblivious to the nature of their connection.

“Very kind of her ladyship too,” Edmund said, dusting a speck of lint from his coat.

Georgina gave him a stony look. “Kind?”

“I believe Mrs. Gardner once did a good turn for the Dowager, Lady Mortimer’s mother. Saved her from a bolting horse or some such thing. But she was living in a poorhouse at the time, you see. When Lady Mortimer located her to thank her after the incident, she found her rather unwell with a chill. They do not heat those places, George.”

A sinking feeling crept over Georgina.

"The Dowager then owed her life to Mrs. Gardner, yet Mrs. Gardner was in a mighty bad way, by all accounts. Very unwell. She may have died if not for the Countess intervening."

Georgina felt the blood drain from her face.

"Her ladyship took her home and restored her to health. Then she set about compensating her for her kindness to her mother. She leased the house for her. Mrs. Gardner has Lady Mortimer to thank for her rising to the fringes of society." He smiled and patted her hand. "Though I do not think her ladyship ever expected that Mrs. Gardner would establish a gaming house. That occurred over time—and only thanks to Ellis and Montgomery."

Georgina listened to his words with increasing alarm. "I assumed Lady Mortimer was *romantically* involved with Mrs. Gardner, and possibly a sponsor of Solitaires."

He screwed up his face. "No, no. The blunt came from Ellis and Montgomery. *They* were always the ones to watch." Edmund leaned closer to maintain discretion. "Word has it, they were nursing some sensitive information about Mrs. Gardner and used that as leverage. Any time she tried to step away, they applied pressure, and she had to toe the line."

Georgina's throat constricted. "But is Mrs. Gardner not Lady Mortimer's mistress?"

"Most certainly not. Her charge, more like. Friendly but not intimate," he said with the conviction of a skillful gossip. "I daresay she did what she could to break her away from Ellis and Montgomery. A lost cause, though, once one is in their grip." He looked down at his own hands that twisted together unconsciously. "We discovered that firsthand."

She buried her face with her hands. "Good God, I've made a dreadful mistake."

"Having made my fair share of those, I daresay you will come about again quickly, George," he consoled her. Edmund, who was insensitive at his best and outright foolish at his worst, disregarded her apparent distress and demanded whether she might introduce him to his idol, Mr. Brummell.

"Talk to him yourself, Edmund," she snapped. "I'm off."

OUTSIDE BROOKS'S, GEORGINA retrieved Artemis and galloped recklessly back to Half Moon Street, heedless of the curious eyes watching her dart at breakneck speed between the carriages crowding the road. Buckby sprang up and seized the reins as she slid from the saddle. Without even a word of thanks, she strode up the front stairs and into the house.

Once inside, and without a clear purpose in mind, Georgina ascended the stairs two at a time. Halfway down the hall, she opened the door to one of the rooms. It creaked, softly inviting her inside. She closed the door behind her with a click.

A few shards of light splintered in from the closed window. Flecks of dust danced in the air where the sunlight played before disappearing into the shadows. A familiar tightness gripped her chest.

Henry's bed towered against one wall. His valet had turned the coverlet down eight years ago, but the bed had remained un-slept in. The room no longer smelled like her brother.

She wandered to his dressing table and leaned against it. His gilt-handled hairbrush rested where he left it to her right. If she looked closely, she could see a few of his fine, dark hairs threaded into the bristles. How soft his hair had been. A ruby cravat pin dulled by a heavy layer of dust sat beside a few coins, a silver letter-opener, and an engraved snuffbox. The attendants had been instructed to leave the room intact.

Georgina traced a pattern in the dust with her finger. "If Elizabeth had let me close to her, I would have only hurt her, anyway." She paused, the bridge of her nose stinging. "I let people down, Henry. I did not look after you."

Her eyes fell on the pair of spectacles that sat open on the dresser. They had been bent slightly and no longer sat flush against the wood. The authorities had returned them after it happened.

"I should have been with you, Henry. My heart tore into a thousand shards that night, and I will never stop trying to put them back together. But you are gone, and it was my fault." She thumped her hand down on the dresser, and everything rattled. "I'm sorry," she whispered.

She paused, as if listening.

"Of course, that's it. You're right. You told me to *always* say sorry. This should be no exception. I need to see her. I must apologize for believing the worst in her, for not trusting her. I must at least say sorry. She deserves that."

Brushing her tears away, Georgina straightened and left the room.

AS SHE ARRIVED at the beautiful town house in Grosvenor Square, a stableboy came to hold the horse. Georgina asked him to walk Artemis for her and pressed a copper into his hand for his efforts. She had not rehearsed her words, and she had no desire to absolve herself of any wrongdoing. Georgina simply wished to atone for the unfair things she had uttered to Elizabeth in her fury-driven rage.

As she hurried up the front stairs, a butler greeted her, regal in his manners.

He advised her that Lady Mortimer had been away from London for three days, and he did not know when she would be returning.

Georgina sighed. Forgetting her whereabouts for a moment, she shrouded her face with her hands, trying to source some mystical solution to her difficulties. About to turn on her heel, she heard a soft voice from behind the butler.

"Is that a visitor, Watson?" A little lady of advancing years stood in the hall, leaning on her gold-gilded Malacca cane. She squinted to see who waited behind the butler.

Watson introduced "Miss Pace" as a caller for Lady Mortimer.

"Will I suffice?" the woman asked with a wry smile. "I was Lady Mortimer before even my daughter."

She nodded and followed the lady into the parlor. Watson disappeared to fetch them both tea. She wished she had Elizabeth by her side when meeting the family's matriarch. The unexpected nature of this encounter sparked Georgina's nerves.

The mature lady sat on the sofa and instructed Georgina to sit near her. "And are you *the* Miss Pace that I have heard so much about? Let me look at you, my dear," she announced and inspected Georgina in the beautifully candid way that only older people can, without causing offense. "She was most accurate in her description. You are exquisite, Miss Pace, if you do not mind my saying."

Her initial nerves abated, Georgina raised the lady's hand to her lips. She placed a feathery kiss on the Dowager's knuckles. "You might compliment as often as you wish. I never tire of praise." Georgina winked. "I am sure you must be fielding admiration all day, as well? Those eyes, shaped just like your daughter's. Silken hair . . . and a figure most of London would envy."

The Dowager chuckled. "Ah, my girl. How droll you are. Elizabeth said you were charming."

The mention drew a smile to Georgina's lips. "Your butler advised me Elizabeth has retired to the country?"

"She has, but only to attend to some business on the estate. My child is a diligent landlady who takes care of her tenants. She is much more proficient at it than I ever was," the Dowager said. "I lack her patience."

Georgina fiddled with the silver buttons of her coat.

"You seem concerned, my dear. Would you like me to send a message to her on your behalf?"

"We . . . we did not part on the best terms. It was a misunderstanding. I'm of the belief that she would not favor contact from me at this moment," Georgina admitted with a small, contrite smile.

The lady regarded her curiously. "She did not mention a quarrel to me, Miss Pace. I daresay she does not share your mindset."

If only this were true. Georgina's stomach knotted. "I am impulsive, my lady. I fear I may have upset her beyond repair."

"She regards you with much esteem, Miss Pace. I should think it is almost impossible that you have fallen beyond redemption in her eyes." Her ladyship smiled. "Elizabeth is a most temperate and patient person. She is unlike me in this way—not the sort of woman to overreact and run away from her troubles. Her main vice, Miss Pace, is that she is rather *too* prudent, too keen to analyze every small thing carefully. I suspect that is why she never married." She surveyed Georgina closely. "I, on the other hand, am impulsive and rush into things."

Georgina could feel her cheeks warming beneath the scrutiny. It seemed she and the Dowager shared these traits in common.

"I had long given up hope of my daughter falling in love and marrying. She has spent her life pursuing charitable work, raising funds for the destitute, petitioning at the House of Peers to improve the lot of the impoverished. She has established large soup kitchens throughout London and advocated to reform workhouses. Not to mention her artists. Her activities have kept her occupied and away from the marriage mart."

Hearing her describe Elizabeth's goodness—when Georgina had thought so poorly of her—filled Georgina with so much feeling, she became desperate to change the subject.

"And do you live here?"

"Only when I stop to visit town, my dear. Most of the year, I reside in the dower house, attached to the estate in Basingstoke. I am not much use in the metropolis these days. Fortunately, Elizabeth visits me regularly and ensures I am well looked after. And when she is not visiting, I receive frequent letters," she said fondly. "It is how I first heard she had met you, Miss Pace."

"She mentioned me in her letters?"

Her ladyship's thin lips curled into a smile. "Certainly, my dear. Elizabeth has spoken of little else in recent times."

Georgina's body grew warm, and yet she could not shake her sense of dread. She bit her lip. "She has?"

"Indeed, Miss Pace. I know you are brave, and you care fiercely about your loved ones. You have a fiery temper but a heart of gold. I even know," the Dowager paused, with a humor in her eyes, "that you bite your lip when you are thinking or worried. Or simply concocting mischief. And that your hair smells like port, and your skin smells like lilies."

Georgina swallowed and tugged at her cravat.

The Dowager chuckled. "Do not worry yourself, my dear. I am old and beyond being shocked. I feel akin to you."

Georgina stifled a laugh. There could be no denying the great level of intimacy she and Elizabeth already shared. Yet it intrigued her that Elizabeth confided so much in her mother.

"I know you protect yourself with liquor and seclude yourself in secret clubs to avoid becoming too attached to anyone. Tell me, has she declared herself to you?"

"Oh no, she has not," Georgina said. She covered her face instinctively. "And I would not expect her to now, my lady."

The Dowager said wistfully, "On the contrary, I expect she will upon her return."

"Might I please have her direction? I should like to contact her, after all," Georgina said, overcome with the need to make amends.

"Of course," the lady responded. She rose and hobbled over to the handsome bureau in the corner, scribbled down the Basingstoke address, and handed it to her.

Watson returned directly with a tea tray and furnished them both with cups and generous slices of lemon cake. The sweetmeat was fragrant and moist, but Georgina had no appetite to enjoy it.

"Miss Pace, one more thing. Before she departed, my daughter did tell me about Henry."

The Dowager's statement caught Georgina off guard, causing her to freeze with her cup of tea midway to her mouth.

"You poor dear. I am so sorry for your loss. Elizabeth did not mention a quarrel, nor any bad terms between you, but she explained you had powerful feelings for the situation of a young friend of yours. And you had made it very much your own crusade to save him. Mr. Coombes, was it? What happened with your brother underpins your desire to help Mr. Coombes. It is understandable." She rested her hand on top of Georgina's. Her fingers were slender, and though her skin was stretched across the bones, depicting her age, her touch was warm and reassuring.

"Understandable even if I have shown her grave distrust and unjustified censure along the way?"

Her ladyship withdrew her hand with a chuckle. "That is something you might show less with age, child. We are both fortunate that Elizabeth is *not* so headstrong."

Georgina nodded uneasily.

"Elizabeth should not have taken herself to the country. You are, in fact, the second person coming in search of her today. Mrs. Gardner called a little while ago, seeking her out. Now that those awful men are in prison, I daresay she hopes to discuss bringing Blair back to town."

A heady sensation washed over Georgina. "Blair?"

"Mrs. Gardner's child, Blair. A darling electora, much kinder in temperament than their mother. They reside in the country. Elizabeth helped keep Blair safe for some time, until those monsters followed Mrs. Gardner on one of her visits. Once they knew where Blair was being schooled, they began to threaten the child's safety, to ensure Mrs. Gardner did their bidding." The Dowager sighed. "Every time Elizabeth attempted to change Blair's location, those men seemed to be one step ahead. It has been a terrible affair."

Georgina's head pounded. Could her assessment of Elizabeth have been any further from the truth? And could it be true that Mrs. Gardner was not a villain, but yet another *victim* in the whole affair? She wanted to swear violently but suffocated it.

Once Elizabeth knew the extent of Georgina's stubborn ignorance, redemption would no longer be on the cards. Sitting here now, the room spun.

Georgina mustered a smile. "And was Mrs. Gardner heading straight off to see Elizabeth?"

Her ladyship maintained strong eye contact. "I believe so. She too requested Elizabeth's direction in the country."

Georgina understood she had placed Elizabeth in an untenable position. Far from being a lady of dubious character and morals, Elizabeth was, in fact, the best of people. But Georgina had pushed her away all the same. Even if Mrs. Gardner reached her first and told her everything, it would be nothing short of the truth. Georgina deserved everything about to come her way.

Georgina nodded. “Very well. Thank you for your time, my lady. I look forward to meeting you again soon.”

With that, Georgina bade her farewell. She knew what she had to do.

40

GEORGINA DESCENDED HER front steps. Even though she intended to travel in the coach, she wore riding breeches, boots, and her most comfortable traveling coat. Her own dark blue post-chaise waited on the street, the coachman having already taken his position at the back of the carriage, while the groom held the reins of four restless horses.

Georgina had only packed one portmanteau, so once Buckby strapped this alongside the large strongbox affixed to the carriage, she climbed in. Buckby jumped up to his seat beside the driver, and the horses sprang forward.

The hours advanced, and they would have to make good speed to stand a chance of reaching Basingstoke before dark. Georgina did not believe in tiring horses to the point of exhaustion, so she made provision for regular changes. The first stop was accomplished in a matter of minutes, with the ostlers speedily swapping the horses, giving Georgina only enough time to swallow a restorative cup of tea and use the privy.

The journey felt interminable but was uneventful, without accident or holdup. Georgina passed much of the daylight flicking through her book, failing to absorb many of the words. The roads were in a constant state of disrepair, and even though her post-chaise was sturdy, it bounced responsively over every bump in the road.

As the day ground on, she dozed, leaning uncomfortably against the frame of the carriage, and when she could not sleep, she stared out the window at the landscape.

She recognized the recklessness of her rushing to Elizabeth's side in this manner, without invitation or notice. However, her need to apologize for her actions diminished all immediate qualms. Her conversation with the Dowager had only reinforced this desire.

They travelled primarily on the London Road; at the midway point, Georgina took herself into a rustic inn and requested a light luncheon. She had very little appetite but picked at the food as best she could, paying her hosts a generous number of coins and returning to the carriage.

As she entered the courtyard, a commotion near her carriage caught her attention.

"Da Missus invited me. Sure as day, she did! Gave me special dispenation!"

"I'll have you turned off, you little scamp!" snarled Buckby, dragging Joshua out of the large box at the front of the carriage.

The boy's face shone tomato-red and glistened with sweat after several hours' confinement in his self-imposed quarters.

Buckby released him when he noticed Georgina step out of the inn. "I did not know the lad hid himself in the carriage, Miss Pace."

"Evidently. Joshua, you are an abomination."

"What's a 'bomnation'?"

Georgina ignored him and addressed the landlady. "Kindly fetch a ham sandwich and some water." She turned to her indignant groom. "Now, Buckby. You have a choice to make. Do you wish to relinquish your seat on the back and travel with me in the carriage, or is that beneath your dignity?"

He scowled. "Can't we leave him here? Or send him back to London?"

"As much as I do not relish what remains of the journey, I am afraid that is not an option. Joshua is a minor and under my protection. I cannot, as you suggest, leave him without a suitable adult guardian. Unless, of course, *you* are volunteering to escort him back home?" She lifted one brow.

This prospect secured Joshua's fate. Within ten minutes, he had dispatched his tasty ham sandwich, a glass of water, *and* some of the landlady's fresh lemonade, relieved himself, and climbed up in the carriage beside Georgina.

Joshua sat on the edge of the seat as the team vaulted forth; his little nose pressed keenly against the window as his eyes tracked features off in the distance. Having only known life in the big town, he asked Georgina many questions. Why was there so much space? How did the farmers keep track of their stock? What happened to poachers? Did she like hunting? Why not? How much did one bleed if caught in a trap?

Georgina pined for the solitude of the initial stage of the journey.

She painstakingly addressed each of his queries to the best of her ability, one after the other. On no less than three occasions, he made her swap seats to afford him a better view of a large windmill, a gaggle of geese that had assembled in the middle of the road in protest, and, most excitingly, an overturned gig.

"Thems below stairs say that you are an elbow-crooker."

Georgina's eyes widened at this candid announcement. "Do they? I daresay there is some truth about that."

"Why?" His wide eyes blinked at her.

Georgina rubbed her earlobe. "Perhaps I enjoy a drink."

"Some people do that when they be unhappy. What made you unhappy, Miss Pace?"

"Do you remember hearing about my brother, Henry? And what happened to him?"

"The banks of the Thames?" His eyes glittered with morbid fascination.

She nodded. "That made me very unhappy, Joshua. Perhaps that is it."

He played with the fringe on the curtain nearest to him. "Would *Henry* like you to be a sad elbow-crooker?"

Georgina blinked quickly, as his innocent question had struck a chord. She shook her head, not trusting her voice.

"I 'spect you want this back then?" From his little coat pocket, he retrieved a silver chain with Henry's delicate fob watch dangling from it.

Georgina clasped her hand over her mouth involuntarily, her eyes brimming. "Joshua! How did you get it?"

He unclasped it and extended it to her. "That Bow Street guv'nor come by with it this very morning when you was out. Saw me in the hall, knew me from when we's met before, he did. Told me to see Miss Pace got her property back. Very special."

Gulping down a sob, Georgina's hands were too shaky to successfully clasp it.

Joshua took it back and attached it. "You know, Miss Pace, you can't change the past. Only the future. Look at what you've done for me. Me whole life's changed, thanks to you. I'm thinking this watch here, coming back to you just now, is a little sign from Henry that it's time to dust yourself off and move on."

Georgina wiped sudden tears from her eyes. "Lady Mortimer did well, helping me to find you, Joshua. Perhaps she knew you would make me feel better."

"We helped each other, Miss Pace. And Lady Mortimer is a right good 'un. I'd guess she wants you to be happy too."

She certainly was a good one.

The closer they got to Basingstoke, the more restless Georgina grew. There was the bothersome question of Mrs. Gardner, who would stop at nothing to sour Elizabeth against her with her vitriolic nonsense. But more beyond anxiety, Georgina felt something else spark within her: a glimmer of hope.

Without the Dowager's encouraging words, Georgina may have abandoned her pursuit of Elizabeth's good graces. Now she found a growing confidence within herself as she contemplated making amends. In the depths of her heart, she realized she had fallen in love for the first time in her life. She wished to embrace those feelings wholeheartedly. Her body ached to tell Elizabeth, even if it meant confronting a rejection.

They traversed dense, forested areas where riotous, colorful wildflowers lined the roads. The carriage trundled across rustic bridges over tumbling streams. They passed vast farmlands with cows, sheep, and horses enjoying the lush green grass. The pleasant weather lasted for most of the journey, save for the last few miles, when the clouds lowered across the already setting sun and pelted rain down on them.

The rain gave Joshua even more to talk about as he traced the droplets of water on the glass with his finger. He chuckled at his good fortune, in contrast to old Buckby, who would be mighty wet by now.

Georgina, hoping to preserve the life of her young charge and maintain the ongoing harmony of her household, suggested that Joshua may wish to refrain from teasing Mr. Buckby, lest he find his ears boxed.

He gave her an impish grin and settled on the seat, peddling his feet backwards and forwards restlessly.

A reluctant smile twitched at the corners of Georgina's lips and she glanced out her own window, determined to enjoy a few moments' silence before their arrival.

Soon enough, the gates of Arlington Park, the country seat of the Countess Mortimer, emerged on the horizon before them. The knot in Georgina's belly tightened, but Joshua's presence forced her to maintain composure she did not otherwise feel. Georgina was grateful for the lad.

White pillars flanked the drive, and an imposing gate blocked their entrance. A groundskeeper emerged from a nearby hut, clearly annoyed at having to leave his warm fireside for the rain. The name of Lady Mortimer's caller meant little to him, but he gestured for the coach to drive through anyway. He closed the gate behind them, mumbling to himself.

An extensive driveway snaked its way through rows of beech trees, shielding the house from sight. Manicured lawns stretched into the distance. A lane branched off to one side, and through the trees, they could see the outline of a house. Georgina suspected this might be the dower house where Elizabeth's mother habitually lived.

The main house came into view, an impressive brown stone façade with white columns at the entrance. Many tall windows reached high into the sky, with Grecian statues towering over them from the roof. A small lake could be glimpsed a short way from the residence, and Georgina could see a discreet church steeple nestled beyond. Elizabeth's home was impressive, indeed.

Joshua licked his lips in appreciation. "Swell."

The coach drew to a halt, and Buckby sprang down, opening the door to aid Georgina. He yelled at Joshua to remain in the carriage. The child grudgingly complied.

The rain had set in, and Georgina's traveling hat and coat did little to protect her from the downpour. She hurried from the carriage and up the steps to the front door. The height of the house afforded her some shelter from the rain. She hammered loudly on the knocker.

A footman presently emerged, looking confused. "Good evening, madam. What can I do for you?"

"My name is Miss Georgina Pace. I have come from London. I am here to see Lady Mortimer."

The footman regarded the chaise dubiously but decided to offer them shelter until Lady Mortimer provided him with further direction. He instructed the coachman and groom to drive the carriage around to the rear of the residence, where they could dry themselves and request some refreshments from the kitchen.

Georgina thanked the footman and followed him inside, out of the punishing rain. The magnificent entrance hall filled her with awe. Immaculate, polished wooden floors stretched out in front of her. The walls were a warm peach color, and the high ceiling was painted with sweet-faced cherubs and adorned with gilt carvings. On either side of the room, doors opened to additional parlors and a ballroom, and a wide staircase in the center channeled towards the upper levels. Georgina wondered how far the house extended out of sight. Joshua would certainly be impressed.

The footman led her to an intimate library, tastefully decorated with thick satin sofas and chairs, large Persian rugs, and ornate tables. Book-filled shelves lined the walls, together with several intimidating portraits and a gleaming Louis XVI mirror. Georgina, damp from the rain, went over to the fire to warm herself. She removed her greatcoat, hat, and gloves, giving them to the footman.

He excused himself and said he would let Lady Mortimer know she had another visitor.

Another. Georgina's stomach tightened. Mrs. Gardner and her unpredictable tongue had arrived first.

41

GEORGINA WAITED FOR what felt like an eternity but was, according to the clock on the ledge, actually only a few minutes. Finally, the door creaked open, and Elizabeth entered, resplendent in a high-waisted, white cotton dress with puff sleeves and embroidered floral vines. She wore a simple silver locket around her neck and a silver bracelet on her elegant wrist.

Behind her, like her nemesis waiting in the shadows, followed the figure of Mrs. Gardner. She appeared to have not long arrived herself, given the curls that framed her face were damp. She had dispensed with any traveling garments and, Georgina noted, looked quite at home.

Elizabeth joined Georgina by the fire, a furrow on her brow. "Georgina, what are you doing here? Would you like a drink? Goodness, you are *wet*!"

"I *did* tell you she might turn up," Mrs. Gardner said.

Georgina, her hair disheveled and her garments damp, looked up at Elizabeth, attempting to ignore Mrs. Gardner. "I must talk to you."

"We are *all* here to talk to you." Mrs. Gardner took a seat, making it clear she intended to stay.

Elizabeth closed her eyes for a moment, as if to gather herself, before fetching them each a glass of brandy and settling down on the sofa beside Georgina. "Very well."

Georgina opened her mouth to speak, but Mrs. Gardner's shrill voice interrupted.

"As I was just saying to you, Elizabeth. I am naturally mortified to be the one to tell you about your little favorite's involvement in the duel, but I could not keep it from you. Miss Pace is guilty of felonious behavior. *Again.* I thought it was only right to warn you before you connected yourself with her further. She's already seen to it that your family name has been maligned *in print* once recently. How much more should you tolerate?"

Elizabeth's gaze was inscrutable. Georgina chewed her bottom lip. She could not deny being present at the time of the duel, though to claim she had been involved was ludicrous.

"I am not sure what your motivation is today, but I need you to cease concerning yourself with my connections to Georgina."

Mrs. Gardner sighed theatrically. "Good. I knew you would not be foolish enough to be taken in by her. I warned you from the outset."

Elizabeth's posture stiffened. "On the contrary. I have full faith my credit will survive any connection Georgina chooses to have with me." She at last looked at Georgina, a small smile touching the corners of her mouth.

If she had not already been sitting, Georgina may have tumbled over, such was her relief.

Mrs. Gardner dropped her glass on the side table with a clatter. She stood up, hands on her hips, facing Georgina. "If you are so innocent, my girl, why don't you tell Elizabeth where you were last night?"

Georgina's eyes clouded over for a moment as she tried to recall the previous night. Everything seemed so long ago. Then she remembered she had been at Prudence's house for dinner, and she wished the floor would swallow her up. Clearly, Mrs. Gardner had followed her.

A peal of snide laughter from Mrs. Gardner brought her back to the present, and Georgina realized she had intuitively covered her face with her hand. She looked at Elizabeth, who regarded her thoughtfully.

"Go on. Tell her."

Georgina's cheeks were on fire. She took a sip of her brandy before speaking. "I dined with Lady Ravenscroft. I did not *stay*."

"So she *claims*," Mrs. Gardner sneered.

Elizabeth held Georgina's gaze without saying a word. Then she stood and paced toward the mantlepiece, her back to both ladies. "Julia, I have been as patient with you as I can bear. You will leave this house and never return."

Mrs. Gardner gasped. "Elizabeth, no!"

Elizabeth turned around. "Yes. I have enabled you for too long. I tried to give you what you needed to live a good life, and you returned my goodwill by involving yourself with disreputable moneylenders and now trying to stand between me and someone I . . . care very much about."

At these words, Georgina stood.

Mrs. Gardner groped in her pocket for her handkerchief and wiped her face as tears sprang from her eyes. "Yes, I have done wicked things. But I have also cared for you, Elizabeth. Truly. I am sorry!"

"Just leave."

"No!" Georgina interjected. The word had tumbled out before she realized she'd spoken.

Both Elizabeth and Mrs. Gardner looked at her in astonishment. Truth be told, Georgina herself was astounded at her words.

"Elizabeth, you are angry. As am I. But if our situation were reversed, you would counsel me to have mercy and treat her with temperance. You have assisted her greatly thus far, and she must take responsibility for her choices. But when you provide someone with resources without the support to manage, you cannot blame her entirely for not knowing how to go along."

Elizabeth blinked. "Are you saying this is *my* fault?"

"No. Only that we might *help* Mrs. Gardner on to a more ethical path and teach her a better way."

Mrs. Gardner's keen eyes were as round as saucers. She was nodding along with every word Georgina spoke now.

"I know about Blair," Georgina said quietly. "Your efforts to keep them safe thus far would be wasted if you cut Mrs. Gardner adrift."

Mrs. Gardner sniffled at the mention of her child.

"With Ellis and Montgomery out of the way, and Mrs. Gardner educated *not* to become involved with their likes again, perhaps it is not too late?" Georgina held her breath.

Elizabeth's expression softened.

Georgina went to Elizabeth by the fire. She took her hand tentatively, pressing her fingers. "This is you."

42

LESS THAN HALF an hour later, they had dispatched Mrs. Gardner to put up at the local inn, and Georgina and Elizabeth were alone at last.

Georgina had carried the weight of her mistakes for so long. The words she had mentally rehearsed in the carriage no longer seemed to adequately express the extent of her feelings and regrets. She regarded Elizabeth's silhouette in the firelight.

"I must tell you—"

"No, Georgina." Elizabeth's words cut her off.

She had been on the verge of saying what she needed to. Dread gripped Georgina once more. Perhaps Elizabeth intended on sending her away as well. She would not have blamed her. She tried to speak, but Elizabeth hushed her once again.

"I will not discuss anything with you in this state. You are cold."

"It matters not. We must talk," Georgina insisted.

"And if a chill carries you off, what shall I tell your father? No. Go upstairs this instant and bathe. You must get warm. Only then will I talk to you."

GEORGINA FOLLOWED AN obliging maid upstairs, down a long passage, and through one of the many doors into a fine bedroom. The chamber was exquisite, boasting a large four-poster bed draped in gray damask curtains and soft, white bed coverings, an elegant dressing table, and a separate sitting area where two maids and a footman were busy filling a tub with steaming water. They erected a screen around the bath and laid out a pile of fresh towels.

The final maid withdrew, and Georgina undressed in front of the fire, discarding her damp clothes in a heap to one side. The fire was bright and warm, but her skin prickled with cold nevertheless. She climbed into the bath, submerging her aching body in the hot water. Georgina closed her eyes, hearing the gentle crackle of the fire and lapping water as her hands swirled beside her. At last, she experienced a moment of tranquility. She allowed her sense of time to slip away.

A soft knock at the door disturbed her reverie. She invited the maid to come in.

"You are *still* bathing?" Elizabeth asked from the other side of the screen. "I thought you might have drowned."

Georgina lurched upright in the water.

"I can return later, if you like."

"No, don't go."

Georgina stood up, the water trickling down her body before she stepped out of the bath and onto the woolen rug, her feet sinking into the soft pile. She peeked over the screen.

Elizabeth stood back a little way. In her hands, she held a decanter and two small glasses. Their gaze locked, and Elizabeth's eyes darkened with desire.

An overwhelming need to be close to her rushed through Georgina. Elizabeth had not come here by accident. A thrill of anticipation buzzed inside her.

"You've brought wine. I thought you did not approve of my drinking."

"I fear you overrate sobriety," Elizabeth replied, laying the glasses down and pouring them both a drink.

At hearing her own words quoted back at her, Georgina chuckled. Her laughter could not combat the nervous energy that presently clenched her belly.

"Fetch me a towel?"

"If you insist."

Georgina marveled at how Elizabeth's tone remained completely devoid of inflection. Did she really intend on roasting her while Georgina stood naked only a few feet away?

Elizabeth reached for a large towel folded on the stand. She closed her eyes and extended it outward.

Anticipation and warmth filled Georgina as she emerged from behind the screen and stood before Elizabeth.

With her eyes still shut, Elizabeth held the towel wide so Georgina could step close to it, then wrapped it around her wet frame and began drying her body. She rubbed the cloth over Georgina's shoulders and arms, allowing her fingers to brush lightly against her skin.

The towel followed the contours of Georgina's body, across the curve of her breasts, down her stomach, over her hips and down her back.

Georgina watched how carefully Elizabeth administered to her drying, without a single stolen peek at her nudity. The buildup of the last weeks tested her. She had never desired someone so intensely. The weight of the emotions she had carried these weeks—these years—lashed her like waves crashing over a ship in a tumultuous storm. Throughout it all, her longing for Elizabeth had been constant. Everything had brought her to this moment.

Georgina swallowed. "Look at me," she whispered.

Elizabeth opened her eyes and gazed into Georgina's. Her pupils dilated, and her breathing quickened.

Georgina shivered.

"Are you cold?" Elizabeth asked.

"No."

With the towel still draped around Georgina, Elizabeth pulled the ends of the cloth towards her, so that their bodies nearly pressed together. She lowered her face to Georgina's, and their lips met—softly at first, and then with building passion.

Georgina reached her hand around Elizabeth's neck, pulling her closer and deepening their kiss. She framed Elizabeth's face with her other hand, allowing her thumb to trace the corner of her mouth as their kiss intensified, their tongues entwining and parting in a dance.

The towel tumbled to their feet as Elizabeth freed her hands to travel over the naked curves of Georgina's body.

Georgina moaned, her muscles stiffening in response to Elizabeth's caress. She deftly loosened the fastening on Elizabeth's gown from behind while diverting her attention with alluring kisses. The sheer white fabric of the dress fell from her body and collected at their feet.

"Georgina," Elizabeth groaned in warning against Georgina's mouth. "Stopping will be difficult."

"Why would I want this to stop?"

Without another word, Elizabeth stepped over her discarded gown and propelled Georgina backwards towards the bed. They kneeled in front of each other on the soft sheets. Georgina leaned in to kiss Elizabeth, working her fingers to loosen her corset and undergarments. Next, she removed Elizabeth's garters and stockings, allowing her hands to slide down the length of her beautiful, long legs.

Now free of her garments, Elizabeth lowered Georgina down onto the pillows and gazed at her as if she were a cherished treasure. Georgina's chest rose and fell. She had never wanted someone so much. Beginning near the foot of the bed, Elizabeth bent and placed a soft kiss on the inside of Georgina's ankle. Her lips made a fluttery trail along the inside of her leg and up her thigh.

Georgina gasped, the tickling sensation intensifying the higher Elizabeth kissed her. It tempted her to laugh, but sheer desire dominated this urge.

When Elizabeth reached the top of Georgina's thighs, she guided her legs to open farther. She glanced up and smiled hungrily before placing a kiss upon Georgina's most intimate spot.

Georgina dropped her head back on the pillows, her mouth parted in wonder. The ticklish feeling dissolved into pure passion. She squirmed as Elizabeth's warm tongue caressed her soft, wet folds, dipping and roaming in unpredictable patterns. The texture of Elizabeth's tongue and lips created a glorious friction and an overwhelming sense of anticipation. Georgina rocked her hips upwards in response, a small moan rising in her throat.

She arched her back, seeking just the right touch as she craned her head so she might observe Elizabeth. Their eyes met for a moment, and the glint of desire that flashed in Elizabeth's gaze made Georgina spiral.

"You're beautiful," Elizabeth murmured, between soft licks. "And quite handsome. Gorgeous, really."

Georgina groaned, digging her fingers into Elizabeth's hair and pulling her closer. Just as she thought she could bear no more, Georgina felt the room dissolve into wave after wave of sheer pleasure as she reached her peak. It crashed through her body in a wave of exquisite relief.

Elizabeth gradually stilled her tongue and moved to lie beside her. Georgina, sensitive from her climax and with a heart quite unguarded, enjoyed the suppleness of Elizabeth's skin touching hers. She perched herself up on one elbow so she could better study her lover.

"That was most pleasurable," Georgina said, struck by the failure of her words to do the experience justice.

Elizabeth stroked Georgina's shoulder. "I am happy you found it so."

"I have a suspicion . . . that . . . I will find . . . much . . . that is . . . pleasurable," Georgina said, punctuating her words with kisses down Elizabeth's neck and throat.

Elizabeth groaned. "Are you sure this is what you want?" she asked, her voice low.

"I am so very sure," Georgina said silkily against her ear.

"Everything? Now?" Elizabeth asked.

While Georgina had enjoyed all manner of physical intimacies with all kinds of women over the years, including more than one velina, she had never found herself wanting precisely what she wanted in this moment. She wished to be as close as humanly possible to Elizabeth, to be completely filled with this woman. Georgina wanted to let every last guard down. And Elizabeth seemed to want this too. Her desire was visible not only in her dilated eyes and the sweat beading on her forehead, but also in an impressive erection that—to Georgina—seemed an outward expression of Elizabeth's grace.

"Yes. Now!" said Georgina, ready.

They kissed again, and Elizabeth deftly adjusted her position so that the most private parts of their bodies could lock as one. Georgina's deliciously wet core allowed them to slide easily together and move in unison. Elizabeth moaned in pleasure. Their breathing quickened as they rocked, holding each other tightly.

Georgina clutched Elizabeth's forearms, her fingers clinging in desperation. Elizabeth was propped up above her, and though the muscles in her arms flexed under her own weight and against Georgina's fervent touch, she seemed to hold herself there with ease. Georgina pressed her face against Elizabeth's shoulder. Her lips opened slightly as she panted. In all her dalliances, she had never met a woman who made her feel this way, driven wild with the need for closeness.

Beads of sweat glittered on Elizabeth's skin. Anticipation was building for Georgina, who felt as though she might float to the ceiling if she weren't pinned in place by her lover. Elizabeth pushed inside Georgina one final time and held her close.

Elizabeth roughly whispered, "*Georgina*," then gasped her own release. Feeling Elizabeth's gratification pushed Georgina to her own edge once again, and she returned Elizabeth's frantic embrace, shudders rippling through her body.

They lay in satisfied silence, save for the sound of their deep breathing. Elizabeth rolled onto her side, pulling Georgina close. Their legs tangled together comfortably.

"Are you . . . was that . . . ?"

Georgina was briefly speechless, and reluctant to ruin the moment with words. But she sensed Elizabeth needed to hear confirmation. She beamed. "That felt most wonderful. *Beyond* wonderful. You?"

Elizabeth gave a deep groan and bundled Georgina against her. "Mmm."

43

GEORGINA WISHED SHE could have lain intertwined with Elizabeth all night. They dozed together in sated comfort for some time before reluctantly unraveling their limbs and climbing out of the bed.

Elizabeth fetched the only gown Georgina had brought in her portmanteau and helped her into it, suggesting they might continue their earlier conversation.

Pouting, Georgina complained that anything they needed to say to each other could just as easily be communicated naked. She shivered as Elizabeth kissed along her neckline at the back of her gown before securing the final clasp.

Elizabeth took a comb from the dresser and tamed Georgina's curls. "I also have a household full of inquisitive retainers, not to mention our respective reputations to consider."

Georgina caught Elizabeth gazing at her through the mirror, and the glint in her eyes filled her with warmth. Perhaps they might not make it back downstairs after all.

But Elizabeth stepped away from her, and so the two restored themselves to a level of respectability, save for the satisfied glow across their cheeks.

The ladies returned to the library, where Elizabeth furnished them both with another brandy and sat down beside Georgina on the sofa.

"Now, what brought you all this way? Surely not simply to ravish me."

The twinkle in Elizabeth's eye made Georgina pause. What she had to say was not meant to be received lightly. She took a breath.

"I came to *apologize* to you. In the past week, I have assumed the most dreadful things about you that were neither fair nor true. I came to tell you how sorry I am to have misjudged you so cruelly." She shrugged. "And possibly to ravish you."

Elizabeth regarded her. "Georgina, I suspect you are given to the dramatic."

Georgina scowled. "I am not. All this time, you have thrown me clues to suggest you were involved with Mrs. Gardner in some way, but you never told me in what manner. I could only conclude that you knew she victimized people like Arthur."

"By the time last Sunday arrived, I realized my lack of communication had led you to that assessment."

"I feared you had deceived me into developing feelings for you, to prevent me from finding out the truth about Solitaires." Saying the words was physically painful.

Elizabeth nodded.

"It was only when my friend Lord Telford apprised me of the *true* nature of your dealings with Mrs. Gardner that I realized what a mistake I had made." Georgina paused. "And then I felt *much* worse."

Elizabeth gave a forbearing smile. "I know I can be difficult to read—and slow to open myself up. Some of this story was not mine to share, which made it more complicated."

"I tried to call upon you in town, but you had already gone away.

Your mother provided me with your direction. She is very sweet, by the way . . . and strangely like me."

Elizabeth's eyes sparkled. "There are similarities. Tell me, did my mother know you were coming here?"

Georgina smothered a smile. "Well, not precisely, but she may have entertained a suspicion to that effect."

Elizabeth took her hand, and Georgina regarded her gravely. "After everything I have done and how I have acted, I know I do not deserve your friendship. But I beg you, please accept my deepest apologies."

Elizabeth sighed. "I cannot forgive you. You have done nothing wrong."

"I caused a scandal when I informed on Ellis and Montgomery to Bow Street. I accused them—rightly so, I might add—of murdering Henry. But I regret that your name was bandied about in the newspapers."

"I was there to witness the serving of the warrant. I confess it was a work of art, and their expressions were haunted when they realized you bested them. I can only wish you had been able to see it unfold yourself," Elizabeth interjected, her eyes brimming. "When the Runner frisked Montgomery and found your brother's watch, it was like the dawning of a magnificent sun as we all realized what you had done. You only played at losing the watch. Of course. As you assured me, you never lose. While they turned on each other with accusations, I almost burst with pride."

Georgina blinked rapidly, refusing the compliment. "Perhaps you've forgotten. I broke *into* Solitaires and stole a faro box. I got arrested. I attended a duel to try to stop my friend being shot," she protested. "I have had more than a few dalliances with married women in my day, and I *did* meet Prudence for dinner." She shrugged. Her list of deficits was an extensive one.

Elizabeth's gaze softened. "Yes. You are a very impulsive, foolish girl. It's part of why I like you."

"I reach conclusions without thinking, and I never consider the consequences."

"Indeed, you do not," Elizabeth agreed. "One only needs to recall the housebreaking."

Georgina looked to the ceiling for assistance with her catalog. "I act rashly."

"Yes, I remember rescuing you from Bow Street."

Georgina sat up straight. "I have decided to establish a home for orphaned children like Joshua. A place where they might be cared for and looked after properly."

Georgina enjoyed the puzzled look she received from Elizabeth, who blinked back at her.

"You have?"

"Another example of my impulsivity. Joshua can consult about how we will operate it. He will love that."

Elizabeth cleared her throat. "I am sure he will. Though do not be surprised if he encourages you to disband formal lessons in favor of pony rides and playing in the park and replace sturdy meals with cake and jellies."

Georgina's smile faded, and she shifted to face Elizabeth. "And of all my failings, I am most guilty of assuming the worst in people."

Elizabeth grasped Georgina's hand and became preoccupied with kissing her fingers. "Indeed. Though distrust can be a necessary precaution."

"Colt did not help matters. He was convinced you were working with Mrs. Gardner the whole time."

"Ah. Colt. The bane of my life."

Georgina tried to concentrate. Elizabeth's lips against her skin made it rather difficult to focus. "He and Sarah are to be married.

Perhaps his impression of you will mellow with *her* positive influence."

"Poor Sarah," Elizabeth said, kissing her palm. "I will have to learn to suffer Colt, will I not?"

A flutter of anticipation rushed through Georgina like a playful breeze. She had a happy thought, then shoved the possibility out of her mind.

"After I returned the faro box to Solitaires, on that awful day we parted, you sent me that odious letter. I thought you might never want to see me again."

"Odious letter?"

"Yes, you wrote '*not everyone is capable of redemption.*' But I *am*. I know I failed Henry. But I am trying to make it up to people."

Elizabeth brought her hand to her mouth in dismay. "Now it is for me to apologize. I was referring to Mrs. Gardner. Never you, Georgina. I wanted nothing more than to call upon you after that day, but I also knew that rushing to talk to you after the incident might only have resulted in further accusations and anger. I hoped that by giving you time to reflect, you would, with any luck, grow calmer. It was a gamble, I grant."

Georgina recognized Elizabeth may have a point on that score. "I wanted to tell you the truth about the night Henry died. But I feared you would hate me as much as I have loathed myself." Georgina fidgeted with her glass. This conversation was never going to be a simple one.

Elizabeth tilted Georgina's chin up with one finger, holding her gaze steadily. "You are not responsible for Henry's death. Only his killers are responsible. You must free yourself of this penance. Henry would not want you to be so unhappy."

Georgina murmured, "That's what Joshua said." She could hardly believe the words she'd just heard, spoken with such softness. "So, you did not turn against me?"

"Well, you are, by far, the most stubborn, hot-headed woman I have ever met." Elizabeth curled her finger around a tendril of hair that framed Georgina's face. "I, therefore, decided not to pursue you in the throes of conflict. And whilst it was difficult, I took myself off to the country where I meant to keep myself occupied until I could hopefully converse with you in a more considered manner."

"How like you, to be so levelheaded."

Elizabeth pinched Georgina's chin. "On the contrary, I have known no one capable of destabilizing me as much as you do. I have spent most of the last few days wondering how to repair my relationship with you. Had I been open about my connection to Mrs. Gardner in the first place, we might have avoided all of this." Elizabeth swallowed and took Georgina's hand. "The truth is, I never expected to become entangled with you. When we met over the gaming tables in St James's Square, you amused me, certainly. I could see that you were an accomplished flirt, and for reasons known only to you, you had seized upon me as your latest mark. And I indulged you but expected little."

Georgina could not deny the truth of this. She put her glass down.

"The day we attended the Royal Academy was the first time I realized I had no choice. You were utterly irresistible, and I was powerless against my desire for you."

Georgina wished such frank dialogue had been available to her weeks ago. "And after we kissed at the masquerade, you subsequently distanced yourself from me. Why?"

Elizabeth's gray eyes flashed up to meet hers earnestly. "No, no. I was in *turmoil*, Georgina. You were running around town, embroiling yourself in all manner of trouble, despite all my advice and urgings to trust me. But not only that. In manner, behavior, and words, you never indicated you intended anything beyond yet another dalliance. I suspected if I continued along the course of becoming your mistress, however tempting, I would soon become another of your casualties."

Georgina lowered her gaze in contemplation. "I think we have both been rather foolish. You are much more to me than that."

"This time apart has been very good for me, Georgina," Elizabeth continued. "It is now clear, beyond any doubt, that I love you and cannot be without you."

Georgina blinked. The room was impossibly bright, as though the sun shined indoors, despite the darkness outside. "You love me?" Delight coursed through her.

"I do. Very much, indeed."

Georgina sat quietly for a moment. Perhaps she would, after all, surrender to the love she felt for Elizabeth and allow herself to be loved back. She reached one hand up to Elizabeth's face.

"There is one more thing we must clear up." Elizabeth breathed in, looking serious. "Be mine?"

Georgina's eyes filled with tears. She had turned into one of those ladies who craved entanglement, after all. She nodded.

"I already am. I love you, Elizabeth."

"Blimey. If it ain't the Missus and her ladyship, in lurve!" an excited voice expostulated from the doorway as the door flung open.

"I will *never* forgive you for cursing me with that child," Georgina whispered through gritted teeth.

Joshua had by this time surged into the room, one hand holding a half-eaten bun. He plunged the other into his pocket. He swept an assessing eye over the room.

"Very nice. Grat'lations. When's the wedding, then?"

"Goodness, what possessed you to bring him here, Georgina?"

"He brought himself." Georgina grinned.

"I got a special dispenation. The Missus were worried about highway robbers. Put me in the strongbox, so I could rumble 'em unexpected like. I could wallop 'em from behind and knock their heads clean off. There'd be much blood, m'lady!"

Elizabeth cocked a brow at Georgina. "You have a singularly macabre interest in beheadings, my love."

Georgina's heart was full to overflowing. She winked at Elizabeth, then turned to the boy.

"You are a wretch, Joshua," she said with a doting smile.

Glossary

**Author-created terms denoted with an asterisk. Other terms were commonly used in Regency London.*

Abigail: A lady's maid.

Box (ears): Little smack / slap.

Box (hunting): A hunting box was a lodge or house located near prime hunting areas. Fashionable people might retreat here as individuals or parties during the hunting season.

Bouncer: A lie / fib.

Bow Street / Runners: Equivalent of the London Metropolitan police of the period (who operated predominantly out of Bow Street).

Brainbox: Head / mind.

Cast Up Accounts: To vomit, be sick.

Chit: A girl, young person.

Claret: Wine, but also a cant expression to describe blood.

Corinthian: A fashionable sports-person. They pride themselves on their prowess with a range of sporting pursuits and while they dressed well, they did not fixate on their appearance (as a dandy would, see below).

Corker: Something very good of its kind (e.g., A good person).

Cotillion: A ballroom dance for four couples, set in a square formation.

Coupe de main: Attack against something.

Cry off: Cancel something, not turn up.

Curricle: A sporting, two-wheeled carriage, pulled by two horses.

Dandy: A person of very high fashion. Generally, dandies considered themselves extremely well-dressed and focused on physical appearance and gracious manners.

Delope: In dueling, the practice of diverting fire away from one's adversary.

De rigueur: Proper, prescribed by etiquette.

Disguised: Drunk.

Dressing down: Scolding.

EO Table: Version of roulette, a wheel with a ball that had Even and Odd numbers.

Elbow-crooker: Big drinker.

***Electora:** Author-created term to describe non-binary individuals. Derived from the Latin words Electio meaning "choice" and Ora meaning "edge/border".

Faro: A French card game that utilized a dealing box. A very popular gambling game during the 17th to 19th centuries.

Flat: A flat is another word for a fool.

Fleece: To take advantage of someone, likely by trickery, and steal their fortune.

Fustian: Nonsense, over the top talking.

Goosecap: Fool.

Green: To be green is to be inexperienced and vulnerable.

Groom: Attendant who assists with horses / carriage.

Hackney / hack: A regency taxi, single-horse and carriage.

***Honorian:** Author-created term to describe individuals with disabilities (broadly). Derived from the Latin word Honor meaning "honor/dignity".

In your Cups: Drunk.

IOUS: see Promissory notes.

Laudanum: Opium tincture of the era, to relieve pain.

Lily-livered: Cowardly.

Lobcock: Lout, blundering person. Curse word.

Loose Screw: Someone who is not put together properly and may seem eccentric, silly, or unstable.

***Lord, Ladies and Electora:** An expression developed by the author to include non-binary identifying characters.

***Lorian:** Author-created term to describe males who were assigned female at birth. In modern terminology, this refers to transgender males. Derived from the word "valor" and the common masculine suffix "ian".

***Mem:** Author-created non-binary personal pronoun, similar to Mr./Miss/Mrs.

Mésalliance: An unsuitable or undesirable marriage.

***Miris:** Author-created term to describe individuals born with Trisomy 21 (Down Syndrome, or similar chromosomal divergence). Derived from the Latin word, Miri meaning "wonderful/to admire".

Ninnyhammer: Foolish person.

On the rocks: Poor, strapped for cash.

Phaeton: An open carriage drawn by one or two horses.

Point Non Plus: To reach the point where you have nothing left to say or do.

Press-ganged: Term for being forced into military service / compelled into service.

Pretty penny: A large sum of money.

Priggish: Uptight, rule-follower, one who irritates by observance of proprieties.

Prinny: Affectionate term for the Prince Regent.

Promissory notes: Written pledges made, in the absence of funds, to repay at a later time. Terms may include interest. Also called IOUs or Vowels.

Ready: Money, cash.

Rum: Alcoholic drink. Can also mean dangerous, nefarious, dodgy.

Sewed up: Cornered, obligated.

Shit-sack: Curse-word.

Shot the cat: Refers to being very drunk.

Superfine: A soft fabric, almost silken to the touch, often used to make jackets.

Stripling: Youth.

Sweetmeats: Sweet confectionaries made with fruit, nuts, sugar and spices.

Tendre: Affection / soft-spot.

Toad-eating: Ingratiating, fawning over someone.

Ton: High, fashionable society.

Too brown, do something: Going over the top.

Une affaire de cœur: An affair of the heart.

***Velina:** Author-created term to describe females who were assigned male at birth. In modern terminology, this refers to transgender females. Derived from Latin word Vellus, meaning "gentle" and common feminine suffix "ina".

***Veris:** Author-created term to describe intersex individuals. Derived from the Latin word Verus, meaning "true".

Vowels: Refers to the vowels "IOU". See also promissory notes.

Watch: The police / constables who patrolled the streets.

Acknowledgements

A huge thank you to my agent, Benython Oldfield, for taking a leap of faith in the quirky rule-breaker from Brisbane and believing in the message of my story.

Thank you also to my wonderful publishing team at Generous Press, specifically Elaina and Amber. I think we're a match made in heaven.

I would like to thank editor extraordinaire, Kelly Rigby. Your encouragement and guidance helped me push beyond my comfort zone and taught me so much about my writing style. You're a star!

Thanks to Mark and Ondina Montgomery for their unyielding support during the creation of this project. Thank you for your guidance and mentoring as I navigated this whole new world.

To my mum, Manuela, Kayt, Kelly M, Louise, Teesha, Gareth Brookes, Kaye Kemp and anyone else who trawled through early versions of the manuscript (sometimes multiple times). I'm very grateful! While the final version may not look much like what you read, I promise I did not waste your time! The various drafts were a necessary journey for me.

And lastly, to my partner and muse, Rebecca. I cannot thank you enough for your patience during the creation of this world. For the countless days when I hit a wall, not knowing how to break it down, and you gave me gentle prompts and made me realize that if I stopped and looked around, I would see there was a pathway around all along, I thank you. Your support and love during my most difficult days is incomparable.

About the Author

J.A. STEVENS is a passionate emerging voice from Brisbane, Australia, dedicated to reshaping historical narratives through the lens of inclusivity. As a mother to a wonderful daughter with Down Syndrome and partner to an inspirational transgender woman, J.A. draws from a well of personal experience that enriches her storytelling.

Her own journey with Autism (ASD), coupled with her love for historical romance, fuels her literary pursuits. Stevens envisions a world where history celebrates all, aiming to craft alternative tales where visibility, equality, and love flourish. Her writings weave together themes of sexual orientation, gender, race, and disability. She invites all to find themselves within the pages of her books.

J.A Stevens is represented by leading literary agent Benython Oldfield of the Zeitgeist Literary Agency.

Learn more at www.jastevens.com

Generous Press aims to please readers like you by publishing lush, high-caliber romance fiction and other books about love by brilliant BIPOC, LGBTQ+, and disabled writers. Together we envision a world in which all people are cherished and free.

Look for Generous Press titles wherever you buy books:

A Change of Pace
BY J.A. STEVENS

Nearly Roadkill: Queer Love on the Run
BY KATE BORNSTEIN AND CAITLIN SULLIVAN

Losing Sight
BY TATI RICHARDSON
(Book 1 of the Boss Chick Village Series)

Someplace Generous: An Inclusive Romance Anthology
EDITED BY ELAINA ELLIS AND AMBER FLAME

Coming Soon . . .

You x Me

BY AYLA VEJDANI

Struck Speechless

BY TATI RICHARDSON

(Book 2 of the Boss Chick Village Series)

Beneath the Sky, Across the Entire Plain

BY JANA PUTRLE SRDIĆ, TRANSLATED BY RAWLEY GRAU

The Treasure Maker

BY CORINNE MANNING